ERASED

Φ

ERASED

Φ

BY LUCAS HEATH

ACKNOWLEDGMENTS

A huge thank you goes to some of the best people in my life, Brock, Todd, Jake, Stefan, and Ben, for their support and encouragement, not only in my writing, but my life.

Another thank you goes to Bev, who has undoubtedly helped increase the quality of my writing and stories.

Contents

The Tower

The Facility

Epilogue

PROLOGUE

It was almost midnight, eleven forty-eight to be exact. The elderly man, needing to quicken his pace, disregarded his cane; he had little time to finish his task. He placed a folded piece of paper into a small, wooden chest, closed the lid, locked the clasp, and lifted the chest off the kitchen table. Carrying it to the basement steps, he descended into the eerie darkness as fast as he was physically able. As he reached the final stair, a dull pain arose in his lower back. His cane would have helped prevent that, but he didn't have time to use it; he was running out of time!

The man flicked on the light and hobbled over to a workbench. He moved it aside with ease, revealing a hole the size of the chest. He braced himself on a wooden stool, lowered to his knees, and slid the container through the opening. Out of a nervous habit, he ran a hand through his thick, white hair and stood. He set the workbench back into place, concealing the hole and its contents, and after turning off the light, preceded back up the stairs.

A groan escaped his lips as he sat down at the kitchen table, the wooden chair welcoming his tired back. He grabbed a permanent marker and pushed up the sleeve on his left arm. There was only one thing to remember. After a moment, he had the numbers 12, 21, 54 prominently displayed in black ink on his skin. The clock on the kitchen wall buzzed as the hour and minute hands met at the twelve. A bright flash outside flooded through the window, filling the whole room and blinding him. The light faded, leaving the elderly man face down on the kitchen table.

THE AWAKENING

DAY ONE: CHAPTER ONE

Ashland; the band poster glued to the white ceiling was the first thing the boy saw when he opened his eyes. He stretched and yawned as he fumbled with removing the bed covers, then propped himself up with his elbows and looked around the room. A dim light peeking through the blinds lit the area, just enough for him to see. Newspaper clippings, band posters, and a small whiteboard calendar littered the navy blue walls. The bed was in the corner of the room, opposite the door. A lamp and digital clock flashing 7:02 sat on a dresser at the foot of the bed. Two sliding-mirrored doors covered half of a closet full of hanging shirts and a pile of dirty clothes.

Across the room was a desk with a computer and large speakers; papers covered the desk, and a backpack lay open on the floor with school books falling out.

He pivoted in bed and placed his bare feet onto the plush cream-colored carpet. With a little push, he stood and then stretched again. A wave of nausea washed over him and he bolted for the trashcan next to the desk, grabbed it, and heaved. Nothing.

"What in the world," the words escaped his lips as the feeling hit him again; it didn't last long, but it made his eyes water. He sat back from the trashcan and used the sleeve of his pajama shirt to wipe snot from his nose. Perhaps he had come down with the flu. He needed to tell his mom to call his teacher.

Anxiety struck at his heart as a realization hit him. He couldn't remember who his mom was. The boy bolted for the door and threw it open, charging down the hall and into the kitchen. "Mom!" he called out several times, but to no avail. Fear replaced anxiety as he realized that the memory of his mom wasn't the only memory evading him. He couldn't remember who his father was or even where he lived. All the details of his life, details he should know, were blank... even his identity. "I can't remember my name," he whispered.

A third wave of nausea overcame him, and the dry heaving started once more. Tears streamed down his face by the time it ended. With frantic speed, he looked around the kitchen, hoping to find clues. Perhaps he had gotten sick, and a virus erased his memories. No, he still remembered things... he was in high school, he had a mom and a dad... at least that was *something*. Oh, and he had recognized his bedroom and the kitchen! Everything seemed familiar to him, but familiarity was as far as it went.

A piece of paper on the granite counter caught his attention, and he raced for it.

Troy,

We headed out early for Detroit and I didn't want to wake you. Don't even think about having any parties. Mrs. Lyons will look out for you until we get back. Hope your date with Kelly goes well tonight.

P.S. There's one hundred dollars for random spending money in the cookie jar. See you in a week.

Love, Dad

Yes, his name was Troy, he remembered now, or did he? Was it a true memory? Or was he so far gone that he would take *any* name? Whatever the answer, he would stick with Troy for the time being. He looked at the clock above the stove and then stared at nothing in particular as he concentrated, trying to process his next steps. He needed to get to the hospital. It wasn't a normal thing for people to wake up without their memory, was it? He needed professional help.

Troy hurried back to his room and opened the closet. Rifling through the colored shirts, he settled on a gray one with the logo of a lion and yanked it from its hanger. Throwing it on the bed, he removed his nightshirt and added it to the pile of dirty clothes. He stared at his body in the mirrored closet door as if he were looking at himself for the first time. He had a thin face and light-brown hair that covered the tips of his ears and part of his forehead. Troy wasn't fat though his abs weren't visible – something he would have to work on later. He was at least five-feet, eight-inches tall, and even though his age remained a mystery, he estimated himself to be sixteen or seventeen – as there was not a hint of facial hair.

As he rotated his wrist, black writing scrawled across it caught his attention. He raised his arm to get a better look. *Troy18*, a simple message revealing his name and he hoped his age. Had he written it? The eight smeared a little, showing the ink wasn't permanent, maybe done by a washable marker.

Troy reached for the fresh shirt and pulled it over his head. He slipped off his pajama bottoms revealing gray boxers. He didn't have time to worry about changing *everything*. Pulling on a pair of loose denim jeans he found in the clothing pile, he looked around for anything that resembled a wallet. Why hadn't he thought of that in the beginning?

The search didn't last long. Troy found a leather wallet with a few dollars inside, but no identification. He ran back to the kitchen, found the money in the cookie jar, and stuck it in his wallet. Grabbing a pen, he scratched a line through his dad's message about the money and wrote to the side, *already took it,* in case he somehow forgot *that* detail.

Troy walked over to the front door, not bothering to check out any of the other rooms in the house. At the moment, he didn't care. He needed to find help and figure out what was happening.

Φ

Jessica Dailey, at least she assumed that was her name, stared at a paycheck on a mahogany dining room table. Her gaze hadn't fallen on the numbers, but at the unfamiliar name printed in black ink.

Erased

An hour earlier, a scream and gunshot out on the street had jarred her from her slumber. She ran outside before she was wide-awake and before her brain told her not to go running toward gunfire. A woman with long, black hair, wearing nothing but a nightgown, pointed a gun at the lifeless body of a man.

"When I woke up, he was in my bed," the unknown woman sobbed as her arms fell limp to her side. "I don't remember seeing him before in my life. I tried to get away, but he chased after me, insisting he must be my husband. He wouldn't leave me alone." She collapsed to her knees, and the gun clattered to the cement.

Jessica had run back into the house to call the police, grabbed the cordless phone on the entry table, and dialed the universal three-digit number. The phone rang several times.

"Thank you for calling the Alpine County police station. All of our circuits are busy right now. Please stay on the line and we will be with you as soon as we can."

Alpine County; that name was not familiar. Where was she? As she had hung up the phone, fear washed over her like a bucket of ice water. Looking around, she had caught her reflection in the entry hall mirror: blonde hair, blue eyes, a round face, thin nose, and full lips, perhaps mid-thirties, but she hadn't recognized the image peering back at her.

Then, at the moment of realization, she became oblivious to her surroundings as she at last embraced the truth; she had no memory of who she was or anything to do with her life! How can a life of memories vanish?

Jessica took a deliberate, deep breath and exhaled to push the fears away. It was not the time to freak out; it was a time to look for answers. Forgetting about the shooting outside, she had searched the house with precision and, having found a basket of mail, sifted through it.

Jessica Dailey was the name listed on every envelope; there were even several letters addressed to Mayor Dailey. Now, she stared at the paycheck and sighed. Her mind flashed back to the woman on the sidewalk next to the fallen body. The stranger had said she had woken up in bed with a man she couldn't remember. Was the woman a floozy, or had she lost her memory too and the poor woman had shot her husband?

Jessica walked back out her front door. The man's body still lay near the walkway to her house; the woman had fled with the gun. Jessica sighed again and stepped back inside her home. She *would* venture outside for answers, but if she was the mayor of Lion's Glade as her mail suggested, she would have to make herself presentable first.

Φ

Troy had taken several steps outside of the house before he realized that he had no clue where the hospital was. He turned around and stepped inside, in search of a phonebook. He didn't understand how he could remember objects, or how things worked, yet everything else escaped him. It was almost as if someone, or something, had targeted those specific memories and erased them.

He gave up the search and grabbed a phone. He would call the police and ask for help.

"Thank you for calling the Alpine County police station. All of our circuits are busy right now. Please stay on the line and we will be with you as soon as we can."

Troy waited for ten minutes before walking into his room and turning on the computer. Perhaps he could find the hospital's address there. The computer booted, but wouldn't connect to the internet like he had hoped.

"Blast it all!" Troy screamed and threw the phone against the wall. The impact didn't leave a dent though part of the phone casing shattered. He left his room and charged back outside into the sunlight. There weren't any clouds above him, just a vast blue sky. He walked down the sidewalk, not knowing where he was going. He stopped and looked at the house he was passing. Perhaps the people there could help him. He ran to the front door and slammed his fist against it several times.

After a few moments, the door opened a crack, and he saw an eye peek out. Troy could tell that it was a man because of a visible beard.

"Please, you have to help me. I need to get to the hospital, but I can't remember where it is. The police are too busy to answer my calls."

The man shook his head. "Sorry boy, I can't help you. I don't know where it's located. Something screwy is going on here." He shut the door without another word.

Troy kicked the door and turned back toward the sidewalk. "Thanks for nothing," he yelled and continued his journey down the road. He looked both ways before crossing the street when a new realization hit him – there were no cars. He had to do a double take and look at all the driveways he could see; not a single car in sight. He continued walking to an intersection. The view was the same; every driveway and street was empty!

If the one-eyed, bearded man hadn't answered the front door, Troy would have thought he was the only person left on the planet. That idea caused a new wave of fear to wash over him. He needed to find someone, *anyone*, who could tell him what was happening. A green two-story house caught his attention and a strange familiarity drew him down the sidewalk toward the front porch.

Before he even had time to knock, the door flew open. An older girl about his age stood at the entrance wearing a white tank top and jeans.

"Oh, thank God!" she yelled as she reached out to grab his arm. She yanked him into the house and shut the door. She dragged him past an ascending staircase, through an archway, and into a living room.

Troy thought it unusual that he didn't have an urge to pull away, but something about this girl brought him comfort. Perhaps it was her green eyes, or long brown hair, two things he liked in a woman. How he remembered that, he wasn't sure, but it brought him reassurance.

"Who are you and what's going on?" she demanded to know as she pushed him onto a leather couch. "Why can't I remember anything? Please don't tell me I'm dead and we're in Hell."

Troy shrugged. All panic and fear drained from his body. "Beats me, but I have the same problem. I was trying to find the hospital. Maybe they can help."

She shook her head. "I called the hospital and police, but nobody answered. Something *is* wrong. What is going on here? Did our country go to war in the middle of the night or something? Why can't I remember anything?"

Troy held up his hand to silence her and stood. "I know, well, I guess I don't know, as much as you do. I woke up with the same problem. It is doubtful a war would have caused this, but a terrorist act might have if it was biological warfare."

"None of this makes sense. I don't even know where my parents are. There is a note pinned to the refrigerator with emergency numbers while they're gone. I also found this." She pulled up the sleeve her arm, revealing the word *Anchor*, written in black ink.

Troy stared in disbelief. "That's *just* like mine! But different!" he pulled up his sleeve, revealing *Troy18*.

"Wait, *you're* Troy?" she gasped.

"I'm assuming so, based on all the clues."

"My name is Kelly. We know each other, or knew each other. I got a text message from my mom saying she hopes I have fun on my date tonight with Troy!"

Even with the seriousness of the situation, Troy laughed. "My parents also left me a note about our date. That's interesting. Even though I don't have a memory of you, you seem familiar. So does your house." He paused and his right eyebrow rose. "You said you received a text from your mom? Did you send one back?"

Kelly nodded. "I didn't want to tell her I couldn't remember her, but I sent a text saying something was wrong. I haven't received a reply yet."

"Well, for what it's worth, I'm here for you. We may not remember each other, but at least we found each other."

She nodded. "What do you think we should do? What if this crisis is happening to everyone else?"

Troy frowned. The possibility hadn't occurred to him. He remembered the man who answered the door said he didn't know where the hospital was. Could he have lost his memory too? "I think we need to start a journal."

"A journal?"

"If we lost our memories because of a virus or something, we don't know if this will happen again. We need to write everything that *has* happened, and *will* happen; starting from the moment we awoke."

Kelly nodded. "Good idea. There are notebooks on my bedroom floor I'm sure we could use."

"Once we write everything down, we can decide where to go from there. Perhaps we can get in contact with someone at the police station."

"That sounds great. I'm glad I'm not doing this alone." She smiled and walked over to the door that led to the front hallway. "Stay here. I'll go get the books."

DAY ONE: CHAPTER TWO

Simon Orson, sheriff of Alpine County, sat at the police station's dispatcher desk, answering the many incoming calls flooding the phone lines. He was already on the one hundred and thirty-eighth call, but the phones continued flashing like blinking Christmas lights. People called in from all over town, complaining and panicking about the loss of their memories.

Simon's problem however, was that he didn't have a single memory himself. He had awoken that morning and realized this when he couldn't remember the woman in his bed. Due to the *Orson M* written in black ink on his left forearm, the *Orson F* written in black ink on the woman's arm, and several framed pictures of the two of them together, they accepted their marriage.

A police uniform had hung on a hook in the corner of the bedroom, revealing his profession. With no hesitation, he had cleaned up and put on the uniform. He was a stocky, middle-aged man with graying, brown hair. He barely reached five-feet, ten-inches tall. His first instinct had been to put aside his own problems and make sure other people were safe. After telling his wife everything she needed to do, he had kissed her goodbye and left.

She had locked the door behind him and searched the house for more information about their life.

After realizing he didn't have a car to drive, Simon had walked, hoping that by chance he would find the police station, as he couldn't remember how to get there. It took almost an hour, but he had made his way into the center of town and found the familiar building. It was next to the town hall.

Simon had used the key in his pocket to unlock the door and stepped inside the building. The lights were still on, making him think that someone should have been there, but he didn't find a soul. He searched until he found his desk located in an enclosed office. It wasn't until he saw the plaque displaying his last name that had he found out his first name. He had a wallet, but it contained no identification.

Being the only one at the station unnerved Simon. Where was the graveyard crew? The police should have one, right? That way, someone could respond if there was an emergency at night. He had jumped when the phone at the dispatcher's desk rang and he rushed to answer.

"Police Department, what is the nature of your emergency?" Simon didn't know if that was the proper thing to say, but at that moment he didn't care. That was the first call; several hundred came flooding in after that, as people woke and called for help, all with the same symptom of memory loss.

"Yes, ma'am, the entire town is affected. Please stay at home and lock your door while we figure this out." After listening to the woman's response, he hung up the phone. The doorbell of the police station chimed, causing Simon to sigh with relief; he could take a break from answering calls. He stood and stretched his legs before walking away from the constant ringing phones.

Simon walked to the front; through the glass door he saw a blonde-haired woman standing with her arms crossed.

She had her hair wrapped into a bun and she wore a navy blue business suit. A pair of glasses rested on the bridge of her nose. Whoever she was, she looked professional.

He unlocked the deadbolt and turned the handle.

The woman shoved the door open and stepped inside, her white high heels tapping against the linoleum floor. "You should put a carpet in front of the door so people can wipe their feet, or this floor will get dirty," she said. She bit her lip and looked around the room. She turned to Simon. "Are you the only one here?"

He nodded. "My name is Simon Orson. I'm the sheriff. At least, I'm assuming I am."

"It figures," she mumbled as she walked toward the back offices.

He followed. "I've been answering people's emergency calls; it seems the entire town is affected with memory loss."

"Sweetie, I am aware of the situation." She spun around and held out her hand. "Mayor Jessica Dailey. At least, *I'm assuming I am*," she said with a playful wink.

So she has a sense of humor. That's good. Simon thought as he let out a small sigh of relief.

"I live up the road, so it was easy finding this place. I knocked on a few doors and talked with others. They are all in a panic."

"And you're not?" Simon asked.

Jessica shook her head. "Not at all," she said. "I do not need my memories to know I have a job to do. I will focus on that problem later."

"It's like your instinct, right?"

"Yes, that is a good way of putting it. My instincts tell me to help everyone I can and worry about myself later. What can I do to help you?"

Simon shrugged. "I don't know. The phones haven't stopped ringing. We need to find an efficient way of informing everyone they are not alone in experiencing memory loss. We're in the same situation, but we need to communicate to them all at once – not one phone call at a time."

"People are dead already. We do not want any more chaos to ensue."

"I agree, but I'm at a loss as of where to start. Not having vehicles adds to the confusion. It makes it hard to get around town."

"True," she said with a nod. "We must figure out why we have no transportation."

Erased

"But that should wait until we can figure out a solution to our communication problems."

"There has got to be a local news station somewhere around here, right?" Jessica asked as she fidgeted with her hair. "People would turn on their televisions, trying to figure out what is happening. Perhaps we can send a message that way."

Simon nodded. "That's a good idea. I saw one on my way here. I can check it out."

"We will go together. I think the people need to see their mayor addressing them and not *some* cop."

Simon rolled his eyes. "When would you like to go?"

"Now. Lead the way."

Φ

"The police still aren't answering. Perhaps we should try heading into town," Kelly said as she tossed the phone on the floor of the family room.

They had moved themselves to the bigger room to have more space. The living room had felt small and confining while the family room was at least three-times bigger and had two couches. Two spiraled notebooks containing the teenagers' writings lay open on the carpet. It was a record of the day's events so far.

Troy rubbed his neck. "If other people are out there without their memories, they could try to hurt us."

"Are you saying my future boyfriend is afraid of people without their memories?" Kelly snapped.

He blushed and lowered his head. "I'm thinking about protecting you."

Kelly smiled and sat forward on the light-yellow, floral couch and reached toward the wooden coffee table. She pulled open a built-in drawer and removed a handgun. "I think I can take care of myself."

"How'd you get that?"

"I found it in this drawer when I was searching the house."

He frowned and his eyebrows furrowed. "Do you think you could use that on someone?"

"I wouldn't have to *kill* anyone, but I could always shoot someone in the leg if they tried harassing me. It's not that big of a deal."

"You would shoot someone in the leg, *just* for harassing you?"

Kelly rolled her eyes and grunted. "You know what I mean!"

"I don't think I do."

She threw the gun to Troy, hitting him in the chest before he had time to react. "Then *you* take it. I'm sure *you* could use it better than *I* would." She stormed out of the room.

"And I wanted to date this girl?" he whispered as he pulled his shirt away from his chest and saw a small red mark where the gun had hit him. He turned the pistol in his hands, studying the design. It was a Beretta M9, which contained fifteen rounds per clip. How Troy could know *that* random information and not his own name was beyond him, but at least it brought comfort to know he hadn't forgotten *everything.*

He set the pistol on the table and glanced at an entertainment center looming against the far wall. The flat screen TV looked to be at least forty-two inches. He grabbed the remote next to the gun and pushed the red button. The screen flickered to life, though after waiting for a time, no images appeared. He pushed the arrow buttons to change channels, but nothing showed on any station.

Erased

"I already tried that. The cable isn't working," Kelly said as she entered the room with a glass of ice water. "Oh, and next time, watch what you say, or I might throw my water at you instead of a gun."

"Go ahead. It might numb the pain of the bruise your gun left," he countered.

"Poor baby, do you want me to kiss it and make it better?" she mocked as she sat on the couch beside him.

"If you want," he said with a grin. The smile vanished when ice-cold water splashed all over him. "I was kidding!"

"Look at what you made me do. Now I have to get more water." Before she could stand, the TV screen lit up, showing a news room. A blonde-haired woman wearing a business suit stood behind a news desk displaying a large yellow five.

"Hello, citizens of Lion's Glade. I am Mayor Jessica Dailey. Calls received at the police station suggest that memory loss has affected our entire town. Let me assure you we are doing everything in our power to get to the bottom of it. What we need from all of you is to stay calm, stay in your homes, and learn everything you can about your lives through letters, records, documents, pictures, and whatever else you can find.

"We ask that you please stop calling the police station, for so far we only have the sheriff on duty. We also ask that if any of you discover that you are police officers, put on your uniform and make your way toward Town Hall. It is the large building with the giant green flag on top at the corner of Langley and Pine Street. Use a map to find it."

"I never even thought to use a map," Troy muttered.

The mayor continued. "We will bring you updates as we receive them. I am sure others will not see this message, so if you run into someone who does not know what is going on, please tell them what I have said. That is all for now."

The image faded to a black screen with the words *'please stand by'* displayed in white letters.

"Well then, what do we do now?" Kelly asked.

Troy shrugged. "I guess we do what she said and wait."

Φ

"Let us hope the announcement will quell any issues that may have arisen," Jessica said when she entered the control room of the television station.

Simon stood in front of a giant panel of flashing buttons, a manual in hand. "This is easier than I thought. It feels like I've used this equipment."

"Maybe you have," Jessica said. "We need to figure out what our next steps will be. Where do we begin?"

Simon set the manual aside and pressed his lips together. His gaze drifted toward the green screen used by the weatherman. "First, one of us needs to head back to Town Hall and see if any more officers show."

Jessica nodded. "That is true."

"Second, we need to check on the citizens and get the hospital functional, or at least a clinic of sorts, in case anyone needs medical attention."

Jessica grabbed a pen and a blank notepad she assumed a reporter owned and scribbled down the ideas. "We also need to contact the Centers for Disease Control to get them out here."

"Do you think this memory loss is an isolated incident? If we *are* dealing with a virus, could it be spreading throughout the country as we speak?"

She bit her lip and shrugged. "I do not have an answer for that."

"Well, let's get started with those ideas for now. Do you want to make one final announcement to the people about the search for doctors and nurses?"

Jessica nodded and sighed. "Yes, let us do that. And then, after you set the announcements on a continuous loop, we can head over to Town Hall."

Φ

"The mayor told us to stay put," Kelly said with a huff of exasperation.

"I want to go back to my place and learn more about my life. Now that I know other people are infected, going to the hospital won't help," Troy responded as he turned off the television.

"You think we are all infected? You don't even know a virus caused this."

"What else would it be?" he asked. "Oh, I know. Maybe aliens have taken over the world and want to screw with or brains!"

"Ok, now you're being stupid."

"Compared to the alien idea, my virus theory doesn't seem so farfetched, does it?"

"How in the world did I ever like *you*?" Kelly asked with another huff.

Troy walked to the front hall toward the door, the notebook journal in hand. He reached for the knob when Kelly pushed in front of him, blocking his exit.

"So you will leave me alone here? I thought you wanted to protect me."

"You have a gun. You can protect yourself, remember?"

She rolled her eyes. "Perhaps, but that doesn't mean I want to be alone."

"Then come with me," he said without showing emotion. "Either way, I'm going home."

"Fine, then go," she blurted and moved away from the door. "But don't expect me to answer if you come back."

Troy turned the knob and opened the door. "Perhaps I'll see you tomorrow."

"Don't count on it," she snapped.

Troy left her house and pulled the door closed behind him. It was early afternoon, and the sun was shining, bathing the neighborhood in light. Large sporadic tufts of incoming white clouds cast shadows upon the ground, creating the illusion that the world was a distorted patchwork quilt.

It took him a while to find his way back home, for he needed time to adjust to the new, yet familiar surroundings. He turned the handle of the front door and pushed it open. He hadn't cared to lock it. The thoughts of his next steps seemed to evaporate the moment he heard movement in the kitchen. He raced toward the noise, hoping beyond all hope that his parents had heard about the crisis and returned. He stopped underneath the arched kitchen entrance.

A man towering at six-and-a-half-feet tall spun at Troy's sudden appearance. The man was tanned, as if he had been living in a desert for quite a while. He had black, slicked-back hair and seemed more muscular than lanky. He wore a black t-shirt and jeans with a bronco belt. A stack of papers were spread out before him on the counter and he had a gun raised and pointed toward the teen.

"Welcome back, Troy," the man said with a thick, Middle Eastern accent, which Troy somehow recognized right away. "I didn't want to search for you, so I'm glad you returned. Now, tell me, where is your father?"

DAY ONE: CHAPTER THREE

The moment Troy saw the gun, every muscle in his body tensed, and he couldn't move.

"I'll ask you again. Where is your father? He's got to be around somewhere. He wouldn't leave his kid alone."

The man must not have seen the note Troy's dad had written about going to Detroit. But then, how could the man know Troy's name?

"So *terrorists* caused our memory loss," Troy uttered, though it escaped his lips before he could think to stop it.

The man burst out laughing and ran a hand over his clean-shaven, dark cheek. "You think *I'm* a terrorist? My boy, if *anyone* is a terrorist, it's your father. Now tell me where he is hiding."

Troy shook his head. "My dad is *not* a terrorist."

"Oh, so you have all your memories, do you? You must be the only one in this town who does."

"No," Troy responded, unsure of how to continue, but his mouth kept moving. "My dad wouldn't do anything to harm people."

Once again, the man laughed, but kept the gun pointed at Troy. "That is yet to be determined. I will do *anything* to find out who erased my memories. Do you understand me, kid? Papers I found in my house say that your dad is one person involved. Now, tell me where he is. If you won't, I may have to take you prisoner until he shows himself."

Whether it was out of instinct or desperation, Troy wasn't sure, but he took a quick step back and dove to the ground, down the hallway. A bullet penetrated the wall and an eardrum-shattering explosion reverberated throughout the house.

Troy's knees throbbed from the impact, but that was the least of his worries. He shoved himself to his feet and ran down the hall toward his bedroom. If the man was chasing after him, Troy couldn't tell, but the fear pounding inside his body propelled him forward. He ran into his room and slammed the door closed, turning the small lock on the handle.

Troy raced toward the window next to the bed and pulled the cord to raise the blinds. Dropping his notebook, he turned the latches and pushed the window open. It swung outward and he jumped through as the sound of splintering wood reached his ears. The man had kicked in his bedroom door. The drop wasn't far and Troy landed on the grass before running around the side of the house to the backyard. He passed a large, inflatable swimming pool and a beach ball as he ran toward the fence that bordered the property.

Troy must have been on the track team at school, or at least practiced parkour, because jumping up and flinging himself over the tall wooden fence felt natural to his limbs. He landed in the yard of a neighboring house and kept running. The emptiness of that backyard and the lack of paint suggested a newly built house still being finished. He may have found the perfect hiding place. He raced toward the deck, and with one jump, cleared the four stairs.

Troy sucked in gulps of air as he tried the sliding glass door, pleading for it to be unlocked. It slid open without resistance and "phew" escaped his lips as he exhaled. He stepped inside and pulled the door shut, flipping the latch. He was correct on the assumption that the house was unfinished. The walls were not yet painted and drywall dust covered the floor. He stood in the dining room, or at least what would be the dining room.

To the right, a large arch led to the kitchen. Granite counters lined the walls of the kitchen, but any appliances had yet to be added. Straight ahead, another large arch led to a hallway. It was similar in layout to Troy's house, but with a second floor. He moved away from the door and turned to peek in the backyard. He didn't see the man or any sign he was still being pursued. Better to be safe than sorry, he checked every possible entrance to the house and secured them.

Erased

The house was two stories high, but if Troy hid upstairs, and the man broke in to search for him, Troy would be trapped. At least on the main floor he had multiple paths of escape. A finished room on the main floor had sliding, mirrored closet doors, like the one in his bedroom; he decided that it would be best to hide behind them. He glanced at himself in the mirror. Sweat dripped down his forehead, and he looked as sick as he felt. He wiped his face with his sleeve and then bent over and lifted his pant legs so he could see his rug-burned knees. They didn't hurt much; it was more discomfort than pain. Troy slid the closet open, stepped inside, and then closed the door behind him, leaving it open just a crack to let in a small amount of light. He sat and leaned against the wall, letting his tired body rest.

Troy closed his eyes and lowered his arms to his sides. His right hand touched a small cylindrical object. Opening his eyes, he lifted it toward his face. How a lone black marker found its way inside the closet, he would never know, but since he didn't have his notebook, it would be best to write what he could. He lifted the left sleeve of his shirt and thought for a moment. After removing the cap, on the opposite side of his arm from *Troy18*, he wrote the phrase *'Dad is a terrorist?'* in case he somehow forgot what the man had said. This would be something he needed to investigate. Then he wrote on his right arm, *'beware the Arab.'* He wasn't sure *who* the man was, but that was the easiest way to describe him. He capped the marker and closed his eyes once more, letting an irresistible sleep overtake him.

Φ

By late afternoon, a large group of doctors, nurses, and police officers assembled in front of Town Hall. Sheriff Orson led his men to the police station to figure out their identities and how they could be of help to the people. Mayor Dailey led the medical staff to the hospital. She had added an announcement to the televised loop that if anyone needed medical attention, they were to go to the hospital where help awaited.

By the time evening arrived, a group of police patrolled the streets, checking up on civilians to make sure they were safe. There were seven reports of death: two homicides, one accidental, and four suicides. Two young cops cleaned up the dead body in front of the mayor's house. That was where the death count stopped, as far as anyone knew.

At seven thirty, Sheriff Orson entered Town Hall for the first time that day and gawked at the enormous foyer. A row of flags representing different nations lined the walls. A few doors partitioned the foyer off from main floor offices and conference rooms, and staircases, which ascended to the second floor, flanked a large reception desk near the front doors on both sides. There was nobody at the reception desk so he made his way up the stairs, walking underneath stunning, golden chandeliers. The plush carpet that covered the floor and stairs was a royal red and almost seemed suited to a king or queen.

Simon reached the top and headed straight back, toward the mayor's office. Thick, wooden double doors blocked his way, and he pulled one open. He stepped inside and yanked the door shut behind him. The office was bigger than he had expected. Three bookshelves lined both the right and left walls. The back wall from the door was glass, allowing the mayor to look upon the town. Her desk was in the center of the room. On it was an antique lamp and a variety of office supplies. There were two blood-red couches in the right-hand corner of the room nearest the door, perpendicular to each other with a small coffee table a few feet away from them. Two black chairs in front of the desk offered themselves to Simon, and the mayor sat in a large office chair behind it, staring out the window.

She swiveled her chair around as he sat in one of the guest seats. "Ah, Simon, I am glad you stopped by, for I was about to call you."

His right eyebrow rose. "You were?"

She nodded and looked toward the telephone on the desk. "I have made many calls to connect with anyone outside of town. I called the CDC, FBI, CIA, and other police stations. It would be pointless trying to name off everyone I attempted to contact. I got recordings, but nobody answered their phone."

Simon shook his head in disbelief. "Nobody is out there to help us?"

She shrugged, showing little emotion. "I believe we are on our own. I assume that everyone else is facing the same issue. They do not know who *they* are. If the citizens of our town can work together, we may return things to normal. The east side of town has large farms with animals and crops. We grow a lot of our own food here. We can survive without outside help if we must, though that is not my pressing concern."

"You don't think food is a pressing concern?"

The mayor shook her head. "Not at this moment. I talked with the owners of a farm, and even though they are affected like us, they know what they are doing. One guy told me he woke up to milk the cows and it took an hour of chores before he realized he had no memory of anything. I have noticed this in the citizens. We may not have memories from before today, but we still seem to fall into routines and life patterns. Any skills we learned have not left us. We should not have a problem getting everything back to normal."

"Okay, then what *is* your pressing concern?"

"I want to learn how this all began. There is no evidence to support the theory we have been like this for more than a day. If what we are experiencing is an effect from a virus, how contagious is it, and how fast did it spread throughout town? As far as we know, *everyone* is affected. I am also curious to find out how long each of us had the virus before our memories vanished. Did we forget quickly or slowly?" She stood from her chair and turned toward the window. "There is another oddity in this mess. Everyone I met today has a single word written in ink across their forearm."

Simon nodded. "I've noticed. Why do you think that is?"

"Is it possible I learned of this coming situation and had people write something on their arms to help them remember? Why would they not write important information on paper instead? I do not know, but it bugs me. There are too many unanswered questions."

"Other than the vehicles, have you noticed there are no newspapers around here either?"

She shook her head without turning. "I did not notice, no. Also, the internet connection is down here."

"It's down everywhere," Simon muttered and ran a hand through his graying, brown hair. "What is going on here, Miss Dailey?"

She turned around and stared into his light-brown eyes. "I wish I knew, Sheriff, for all of our sakes."

Φ

Kelly eyed the strange meat in her refrigerator and pulled it out. It looked better than the rest of the food. She grabbed the mayonnaise and shut the fridge door before setting them on the counter. It was almost nine, and the sky had faded to black.

Troy hadn't returned like she had hoped he would. She had searched the phonebook for his phone number before realizing she didn't know his last name. She sat in the family room feeling frustrated, watching for any new announcement from the mayor. There was nothing else to do, and she had ended up falling asleep with the gun by her side.

A change in the televised announcements woke her; it was the sheriff's voice explaining the evening procedure. Earlier, the mayor had suggested that everyone stay inside, but now the town government forbade anyone from leaving their homes until they made another announcement in the morning. Kelly's stomach growled, informing her of its wish to consume food. She realized she hadn't eaten for most of the day, which was enough to get her to the kitchen. She finished making her sandwich and placed the meat and mayonnaise back into the fridge. Taking her food to the family room, she set the plate on the table next to her glass of water.

Kelly walked over to the television and grabbed a movie from the entertainment center's shelf. She removed it from the case and slid it into the DVD player. Two hours passed, and when the movie ended, she couldn't utter a word. The world and story woven together was spectacular and breathtaking. She wasn't sure how to absorb it all. The concept of a movie wasn't new to her, but she had no memories of seeing any. She needed to find Troy and get him to watch a movie with her!

Her thoughts snapped back to reality when the cell phone in her pocket vibrated. Kelly removed it and flipped it open, revealing a text message. "From Mom," she read, and then she hit the center button on her phone to read the message.

Kelly,

Remember to stay Anchored in reality. Find the clues to your problem. Love you. Stay strong.

-Mom-

After reading the text message, Kelly looked at the word anchor on her arm and shuddered. She typed a short response, unsure of what else to say.

Mom, come home, NOW!

Kelly sent the text and took the empty plate and glass into the kitchen, setting them in the sink. After retrieving her notebook journal, she journeyed upstairs, brushed her teeth, and changed into sweat pants and a tank top. She plugged her cell phone into the charger, making sure that there wouldn't be any reason for the battery to die. Climbing under the covers of her queen-sized bed, she snuggled in, making sure she kept her journal clutched in her grasp. She had written all she needed to for the day.

Moments before she drifted off to sleep, she heard her phone vibrate. She pushed herself up with reluctance and reached toward her phone on the nightstand. She flipped it open and read the new message from her mom at least five times, trying to comprehend the meaning behind it.

Kelly,

I can't come back. It's not safe. Please be careful. Be cautious of Mayor Dailey.

-Mom-

Φ

Sheriff Orson stood on his back deck looking up at the starry night sky. His wife, Bonnie, stood by his side. He wrapped his arm around her shoulders and kissed her on the cheek. "I'm glad I'm not alone in this," he said as he pulled her close.

"So am I. I hope there's a way to reverse this. Not being able to remember our life together makes my heart ache," she responded.

"What if there's no cure? Would you be willing to stay with me and make new memories?"

She smiled and looked up at him. "Of course! But getting my memories back would be great too."

Simon chuckled and kissed her again. He couldn't remember her, but being with her felt right. He wouldn't want to be with any other woman on the planet; that was something he knew without doubt.

"So, if the mayor can't contact anyone beyond our town, what happens next?"

He shrugged. "We haven't gotten that far yet. We spend today focusing on avoiding chaos. It's amazing that we didn't have more issues with people. There were several deaths, but no riots and no major conflicts. Today, talking with the doctors and nurses, they almost seemed robotic as though they lacked any emotion. It's almost creepy when I think about it. I *know* they aren't robots, but without their memories, they seemed void of personality. I see that in Jessica Dailey too. At first, I thought she had a sense of humor, but only for a moment. She shows little emotion."

"You and I have personality," Bonnie said with a small laugh.

He nodded. "Yeah, I suppose we do. Perhaps it's because they are doctors. I don't remember meeting a doctor with a personality."

Bonnie laughed even harder. "I don't *remember* ever meeting a doctor with a personality either." She continued to laugh at the joke and readjusted the small gold-plated watch on her wrist. "It's about midnight. Perhaps we should head inside and get to sleep. You have to wake up early tomorrow."

He nodded, but his eyes maintained their focus on a cluster of stars.

"Simon, what is that?" Bonnie asked as she pointed toward the horizon.

He turned to where she was looking and had enough time to see the bright light before it consumed them. They collapsed to the ground, unconscious.

DAY TWO: CHAPTER FOUR

The unpleasant blare of an alarm clock startled Troy awake. The first thing he saw when opening his eyes was the band poster glued to the ceiling: *Ashland*. His heart beat at a rapid pace as he fumbled with removing the bed covers to reach for the clock and end its tyranny. With a successful pat of the off button, he fell backward, his head hitting the pillow. He stretched and yawned, and yawned once more, and then groaned. The clock flashed 7:30. It was way too early for school.

He remembered having a dream about a cute girl with sparkling green eyes and brown hair. What he would give to meet somebody like that someday. He focused on the dream for a while, and then he propped himself up with his elbows. He sat up and pivoted in bed, placing his feet onto the ground. One foot landed on the plush carpet, while the other found its place on a green, spiral notebook. He reached down and moved his foot to pick up the notebook.

"Memories," he read the title written in black ink across the front. He couldn't remember ever having a spiral notebook. It was in that moment panic settled in as realization hit him; he didn't know who he was, he had no memories of his life. Troy stood, notebook clutched in hand, and raced out of his bedroom, hitting his side against the door's corner as he tried to squeeze through without completely opening it. "Mom!" he yelled through the house. Forgetting his mother scared him more than not knowing who *he* was.

He raced through every bedroom, searching, hoping that somehow, someone would be there to tell him what was happening. He ran to the kitchen and his eyes spotted the note.

Erased

Troy,

We headed out early for Detroit and I didn't want to wake you. Don't even think about having any parties. Mrs. Lyons will look out for you until we get back. Hope your date with Kelly goes well tonight.

P.S. There's one hundred dollars for random spending money in the cookie jar. See you in a week. **Already took it.**

Love, Dad

Troy shook his head in confusion. This was too weird. He ran back to his room and looked around until he spotted a wallet on the dresser. He grabbed and opened it. The one hundred dollar bill was there. An emotion bubbled up inside him; a mix of a scream and sob, but he bit his tongue and held it back. Perhaps he received a head injury, and it caused amnesia. That sounded more logical than not. Maybe he was sick, and a virus was messing with his brain. Either way, he needed help. He rushed to find a phone, and the moment he found one he dialed 911.

"Thank you for calling the Alpine County police station. All of our circuits are busy right now. Please stay on the line and we will be with you as soon as we can."

Troy walked back to his room and fell onto the bed. He waited for what seemed like forever, and yet nobody answered. No one would come to his aid. He hung up the phone and tossed it to the floor. It was then he remembered the spiral notebook gripped in his hand. He opened it, wondering if it held a clue to his crisis. After all, the notebook had the title *Memories*, and he had found it next to his bed.

For the next ten minutes, he read five pages of his own handwriting, which explained small bits of information about himself and everything that had happened the previous day. The entry ended with him and Kelly watching the mayor on television explain that the whole town lost their memories and that people should stay in their homes. He had also included the street names to find Town Hall, and a note to use a map to get there.

Troy's anxiety faded. "So I ended up forgetting again. I must keep writing in this thing," he muttered and stood, leaving the notebook on the bed. He needed to take a shower, and then he would go see Kelly.

He grabbed clean clothes and carried them to the bathroom. As he removed his shirt the black markings on his arms grabbed his attention. "What in the world?" There was *Troy18* that he had read about in the notebook, but two new markings caught his attention. *'Dad is a terrorist?'* was on the opposite side of his arm from *Troy18,* and on his other arm was the phrase *'Beware the Arab.'*

Questions swarmed through his head like a hive of bees as the warm water hit his body. He was careful to avoid washing off the writing though he doubted the thick marker ink would rub off his skin with just one cleaning. "Why didn't the notebook mention these phrases?" he wondered aloud. "What made me write these on my arms and not on paper?" Troy finished his shower and dressed before returning to his room. He made sure the wallet was snug in the back pocket of his jeans, then looked at himself in the mirror and adjusted his hair with his hand. He stared at the white lion on the gray shirt for a moment; the lion seemed familiar. He found a ballpoint pen, and after opening the notebook, turned to the next available page.

Day Two, he wrote, and described his feelings when he awoke. He also mentioned the new, temporary tattoos on his arm. Could he have been on to something? Was his dad somehow connected with people losing their memories, or something more heinous? Before he went to see Kelly, he needed to search the house and find every bit of information about his father.

Φ

Jessica Dailey slept through most of the morning, for there weren't any gunshots or screams to wake her. A clock on the wall informed her it

Erased

was ten o'clock when her eyes fluttered opened. She yawned and, with reluctance, pulled herself out of bed. The need for coffee pushed her forward. She walked to the kitchen and prepared the machine to make the delectable caffeinated drink. It was too early to think about anything. Her mind felt blank, but she contributed the emptiness to the fact she wasn't functional without her morning java.

It wasn't until the first cup of coffee was in her stomach and the caffeine flowed through her veins that she realized her problem. She needed to figure out the day's events, but when none came to mind, the reality of her dilemma hit her. "Talk about identity crisis," she muttered as she tried with all her power to recall her name, or any memory of her life. She sat on a sofa chair in the living room and tried harder, going through a list of logical things she should remember. Her birthday, her name, her address, her parents, her childhood, but nothing surfaced. She knew she had known all those things at one point, but now, Jessica couldn't remember. Even more strange was that she felt no emotion about it.

Perhaps relying on her brain was a stupid idea. Jessica stood and searched through the house for information, hoping that she would find *something* to help trigger her memories. She came across a pile of letters that shed light on her identity. She was a mayor though she wasn't sure if she could run things in her condition. Perhaps she suffered from a brain disorder, or a tumor. Those were two possible conclusions. Her house and everything in it felt familiar, but she had no memory of living there.

After finding a phonebook underneath the entry table, she searched for the number of the hospital. She didn't want to declare her amnesia an emergency and call for an ambulance, at least not yet. She dialed the number and waited. The phone rang several times before somebody answered.

"Thank you for calling Lion's Glade Medical Center, how may I help you?"

Lion's Glade? Yes, that was the town listed on her mailing address. "My name is Jessica Dailey. I am not sure if you can help me, but I seem

-40-

to have amnesia. I do not recall bumping my head or doing anything that may have caused this, and I need to know if it could be a potential emergency."

"You're not the only one," the woman said with a hint of despair in her voice. "From what the sheriff told me, the entire town is facing the same problem. Nobody has any memories of their identities or lives."

Jessica wasn't sure of the exact feeling that blanketed her, but a shiver shot through her body. "So *everyone* is inflicted with this problem? What about you and the sheriff?"

The woman on the other end spoke with a slight southern twang in her voice. "Oh, don't get me wrong, ma'am. We don't have memories either. However, when we woke this morning, we figured out who we are and went to work. My name is Bonnie. I'm a nurse here. I'm the only one who has shown up so far. Simon Orson is the sheriff *and* my husband."

Jessica looked down at her golden, silky night pants and closed her eyes. She inhaled and let out the breath. She felt a spark of sorrow deep within, but pushed it away, smothering it before it had time to reach the surface. "Well then, I suppose I should get ready and head to the police station."

"Is there anything else I can help you with?" Bonnie asked.

"No, you have done more than enough. Thank you." Jessica hung up the phone and set it on the cradle to keep it charged. She proceeded up the stairs and searched through her room. It was tidy and organized; a fact that brought her comfort.

She walked to the closet and removed the articles of clothing that completed a lady's business suit and then walked to the bathroom. She removed her nightshirt and stared at the black ink on her white skin. *SG-H30*; a strange set of letters and numbers covered her wrist. She licked her thumb and ran it over the zero, smudging it. It wasn't permanent. Could it have significance to what was happening?

Erased

Jessica once again shoved the emerging emotions aside. At the moment, she needed to forget the message on her arm. Her duty as Mayor was to keep her cool, and to help the citizens. No matter what it took, she would do just that.

Φ

By late morning Troy had amassed a large collection of evidence and spread it out on the dining room table. He had removed the flower vase and set it on the kitchen counter to give him more space. He had the birth certificates of his parents and himself, a family photo, a locked safe he found underneath his parent's bed, documents he had found in a filing cabinet, and the note his dad wrote for him. None of the files he read answered whether his dad could be a terrorist, or why people's memories disappeared. The safe might hold a clue, but he needed to figure out the digital code to unlock it.

That Troy even cared as much as he did, surprised him. Perhaps he had a deep sense of family loyalty. Perhaps in a subconscious way, he remembered his dad and needed to protect him. Whatever the reason, he needed to prove or *disprove* the theory that his dad might be involved. How did the phrase *beware the Arab* fit into all of this? Troy decided that he couldn't do it on his own. He needed to go see the girl he described in his notebook; he needed to meet Kelly.

Troy ran out of the dining room, through the kitchen, and down the hall, passing a black hole in the wall the size of a dime. He ignored the puncture and entered his room. He snatched the backpack from the floor and emptied its contents before returning to the dining room. After shoving all the information he had found into the backpack, he zipped it closed and slipped his arms through the straps.

He would have to carry the safe by hand. He picked it up and almost dropped it when he moved. The safe was two feet long and wide, and one foot high, with at least seventy pounds of metal, and who knew what else he would find. Troy had to set it down to open the front door. It was difficult to manage, but after a while, he set the safe on the porch of Kelly's house. His muscles would hate him in the morning. The door opened before he could knock.

"It's about time!" Kelly snapped as she examined him. She was the girl he had seen in his dream. "You don't look like I thought you would, but that's all right. We can work with that later. Just get your butt in here!"

Was she this demanding yesterday? Troy wondered as he picked up the safe and carried it into the house. He set it on the floor of the family room and breathed a sigh of relief when he sat on the carpet and leaned back against the couch.

"I expected you to be here hours ago!" She said as she folded her arms and eyed the young man.

"You knew I was coming?" Troy asked.

"Obviously," she said and rolled her eyes. "I wrote about you in my journal, and I'm sure you wrote about me in yours. I figured you would wake up, freak out, read your journal, and come see me right away."

Troy couldn't help but chuckle. "I'm sorry to disappoint you, but I searched my house for clues about my dad. Has the mayor been on television yet?"

Kelly shook her head. "Not yet. I've kept it on the same channel as yesterday too."

"Something different must have happened today then. She might not come on at all. We *will* need to warn them at some point."

"About?"

"About the fact that our memories reset every day; at least, it happened last night." Troy opened his backpack and pulled out the documents and clues he found at home. He spread them onto the floor.

"What is all this?"

Erased

"After I left here yesterday, something happened. My journal doesn't tell me what occurred, but I found these new clues on my arms." Troy slid the sleeves up his arms and showed the words written in black ink.

Kelly's eyes grew wide, and she sat by his side. She grabbed his arm and turned it to get a better look. "So you think your dad is involved with this?"

Troy shrugged. "I did yesterday though I'm not sure why. I'm hoping this safe might have answers."

Kelly looked at the metal box and saw the electronic keypad on the front. "Maybe we can hack it," she suggested.

"You know how to hack electronic safes?" Troy asked as his right eyebrow rose.

"Well… no, but we could try."

"We would have better luck trying random combinations," he said with a sigh. "Perhaps there's a clue to the code in these files. That's why I brought them."

A sound coming from the television caused the teens to turn toward the screen. The Channel Five Studio was visible and a man wearing a police uniform stepped into view.

"Citizens of Lion's Glade; my name is Simon Orson and I am the sheriff. By now, I'm supposing you are all awake and have concluded you no longer have your memories. You aren't the only ones. I have talked with over a hundred people in the past several hours who are all experiencing the same thing. Please stay as calm as you can in this challenging situation and search for information about your lives.

"I am the only police officer on duty, so if anyone who's watching figures out they are part of our law enforcement, please come to the police station and help. It is next to Town Hall, the largest building in town with the giant green flag on top. It is at the corner of Langley and Pine Street, so you can use a map to find it. We will do everything we can to sort this out. Thank you." Simon walked out of the camera's view and the screen went black although the message would most likely repeat in the next couple of minutes.

"Something changed today. I wasn't expecting the sheriff to be the one addressing the town," Troy muttered.

"Do you think something happened to the mayor?" Kelly asked.

"I doubt it," he mumbled. "This *isn't* time travel. We just don't have our memories. Even if our memories reset every day for the rest of our lives, our decisions will almost always be different."

"Should we write this down in our journals?" Kelly asked after a short silence.

Troy nodded. "Yes. And then we need to get in contact with the sheriff. He needs to be informed about everything we know."

DAY TWO: CHAPTER FIVE

By the time Simon left the news building and returned to the police station, the mayor was standing outside, waiting for his arrival. She held out her hand the moment he was within reach. "Jessica Dailey. I am the mayor of Lion's Glade."

"And I'm Simon Orson, the sheriff." Simon shook her hand and then used a key to unlock the deadbolt. He shut the door as soon as they stepped inside. "I wondered if there were any others in government here. I would have hated to be the only one."

She nodded. "With a problem this big, I do not blame you. Your wife told me that the entire town is affected."

He nodded. "That's no exaggeration. I've been answering calls all morning and then had the idea to use the news station to relay a message to anyone who watches. I've met a few people on the road, but most have stayed in their homes."

"People fear the unknown. They are too afraid to venture outside, not knowing where they are or anything around them."

The sheriff shrugged. "It's possible. I know little about psychology though."

"It is only a theory. I saw your message, and it is rather good. That should keep the peace a while longer."

The sheriff walked into the back room and sighed when he heard the phones ringing. The rear of the police station contained at least twenty cubicles. Two of them were dispatcher's boxes, and incoming calls forwarded to both phones. The rest of the partitions were silent. There was one office space with a window and door that the sheriff occupied. The white walls seemed to shine from the incandescent lights evenly spaced along the ceiling. The building was smaller than it appeared.

"So, what is the next step?" Jessica asked as she stared at the ringing cubicles.

"Well, I set the recording on a continuous loop. Anyone turning on their televisions will hear my announcement, and I hope that, after a while, the rate of calls will slow. I think trying to reach someone outside of town will be our next course of action."

Jessica nodded. "I agree. I should head to my office and do some research. We must get the CDC out here and figure out what erased our memories."

The sheriff nodded. "In the meantime, I will continue to answer the phones until the deputies arrive. Then we can focus on helping the citizens."

She nodded and turned away. "That sounds good."

Simon watched her leave and pressed his lips together. He couldn't quite place it, but something seemed off about the mayor. She seemed almost robotic; her monotone voice never fluctuated in pitch and she didn't even use contractions. Simon decided she had the personality of a turnip. When the front door closed, he walked over to one of the ringing phones and groaned before answering. "Alpine County Police, what is the nature of your emergency?"

Φ

A cold blast of wind struck the man in the face, waking him from his slumber. He sat in the driver's seat of a red 1995 Toyota Tacoma, with the windows rolled down. He gripped a set of keys in hand and noticed a smear of blood where a key had jabbed into his palm, scraping off a chunk of skin. After blinking a few times, he rubbed his eyes and then reached to scratch the top of his head. His muscles jerked when something crawled on the back of his hand and he brought his other hand down on top of it. The spider didn't have a chance. He wiped his hands on his red plaid, short-sleeved shirt and looked down at his holey jeans.

Erased

His head felt like it was on fire and throbbed to the rhythm of the rock song playing through the iPod at his side. He rubbed his temples and opened the truck door, stepping out onto the pavement. He had parked on the side of the road. The highway extended from horizon to horizon, with rocks and desert land as far as the eye could see.

He fell to his knees as pain surged through his skull. He screamed and clutched his head. As his hand brushed against his forehead, he could tell that he had a fever. The pain subsided, and he noticed a cotton ball tinted red with blood taped to his arm. Had he been in a hospital? He reached for his back pocket and removed the wallet. According to the ID, he was Mark Hood, and he was from the State of California.

A second spike of pain pierced his head as a memory surfaced. A woman had put up a request on a community bulletin board, hiring someone to move furniture from California to Kansas. The pay looked good, and he had taken the job; it sounded simple enough. The memory faded, leaving Mark back on the deserted road. As soon as the pain left, he stood and peered into the back of his truck. There was no furniture, so he must have delivered it.

He froze as another memory rose from the depths of his mind. He had delivered the furniture to the woman and stayed in town for the night, renting a motel room. That's where everything went fuzzy. The next thing he remembered, though even the memory was unclear, was waking up strapped to a hospital bed with a tube and needle injected into his arm. The doctors said he had a virus though they wouldn't say anything more. He had freed himself from the restraints, took the needle out of his arm, taped the cotton ball over the puncture wound, and escaped. How he found his truck and got away, he may never know. He couldn't remember what happened after that.

Mark pushed the memories away and walked around his truck, checking for any damage; everything looked fine. Climbing back in, he hit his knee on the steering wheel, placed the key in the ignition, turned it, and the vehicle roared to life. He shifted gears and began his journey home. It wasn't long before he passed a sign. *Welcome to Lion's Glade.*

Mark couldn't explain the sudden shift in his mind, but he spun the steering wheel all the way to the left, forcing the truck into a sharp U-turn, almost causing it to rollover. He punched the gas as soon as he had straightened his trajectory and reached seventy miles an hour before he felt safe. He wasn't sure why, but he knew that he needed to get as much distance as possible between himself and Lion's Glade.

Φ

"Maybe we have parasites in our brains," Kelly suggested as she finished writing in her journal.

Troy looked up from his paper and his right eyebrow rose. "Excuse me?"

"It's a logical idea!" she said with more enthusiasm than Troy had seen since arriving earlier that day. "They might be in the water. We all drink water! At least, I *hope* we all drink water. My point is, maybe there are parasites in the water and they somehow made their way to our brains and began eating them."

"You think parasites are eating our brains," Troy repeated, trying to make sure he understood her idea.

"That would explain why we lost our memories while we slept. Perhaps they feed on memories."

"Are these supposed to be aliens from a science fiction movie that need our memories to survive? Isn't there already a dream eater out there somewhere?"

Kelly rolled her eyes. "You don't have to be sarcastic. I'm trying to be logical. Perhaps the parasite feeds on the area of the brain that has memories, and all the new memories we make are eaten when we go to sleep."

Erased

"I may see slight logic in that, but I refuse to believe a microscopic bug is eating my brain. That's gross. I'm not even going to include that theory in my notebook. I don't want to remember this tomorrow."

Kelly sighed and turned to the television. The same clip of the sheriff had been playing for two hours already and Troy had muted the sound.

"I've written a possible list of combinations for the safe's password," Troy said as he tore out a piece of paper from his notebook.

"It's a good thing we only need to look for a number combination and not anything with letters." Kelly sighed again.

"Thank you for calling the Alpine County Police Station. All of our circuits are busy right now. Please stay on the line and we will be with you as soon as we can," the telephone on the table informed.

"I would have thought that after an hour of being on hold, someone would answer the phone," Troy said with a huff matching Kelly's. "Perhaps we should go to the police station and talk with the sheriff in person."

"That's what I suggested an hour ago," she said and rolled her eyes. "The quicker they know about this, the easier it will be for them to prepare. The safe and its contents can wait for now. We have all the time in the world to figure this out."

"That's true," he agreed. "Oh, I forgot to ask. Did your mom ever reply to that text message you sent her yesterday?"

"I forgot to look!" she said as her pupils grew bigger. She ran to her room and grabbed the phone from the nightstand, flipping it open. No new text messages. She flipped through the history and grunted when she saw an empty inbox.

"I'll take that as a no."

Troy's voice made her jump, and she spun toward the door. "Don't scare me like that!" she rebuked.

"Nice room you have here though the pink walls have already given me a migraine." Troy glanced at the stuffed animals on the bed. "You have a stuffed turtle with wings? You learn something new every day."

"Get out!" she demanded and pushed him from the room.

"Who comes up with those dumb stuffed animal designs? I would like to know."

Kelly slammed the door shut as soon as they were in the hall. "You listen here, Buster," she said as she waved her hands at him. "This is *my* room, and I don't want you in here, all right? Especially if you insult my stuffed animals."

"So you don't mind if I insult the room's color?" If looks could kill, Troy knew he'd be dead. "All right, I'm sorry."

"You're forgiven. Now, let's get going, and grab a map. I want to be at the police station as soon as possible."

Φ

Jessica Dailey sighed although anyone who heard it may have mistaken it for a groan. She stood at the large window that doubled as a wall and looked out at the town. There had been no reply to any of the messages she had left, from anybody outside of town. It was a conundrum that led to one conclusion; whatever was happening in Lion's Glade wasn't an isolated incident.

Her frustration caused her emotions to bleed through the cold exterior she tried so hard to protect. She didn't have an answer to why she needed to build a wall around her heart; she assumed it was part of her personality, and that was fine with her.

The phone on her desk rang, and she spun around, grabbing it from its cradle and lifting it to her ear. "This is Mayor Dailey speaking."

"Mayor, this is Sheriff Orson. I wanted to inform you I have at least ten deputies on duty. I'm sending them throughout town to help keep order and see how our citizens are doing."

Jessica nodded. "That sounds excellent. I have yet to reach anybody on the outside, but I have not given up hope. I will continue to make calls."

"That sounds good, ma'am," like his wife, a hint of a southern twang escaped from his voice. "I will keep you updated."

"Goodbye, Sheriff," she said and hung up the phone. She collapsed into the big office chair and looked at the list of thirty numbers she had already tried calling. Did a world outside of their town even exist anymore? Jessica couldn't prove it one way or the other, but she doubted anyone was left to help them.

Φ

"Sir, when do you expect to launch an investigation into what is happening with our town?" Landon, one of the younger deputies asked as he entered Simon's office.

"We need to worry about our citizens first. Once the mayor gets in touch with the CDC, they will arrive and begin the investigation. We can't do much right now."

"I suppose, but I feel like we should do more!"

Simon chuckled. "You're paid to do as you're told, not do what you feel."

"You're right. I'm sorry sir," Landon said as he ducked out of the room.

Simon stood from his seat and left his office. He looked toward the dispatchers' cubicles and saw the young man and woman who volunteered to help. If he remembered correctly, her name was Loraine and his name was Bobby.

Loraine turned to Simon as she hung up the phone. "We received a report of a stabbing in the Less Is More grocery store, over in the east part of town."

"Contact Deputy Richards and send him over there to check it out. I'll call my wife and have her send a nurse she recruited to see if they can help."

Loraine nodded and lifted a handheld radio to her mouth, giving the instructions.

Simon returned to his office and dialed the hospital. Bonnie answered on the first ring, and after he informed her of the situation, he said goodbye and hung up, letting her get back to work. Four people had already arrived at the hospital with severe injuries though there were no reports of death. His desk phone beeped and a red light flashed. The secretary at the front desk was trying to contact him. He hit the corresponding button. "Yes?"

"Sorry for the interruption, sir. There are two kids here to speak with you."

"Terrific," he muttered with a quiet grunt. "Send them in."

Within a few moments, Landon escorted Troy and Kelly into the office. They each took a seat in front of the sheriff's desk.

"My apologies; when the secretary said two kids were here to speak with me, I thought she meant *kids.*"

"Trust me, he still acts like a kid," Kelly said, glancing in Troy's direction.

"Says the girl who poured ice water over me," Troy replied.

Kelly's eyebrows rose for a split second as her mouth fell open.

"What? You thought I would forget about that?" Troy asked. "Well, I did, but I wrote about it in my journal."

"I think I need to rip pages *out* of that journal," she muttered.

Erased

"Why did you need to see me?" Simon asked, trying to get the youths back on topic.

They both turned to him and sighed in unison. "Do you want to tell him, or should I?" Troy asked.

Kelly shrugged. "Doesn't matter."

"Sir, my name is Troy, and this is my friend Kelly. We have come across important information." Troy removed a folder from under his shirt. "I found this folder inside of a metal safe underneath my parents' bed. It holds important documents."

"All right," the sheriff said as he held out his hand to take the folder. "What's so important about them?"

Troy cleared his throat. "They offer the answer to why everybody has lost their memories." He paused. "And it turns out my dad is involved."

DAY TWO: CHAPTER SIX

The teens had been at the police station for a few minutes before the sheriff led them to Town Hall. They sat around the mayor's desk and waited until they had her complete attention. Troy began to explain.

"They named the fungus Sporrid Hychoryst. It was a genetically modified fungus created by my father and other scientists in a laboratory somewhere in town. From what the documents state, a company called Midas hired them to produce a biological weapon that erased memories. From the data I read, the fungus begins as a spore the size of pollen. It's released into the air and carried by the wind. Once inhaled, and I'm not sure how this works, the fungus makes its way to our brain."

"I told you my parasite theory wasn't *that* farfetched," Kelly said with a smirk.

He turned to her and nodded with a grim expression on his face. "You were right in a way." He turned back to the mayor. "When the fungus reaches the brain, it cuts off access to the memory center, preventing you from retrieving any previous memories."

"What about your intuitions, your skills, feelings, emotions, et cetera," the mayor asked.

"I'm not sure. The files never discuss that. All I can do is assume that your skills, feelings, and everything else are separate from memories and are in a different part of your brain. Perhaps it's like muscle memory. When I was searching my home earlier today, I found a book on my dad's desk about memories. There was a sticky note he put on a chapter about trauma. Sometimes, when someone goes through a trauma, they block it out and don't remember the event, but the feelings and emotions related to that trauma still exist. For instance, let's pretend that you almost drowned when you were a child. You may block out that memory, but whenever you see water, you may become frightened without understanding why."

Erased

"Can you explain why our memories are erased again when we sleep?" the sheriff asked. "If that piece of information is true, it will devastate everyone."

"It's true," Kelly said. "Our notebooks already proved it."

"According to the research in the files, everything that happens during the day gets put into our short-term memory. When we sleep, the day's information gets converted into long-term memories, and anything left in our short-term memory banks resets for the next day. Our problem is that if we can't access those long-term memories, we are stuck in a dangerous loop of waking up with none at all."

"So, what if we do not fall asleep? What would happen then?" The mayor asked.

Troy shrugged. "I only know what I read from these papers. I'm not a scientist."

"So are we justified in assuming that someone released this fungus on our town and everyone is infected?" the mayor asked.

"It's the logical conclusion," Kelly said. "What other explanations are there? You have the answer right *here*."

"Actually, you don't."

The sudden deep voice caused the teens and sheriff to turn. The mayor looked past them to the door. A man wearing a navy blue business suit stood at the office entrance. He had slicked back, black hair, a tall and slender build, and looked to be in his early forties.

Troy recognized him from the family photo. "Dad!" he yelled and jumped up, knocking over his seat. He rushed to embrace him in a hug.

"So you're Troy," the man said as he looked down at the teen.

"You don't remember me?" Troy asked as he pulled away.

The man shook his head. "I'm sorry, son, but I don't. There's a photo of you on my work desk."

"Did you come here to find me?"

"No. I've wanted to, but work has kept me preoccupied." He turned to the others. "My name is Peter, and I'm a scientist who helped create that fungus."

"Please, take a seat," the mayor said, motioning for him to take his son's chair. "Tell us what you know."

Peter set the chair back up before sitting. "The project was a failure. After two days, the fungus kills all life exposed to it, and then produces more spores to discharge. We realized that if this were to be released *anywhere*, it would be uncontainable and spread throughout the planet on wind currents. We destroyed it and burned the entire project. Our work isn't what's causing this."

"How do you have memories of *that* and not of your own son?" Kelly asked.

"Oh, I have no memories of anything. However, we recorded videos of everything we did in the laboratory. We documented everything, and I burned every inch of that room to kill every spore. I have access to the video logs in my office and I've been reviewing them and taking notes. I can say with all certainty we are dealing with something different."

"How is that even possible?" Troy asked from where he stood, behind Kelly. "We are dealing with a problem, and the only solution that presents itself is wrong? Are we being manipulated, or what?"

The mayor bit her lip and stood. She turned toward the window and stared at the sunset. "I do not think it is manipulation, but it *is* an odd coincidence. Peter, are you sure that your work could not be duplicated in any way?"

"Without my memory, I can't be sure of anything, but I doubt it. I watched the videos. Amongst the scientists, it was a unanimous decision to destroy the project with no hesitation. I doubt any of the others would try duplicating anything."

"I suppose we will find out tomorrow, huh?" Kelly asked. "After all, if we *are* infected, two days will have passed and we will all be dead."

"That's a pleasant thought," Troy muttered. "Dad, if you were at your lab, then where is mom? I found a note in the kitchen saying you two went to Detroit."

Peter shrugged. "I can only assume she went on without me."

"We need to worry about the problem at hand," the mayor snapped. "If our memories reset every day, then we need to warn our citizens to prepare. They need to make notes for themselves."

"I can make another announcement and keep it on repeat for the rest of the day," Sheriff Orson suggested.

"There are few hours left in the day," she said with a sigh. "It will have to do though. Make sure you inform your police force about this. Perhaps they can help warn people. We may not reach everyone right away, but if we *are* still alive tomorrow, we can continue to spread the word."

The sheriff nodded and stood. "I will get right on that." He hurried from the room.

"I told you we should have gotten here earlier," Kelly said as she tilted her head back to glare at Troy.

"I'm sorry, but once I got those files, I needed to read them."

"It was *your* fault for even trying a password right before we were about to leave. You should have waited!"

"The password worked, didn't it? Sure, we may be back to square one, but at least now we know the truth."

"Which we would have found out anyway, because your dad would have *still* entered this office," Kelly countered.

"Enough!" The mayor yelled and turned. "I appreciate you coming forth with this information, but you are now giving me a headache. Please leave my office."

Kelly stood from her seat and turned to Peter. "Are you coming, sir?"

"You go ahead. I would like to talk with the mayor alone for a moment," he responded with a warm smile.

The teens left the office, shutting the door behind them.

"What would you like to talk with me about?" Jessica asked as she returned to her seat.

"I would like people brought to my laboratory for testing. I'm sure the CDC will have enough on their hands when they arrive. Until then, I should try to find the problem and perhaps create a cure."

"You will need to do that because nobody is coming to our rescue. I called every agency I can think of, and I only get recordings. I doubt we are the only ones being affected by this," she paused, "whatever *this* is."

Peter leaned forward, placed his elbow on his leg, and rested his chin on his fist. "It's possible, but until we know more, we can only speculate. Perhaps tomorrow we need to begin a real investigation to learn more about the town and our location."

The mayor nodded. "That sounds like a great plan. Also, I suggest that if you want test subjects, you take your son and his girlfriend. That would shut them up for a while."

"That's his girlfriend?" Peter asked as he turned his head toward the door. "They act like siblings, but I suppose I didn't have a picture of *her* on my desk."

"Let us not worry about this tonight. I am tired enough as it is. For now, I need to write down everything I learned today so I will relearn it with ease tomorrow."

Peter chuckled. "That's fair enough. Well then, I will leave you to your work. Have a good night." He stood and left the room, joining the teens in the hallway.

Jessica sighed and pulled open one of the desk drawers, removing a bottle of ibuprofen. She grabbed the neglected glass of water by the phone and took two pills. It would be a long rest of the day.

Φ

Mark's eyes opened and his head throbbed. He had had another migraine and pulled to the side of the road to wait for it to pass. He must have blacked out for quite a while because now the sun was almost invisible behind the vast landscape. Had he driven very far? Something told him he hadn't. It almost seemed that the further away he got from Lion's Glade, the worse the headaches became. He opened the truck door, stepped out onto the highway, and within moments, his vomit splattered against the cement. The doctors in the hospital had said he was sick. What did he have? Could it be the swine flu, or something worse? Whatever it was, it was affecting his memory. He remembered almost nothing.

"My name is Mark Hood," he said aloud. "I am from San Diego, California. My dad's name is," he paused. He couldn't remember his father's name. He tried harder. "My dad's name is," he repeated, but the word wouldn't show itself. He climbed into the bed of his truck. Sleep was what he needed. Every muscle in his body ached. Perhaps if he felt better tomorrow, he would continue his trip. He needed to get home to his family, needed to get help. He needed to… wait, what did he need to do again?

Φ

The rest of the evening in Lion's Glade was uneventful. The police had to deal with a few break-ins, but no deaths had been reported.

Sheriff Orson recorded another announcement and played it on a continuous loop, hoping that enough people would see it and follow the instructions. He left the station for the night and met his wife Bonnie at home, to spend quality time with her.

The mayor wrote several to do lists before heading home and then wrote herself a five-page letter explaining what was happening. She taped it to the inside of her bedroom door, so that after waking up, she would be sure to notice it before doing anything else.

Citizens who watched the sheriff's announcement also wrote messages and letters to themselves. Some taped their notes to their bedroom ceiling so it would be the first thing they saw when their eyes opened. Others attached messages to their bedroom doors. Still, others went a step further and wrote on their arms, just in case they somehow didn't see the paper.

After visiting their house, Troy and his dad spent the rest of the evening with Kelly at her home, playing card games they made up on the spot, and writing about everything else that had transpired. Sure, Troy didn't remember his dad, but he could feel the father-son connection. There was a bond there, something that nobody could take away by removing his memories.

"Hey, do you want to watch a movie?" Kelly asked as she closed her notebook.

Troy looked at the clock and shrugged. It was almost eleven, not too late to watch a movie. Besides, he wasn't even tired. "Why not?" He turned to his dad. "Would you like to join us?"

Peter shook his head. "No, thank you. You kids have fun. I will head home and check on things. Perhaps I can find something that explains what happened to Mom."

Troy laughed. "I'm sure she's fine, dad. Like you said in the mayor's office, it's possible she went on without you. Maybe when you were about to leave for Detroit, you got a call from the lab and had to stay."

Erased

A chill rippled through Kelly's body and goose bumps formed on her arms as a realization hit her. "There's a problem with that theory," she said.

Troy turned to her, his eyebrows furrowed. "What's that?"

"It was something you mentioned yesterday. I wrote it in my journal." She turned to the page and held it out for him. "Where are all the vehicles?"

"You know, I noticed that something was off on my way to see the mayor, but I thought little about it," Peter said as he and his son stared at the writing in the notebook.

Kelly continued. "How did you plan on getting to Detroit without a car?"

"If there aren't any vehicles, then she must still be in town somewhere," Troy breathed.

"*Or* there was another way to leave," Peter said with a frown. "Like a horse or something. Maybe we were the only family in town who owns a vehicle. I don't know. There are too many unanswered questions."

Troy sighed. "I suppose you're right. Tomorrow we will have something to do; though, I wish we could find her now." He wrote *Find Mom* in his journal. Several seconds passed with no one saying a word.

A small cuckoo clock on the wall broke the silence as it chirped in the twenty-third hour of the day. A glow outside the window caught Kelly's attention, but before she could say anything, a light enveloped the room, rendering them all unconscious.

THE TOWN

DAY THREE: CHAPTER SEVEN

Kelly awoke with a start when the alarm clock on her nightstand blared. Her hand clutched a notebook. Had she fallen asleep while writing? She swung her empty fist, hitting the snooze button, and knocked the clock off the small wooden table. When her vision wasn't so blurry, she lifted the notebook to her face. The title *Read now!* on the front in bold black letters showed its importance. She flipped it open and read, digesting the information.

If it wasn't for the fact she couldn't remember anything, Kelly would have thought someone losing all of their memories was insane. However, as she read, she understood her predicament. There wasn't any reason to freak out, for she had already lived through two days of this horror; not to mention she had a great boyfriend taking care of her. At least, that's what she wrote the previous day. She looked at the displaced alarm clock and groaned. 7:03 AM was not a time people should be awake.

She reached for the cell phone on her nightstand and brought it to her face. On day one, she had sent a text message to her mom. So far, she hadn't received a reply. The inbox was still empty. She closed the phone, seeing the time displayed on the digital bar on top. 8:05 AM?

Kelly leaned over the side of the bed and looked at the alarm clock again, seeing the 7:05 AM flashing in red numbers. There was an hour difference. She pulled the covers away from her body and slipped off the bed. She looked at her phone again and then back to the clock. Cell phones were almost always more exact so she changed the time on the alarm clock before setting it back on the nightstand.

She spent the next two hours preparing for the day. She ate breakfast, changed every clock in the house by one hour to match her cell phone, took a shower, spent at least twenty minutes deciding what to wear, put on makeup, and around ten thirty, she was all ready to take on what the world threw at her. The lack of memories didn't faze her. She knew what had happened the past two days and visualized the events that took place, except she had no idea what anybody looked like, which made her nervous.

She turned on the television to channel five like her notebook instructed and saw two people on the screen. They introduced themselves as the mayor and sheriff of Lion's Glade. They talked about the situation everyone was dealing with and gave people suggestions on what to do, the biggest one being to take notes throughout the day. Even though the citizens may not have memories of the previous day's events, they would have a hard copy. Soon, people would return to work and their normal lives. At least, that was what the mayor and sheriff hoped.

"It's a pipe dream," Kelly said aloud. "Nobody will ever be able to return to their normal life after this." She watched for a while longer as the sheriff talked about starting an investigation to look into the town's history, and other things that didn't interest Kelly. The doorbell rang.

She took her time to answer. "It's about time you got here," she said as she yanked the door open.

"Really now?" asked a tall, dark-skinned man with a heavy, Middle Eastern accent. "Do tell."

Φ

"So, let's go over what we know," Sheriff Orson said to a small group of police officers seated in his office. "Either the outside world is dealing with the same crisis we are, or we are cut off from contacting anyone beyond Lion's Glade. Either way, we are on our own."

"From what the mayor wrote in her notes, we aren't cut off from anyone. Nobody responded to her calls, and she kept getting prerecorded answering machines," Landon, one of the younger deputies said.

"Either way, that's a problem. There's no way we can let the public know that detail." The sheriff sighed as he looked at the plaques on the wall. He had received an award for heroism on four different occasions and he wished he remembered those moments; he needed a boost of heroism right now.

"What would you like us to do, sir?" Landon asked. It was clear the others had chosen him to be their spokesperson.

"Go to the library and find any history books you can on our town. Also, for the heck of it, bring back any books about our country's history. There may be useful information there."

Landon nodded, and the group left the office.

"Sheriff Orson," the dispatcher, Loraine, called out from her cubical. "I have somebody on the line for you."

Simon poked his head around the doorframe of his office. "You can transfer the call. You don't need to yell across the police station."

"My apologies, sir; I will transfer the call."

The sheriff returned to his chair and rubbed his forehead when the phone rang. He answered. "This is Sheriff Orson; how can I help you?"

"Sheriff, my name is Peter Benet, we met yesterday."

The sheriff looked down at his notes. "Yes. I can't say I remember you, but I know we talked. What can I do for you?"

"I need to see you right now. It is very important."

Simon moved the phone away from his mouth and coughed. He cleared his throat before answering. "I'm at the police station if you want to stop by and talk."

Peter grunted. "No, I need you to come to *my* location, and hurry."

Simon chuckled. "I'm needed at the station to continue coordinating things. Perhaps later this afternoon I can get away. If you like, I can send somebody else."

Lucas Heath

The tone in Peter's voice lowered. "Sheriff, get your butt out of your chair and come to 1521 Woodland Drive. I expect you here within the next thirty minutes."

The sheriff rolled his eyes. "Perhaps I haven't made myself clear," he began, but Peter interrupted.

"No, let me make *myself* clear, *sir*. I'm the *only* scientist right now who can help find a cure for this problem of ours. If you want my help, then get yourself down here. Either that, or I can call the mayor and get her to send you herself." The line went dead.

Simon returned the phone and stood, brushed a few bagel crumbs from his uniform, and left his office. He walked out to the front lobby where a young secretary sat behind a desk, playing solitaire with a tattered deck of cards. "When Landon checks in, have him call my cell. The same goes for anybody else that needs to get in contact with me."

The secretary nodded without looking up from her game.

"You have my cell phone number, right?"

She continued to stare at the cards, but pointed to a sticky note attached to the computer screen.

Satisfied, the sheriff left the building and removed a map from his back pocket. The town was rather large, with an estimated population of 1305 people. At least that's what the 2015 census showed. According to the calendars, today was March 13, 2017, though the fact it was March amazed him, considering the weather's warmth. Perhaps that gave him a clue as to the town's location. The town map gave no information other than street names and which direction was north.

Another thing he discovered that morning was that Daylight Savings Time had begun though it was only by the fluke of finding his cell phone. He had been reaching for his watch, but bumped it, knocking it behind the dresser. It was there that he found his phone. The time difference confused him at first, but it clicked once he saw the calendar. In fact, he realized that

Erased

Daylight Savings had begun the day before, though he guessed that, with everything that happened yesterday, nobody would have noticed. *He* sure didn't, because all the clocks at home and in his office still needed to be changed.

He found the street name Peter gave him on the map and made his way there while keeping a close eye on every sign he passed. Maybe they had a bike shop around there somewhere. A bicycle would be very helpful for getting around town.

It took thirty minutes for him to arrive at his destination. Peter stood on the front porch of a green two-story house, his arms folded. He wore a navy blue business suit and a black tie. "We have a problem."

Simon used his sleeve to wipe his sweaty forehead. "And you couldn't tell me this over the phone?"

Peter shook his head. "I don't know who to trust, or if anyone may listen to our conversation."

"We are in the middle of a frightening crisis, and you think people tapped the phone lines?" Simon held back an annoyed groan. "What can I help you with, Mister Benet?"

Peter pointed to the house. "My son and his girlfriend are missing."

Simon's left eyebrow rose. "You got me out here for that? They might be *anywhere* for a multitude of reasons."

"Well, someone kicked in the front door of my house and Troy is gone. Kelly's journal is in the middle of her living room floor with the television on, yet she's nowhere to be found, oh, and her front door was wide open. But you're right. They could be *anywhere* for *many* reasons."

"Being sarcastic with me isn't helping my mood," Simon said with a frown.

"In all honesty, I couldn't care any less about your mood. I'm trying to find my son. And until I do, I will not look for a cure. So act like a cop and investigate."

Simon sighed. "All right, move aside." He passed Peter and walked into Kelly's house. Everything looked to be in order. He walked into the living room, seeing every throw pillow in place. The white carpet was spotless as if nothing unclean had ever stepped upon it. He moved into the hall and entered the kitchen. There were no dirty dishes anywhere. The sink was empty and the granite counters were bare though they had a distinct lemon scent. The house looked perfect.

From the kitchen, he walked through the dining room and into the family room. The television was still on, replaying the message he and the mayor had recorded earlier that morning. A notebook lay open on the floor. Two pillows had fallen off the couch, but nothing else seemed to be disturbed. He leaned down and picked up the notebook, reading through a few lines. He turned to see Peter standing by the door, arms still folded.

"I can only guess that something scared her to run out of the house if she left the television on and her memory journal here."

Peter shrugged. "No need to look in other rooms, I've already done that. It's almost creepy how perfect everything is, but there weren't any clues. Come with me to my house."

The sheriff nodded and grabbed the remote from the couch and hit the power button, turning off the television. They left the house, shutting the front door behind them.

Peter held a small book of his own. He led the way to the blue, one-story house he and his family had lived in, before everyone forgot. The damage to the doorframe was noticeable, with a giant shoe print in the dead center of the door. They entered the house, which almost seemed as perfect as Kelly's. Everything was in its proper place, at least until they got to Troy's room. A backpack lay on the floor near a desk, with several books poking out. A pile of clothing could be seen in the closet. An alarm clock was on the floor and the comforter hung off the bed.

"What clues are you expecting me to find? You've already been here and searched."

"This isn't all I have to show you." Peter once again led Simon down the hallway and pointed to a hole in the wall. "That, if I'm not mistaken, is a bullet hole."

"I don't know if I would assume that," Simon said. "Even if you are right, that hole could have been there for a long time and you just don't remember. If you have a picture of your kid and his girl, then we can make copies and give them to my men so they can keep an eye out. I will admit something weird is happening here, but do you think somebody kidnapped them?"

Peter nodded. "I do. That is why I called you."

"Perhaps I'm a little slow this morning. I didn't get my coffee. Why would somebody want to take your son?"

"I think this will answer your question," Peter said as he removed a folded piece of paper from his pocket. "I wanted you to conclude that there is a problem before I showed you this. That way, you would understand why I asked you here. I figured you would dismiss the letter altogether without seeing this for yourself. After all, you *are* a cop."

"You have an unhealthy mistrust of the police, Peter," Simon said as he held out his hand. "You could have come to the station and let me read it without bringing me out here."

"I needed you to come here." He placed the letter into the sheriff's hand.

Simon unfolded the paper and read.

Peter Benet,

I have your son. It's a scary thought, isn't it? I control his fate, just like you controlled the fate of many when you developed your fungus. You are the reason I can't remember my life. You are the reason my wife left me a note and then killed herself. Either you will pay, or your son will pay. It's your choice. I want you to contact Sheriff Simon Orson and bring him to your home and...

Simon read the rest of the sentence and his eyebrows jumped for a second from surprise and then furrowed in frustration. "He can't be serious!"

Peter nodded. "He wants you to execute me."

DAY THREE: CHAPTER EIGHT

The sheriff finished the rest of the letter.

I want you to contact Sheriff Simon Orson, bring him to your home, and have him put a bullet through your head. After that, he can announce on television that the one who created this whole mess is dead. The people will have their justice. Only then will I let your son go. It's your choice, Peter.

The sheriff finished and shook his head. "I don't understand his thinking."

"Do what he says," Peter replied with a sullen frown tugging at his lips.

"I will not kill you!" Simon said, exasperated with the situation. "Why wouldn't this man kill you himself? Why does he want *me* to do it?"

Peter shrugged. "Perhaps he sees it as legal justice for the sheriff to be the one to pull the trigger. I can't tell you what's going on in his mind, but if you don't do what he says, he won't release my son. He has given me two options: revenge or justice."

"Either you die, giving him justice, or he will get revenge and kill your son?"

Peter nodded. "That's what I'm thinking."

"So, you must have a plan. After all, you realize we need *your* help to figure out what's causing our memory loss and create a cure."

Peter shrugged. "Shoot me."

"That's your plan?"

"I said shoot me!" Peter said and shoved Simon.

"I will not kill you!"

"My son's life is on the line! Take your gun, point it at my head, and pull the trigger!" Peter shoved Simon again.

Simon grabbed his gun from its holster and pointed it at Peter. "Is *this* what you want? Even if you die and I get your son back, we would still lose our memories every night. That's no way for anyone to live! You are trading your son's life for everyone else's, and he'll still be stuck in the same nightmare! How could you trade the lives of everyone in town for one person?"

Peter shook his head. "You underestimate the bond between a father and son. I don't even remember raising him, or spending time with him. I only have a picture of him on my desk at work. However, every fiber of my being is screaming at me to save him, and I will, even though it will kill me."

The sheriff shook his head. "Get on your knees." Peter obeyed and Simon lowered his gun, aiming it at the scientist's head.

"Thank you," Peter whispered. "Perhaps you can find the other scientists that worked on the project and get them to help you. All that information is back at my laboratory. The address and keycard are in my notebook." He lowered his head toward the ground.

"Oh, I'll find them, but you aren't going anywhere either." Simon grabbed the barrel of the gun and swung; the handle collided with Peter's head, knocking him unconscious.

Φ

Mark awoke; his face pressed against a steering wheel. His head throbbed to the rhythm of the music blaring through the iPod at his side. He stared through the windshield at the rising sun and then glanced through the side windows. Rocks, cracked dry land, and a highway extended further than the eye could see. Where was he? How did he get there? He remembered his name; Mark Hood, but an avalanche of darkness within his mind buried everything else.

As he concentrated, a partial memory surfaced. He had been sick at a hospital, which made sense. Something felt wrong with his body *and* his head. He clutched a set of keys in hand and slid the truck's key into the ignition, starting the vehicle. Where would he go? He must have been heading *somewhere* before his mind became hazy. Perhaps driving forward until he reached a town or city would be the best idea. He put the vehicle into drive and stepped on the gas. Before long, a welcome sign came into view. Only when he see the town name did his foot slam on the brake.

Welcome to Lion's Glade, the sign read. Fear rippled through his body. Every hair stood on end and he shivered. His instinct told him to escape. Escape to where though? His mental and physical health already suffered. Perhaps he needed to push past the fear and ask for help. Stepping on the gas once more, he did his best to ignore the feelings that screamed at him to escape. He passed the sign, heading toward the town in the distance. He could only hope and pray that he made the right decision.

Φ

Kelly moaned as she tried opening her eyes. She felt groggy and her head ached.

"I wondered when you would wake up," a boy said. "You've been out for a while."

After a several minutes, she could keep her eyes open; they adjusted to the minimal light entering from a small window near the ceiling. The cement floor and walls, support beams, and wooden stairs showed that she was in a basement. Duct tape bound a shirtless boy to a chair, and he had a smile on his face. She noticed a giant word written in red across his chest; *kidnapped.* She realized she had stared at it for too long when the boy spoke.

"Do you like what you see?" he asked with a wink.

"You should join a gym and work on your pecs. You've got a little flab going on there," she responded without hesitation.

"Yeah," he said and dropped his head with a sigh. "I'm Troy," he spoke after a moment of silence. He looked up and watched her.

"I somewhat assumed though I didn't know for sure. I'm Kelly. It's nice to meet you, for like the fourth time." She attempted to move her hands, but found them bound behind her back with tape. The man had also secured her legs in the same fashion.

Troy nodded in understanding. "I wonder why he would take you too. You and I are friends, but what's the purpose of your abduction?"

Kelly shrugged. "What happened to you this morning? I expected *you* to show up, and I got that crazy guy standing at my door instead. He grabbed me and put something over my face for several minutes, and then I woke up here."

Troy nodded. "The man called it chloroform. He would have used it on me, but I cooperated. When I woke up this morning, I read my notebook and got ready to see you. That *pervert* had the nerve to enter the bathroom while I was taking a shower. He pointed a gun at me and barely gave me time to put on my clothes. I forgot to bring a shirt with me to the bathroom and he wouldn't let me get one. He didn't let me put socks or shoes on either!"

It was only then that Kelly noticed Troy was barefoot. "I'm surprised he let you put on pants. *That* would prevent you from even *wanting* to escape."

Troy's eyes narrowed. "Don't give him any ideas. Are you normally such a smart-aleck?"

"It's a natural tendency," she said with a giggle. "So, what does he want?"

"I don't know, but he's been yelling upstairs for the past couple of hours about the stupidity of police officers not following simple directions. He stopped ranting a few minutes ago."

"What is he waiting for? What does he want?"

Troy shrugged. "Beats me. I'm not sure what he's after, but I hope he gets it and sets us free. At least I understand what *beware the Arab* means now."

They sat in silence for several minutes before Kelly spoke. "Okay, I *have* to ask. Why the word on your chest?"

Troy chuckled. "When I first got here, I asked Mister Arab Guy if I could use the bathroom. I grabbed a tube of lipstick near the sink and wrote the word *kidnapped*, so I would have an idea of what was going on if he keeps me here for more than a day and our memories reset. He saw it, but didn't care enough to make me wash it off."

"Oh," Kelly said. For a short while, they sat in silence, waiting for what came next.

Φ

Peter sat on a cot, staring at a large mechanical clock, watching the second hand spin. He had woken up an hour earlier in a jail cell, with his wrists still cuffed behind him. The sheriff's betrayal fueled Peter's fury, but with nobody near to unleash his anger upon, and nobody there to witness his breakdown, he let the tears flow. He was sure the kidnapper had killed his son; a son he had no memory of, but that didn't break the bond they had. His wife never entered his thoughts. He only wanted his boy.

Sheriff Orson sat at his desk, looking over reports his secretary had printed out for him. They had already distributed the pictures of the teenagers, but maybe there was more Simon could do. The phone rang, interrupting his thoughts. He lifted it from its cradle and answered. "Sheriff Orson speaking, how can I help you?"

"Hello, Sheriff." A man with a thick, Middle Eastern accent spoke. "I am sorry that you decided my demand is negotiable."

"What demand?" The sheriff asked.

"To have Peter killed. I fail to see the reason you have traded his son's life for his."

"Peter may have the skill we need to fix this problem with our memories and return things to normal. It would be a huge mistake to kill him. If there's any hope of finding a cure for this, we need him alive."

"There *is* no hope for us," he hissed. "There was no hope for my wife. Peter's son still lives; so does the girl. I want your decision by midnight, or they both die."

Simon hung up the phone when the line disconnected and he sighed. He stared at the papers on his desk and a knock on the door startled him.

"Sir, may I enter?" Landon, the young deputy asked.

"Enter," Simon said as he read another report.

Landon stepped inside, but approached no further. "Sir, we found many books on American history. They answer a few of our questions. We could only find one book on the town's history; it was open on a table as if someone had been reading it before we got there."

The sheriff nodded. "Place those books in conference room A. If you guys want to take time and patrol, go for it. If not, then read and take notes."

Landon nodded. "Thank you, sir. I'm sure they would like to read. We are all curious about where we live." He took a step back without turning away from the sheriff. "I will give my report to you later this evening."

Simon nodded and waved Landon away. He watched him go before returning his focus to the documents in front of him. After scooping them up, he left his office. He passed by the dispatchers' cubicles, hearing them chatter away with people asking for any new information. Neither he nor the mayor had televised any updates since the morning. In fact, he hadn't heard from the mayor since they parted ways after the first round of announcements. Perhaps after talking with Peter, he would head over and record another update.

He pushed the bar on a large metal door and stepped inside the jailhouse of the station. There were five cells in all. Each one was eight by ten feet, with thick iron bars that extended from floor to ceiling, every five inches. Each one contained a small cot and a toilet. He walked to the end where Peter sat staring at the clock.

Peter looked at Simon and then turned back to the timepiece.

"He called here a few minutes ago."

Peter's eyes shifted to the sheriff. "Did he kill my son?"

The sheriff shook his head. "No, he has given us until midnight to decide, and he left no room for interpretation. It's your life or Troy's. I think I may be on to something though and I want your input." The sheriff stuck his hand through the bars and laid out the first few papers on the ground. "The man claims his wife committed suicide. We had four reported suicides in the past two days since we believe this started. Two were male, and two were female."

Peter looked at the report on the first woman's suicide. It included a picture.

"I know that you have no memories of her, but I have to ask, does that woman seem familiar in any way? Perhaps like an instinct you knew her, or a strange familiarity?"

Peter stared at the picture of the lifeless face. He shook his head. "No, why would you ask that?"

Simon looked at the next three pages in his hand. "Something is wrong with this whole thing. Why would a normal town citizen think you were the reason his wife killed herself? Why would he think you had something to do with people's memories being erased?"

Peter shrugged. "I don't know. Why?"

The sheriff put the second set of documents onto the floor; once again it included the woman's picture. "We don't have her name or where she lives. According to the report I wrote two days ago, she jumped off a building. There was no identification on her."

Peter looked down and knelt to the floor, scanning her picture. "No, it can't be," he gasped. He shook his head and then studied the other documents. "I don't understand this. Why would she…" he paused and looked up at the sheriff. "What did the man sound like?" he asked with a sense of urgency in his voice.

"The man?"

"The man who kidnapped my son; you said he called you. What did he sound like?" he pressed.

Simon's eyebrows furrowed. "He spoke with an accent. It almost sounded like he was from the Middle East."

"This is his wife," Peter said with several rapid nods.

Simon felt a chill shoot through his body and he shuddered. "How do you know? Do you recognize her?"

Peter nodded. "Yes. Her name is Elizabeth. She was a brilliant scientist. She helped create the fungus."

DAY THREE: CHAPTER NINE

Mark had driven for a while before he pulled into a gas station. The town roads were void of any vehicles, and the few people he saw walking along the sidewalks gawked at his truck as he passed them. He climbed out of the driver's seat and removed his ID from his wallet. He swiped it through the machine and waited before he could fill up the tank. The needle pointed near the E, and he figured that if he wanted a quick escape, he better make sure he had fuel. He returned the nozzle after a few minutes and climbed back into the truck. His body ached though he did his best to ignore it.

Where would he go, the hospital? Even the idea sent a ripple of fear through his body. He needed help, and as scared as he felt, he needed a doctor. How would he even find it? How big was the town? Did Lion's Glade even have a hospital? The questions surged through his mind, making his head hurt even more. He climbed back out of the truck and walked toward the gas station door. It was unlocked, and he stepped inside the building. Nobody was there.

"Hello?" he called out. The place was silent, except for the hum of refrigerators in the back which held many varieties of sodas, alcohol, milk, and energy drinks. His stomach growled from hunger and he walked down one aisle, past the candy, to the assorted nuts. He grabbed a couple bags and proceeded toward the refrigerated section, grabbing a bottle of milk. He made his way to the front register and saw a town map in a cardboard box. Grabbing a map, he glanced around for the attendant. Nobody stood behind the counter. He pulled out his wallet and set a ten dollar bill on the counter, figuring it would cover the expenses, and returned to his truck.

He ate. His throat was on fire though the milk helped sooth the pain. He opened the map and studied the roads. Looking through his windshield, he saw signs in the distance and read the street names with ease. He was at the corner of Penn and Dunn. The hospital was across town. He doubted it would take him long, considering there weren't any cars on the road and he didn't see a single stoplight. Sure, he would have to stop at stop signs, but oh well.

He did just that, making his way toward the hospital. The closer he got, the more he shook. As soon as it came into view, a memory jabbed at his brain. He had been here.

Φ

At the Midas Tech Laboratory, near the south edge of town, Peter retrieved a keycard from his wallet and placed it near a scanner. A large metal door slid into the wall. As they stepped in, a hallway light flickered to life; the door shut behind them after they entered.

"Welcome back, Peter," the voice of a woman transmitted through a speaker in the ceiling. It sounded almost human though a strange break and fluctuation in her words exposed it as a computer-generated voice.

They headed down a solid gray hall, toward a flight of stairs. Their footsteps echoed on the plain cement as they walked. Peter used his card at another scanner by a metal gate and the chain link door unlatched. He pulled it open and shut it once they were on the other side. They continued down a second flight of stairs before coming to a metal door. Peter pushed a button in the shape of a down arrow.

"This is a lot of security," Simon said as they waited for the elevator. He tugged on his shirt and straightened his badge.

Peter nodded. "If you knew about the experiments we conducted here, it's not that shocking."

A bell dinged, and the doors slid open. They stepped inside the elevator. While the halls and stairs had been concrete, the elevator had a carpet. Peter scanned his card once again and typed a seven digit number into a small keypad. The elevator shook as it started its decent further underground.

"You remembered the code?" the sheriff asked.

Erased

Peter shook his head. "I found it on my desk when I woke up this morning. I watched a few video logs and then went to find my son."

The cell phone in Simon's pocket vibrated, and he removed it. "Sheriff Orson speaking," he said as he flipped the phone open.

"Sheriff, it's Landon, the mayor called and wanted to…" Landon's voice vanished as the reception ceased to exist.

"Most radios and cell phones don't work down here," Peter said. "Especially the cheap kind like yours."

"Thanks for the warning," Simon muttered.

It took another minute before the doors behind the two men opened. Peter turned around and walked into an office space. Simon followed.

"The laboratory is further inside, but we don't need to go there. We need to find Elizabeth's file and get her address."

They walked past cubicles, toward the private offices.

"What did he say?" Simon asked.

"Who?"

"Elizabeth's husband; you said he left a message on her office answering machine. That's how you knew he had an accent. What did he say?"

Peter shrugged. "He sounded freaked out. His call this morning woke me. Elizabeth's office is right next to mine. He said he didn't remember her, but he loved her anyway, or something like that. I didn't erase it. You can listen if you wish."

Simon shook his head. "No, thank you."

They reached her office and entered. It wasn't a big space, but it contained a desk with a computer, two filing cabinets, and a chair for guests. A creamy yellow painted the walls and the ceiling tiles were solid white, making them look almost new. To Simon, *everything* seemed new, as if nobody had ever been there.

Peter walked over to a filing cabinet and sorted through the useless information. "Can you flip that switch for me, please?" he asked and pointed. A moment later, light bathed the room in an eerie glow. It took time, but Peter came to the folder he needed. He yanked it out and shut the drawer. He walked to Elizabeth's chair, sat down, removed the papers, and spread them out on the desk. Simon joined him and read over his shoulder. "Ahmed Muhammad," Peter read aloud. "That's her husband's name. I have the address."

"Is it possible to use one of these office phones to call out? I can get my men over there right away."

Peter shook his head. "This man doesn't understand what his wife did here."

"Do you believe she killed herself because she thought someone released the fungus?" Simon asked.

Peter shrugged. "I can only speculate. The question running through *my* mind is, did she jump before everybody lost their memories, or was it after this happened? The report states a deputy found her body on the sidewalk. How long was it there?"

"Why does it matter?" Simon asked.

"Because, if she jumped before, we have a solid clue she saw what happened and that our project *caused* this. Perhaps it's a modified version of the fungus which doesn't kill its victims after two days."

"If she jumped *after* everybody lost their memory, what would that tell us?"

Peter pressed his lips together in thought. "Perhaps she freaked out when she couldn't remember anything and decided she didn't want to live that way. Right now though, we need to focus on getting my son away from Ahmed."

Erased

"Which goes back to my question; can I use one of these phones to call out of this facility? I can give my men the address and have them search the place."

Peter shook his head. "If Ahmed sees the police coming, he might kill Troy and Kelly. I don't want them involved. I want to go in myself and stop him. Perhaps I can convince him I had no part in the releasing of this experiment."

"Do you think he will listen? I wouldn't like sending you in alone. We still need you to figure out what's causing this problem and fix it." The sheriff stood behind Peter and could have hit him in the back of the head again. It was a wonder Peter hadn't gotten a concussion from the first blow.

Peter sighed as he continued to look at the papers in front of him. "You could knock me out, destroy my journal, convince me I need to help the town, make me forget about my son, and that could work. I beg you though, please let me save Troy. My wife is also missing. At home I found a note I wrote to Troy, telling him she and I were leaving for Detroit. I don't know what happened after that. I can't lose both of them." Peter stood and turned to the sheriff. "I will help you figure out this problem, and I will create a cure, but I need my son back first."

The sheriff eyed Peter before speaking. "It amazes me you don't have your memories, yet you still have such a strong bond with your son. However, you show little emotion."

Peter nodded. "I know," he mumbled. "I don't understand it either. My emotions are erratic, and I'm not sure what to feel. But, I *need* to make sure he is safe."

The sheriff nodded. "Fine, I will let you go, but I'm coming with you. I won't let you face this guy alone. For all you know, he could kill you *and* the teens."

A slight grin formed at Peter's lips. "Well, I have the address. All I need is a gun and we are good to go."

Lucas Heath

Φ

The sun had disappeared behind the landscape by the time Mark had pushed past the fear and left the truck. Many times he had told himself he was fine and ended up getting into arguments with a voice in his head telling him to suck it up and ask for help. His truck was the only vehicle in the parking lot, which made him wonder if the hospital had any employees. The town already seemed desolate. Something was wrong; he couldn't ignore the eerie chill down his spine.

His legs trembled as he shut the truck door and approached the hospital's entrance. The building looked small from the outside, but Mark assumed that, for a town as big as this one, it had what it needed to accommodate the citizens. The automatic sliding glass doors opened as he approached. He walked inside and saw a counter to his left. A woman wearing a light blue shirt and pants sat behind the counter, reading something on a computer monitor.

"Excuse me," he mumbled.

She looked up and smiled. "Hello," she greeted. Her voice had a tender warmth that soothed his mind. "How can I help you?"

"My name is Mark Hood, and," he paused. What else was he going to say? That he was losing his mind? That his memories were disappearing? That he had the flu and needed medication? He rubbed his forehead. "Something is wrong with me," he said. "I'm sick. I have the flu or something and I'm losing my memories. There's also this strange voice speaking in my head." The woman would either think he was crazy and have him committed, or think perhaps he had the flu and that the fever was affecting his mind.

She picked up a phone. "Diana, we have another patient. Please get out here." Her voice broadcasted through speakers installed into the hospital ceiling. She hung up the phone and left the booth, approaching Mark. "So you say you're losing your memories? Don't you mean you *lost* your memories?"

Erased

Mark shook his head. "No," he said. "I remember small things, like my name and that I'm from California. I also remember that I was at a hospital and they said I was sick." The nurse's eyes grew wide, and Mark wasn't sure if she thought he was insane, or understood his problem.

Another woman appeared from a swinging door on the other side of the waiting room. "What's wrong with this one, Bonnie?"

Bonnie turned to Diana. "He still has partial memories. He thinks he has the flu."

Diana's eyes shot open for a split second. She waved Mark to follow. "Come with me please," she said with such a commanding voice that Mark felt obligated to obey.

"Don't I need to fill out paperwork?" he asked.

The woman stared at him for a moment before answering. "We will worry about that later; please come with me."

Mark complied and followed her, walking deeper into the hospital.

Bonnie returned to her station behind the counter and picked up the phone. She looked at a small sticky note taped to the computer monitor and dialed the number.

"Sheriff Orson speaking."

"Honey, it's Bonnie," she said, hoping he hadn't forgotten her.

"Yes, dear, what can I do for you?"

"I wanted to let you know that a man just entered the hospital, and he still has some of his memories."

There was a pause on the other end. "She said a guy showed up at the hospital and he still has some of his memories."

"That's good news!"

Bonnie heard a second voice in the background. She heard a shuffling of the phone.

"Bonnie, my name is Peter. I am a biologist assigned by the mayor to work on finding a solution to this problem. While this mystery man is in the hospital, I need you to take blood samples for me."

Bonnie listened to the instructions and wrote them all down on a notepad by the phone. She hung up and tore the paper from the pad. She picked up the phone and pushed a red button. "Diana, please come to the front desk," she asked over the PA system. She replaced the phone and looked over the list again. She would make sure that Diana delivered the instructions to the doctor.

If this man, Mark, still had memories, then perhaps his body somehow fought against the cause of their memory loss in the first place, which also made him sick. Or maybe he had the flu, which prevented him from losing all of his memory. There were many possibilities, but excitement still gripped Bonnie. They were one-step closer to a cure.

DAY THREE: CHAPTER TEN

"If that man still has some of his memories, do you know what that means?" Peter asked as he looked at his notebook. He scribbled down information he had seen in the laboratory offices. That way, if something happened to him, the town wouldn't be without hope. At the moment, he and Simon walked across town toward the address where they assumed Ahmed held Troy.

The sheriff nodded and looked at his cell phone. It was late already, and they didn't have time to waste. They still had a midnight deadline, given by the kidnapper. Simon called the police station to get the latest news. Ahmed had called twice, asking for the sheriff. Each time the dispatchers told him that Simon had left the office, he would repeat his threat of wanting Peter's body by midnight, or the boy and girl would die. "If he calls again, transfer the call to my cell phone," Simon had told Bobby the dispatcher.

"The man in the hospital might be the answer," Peter said. His mind raced with ideas. "Well, not *him*, but his body, his blood."

"Peter," the sheriff said and stopped walking.

Peter halted and turned to Simon.

"Do you want to save your son, or do you want to go talk with this new guy at the hospital?"

Peter frowned and his eyebrows furrowed. "Why would you ask such a thing? I want to save my son!"

The sheriff nodded. "All right, then you need to switch gears now. Focus on the man later. We need to come up with a plan. I don't think we have the skills to do this by ourselves. Every bone in my body says to call for backup."

"But you can't," Peter said. "You're right though. I can think about science later. You're the sheriff, how should we proceed? It's not like we can knock on the door, can we?"

"Let's keep walking while we talk." The sheriff continued on and Peter followed. "We need to make sure that's where Troy and Kelly are being kept. What if he is holding them elsewhere, in case we figured out his identity?"

"He won't be thinking about that," Peter said. "Nobody in this town has their memories. There's no way he would expect us to figure out who he is, let alone *where* he lives."

Simon ran his hand over the slats of a white-picket fence as they passed. "You know, I have an idea, but first I need to pee."

Φ

Mark felt exhausted and his head continued to throb. Fear prevented him from sleeping. He lay on a hospital bed with an IV stuck in the crook of his arm, right where the cotton ball and tape had been. Something seemed to click in his head. That's right! Yesterday he had a blood-covered cotton ball taped to his arm.

Did that happen yesterday? He couldn't remember. This morning when he awoke, there was no cotton ball on his arm. He had forgotten about it until now. Did he rip it off in his sleep? Why did he care? That constant voice seemed to ask him countless questions. He needed to silence the little man in his head.

A doctor, whose name Mark had already forgotten, entered the room with a clipboard. He wore a long, white coat over navy blue pants and a matching shirt. A stethoscope hung from around his neck. "We are testing your blood to figure out what's wrong, but we expect the test results won't come back until tomorrow sometime. I hope the biologist shows up to look them over. For now, you can relax and get some sleep. A nurse is right outside if you need anything." He placed the clipboard in a holder at the end of the bed and left.

Erased

Mark looked around the room. It appeared dreary with gray curtains over the windows, a sick cream color for the walls, and a yellow-tiled floor. The room felt rather small and contained the hospital bed, a single chair for a guest, and several machines near his head, though Mark wasn't sure of their purpose. He closed his eyes, hoping that he could sleep.

Φ

"Doctor Kale, please come here," Diana called out as the doctor walked by the nurses' station.

He turned to her and rested his arms on the counter.

"There is something you should see. I thought the name Mark Hood sounded familiar, and I figured out why." She lifted a folder from her desk and passed it to him. "I should have found it sooner, but there were too many distractions, and I didn't think about it. When I remembered where I had seen the name, I did a search. His name is on a list I filed earlier this morning. I didn't think we would need it since everything had changed."

"What list?" the doctor asked as he opened the file and gave it a glance.

"A list of earlier patients," she said. "Mark Hood was in *this* hospital, in that *exact* same room, a few days ago."

Φ

"That's the house," the sheriff said in a whisper. Both he and Peter were hiding behind overgrown bushes across the street and a few houses away from the target. Large, thick drapes covered the windows though light escaped a thin crack. The two-story house had a covered porch with a bench swing, and a sapling grew in the front yard. Darkness concealed all other details.

"How much time do we have left?" The question was almost prophetic, for the cell phone in the sheriff's pocket rang.

He removed it and flipped it open. "Sheriff Orson speaking," he answered.

"Sheriff," the voice was distinct and unmistakable.

"What can I do for you?" the sheriff replied.

"I've been trying to contact you. You've been very elusive."

"I've been dealing with a town-wide crisis," the sheriff's cold reply caused the man to pause.

"Yes, you have, though I have to wonder what you've been doing. You have yet to execute Peter Benet and leave his body at his home. You realize you have less than thirty minutes, right?"

"How do I know you will release the teens once you get what you want?"

"You don't, but I am a man of my word. I wouldn't slaughter innocent children without purpose. If the boy's father dies, there will be no reason for me to harm them. I will let them go."

Simon looked at Peter and nodded. "Then I will kill him. I can't let two teens die because of one man's mistake."

"I'm glad you finally see reason." Ahmed's chuckle unnerved the sheriff and it felt as if icy tendrils wrapped themselves around his neck. "Make sure to kill Peter in his living room. That's the easiest place to confirm his death."

"Fine," the sheriff said. "Is there any way you can extend the deadline? It will take me a while to get Peter there."

"Then *run*," Ahmed said, and the call ended.

The sheriff set his phone on silent and closed it before slipping it back into his pocket. "No extensions," he said. "I'm wondering if we are at the right house."

Erased

"Why would you say that?" Peter asked.

"He said I needed to kill you in the living room of your home so it's easier to confirm your death, which means he's watching your house somehow. Perhaps he's stationed in a house near yours."

Peter shook his head. "If he is, then we have lost. This is our last chance to find them."

The sheriff sighed. "All right, let's go."

Φ

Mark forced his eyes open and a wave of exhaustion tugged at his mind, doing its best to drag him into the world of dreams. He tried moving his right arm, but it wouldn't budge. He tried moving his left arm, but with the same results. Someone had strapped his arms and legs to the bed. He wanted to yell, but he couldn't; he was too tired. He saw Nurse Diana at his side, holding a syringe, injecting something into the tube that fed a liquid into his arm.

"I'm sorry," she said with a voice full of remorse. "But you're patient zero. You're the one who started this whole thing. We will need you for testing."

Whatever she injected into the tube worked fast; before Mark responded, he fell fast asleep.

Φ

It took several minutes, but Peter and Simon made it through the shadows to the side of the house. They had figured that if Ahmed kept the teens anywhere, it would be in the dark. A basement would be the best place to keep them disoriented.

Peter heard a television on inside the house, repeating a message the sheriff and mayor had recorded earlier that morning. No fence bordered the property, allowing them to reach the back of the house without a problem. The target window was at ground level and locked tight. It was two feet by one foot and led to the basement. Peter removed his blue suit jacket and dropped to his stomach on the grass. He turned on a small flashlight he had taken from the laboratory and shone it through the glass.

"Are they in there?" Simon asked.

Peter panned the flashlight from right to left, spotting the half-naked boy taped to a chair. "Yeah, Troy is here," he said as he returned to his feet.

"Perhaps he left Troy, but took Kelly with him to witness your execution. That way he had at least *one* hostage with him."

Peter shook his head. "That makes no sense. He would take Troy if that were the case, not Kelly."

"Then what do you want to do? We have ten minutes until midnight. We can take the risk and follow our plan, or we can come up with something new."

"Sir," a voice called out in a hushed whisper as a dark image rounded the corner of the house.

Peter raised his gun and pointed it at the three approaching men.

"Lower your weapon, Peter. They are my deputies."

"I told you we would do this alone!" Peter snapped. "When did you even have time to call them?"

"When I took that bathroom break," Simon admitted. "Going in without backup is a stupid idea. We now have a better chance of capturing Ahmed alive before he hurts your son." The sheriff turned to Landon and his group. "Glad you made it. We have a visual on the hostage. He's alone. We don't know who else is in the house."

Landon nodded. "Tell us what you want us to do."

Erased

"I want you to stay in the back. I'll take Barns with me to the front. The moment I ring the doorbell, we break down both doors. We want to keep this guy alive."

"And you want us to break down the door, how?" Landon asked.

"God gave you legs to kick with, son, and you will use them. This house is older than most I've seen here in town, and the doors don't look like they would withstand two men kicking it at once."

"What about me?" Peter asked.

"This is why I had my men meet us. I do not want you going in, especially if there's a possibility you could be hurt. We will save your son. I promise."

Peter sighed and shook his head. "And you wonder why I don't trust cops," he said.

They had little time left. Within minutes, the sheriff and Deputy Barns stood on the front porch. Landon and another young deputy stood at the back door.

What could Peter do, take on the cops himself, just to save his son from a different enemy? The idea seemed stupid. He could only stand and watch how events unfolded. He flicked the gun's safety off and kept the weapon clutched in his hand, hoping there would be no need to use it.

What came next happened fast, and it left Peter in a state of shock. The doorbell rang through the house as the sheriff pushed the button, giving Landon and his partner the signal to break down the back door. The sound of two gunshots blended with splintering wood as the police kicked in the doors.

"Officer down, the sheriff is down!" Barns screaming from the front. Landon and his partner were already inside the house. A few more gunshots pierced the silence of the neighborhood.

Lucas Heath

Sudden light flooding through the basement window drew Peter's attention. He dove to his stomach and looked through the glass, seeing a dark-skinned man running down a flight of stairs on the opposite wall from the window. The rest, Peter attributed to instinct. His face was a foot away from the glass though that didn't stop him. He lifted his gun, pointing it at Ahmed who had stopped in front of Troy and raised a knife. Peter pulled the trigger three times. The bullets shattered the glass and hit the intended target twice. The third bullet embedded itself into the wall behind him.

Landon ran down the stairs as Ahmed collapsed to the ground, the knife still clutched in his hand. Landon looked toward the window, seeing Peter, and then back to the man on the ground with two bullets in his back.

The thick accent escaped Ahmed's lips as he spoke. "I wanted justice for my wife, and yet you people protect the guilty while the innocent suffer." He closed his eyes and said no more.

Landon stepped on the hand that held the knife to protect himself from a possible attack. He used his pointer and middle fingers to check for a pulse. He looked up at Peter and shook his head. Ahmed was dead.

Troy stirred in his chair. A strip of tape covered his mouth, preventing him from talking.

Peter jumped to his feet, leaving the gun by the window, and ran into the house. He wished to comfort Troy and remove all the tape from his body, setting him free, but the corpse of Landon's partner made him stop.

"Stay with me, sir, you can't die on us," Barns yelled from the front.

Peter made his way through the dining room and down a hall to the front door, passing pictures of Ahmed and Elizabeth on the way. Sheriff Orson lay face up on the carpet, eyes closed, two bullet holes in his chest.

Barns, a somewhat chubby, young redhead, who looked to be in his mid-twenties, had tears in his eyes. "I'm sorry," he said as he clutched Simon's lifeless hand.

Erased

Peter stared at the body and shook his head. Two police officers had traded their lives for his son. He could never repay something like that. He wandered into the living room, trying to find the steps that led to the basement. He didn't get very far, for as the clocks brought in the midnight hour, a light filled the sky, bathing the town, rendering everyone unconscious. Day three had ended.

DAY FOUR: CHAPTER ELEVEN

The alarm clock blared at six in the morning, rousing Bonnie from her slumber. After rolling over to the other side of the bed, she reached out toward the sound, trying to find the snooze button. She fumbled around until she found a little switch, turning the alarm off altogether. She rolled back onto her side of the bed and attempted to keep her eyes open for more than a few seconds. After a yawn and a moment of stretching, she guided herself out from beneath the covers. She placed her feet on the floor, finding two pink fuzzy slippers to slide them into, and made her way to the bedroom door.

She found a white piece of paper taped to the handle and removed it, lifting it to read.

We are Simon and Bonnie Orson. Due to a strange occurrence in our town of Lion's Glade, the entire population has lost their memories. There is a notebook on the kitchen counter with everything we have figured out about our life together. Read it.

Bonnie replaced the paper and looked around the room; no Simon to be seen. A neatly pressed police uniform hung from a hook in the corner, near a closet. Perhaps Simon stepped out, giving her more time to sleep. She opened the door and walked down a familiar, yet unremembered hall, and after looking around, entered the kitchen. She found the notebook on the counter and picked it up, took it to the living room, and sat in a recliner.

Our Life Together, she read the title on the front of the notebook. Bonnie flipped it open and read. It included information on the events that took place the past couple of days, summaries of letters, and several documents she found in the house on day one. It explained that she worked at the hospital as a nurse, Simon was the town sheriff, and the notebook contained a short note that said she loved Simon more than life.

Erased

Bonnie stood and set the notebook on the coffee table. According to the information, she started work at noon, but until then, she would look for her husband.

Ф

The alarm clock blaring at 7:00 AM rattled Kelly awake. She swung with all her might toward the sound without opening her eyes and knocked the alarm clock to the floor. She missed the snooze button, and it continued to shriek out of her reach. With a groan of frustration, she left the comfort of her bedding and slipped to the floor. She hit the snooze button, silencing her enemy, and laid on the floor.

The dream from which she awoke tugged at her mind. Someone had locked her in a bathroom though she didn't know why. She tried escaping, but the bathroom had no windows. Within a few minutes of searching for a way out, she heard gunfire below her, and then she woke to her alarm.

After several minutes she forced her eyes open and stared at the blinking clock in front of her – 7:10 AM... a time suited to early birds, which she wasn't. At least, she didn't think she was. She couldn't remember. She sat up and leaned against the bed. Her wrists and the skin around her mouth throbbed. A notebook several inches from her hand had *Read Now!* written on the front in bold, black letters. She reached for it and caught herself from falling over, and then grabbed the metal binding. She pulled it over, opened it, and read.

Ф

Troy awoke with a start as if a jolt of electricity had shot through his body. His heart pounded at a rapid pace as adrenalin filled his bloodstream. Drops of sweat cascaded down his cheeks, and he kicked the covers away from his body. He stared at his naked torso, seeing the word *kidnapped* and droplets of sweat across his chest. Troy wore blue shorts, and they too were soaked. He thought he may have wet himself. His hand held a tight grip on a green spiral notebook.

Lucas Heath

He spun out of bed and stood to his feet. His body shook with such intensity, he had difficulty moving. He made his way to the trashcan by his desk where he dry heaved. After a moment of rest, his stomach settled, and he looked down at the notebook in hand, which had the title *Memories* written in black on the front cover, and the sentence, *Troy READ NOW*, written underneath the title. He followed the instruction and opened the notebook. His entire body ached from the adrenaline, but he tried to ignore it so he could read. His muscles loosened and his heartbeat slowed as he digested the information written on the pages. Without knowing why, he believed every word. The one question nagging at his mind had to do with the word on his chest. He had written nothing about it in the journal.

Troy stood, tossed the notebook to the floor, left his room, and walked down the hall to the bathroom. He stripped the shorts and boxers off his body and stepped into the shower, pulling the glass door closed behind him. He turned a knob until ice-cold water poured over his skin. Goose bumps rippled over his body, but the cold water had a strange, calming effect. He grabbed a brush hanging from a small clip in the corner and tried scrubbing the red word off his chest. Perhaps something *had* happened, but whatever caused him to feel this way, he knew he wouldn't want to remember.

Φ

It hadn't taken long for Bonnie to realize her husband wasn't at home. She assumed he had already left for work, so she dressed, straightened her hair, grabbed a set of keys and directions to the police station on the kitchen table, and left the house. After a short time, she reached her destination.

Ten police officers stood outside the station.

"What's going on?" she asked the nearest officer as she approached. He looked rather young, maybe in his early twenties.

Erased

He shrugged. "I'm not sure. We all woke up without our memories, yet had instructions we wrote to ourselves telling us to put on our uniforms and come to the police station."

"No, I mean, why are you all standing out here?"

He shrugged again. "It's locked. We are waiting for the sheriff, I suppose."

"He's not here yet?" Bonnie pressed her lips together. She didn't understand why she had such a strong longing to find Simon, but she needed to see his face in person and hear his voice. Perhaps true love kept her searching. She had no memories of him, but that desire to see him never left.

"Not that I'm aware of. I'm Landon."

She shook his hand. "It's nice to meet you." She thought for a moment. "Shouldn't there be a night crew in the station?"

"I am scheduled for the night crew." Another young man stepped forward. "At least, that's what the paper said. I'm supposed to get here at midnight. I came this morning to confirm with the Sheriff."

"But what about last night's crew?" Bonnie asked. "They should still be inside, right? Unless they never selected a graveyard crew in previous days."

Landon shrugged. "I didn't write about it in my notebook."

"Is it me, or is something wrong here?" Bonnie asked as she shoved her hands into her jean pockets.

Landon shrugged. "Other than waking up without our memories?"

Bonnie shrugged. "I can't explain it; it's like..." she paused when her fingers embraced the keys she had grabbed from the table. She removed them from her pocket and studied each one. Engraved into one of the keys were the words *Do Not Duplicate*. She walked through the group of officers and slid the key into the lock. It turned, unlocking the deadbolt.

There were grunts and nods of approval as she opened the door, letting the men enter. Landon stopped by her side. "I didn't catch your name."

Bonnie gave a nervous laugh. "I suppose you didn't. My name is Bonnie Orson. The sheriff is my husband. At least, that's what my memory journal says."

Landon smiled. "Well, Mrs. Orson, I look forward to meeting your husband."

"That makes two of us," she said with a sigh.

"Are you doing all right?" Landon asked as his brows furrowed.

She shook her head. "Are you really asking me that question? Of *course* I'm not all right. I can't remember a danged thing and my husband is nowhere to be found."

"I'm sure he's around here somewhere," Landon tried reassuring her. "Until he shows up, I'll set up tasks for the rest of the deputies. I took detailed notes on what has happened the past few days."

She nodded and turned her head, scanning the streets. A blonde-haired woman dressed in a dark blue business suit approached. To Bonnie, it looked like the woman had lost a battle with her weight and leaned toward the pudgy scale.

"Hello, my name is Jessica Dailey, the mayor of this town," she said to Bonnie and Landon when she stepped within handshaking distance.

"Officer Landon Davis, ma'am," he said as his posture straightened.

"And I am Bonnie Orson, the sheriff's wife."

"Ah, Sheriff Orson; I wrote a lot of good things about him. Is he in the police station? We need to record an announcement for the citizens."

Erased

"Ma'am, Sheriff Orson has yet to arrive. Bonnie here has been looking for him."

"Bonnie?" Bonnie asked with her right eyebrow raised.

"I'm sorry," Landon stammered. "Mrs. Orson has been looking for him."

"Well then, I must record the message myself. Let me know when he arrives. I would like to speak with him." Jessica glanced at a piece of paper in her hands, focused her gaze down a road for a moment, and began walking.

"If you will excuse me, I should get inside and talk with the others." Landon gave a farewell nod and entered the station, shutting the door behind him.

Bonnie watched the mayor until she disappeared around a corner. *That suit really doesn't fit well,* she thought before exhaling an exasperated breath and heading home. Perhaps Simon had returned.

Φ

Peter awoke with a start to a telephone ringing. He lifted his head from a metal desk and saw a puddle of drool formed into a perfect circle. He wiped his mouth and grabbed the phone before his brain clicked into place. "Hello," he answered.

"Dad, is that you?" a boy's voice blared through the phone.

"Who?" Peter asked. A misty barrier clouded his thinking, and it took a moment to clear the fog.

"Is this Peter?"

"I don't know," Peter drawled as he realized he didn't have his memories.

"Oh no," a sigh came from the other end. "Are you sitting at a desk?"

"Yes," Peter responded as he looked around the room. He sat in an office. It had a small metal desk with a computer monitor and a bunch of papers with a small notebook on top. Two filing cabinets stood against the wall behind him and a potted plant sat next to the door.

"Is there a notebook near you?"

Peter cleared his throat. "Yes."

"Read it."

Peter picked up the notebook and flipped it open. The person on the other end waited for Peter to read. "You must be Troy."

"Yes, sir," Troy said.

"If you're calling me, then you must be safe," Peter said.

"Safe?"

"You're safe from the man who kidnapped you."

Troy didn't respond for several seconds. The word he had scrubbed from his chest entered his mind. "Yes, sir. I woke up in my bed this morning."

"Good!" Peter said. Satisfaction bloomed in his heart. "What about Kelly?"

Troy gave a nervous laugh. "I called her right before I called you. She is fine."

"Make sure you thank the sheriff if you see him. He helped save you."

"Dad, what happened yesterday? I'm sure you have it all written out." Troy wasn't sure he wanted to know, but the question nagged at him.

Peter spent the next few minutes reading everything he had written down from the past few days. The events of the police assault on the house were a mystery, but he assumed it was a success if Troy and Kelly were free. "If I'm supposed to figure out what's causing our memory loss, I should get to work. Will you be okay?"

Troy sighed. "Yeah, I will be. I'm headed over to Kelly's."

"That sounds like a good plan. I have her cell phone number written down here. I'll check in with you soon."

"All right," Troy paused for a few seconds. "I love you, dad."

"I love you too, son." Peter hung up the phone. His heart pounded from anxiety. There had been a strange tension while talking with Troy, which made sense considering they had no memories of each other, but perhaps there was another reason. Whatever had happened the day before, it affected Peter deeper than what could be confined to memories, it went right down to his soul. Reading about the sheriff caused Peter's muscles to tense. He took an extended breath and exhaled, hoping it would help him relax so he could focus on the problem at hand. He needed to figure out what caused the town's memory loss and then create a cure.

DAY FOUR: CHAPTER TWELVE

"So what did your dad tell you?" Kelly asked as she sat next to Troy on her family room couch, a glass of water in hand. They had turned on the television and watched the mayor's announcement twice before muting it.

"I don't have all of the details, but a man kidnapped us yesterday. That's why we have nothing written down in our journals."

"Should we at least write that part down so we know why a day is missing?" Kelly asked.

"You can," Troy said. "But I want no memory of it."

"You *don't* have a memory of it," Kelly said. "Right?"

"You're right," Troy said with a sigh. "You are *very* right. I don't remember it with my brain," he pointed to his head and then pointed to his chest. "But it's almost as if my heart remembers. I can't explain it, but I woke up this morning and my heart was pounding so hard I felt it in my throat. Dread overwhelmed me. Every part of me screamed that something bad had happened."

Kelly's eyebrows furrowed. "That's creepy," she whispered.

Troy nodded. "Yes, and I still feel that fear. I need to calm down and I don't want to sit around the house all day. How about we go explore the town and thank the sheriff for helping my dad save us."

Kelly nodded. "I agree. We should get fresh air. We're confined here."

Troy stood and stretched. His muscles ached as did his wrists and mouth. He assumed it was from tape the kidnapper had used, considering Troy didn't have hair on his wrists while the rest of his arms did.

"Should we leave our notebooks behind or take them with us?"

Erased

"Take them," Troy said with a firm nod. "I want to record every detail."

Φ

Jessica Dailey sat in her large roller chair, looking through several lists she had no memory of writing, when a knock came from the office door.

"Mayor Dailey, may I step in?" Landon asked as he poked his head into the room.

"You may enter," she said and a smile spread across her lips as he approached. "What can I do for you?"

"I need to inform you that the sheriff still hasn't arrived for work. I took the initiative and gave tasks to the others."

"Superb," she said with a nod. "How many officers are on duty?"

"Ten, which includes myself," Landon reported.

The mayor's right eyebrow rose. "We have that many?" she said and pressed her lips together.

"We should have twelve, but the sheriff and one other deputy have not arrived."

She looked down a stack of papers. "That seems like a lot of police for a town with a little over a thousand people."

Landon shook his head. "Not at all, ma'am," he said. "The way I figure it, there are always two cops on active duty twenty-four hours a day, plus a dispatcher who stays at the police station, though he can double as a deputy if the need arises. The shift changes every eight hours, which makes nine officers that work in a five-day week. But then we have the weekend crew who comes in, which adds another nine officers to our payroll."

"Are they paid per hour, or what?" the mayor asked.

"Does it matter?" he wondered. "I understand that you want everything to return to normal, and I do too, but money should not be a concern. The men on duty right now are here to help our town in this crisis, not for the pay. We can figure all that out at a later time. We need to worry about the citizens and figure out where we live."

The mayor nodded. "Truer words were never spoken. None I *remember* anyway," she said with a wink.

"I sent a few of the men home so they can be ready for tonight. Something Bonnie Orson said bothers me. Last night we didn't have a crew working graveyard shift, so I am making sure we have a crew working tonight. They will be in at eleven o'clock."

"That sounds good," she said as she folded her hands and rested them on the desk. "Is there anything else?"

Landon nodded. "Have you made any progress trying to contact anyone from the beyond the town? Sheriff Orson had notes on his desk saying you haven't been able to reach anyone the past couple of days."

She shook her head. "No. I believe that what affected us reached the world beyond our little town."

"Well, I propose that we find out."

The mayor's right eyebrow rose. "How do you suppose we do that?"

Landon sighed. "I want to travel to the next town to see if anybody else is having the same problem."

The mayor nodded. "That sounds like an excellent idea, though without a vehicle, that will be difficult. We do not know how far you would have to walk. We don't even know where *our* town is located."

"I found a bike in my garage, which is how I got to work this morning. Deputy Barns is in command until either I or the sheriff returns. He and two others are going over some books on the town *and* our country's history. The rest on duty are out on patrol, making sure things stay peaceful."

The mayor nodded once more. "Good, then I wish you luck on your venture."

Landon smiled and bowed. He turned around and headed toward the door.

"Oh, and Landon, be careful out there. For all you know, there may be zombies walking around," she said with a laugh.

"I don't think it matters," he said without stopping or turning. "We're all pretty much zombies already."

Φ

Peter peered through a microscope, staring at his own blood on a plastic slide. He studied it awhile before pulling away and writing down his observations in a notebook. There was nothing in the blood that suggested anything had infected it. But then again, if the fungus he created *was* responsible for their memory loss, it would make its way to the brain and disappear from the blood stream. The only way to continue his research was to study somebody's brain. He flipped back several pages and found a phone number. He lifted the phone from the receiver and dialed.

Φ

Bonnie sat at the dining room table with a plate of scrambled eggs in front of her. She had to force herself to eat because not knowing Simon's location reduced her appetite. Her muscles tensed when music played nearby. She tilted her head, trying to figure out from where the sound was coming. She stood and followed the tune back to her bedroom. It sounded like a classical symphony, full of violins and other instruments she couldn't name. She looked around, trying to find the source of the music.

Lucas Heath

The music stopped, leaving Bonnie alone in silence. She turned her head several times, hoping to spot what had made the enchanting melody, and frustration jabbed at her heart. As she turned to leave the room, the music started again. She spun around and closed her eyes. It was coming from her left, near the dresser. She hurried toward the sound. It seemed like it was coming from *behind* the dresser. She grabbed the piece of furniture and gave it a tug, pulling it away from the wall. Bonnie found the ringing phone and reached for it, snatching it up. *Blocked Call.* She flipped it open. "Hello?"

"Hi, my name is Peter Benet. Is Sheriff Orson available?"

Bonnie's heart sank. She was hoping it had been her husband. "No," she whimpered. "I don't know where he is. Nobody has seen him today."

"That's odd," Peter said. He sighed before continuing. "Are you his wife Bonnie?"

"Yes," she said and tears formed in her eyes.

"Perfect! You work at the hospital. The mayor hired me to figure out what's causing our memory loss. However, right now I need access to your morgue. Can you help me with that?"

"You want access to the morgue? For what?"

"I don't think you want me to go into detail," he said. "But I need to check out the brains of several corpses. Can you help me?"

She wiped the tears from her eyes. "Yes, I can help you. I'll be at work around noon. You realize you could always ask another nurse at the hospital to help you, right?"

"Well, after what the sheriff did yesterday for me and my boy, I trust him to help me; and since you are a nurse, I thought it would make things easier. I will be at the hospital around twelve. Thank you."

"Wait, what did Simon do for you yesterday?" The phone clicked, signaling Peter had ended the call. Bonnie let out a frustrated scream and then shoved the phone in her pocket. She looked at the clock. It was eleven. Could Simon's disappearance have anything to do with what he did the previous day? She planned to find out.

Ф

Landon sat on his bicycle seat with one foot on the ground. He reorganized the contents in a knapsack so that the flashlight inside wouldn't dig into his back. He unfolded the town map and studied it for the fifteenth time in the past hour. There were three possible routes. He could head along the highway to the north or south, or head east through the farm lands and hope he reached another town or city. Heading north sounded better than the other options, and with that decision, he folded the map and began his journey down the road.

Ф

Troy and Kelly stepped up to the police station door and peered through the window. A young woman sat behind the front desk, a deck of cards in hand. Troy grabbed the handle of the door and pushed it open. He stepped inside and Kelly followed.

"Hey, we are here to see Sheriff Orson," Troy said as they approached the front desk.

"Sorry, but he hasn't come in today. Nobody knows where he is," the woman said without looking up from her card game.

"Are you sure?" Kelly asked.

The woman glanced at the teens. "I'm sure. Now get lost," she snapped.

"*Somebody* woke up on the wrong side of the bed," Kelly whispered. The teens left the station and stared at a battered American flag in the distance, waving in the gentle breeze. "What should we do now?" Kelly asked.

Troy shrugged. "What else *is* there to do? If nobody knows where the sheriff is, then let's go search for him!"

Φ

Every muscle in Mark Hood's body spasmed, slamming his face into a steering wheel and waking him. A horn honked, and he pulled his head away. His eyesight blurred and fatigue overwhelmed him. He longed to cry though the tears wouldn't come. He grabbed a handle and pulled on it, opening the door. When he tried stepping out, his legs collapsed, and he went sprawling to the cement. He looked up at the red truck before him. It looked familiar though he wasn't sure why.

He let his head rest on the concrete for several minutes as the rays of sun comforted his body. After a time, he sat up and looked at his surroundings. He was in the middle of nowhere, with a road extending in both directions farther than his eye could see. Hadn't he been at a hospital? Or was that a dream? Was *this* even real, or was he in a nightmare?

"Come on, Mark. Let's go. Pick yourself back up, get in your truck, and drive." A voice from within prompted him. "Drive forward until you are in Lion's Glade."

Mark stood on feeble legs and climbed into the vehicle. His body ached; he needed help. Perhaps he should search for a hospital.

"You've been there before," the small voice warned. "You can't trust them. They will strap you down and hurt you. You need to find somebody who will help."

Mark clutched his head as a spark of pain shot through his body. He waited until it subsided. "Who would I even go to?" he asked aloud, hoping that his brain would answer the question for him.

"You need to find Peter Benet," the voice responded with such clarity it almost sounded audible. "He's the only one who can help you."

DAY FOUR: CHAPTER THIRTEEN

"If we search for the sheriff, where would we even look?" Kelly wondered as she followed behind Troy.

Troy stopped and sat at a bench in front of the town park. He removed his backpack from his shoulders, unzipped it, removed his journal, and then set the pack on the ground.

"This place is beautiful," Kelly said and joined Troy on the bench. She gawked at the lush, green grass and trees spread throughout the property. It was several blocks from the police station and was at least the size of a football field. A single concrete path curved its way through the park, making it easier for bikers to ride through the middle.

Troy flipped through several pages and held out his hand. "May I use your cell phone?"

Kelly reached into her pocket, removed the pink flip phone, and handed it to him.

"Gross, I hate the color pink," he said with a grunt.

"Do you want to use my phone, or not?"

Troy nodded and flipped open the phone. He dialed a number he had written down in his notebook. It rang several times before somebody answered.

"This is Peter."

"Hey, dad, it's Troy."

"Is everything all right?" There was obvious concern in his voice.

"Yeah, Kelly and I are fine. We are going to search for the sheriff. Nobody at the police station knows where he is."

"That's curious. His wife Bonnie doesn't know where he is either."

"I had a thought and decided I should call you. Do you think that something happened yesterday that caused his disappearance? After all, you both came to save Kelly and me."

Peter hummed over the phone for a moment before responding. "It's possible. I wrote my last entry yesterday right before we assaulted the kidnapper's house. I don't know why I wouldn't have recorded the details of what took place, especially if I returned to the laboratory afterward."

"Is it possible you didn't want to remember what happened so you didn't write it?" Troy wondered.

"I could say *anything* is possible. I wouldn't worry about it though. You two are safe. That's what matters."

"Would you give me the address of the kidnapper's home? I'm sure you have it with you."

There was a long pause. "I have it, but I don't think you should go there."

"Dad, if something happened to the sheriff, we need to find out. Nobody else seems worried about him. Perhaps he's fine, or maybe he's in trouble. I doubt the police will search for him until he's missing for more than a day. Kelly and I have nothing better to do. Please give me the address. If the kidnapper is still there, he won't mess with us. We have a gun."

"Where did you get a gun?" The tone of Peter's voice rose.

"It's Kelly's." Troy looked over to see Kelly glaring at him.

"Troy, it's far too dangerous. Who knows what that maniac is doing?"

"What part of *we have a gun* don't you understand? We can defend ourselves. We *need* to help find the sheriff. Trust me, dad. We will be fine. *This* is something I have to do."

Erased

There was a dramatic huff from the other end of the line. "All right," Peter agreed. He gave them the address and a strict command to call him at the first sign of trouble.

Troy flipped the phone closed and handed it back to Kelly. He wrote the address in his journal with a pen that stored within the spiral wire and then removed a map from his backpack.

"Are you sure you want to go there? You told me this morning that whatever happened yesterday affected your heart. It seems like a bad idea."

"Maybe," Troy mumbled. "But perhaps it will give me closure or something. It's not like we have anything better to do."

"We can search for your mom," Kelly said as she placed her hand on his. "I saw your journal this morning when you went to use the bathroom. You wrote a note to yourself saying you needed to find her."

Troy shook his head. "I don't know why I wrote that. Where would I even look for her? Is she even in town? I would need more details. Looking for the sheriff is the only thing we can do." He slipped the notebook into the backpack and zipped it closed. "I know where this street is. We passed it on the way here. Let's go."

Φ

Landon peddled at a slow pace, enjoying a nice cool breeze that caressed his bare arms. The uniform shirt he wore had short sleeves, and considering how warm it was, he didn't mind at all. He kept riding, shooting past stop signs without bothering to look both ways before entering the intersections. As he approached one road, the name on a street sign caught his eye. He pulled on the hand brakes, came to a stop, and placed both feet on the ground before taking off his backpack.

He removed two small notebooks he had been writing in and opened the first one. After scanning through the last couple of pages, he closed it and slid it back inside the pack. Landon opened the second one and flipped to the end.

He remembered reading yesterday's final entry earlier that morning, but had thought little about it. The day before, the sheriff had called him to gather a team and meet him at a home address. A man had kidnapped two teenagers, and the sheriff assumed they were at that address. Landon wrote that he had gathered the team, and they were meeting up with the sheriff, but no other entries came after that. How did things play out? Did Landon even get to the house? He pressed his lips together. The name on the sign matched the street name of the address. Could the sheriff be there?

After contemplating the situation for several moments, he slid the journal into the backpack and folded the map. Checking out the home wouldn't be a bad idea. He slid the map into his back pocket, zipped up the backpack and, instead of riding forward he turned to the right and began a course to his new destination.

Φ

Mark put little pressure on the gas pedal as he eased his way through the streets of Lion's Glade. He needed to find Peter; at least that's what the voice in his head kept telling him though he had no idea who Peter was. No images came with the voice, only a name. At least he knew where to begin his search. If Peter could help him, he must be a doctor. Perhaps he could be at the hospital, or at least someone there may know how to find him. The thought of even going near the hospital sent a shiver of fear down Mark's spine.

He parked his truck on the side of the road and closed his eyes before a sharp pain shot through his head. He groaned as his stomach muscles spasmed. His body was falling apart; that much was certain. How long had it been since he had eaten? He could hardly even remember his own name. When the pain subsided, he looked out the vehicle windows. There was a grocery store to his right. His stomach growled as he thought of food. As there weren't any cars in the parking lot, it was most likely closed.

"Sir, step out of the vehicle."

The voice shattered Mark's thoughts about food. A man in a police uniform stood in front of the truck, a gun raised and pointed at him.

Was the officer talking to *him*? What did he do?

"I said step out of the vehicle and get your hands in the air!" The cop yelled.

Mark obeyed and opened the door, stepping out of his truck. He raised his hands.

The next few moments were a blur, making it impossible for Mark to respond. The cop handcuffed him, placed him under arrest, took the vehicle keys, and forced him into the passenger seat of his own truck. The officer got in the driver's side and drove.

"Where are we going?" Mark asked.

"The police station," the man replied. "Now that you're here, we'll figure out where you've come from and what's going on outside this town."

Φ

Landon applied the handbrakes, bringing the bike to a stop in front of the address he had retrieved from his book. The light blue house rose two-stories high with a bench swing in the corner of a covered porch, and a sapling in the center of the front yard. Landon climbed off the seat and set his bike on the grass. He removed the gun from its holster and approached the porch. Drapes covered the windows, preventing him from seeing into the house.

He wasn't certain how to continue, but opted to ring the doorbell. A chime rang from within, though after a lengthy wait, nobody answered. Landon circled around back, keeping an eye out for anything suspicious, and a detailed log in his mind of what he saw. A set of stairs led up to a wooden deck and back door. Close to the deck and near the ground, a small window caught his attention. He walked over to it and knelt down so he could peer into the basement. It was empty, but other than that, there wasn't anything unusual.

He pushed on the glass, but an inside latch kept the window from opening. Landon stood and climbed the deck stairs. He tried the back door and was pleased to find it unlocked. When he stepped into the house, he found himself in the kitchen; except for a phone and notepad, the counters were bare. He walked through the archway to the back hall and continued on, passing two doors, until he came to a living room.

As the heavy curtains blocked out all natural light, Landon groped around for a light switch and flipped it when his fingers found the button. He could now see the unusual décor. The furnishings were basic and comprised a couch, a small table, and a floor lamp, but a plethora of strange items covered the walls including: wooden masks, spears, and dream catchers. However, there was nothing to offer any clues to what may have happened last night.

Landon proceeded through an opening on the far right of the living room and found himself in the foyer, he flipped on another switch to illuminate the area. Blood. Dried blood coated the carpet, and considering how well kept this house was, the blood hadn't been there long.

He walked down the front hall toward the dining room, when a polished, wooden pocket door caught his eye. He grabbed the handle and moved it aside, revealing two staircases, one ascending, and the other descending.

"Who in the world designed this house?" he whispered as he mounted the stairs. He reached the top and turned on the lights. Feminine hygiene products littered the floor of an open bathroom in front of him. As he checked out the rest of the doors, they led to either bedrooms or closets with supplies. He decided that it was safe to declare the top floor empty.

Landon returned to the ground floor and walked through the dining room and back into the kitchen. There were two doors he had yet to check out in the back hall. The first led to another bathroom. A second pocket door opened to an office. He stepped inside and observed the pictures along the walls of a man and his wife. The man looked to be of Middle Eastern descent while the woman was Caucasian. They were both smiling in the pictures, but where the husband appeared happy, the wife's smile seemed forced. Shakespearian literature and other random books filled two bookshelves against the right wall.

A potted plant sat against the empty wall to the left. Above the plant, the wall had a distinct indentation, suggesting that the large, taxidermy moose head, now hanging across from the entrance, had once hung there. Why anybody would want the head of a moose behind them while working at their desk was beyond explanation. It would feel like someone was looking over your shoulder the whole time. It seemed out of place, and if Landon had lived there, he would have gotten rid of the head altogether.

In front of him on the desk, a computer monitor drew Landon's attention. He approached to sit behind the desk and moved the mouse to clear the screen saver. Feeling the eyes of the moose staring at the back of his neck, he shivered, but what he saw on the screen made him forget all about the creature. "What on earth?" he whispered, but froze when he heard the back door open. Someone had entered the house.

Φ

Several minutes after twelve, Peter sat in the waiting room of the hospital. He stood when a short, thin woman approached. She had brown hair down to her neck and looked to be in her late forties.

"You must be Peter," she said as she held out her hand. "I apologize for the wait. I attempted to find the morgue."

Peter shook her hand. He then swept his other hand through his slicked-back hair, making sure it hadn't deviated from its original style. "Checking out these bodies could be very helpful in figuring out a cure for our memory loss."

She nodded. "Follow me. We have no one on staff in the morgue, but according to our computers we have six bodies back there."

Peter followed her through swinging doors.

"What did my husband do for you and your son?" she asked. The question had been nagging at her since she had gotten off the phone with Peter.

He recapped the information he had told Troy earlier that morning as they turned several corners. "People are looking for your husband. I'm sure they will find him."

"I hope so," Bonnie mumbled. She led Peter through another set of swinging double doors, into a dim hallway. "It took a while to find this place." She opened a door to her right, and they entered a chilly, yet bright room. "The bodies are over there." She pointed to a large, metal, built-in cold-chamber with twelve small doors. She handed him a clipboard. "I don't want to see the bodies, but I printed out a list for you, identifying which people are in which compartment."

"Thank you, Bonnie. I appreciate this."

She smiled and hurried from the room. Peter read the list over and selected the first person whose brain he would study. Elizabeth Muhammad.

Φ

Bonnie had returned to her station, answered a phone call, and had begun a game of FreeCell on the computer when Peter burst through the doors leading into the waiting room.

"They're not there!" he yelled, startling Bonnie and making her jump.

"What?" she asked with a tone that suggested she didn't appreciate his outburst.

"The bodies in the morgue," he said again, his tone more than frantic. "There's not a single one in there! They are *all* gone!"

DAY FOUR: CHAPTER FOURTEEN

"I don't think we should be in here," Kelly whispered as they entered the home of their supposed kidnapper. She shut the back door behind them. They stood in a kitchen, unsure of what to do next.

"Don't worry. I have the gun," Troy replied as he stepped in front of Kelly, making sure he would be a shield, if needed. He felt like throwing up, but took deep breaths to push the feeling away and regain his composure.

"I know that," she said with a sigh.

"Where do you want to go; left or right?" Troy asked.

Kelly shrugged. "I don't care."

Troy walked toward the dining room when a noise from the left hallway caught his attention. He tilted his head to see if he could hear anything else. Sure, they had seen a bicycle out front, but they didn't think there would be anybody inside the house; not alive anyway.

Before he could react, a man wearing a police uniform rounded the corner, his gun pointed at the teens. "Freeze!" he commanded.

Troy obeyed and dropped the gun, letting it clatter to the floor. He shot his hands in the air as did Kelly.

"We didn't mean to break in!" Kelly blurted. "We are looking for the sheriff!"

"We didn't break in, the door was unlocked," Troy whispered.

"The sheriff?" Landon asked as he lowered his gun. "Why would you think the sheriff is here?"

"Because he saved us from a kidnapper yesterday," Troy answered. "He's missing, and we want to find him."

Lucas Heath

"So you're the teens we came to help." Landon slid the gun into its holster and took a breath. "I came here looking for the sheriff as well though I found something a lot more complicated. You two should head home. I'm looking into this."

"What did you find?" Kelly asked.

"It doesn't matter," Landon replied. "As a police officer, I am ordering you to go home."

Troy sighed. "Fine, come on Kelly, let's go." He leaned down and picked up the gun.

"You're letting him kick us out?"

Troy nodded. "I hope you find the sheriff, sir." He turned back toward the door and opened it, waiting for Kelly to exit first. He followed after her and shut the door, leaving Landon alone.

"Are we *really* going to leave?" she asked.

Troy nodded. "We are. He's a policeman looking for the sheriff. Why should we rebel? He's trying to help and keep us safe. I don't want to go home, but I will not disobey his orders."

"Why do you have to be so moral?" Kelly asked with a groan.

"I don't know. Maybe my parents raised me to be. Let's go get food. I'm hungry." He paused for a moment. "I forgot to ask, but did you ever receive a text message from your mom? You sent her a text a few days ago, didn't you? Did she ever reply?"

Kelly shook her head. "No. I sent her a message this morning saying there was an emergency, and I needed her to call me. I tried calling multiple times, but she never answered."

Troy sighed. "Let's get something to eat and figure out what to do from there."

Kelly's eyes widened. "Let's watch a movie!"

Troy grinned. "That is a great idea!"

They walked down the porch steps and left the property.

Landon sat behind the desk in the office, staring at the computer monitor. He removed a cell phone from his pocket and selected a number he had added into his contacts that morning. The phone rang for a short while before somebody answered.

"Hello, Jessica Dailey speaking," she said.

"Miss Dailey, this is Deputy Landon, we talked earlier this morning. I found something you have to see."

Φ

Peter and Bonnie stood in the morgue, staring at the bulky cooling chamber. Peter had shown her each compartment, and they were all empty.

"I don't understand it," Bonnie said as she shook her head. "Our system shows that the bodies should be here."

"Perhaps somebody else took them to find a cure to our problem," Peter suggested. He hoped that was the answer.

"I couldn't tell you," she said. "First, my husband goes missing, and now dead bodies disappear? What is wrong with this town?"

Peter placed a hand on her shoulder. "I'm sure there are simple explanations."

She pulled away and walked toward the door leading to the hall. "Well, I'm sorry I couldn't help you. You will need to find your own bodies to dissect." She paused and turned to look at him. "And don't assume that I'm giving you permission to kill someone." She exited the morgue leaving Peter alone.

He shook his head and tried formulating a plan. He couldn't do anything more at the moment, and until someone else died, there would be no cure.

Φ

Mark groaned as pain pierced his abdomen and his headache worsened. He rested on a cot in the police station jail with his eyes closed. He attempted to sleep, but the discomfort kept him from resting. According to the police officer, the United States government had outlawed vehicles a few months prior, due to gas consumption and global warming. None of the information made sense to him. By driving his truck, he had broken a federal law, which was why the police officer arrested him.

Deputy Barns sat at the table in Conference Room A, talking with the arresting officer. "You didn't have to arrest him, Kyle. He doesn't even have his memories. How would he know about the laws?"

"He's from California." Kyle said as he adjusted the name badge on the left side of his uniform. "I thought arresting him would be the easiest way to get information. Until I realized he *doesn't* have his memory. We now have proof that whatever is happening to us is happening to the country!"

"I wouldn't go *that* far," Barns said as he set down a book in his hand. At least thirty books on American History, and a single one on the town's history, littered the table.

"I would. We don't know the potential danger this man has brought to our town. He's sick. I contacted the hospital to send someone to check on him."

"When Sheriff Orson shows up, he might not be happy about this. I hope you're ready for that."

"He's not here though, is he? Deputy Landon is the closest man to being in command, and he left to do who knows what?" Kyle shrugged.

Erased

"He is trying to make it to another town to see if they are in trouble like us," Barns informed.

"But with this Mark guy, we already have that answer. Landon is wasting his time now."

"And yet, we *don't* have that answer, do we? We are making assumptions; just like our government." Barns sighed and stretched. "According to this, the government decided they wanted no one spreading false news against them, so they limited the media. They outlawed newspapers, magazines, and cut down on the news stations to make sure no negative propaganda would spread. The government implemented strict regulations for the remaining news stations."

"What's your point?"

"They did all of this out of an assumption that others would rise to hurt them through mass media. They even outlawed the internet. We need to stop *assuming* and do what's best for the town."

"That's true, and putting a man we know nothing about behind bars is the best thing for our town."

"We don't know anything about *anyone*!" Barns said in exasperation. "We have no memories!"

"Deputy Anderaos, someone from the hospital is here to check out the prisoner," the secretary yelled from across the station.

"That would be for me," Kyle said as he stood from his seat. "I'll talk with you soon." He left Barns alone in the conference room and walked to the front of the station. A man dressed in a navy suit and matching tie stood at the reception desk. He held a briefcase at his side. "Hello, I'm Deputy Kyle Anderaos."

"I'm Peter Benet. It's nice to meet you."

They shook hands and Kyle stepped back to study the newcomer. "You're from the hospital?"

Peter nodded. "I'm the scientist working on solving our memory problem and I'm also a certified doctor. I was at the hospital when you called them, so they sent me."

Kyle nodded. "That works for me, but I must warn you, he's sick."

"I'll be careful," Peter reassured as Kyle led him to the jail. The back room with the cells had dim lighting, making it harder to see.

"His name is Mark, and he's at the end," Kyle informed. "I have work to do, so I'll leave you to it."

"You're leaving me alone with him?" Peter asked as his right eyebrow rose.

"He's very weak right now from whatever sickness he has. I'm not too worried. Here's the key." He passed the small metal object to Peter before leaving the room.

Peter walked to the end cell and saw the man. Even in the faint light, he could see the paleness of Mark's skin. He slid the key in the hole and turned it. He pulled the door open once the latch unlocked and stepped into the cell.

Mark opened his eyes and stared at Peter without saying a word.

"My name is Peter, and I'm here to help you."

"*You're* Peter?" Mark asked as a smile spread across his lips. "What are the odds?" He closed his eyes again and exhaled.

"The odds of what?" Peter asked.

"What are the odds of meeting you without having to look for you?" Mark laughed. "You're the one who can help me."

"Help you with what?" Peter wondered as he crouched down at Mark's side and opened his briefcase. He removed a stethoscope.

"You can help cure my sickness and memory loss."

Erased

Peter placed the eartips into his ears and listened to Mark's heart. He returned the equipment to his briefcase. "Who told you I could help you?" he asked.

"The voice in my head," Mark whispered. "I sound crazy... I know that. But I keep hearing this voice saying you will help me. I have a few memories of my life. I remember my name and my dislike for hospitals and doctors. You even seem familiar. I mean, I don't remember you, but I must have a subconscious memory if I keep hearing your name in my head."

Peter's heart beat faster. He latched his briefcase and stood. "Mark, come with me."

Mark pushed himself to a seated position. "We're leaving?"

Peter nodded. "Yes, we are going to my facility where I can do a thorough checkup. I heard you arrived in a truck?"

Mark nodded. "Yes, but the police have my keys."

Peter nodded. "Not for long." If Mark had his memories, he could be the answer to the problem; he could be the cure. At the moment, Mark was Peter's test subject.

Φ

It took a while for the mayor to arrive at the address Landon had provided, and before she even had time to knock on the door, he had flung it wide open, ushering her to enter. He led her past the dried blood on the floor, through the exotic living room, and down the hall to the office.

"What was so urgent that you pulled me away from my duties? I almost didn't have time to finish recording this afternoon's announcement."

"Trust me, ma'am, you will want to see this." Landon sat her on the chair behind the computer. He had removed the moose head from the room before she arrived.

Jessica looked at the computer monitor and shrugged. "Why am I here?"

Landon clicked on the screen and brought up a program. "This house belongs to a man who kidnapped two teenagers yesterday. His wife was a scientist who created the fungus with Peter Benet."

"What does that have to do with this computer?"

Landon clicked several times and brought up a screen.

"Wait, is that," she asked, but her sentence trailed off as she stared at the image of the police station.

Landon clicked again, and after a few seconds, clicked again, continuing the process multiple times.

"These are all live?" she asked as she looked up at the young deputy.

He nodded. "Yes ma'am. There are cameras spread throughout the entire town, and they are recording *everything* we do."

DAY FOUR: CHAPTER FIFTEEN

The mayor paced around the home office for a while, thinking about the situation. "Is this man, Ahmed, the only one who had access to these cameras? Or do you suppose he is working with somebody?"

Landon shook his head and sighed. "I don't have the answer to that." He sat at the desk and watched a live camera feed of the police station. A man dressed in a navy suit argued with Deputy Anderaos. None of the cameras had sound, only video.

"Does this computer have access to saved recordings?"

Landon nodded. "Yes, but they only go back until zero six hundred hours on day one. Also, the cameras are limited to building entrances, offices, and family rooms. There aren't any in bedrooms, bathrooms, or even outside buildings; at least, if there are any, this computer doesn't have access to them."

"Well *that* is convenient," Jessica snapped. "What is going on here, Deputy, and *where* is the sheriff?"

Landon turned his gaze for a few moments before looking at the mayor. "There are cameras in this house too. One is embedded into the light fixture, pointed at the front door. A clock facing the back door holds a second camera. The third is on the far wall in the basement, and the final one is inside a giant moose head that was against the wall behind me; I moved it."

"Why would a man have cameras in his own house? Was it to have proof of who entered and left?" Jessica fidgeted with her hair, making sure the bun stayed in place.

"Once again, I don't have the answer, but I am aware of what happened to the sheriff. Last night, he called and ordered me to gather two men and meet him at this location. I watched through the videos of the events that transpired because I didn't write them in my journal. The sheriff died in action, saving the boy and girl Ahmed had kidnapped."

"Are you positive?" Jessica asked as she walked around the desk to watch the screen.

Landon replayed the video and she let out a gasp when the bullets hit Simon in the chest. Landon exited out of the recording. "He's dead, ma'am."

"Well then, I must tell his wife," she said. A tear escaped her eye and dropped down her face.

"Are you all right, ma'am?"

She nodded and wiped the tear from her cheek. "I am fine. What happened after that?"

Landon shook his head. "I can't tell you. The cameras shut down at midnight and didn't reactivate until zero six hundred."

"So there *is* a period when the cameras are not recording," she said and pressed her lips together. She walked around the desk toward the office door. "I will locate the sheriff's wife and tell her what we found."

Landon nodded and kept his gaze focused on the screen. "What should we do about the cameras?" He pulled his attention away from the computer.

She stopped and turned. "I want at least one officer here at all times. This could be our surveillance system for the time being. That way, we see what is going on in town."

Landon nodded.

"I am also declaring you the sheriff until this crisis is done. I will inform the other deputies once I return to Town Hall."

"You want *me* to be the sheriff?" he asked, dumbfounded.

She nodded. "You seem to be the obvious leader with the sheriff gone. Is there any reason you should not be?"

Landon shook his head. "No, ma'am."

"Good, then you are the new sheriff. Congratulations." She walked out of the room without saying another word.

Landon turned to the computer once more. "Well then, how can I argue with that?"

Φ

"I can't believe you punched him," Mark said from the passenger seat of the red Toyota Tacoma.

Peter chuckled. "He didn't give me much of a choice now, did he?"

"But he's a cop," Mark responded.

"Not a good one," Peter countered. He slowed down at a stop sign to let a woman dressed in a pink tank top and light blue shorts cross the road.

She eyed the vehicle before running to the other side.

Peter pressed his foot on the gas pedal and continued.

"So what are you going to do?" Mark asked.

Peter sighed. "I'll be honest with you, Mark. You may be our only hope of finding a cure to this problem. Until I heard about you, I thought that all hope might be lost. Either that, or I would have to murder somebody."

"You're kidding, right?" Mark asked.

"Sort of," Peter responded. "I may have to sedate you and look at your brain."

Every muscle in Mark's body tensed. "My brain?"

"Don't worry," Peter tried reassuring him. "It will be painless and I'm not even sure I will need to."

Mark relaxed. "Why did you choose me? Couldn't you check out somebody else's brain?"

Peter shook his head. "I wouldn't want to risk killing them on accident."

"What about me?" Mark asked as his muscles tensed again.

Peter shrugged. "I can always take you back to the police station where you will sit in that cell and live a miserable existence for however long they keep you in there, or you can come with me and let me try to figure out what is wrong with you."

"So, you chose me because you could blackmail me?"

Peter shook his head. "Not at all," he responded. "I chose you because you still remember things. I need to figure out why you're special and why everyone in this town has forgotten everything."

Mark took a breath and let it out. "All right, I'll do it. Just please don't kill me."

Φ

After an hour, the mayor arrived at the police station. Someone had propped open the front door and, as she entered, her high heels tapped against the linoleum floor.

The secretary looked up from her card game. "May I help you?"

"I am Mayor Jessica Dailey. I need to search through the sheriff's office."

The woman nodded. "It's the enclosed room with a glass window and desk."

Erased

Jessica thanked the woman and walked to the back room, passing three officers who turned to study her. After a moment, she spun around and stared at the men. "I know I am attractive, but keep your eyes to yourself." She stomped into the sheriff's office and searched through papers on his desk until she found one which contained Bonnie's information. She was a nurse at the hospital.

Jessica left the space and stopped in front of the three officers still talking around a desk. "I want to let you all know that Sheriff Orson died in the line of duty last night while saving two teenagers. Landon is now the sheriff of Lion's Glade. Make sure that everyone else is informed of this and writes it in their logs."

"And who are *you* to be telling us this?" one man asked with a smirk.

Jessica walked up to him, her hands resting on her hips. "Don't you have a television?"

He stood, revealing his height to be over six-feet; a giant compared to her. "I do, but it's broken."

"I am Mayor Jessica Dailey, the one running this town and signing your paycheck. So I would suggest you sit down and shut up while your friends here do as I say and inform everyone else of Landon's promotion." She turned to the others. "Get on it!"

They obeyed. One stayed to make the radio calls while the other made his way to another room.

Jessica left in silence and headed toward the hospital.

Φ

Peter ran a hand through his hair as he read over a document he printed. He had used one of the laboratory machines to compare Mark's blood with his own. According to the data, there were no anomalies in either of their blood.

Mark sat in a chair in Peter's office, waiting for what would come next.

"I don't understand it. I expected to find *something* strange in your blood."

"It's normal then?" Mark asked as his eyes grew wide and brows furrowed.

Peter nodded. "While that's good for you, it's *not* for the rest for us. Now I *will* need to look at your brain."

"Don't they have equipment at the hospital that scans a human brain?"

Peter shook his head. "I already thought about that, but they don't. I'm not even sure what I'm looking for will show up on an MRI anyway."

"What *are* you looking for?" Mark asked with a hint of exasperation in his voice. His head still throbbed and his body ached.

"Do you *really* want to know?" Peter asked.

Mark thought about it for a moment and shook his head. "No, I don't."

Peter chuckled. "Well then, all that's left is to head into the laboratory and begin the procedure."

Φ

It didn't take long for Jessica to arrive at the hospital and tell Bonnie the news about her husband's death. Bonnie began sobbing and Jessica joined her moments later. The emotions Jessica tried so hard to suppress flooded to the surface.

Diana, one of the other nurses, let Bonnie go home for the night and took over her duties while she waited for a replacement to arrive.

Bonnie didn't have the strength to argue, and with Jessica's help, she made it home. "Thank you," she said as she approached the front door to her house.

Erased

"You're welcome. From everything I wrote about him, he seemed like a decent man," Jessica said and forced a smile. "Are you going to be okay by yourself?"

Bonnie nodded. How a man of whom she had no memories could affect the depths of her heart reached beyond her understanding, but her heart felt so broken. "I need time alone," she said and inserted a key into the lock.

They said their goodbyes and Jessica journeyed back to Town Hall.

Bonnie walked through the door and shut it behind her. The pictures of her and Simon in the entry hall were almost haunting. After setting her purse down by the door and walking into the living room, she saw the notebook she and Simon had written together and a new river of tears flowed. She knew what she had to do.

Φ

Night had fallen on the town of Lion's Glade by the time the third movie ended. Troy laid on the couch with a sleeping Kelly cradled in his arms. The rush their senses got from the action in the first movie ignited their longing to watch more, but Troy made a point to write down the day's happenings before they turned on another. He would not allow a day to go by without writing about it.

He looked down at Kelly who snuggled closer, and his heart skipped a beat. There was no doubt about it; he knew he was experiencing love. He rested his head on hers, and after an unstoppable yawn, let sleep overtake him.

Φ

The mayor returned to her office and wrote down detailed notes about the day's events. It seemed the more they learned, the more questions that arose. There was something weird about the whole situation. If Deputy Anderaos hadn't discovered the outsider, which proved that the rest of the country had the same problem, she would have assumed someone had targeted her town. Then again, Landon never had time to venture out to see if another town besides Lion's Glade lost their memories. Even with Mark's arrival, they still didn't know for sure. Perhaps she would send somebody out in the morning.

Φ

Around eleven thirty, a deputy working nights replaced Landon from watching over the new surveillance system. Landon made a note in his journal that the night crew had arrived for duty, and then he went home. He continued to write about his day and included ideas to improve the efficiency of their investigation. The writing lasted until he couldn't keep his eyes open and he fell asleep on the couch.

Φ

Bonnie stood on her back porch and observed a bonfire burn everything that even hinted at Simon's existence. She spent hours rewriting her book of memories and the notes she needed to remember. She got rid of every object or picture she could find; all documents with his name on them, his cell phone, wristwatch, and clothing. They all burned in the fire. She couldn't help but cry as the last of his belongings turn to ash. When she woke in the morning, she wouldn't know he ever existed. It was best that way.

Φ

Peter sat at his desk, looking over several papers when another man entered the small office. "So, did you find out?" he asked.

Peter looked up from the documents and studied the man. He looked to be in his mid-thirties and had short, spiked hair. He wore black jeans and a black t-shirt that peeked out from underneath a white lab coat. The gray of his eyes was visible in the light. A smile spread across his lips as he waited for Peter's answer.

Erased

"I have good news and bad news for you," Peter said as he stood. "The good news is that the fungus has nothing to do with our memory loss."

"I already knew that," the other man scoffed.

"The bad news is that I still don't know what's causing our memory loss."

The man bit down hard on his lip until he tasted blood. "What about Mark? Why has he remembered things and not others?"

Peter picked up the papers on the desk and handed them to the man. "I didn't find the fungus in his brain, but I found something else."

The man looked the data over and his face registered shock. "He has a brain tumor?" he asked.

Peter nodded. "Yes, Mark has a brain tumor."

Φ

The rest of the town settled in for the night as the clock struck midnight, and for the fifth time, a brilliant light filled the sky; as it bathed the town, it rendered everyone unconscious, ending the fourth day.

DAY FIVE: CHAPTER SIXTEEN

The next morning began with an abrupt clap of thunder, yanking the citizens of Lion's Glade from their slumber. Sheets of rain fell from the sky, filling the town with a fresh aroma of water on concrete. Troy and Kelly awoke in their own beds, both clutching their journal.

Oblivious to the storm, Peter slept at his desk in the laboratory office underground, stirring only once to the sound of a bell from the elevator.

The mayor, awake and alert, prepared for another day of problem solving. She couldn't remember what the previous days had held, though based on how her body felt, she knew they had been exhausting. Even with the rain, she would need to walk to the television station and record an announcement. As she slipped on a trench coat, the writing on her arm once again caught her eye. SG-H30; a strange mix of letters and numbers. What did it mean? Why did she write it on her arm? It was another question she would add to the plethora of mysteries.

Landon, the new sheriff, stared at himself in the mirror as he slid a razor down his face, shaving every whisker on his cheek. He had pulled the razor away from his skin to rinse it off when the house shook from the thunder. He needed to hurry to the police station to dismiss the night crew and then send someone to watch over the surveillance system they found yesterday. After grabbing a set of keys from the kitchen table and shoving them into his pocket, he snatched two pastries from the toaster. He flipped the hood of his jacket over his head, picked up an umbrella from a basket by the front door, and walked out into the storm.

Φ

Landon arrived at the police station around seven, and by then, the rain had turned into a fine mist. He shook the water droplets from his umbrella and closed it before pushing on the door to enter the police station.

Erased

Somebody had locked the deadbolt. He pressed himself against the glass and peered into the darkness. The lights were off and the place was empty.

"Nobody is here!" A man wearing a police uniform called out from underneath a store's awning across the street. He left the canopy's protection and walked over to the new sheriff.

"We should have a night crew though," Landon said as he continued to peer through the window. He knocked on the door several times.

"I already did that. I didn't get a response. Nobody is home."

"That's odd," Landon said as he turned to look at the man.

The other cop was a bigger guy though he looked to have more muscle than fat. He was five-feet, nine-inches tall, had ruffled red hair, and a chubby face. "I'm Deputy Barns," he said as he reached out his hand.

"Sheriff Landon," Landon replied.

"Ah, so you're the sheriff. Do you have the station keys?"

Landon shrugged. "I don't know." He removed the keys from his pocket and studied each one. A gold key stood out with the words *do not duplicate* etched in the handle. What would it hurt to try it? He slipped the key into the lock and turned it, hearing a click. He turned the handle, pushed the door open, and grinned. "I guess I do."

He and Barns both entered and walked into the back room, flipping a group of switches and turning on the lights.

"I wrote down yesterday that the night crew arrived for work at eleven. Am I wrong?"

Barns shook his head. "I don't think so. I also wrote that someone relieved me from duty at eleven."

Landon sighed. "Then where is the night crew?"

Φ

"Peter," the deep monotone voice pulled Peter from his dream. He opened his eyes and stared at the man leaning over him. He sat up and wiped drool from his mouth. "Who are you?" he asked. He blinked a few times and rubbed his eyes. He was in an office.

The man grabbed a notebook on the desk and shoved it into Peter's hands. "Read this." He turned and left the room.

Peter sat in a roller chair, staring at the notebook. After the fog cleared from his eyesight, he opened the journal and read.

Φ

The mayor yawned and stretched as she laid on the blood-red couch in her office. She had arrived after recording and broadcasting the morning announcements. If it wasn't for her detailed notes on how to work the television equipment, it would have taken her hours to figure it out.

Her muscles ached from all the walking she had done the past few days. If only they had vehicles to use, it would make things so much easier. However, according to what the police learned, the government had passed a law to reduce carbon emissions, making gas powered vehicles illegal. It made little sense to Jessica, but there weren't any vehicles around so it's not as though she could question the legitimacy of the info. Would they not have made electric cars to use? Why wouldn't they at least have emergency vehicles at their disposal? A knock at the door helped shift her thoughts back to reality. She stood and walked over to her desk. "Come in."

"You wanted to see me?" Landon asked as he entered the room.

She nodded as she fixed the bun holding her hair in place. "Yes. As I am sure you recorded in your notes yesterday, you were on your way out of town to see if what we are experiencing extends beyond Lion's Glade. I know you put that mission on hold, but I would like it to be continued. Since you are the sheriff, I'll need you here. Select one of your deputies and send them out."

"Sounds good, ma'am," he said with a nod. He almost spoke again, but hesitated.

"Is there something you would like to say?"

"Well, there have been odd occurrences with my deputies, and I'm not sure how to react to them."

"Like what?" she asked.

"Well, those I chose to work the graveyard shift weren't on duty when I got to the station this morning. I called two of them and they had woken up at home. Their journals stop right before midnight."

The mayor's right eyebrow rose. "That is interesting."

Landon nodded. "I wrote down in my notebook that the town surveillance system we found yesterday shuts down between the hours of midnight and six in the morning. So far, amongst the people I've asked, nobody has any record of those hours."

"Sounds like a coincidence," she said. "I think this whole chaotic situation is enhancing our paranoia. It is normal for people to sleep during those hours. Perhaps the deputies on duty could not handle the shift and went home."

"It's possible, but something feels wrong. I have a theory that I want to test tonight to see what happens after midnight."

"Do what you need to and then report your findings. Is there anything else?"

He shook his head, "Not at the moment, no."

"Then you may go. And make sure you send somebody out in search for another town." She paused and looked down at her notes. "Oh, and one last thing; I want a summary report on what your deputies found out about our country and town by this evening."

Landon left her office and sighed. He already sent Barns to watch over the surveillance system. He also sent a bunch of the other deputies on patrol, except for Kyle Anderaos, who was busy reading the history books and taking notes in the conference room. Unless another deputy had shown up at the police station, Kyle would be the one sent out of Lion's Glade to search for answers.

Φ

Kelly groaned when she finished reading her journal. There was so much information to absorb, and in less than twenty-four hours she would have to learn it all again, including the current day's events. She looked at the digital clock she had silenced and yawned when she saw the time. Her eyes fell to the cell phone on the nightstand when it vibrated. She snatched it up and flipped it open, looking at the name on the screen. She hit the green button to answer. "Mom?" she squeaked.

The voice sounded inaudible, as though a strong gust of wind drowned out the words, but she clearly heard a woman's voice. "Kelly," her name stood out in the chaotic noise. "Find," static overwhelmed the words. "Schools for," the rest couldn't be heard before the phone connection died. Goose bumps covered Kelly's body and a tangible eeriness fell upon the room, making her feel insecure and alone.

Φ

"You want me to do what?" Deputy Anderaos bellowed as Landon informed him of his new task. "You realize there's a storm outside, right? I could be struck by lightning!" He rubbed a hand over his forehead and winced when his pinky touched the skin around his prominent black eye.

Landon nodded. "I understand, but the mayor wants it done."

"How do we know she's who she says she is? She could be *anyone* claiming to be the mayor! We don't remember who the *real* mayor is!"

"Regardless of whether she's the real mayor, she's trying to help this town the best she can. We need to know if we're the only ones in trouble, or if there's another town close by that's dealing with the same thing. If that's the case, we can assume the whole country is affected. Then it will be easier to figure out how to proceed. As your commanding officer, I'm giving you this order."

"You're only the commanding officer because the mayor made you the sheriff. If she's a fraud, then so are you."

"And if you don't go, I'll throw you in jail."

"You wouldn't abuse your power that way," Kyle scowled.

Landon shrugged. "It's not abuse. I will have perceived a threat to the tranquility of our town and dealt with it. Trust me; nobody will see that as abuse."

Kyle grunted and stood from his spot at the conference room table. "Fine, I'll go, but I at least get a bike, right?"

"Wouldn't that make you more of a lightning rod, riding on metal?" Landon asked as he tried to suppress a smile.

"Oh, so you're a comedian now?" Kyle mocked.

Landon shrugged. "I have my moments. It looks like the sky is clearing up toward the south. Perhaps you should head that way."

Kyle sighed and pushed past Landon as he walked out of the room. "Just give me the stupid bike."

"I didn't ride mine in today because of the rain, but there's a bicycle shop when you head toward the shopping mall. That's what Barns told me anyway."

Kyle mumbled something under his breath and left the station.

Landon approached and sat in Kyle's chair. The book open before him was the only one they had found on the history of Lion's Glade, and on every page, there was a different word underlined. Yesterday, Landon and a few others had thought it could be a code, but nobody could figure out what it was. None of the words made any sense together. Perhaps it was nothing. Landon flipped to the book's beginning and read.

He got through the first page when the cell phone in his shirt pocket rang. He grabbed it and answered. "Sheriff Landon speaking."

"Landon, its Officer Barns."

"Doesn't anybody use the police radios anymore?" he asked.

"I tried to, but you weren't answering."

Landon looked down at his side and rolled his eyes. "I forgot to put one on this morning. Sorry about that. What do you need?"

"What was the address you gave me this morning for the house that had the town surveillance system?"

Landon recited it by memory, which impressed even *him* considering he had only read it in his journal once that morning.

"Are you sure that's the right one?" Barns asked with a hint of annoyance in his voice.

"That's what I have written. Why do you ask?"

"Because I'm here now, and I can't find the computer."

"It's in the office. You know the room with the bookshelves, books, and desk."

Barns grunted. "See, that's the problem. Every room in this house is empty. It doesn't look as if anyone has ever lived here. There's no carpet and these walls have a fresh coat of paint, and I'm willing to guess that nobody ever lived here. I don't know if your surveillance system was ever here, but if so, it's not any longer."

DAY FIVE: CHAPTER SEVENTEEN

Peter finished reading his journal and stood from his chair. His lack of memories provided enough proof that what he wrote held true. He set the notebook down and left the office, looking around the large space. A ceiling light flickered in the office next to his and the odd man who had woken him sat at the desk, reading something on a computer monitor.

"Did you finish?" the gray-eyed man asked.

Peter nodded. "I assume you're my boss?"

"Haven't you heard the proverb *never assume*?" the man asked as he turned to Peter. His gray eyes had a strange coldness about them. "Of course not; you just woke up and wouldn't remember that."

"Then who are you? I didn't write about you in my journal."

"Which is a good thing," the man said. "I told you never to write about me."

"All right," Peter said as his left eyebrow rose. "Then what do you want."

Gray Eyes turned the computer monitor so Peter could see. A video played, showing Peter standing over a man on a stretcher. "His name is Mark," Gray Eyes said. "You should have read about him in your notes. You looked at his brain yesterday and discovered he has a tumor."

Peter nodded. "It's good to put a face to the name."

Gray Eyes hit the button to fast-forward through the video. Several minutes passed as the video showed Peter closing up a small part of Mark's head and stapling his skin together. He then studied the monitors to make sure everything was all right and left the scene. They continued watching Mark in bed.

"Nothing is happening," Peter said.

"Keep watching," Gray Eyes commanded.

They waited as the video continued to fast-forward. The screen blackened.

"What happened?" Peter asked.

Gray Eyes answered as he stood. "The camera shut down at midnight."

"If the camera isn't working, did you check on him?"

"The camera began recording again around six this morning. And yes, I went to see him; he's gone." He clicked a red x in the corner, exiting out of the video, bringing up a live view of Mark's room. The stretcher was empty. "Now, Peter, tell me. Where would a man who *just* had his head opened, go?"

Φ

"It was so creepy," Kelly whispered as she snuggled up to Troy on his living room couch. She had decided the emptiness of her own home was too much for her to handle, so she dressed and raced over to Troy's.

"She said something about school?" he asked as he wiped a droplet of water from his face. He had just finished taking a shower when the doorbell rang, and rushed to dress, not taking the time to dry his hair.

"She said, *'Kelly... finding... schools',* and then the phone went dead."

"That's disconcerting. After all this time of her not answering your text messages and phone calls, why would she call you about school?"

Kelly shrugged. "It made me feel so alone."

"Well, you have me," Troy said with a nervous laugh.

"That's a start," she said. "I think it's time we try finding our friends. I mean, we've got to have more than *just* each other, right?"

Erased

Troy nodded. "I've never thought about that."

"That's why *I'm* the woman, and *you're* Troy."

"Ouch," he said as he swung his fist against his chest, portraying mock hurt. "You don't even have the decency to call me a man?"

"I would, if I were looking at a man," she said and stuck out her tongue. She grabbed her pink phone and flipped it open, then scrolled through the contacts.

Troy ignored the comment. "So you're going to call random people in your phone until you learn if they were your friends or not? You realize that they won't remember you either, right?"

"Then what am I supposed to do?" she asked as she threw her hands in the air, almost letting go of the phone.

"How about instead of calling them, we go introduce ourselves in person."

"And how do you expect to do that if we don't know where they live?"

Troy gave a devious grin. "That's why *I'm* the man and *you're* Kelly."

She squinted and glared at him. "I wish I had ice water to throw on you right now. How do you expect us to find out where they live?"

Troy shrugged. "I think we should go get their addresses."

"And *how* do you suppose we do that?"

Troy snickered. "We will take a cue from your mom. Let's go visit the school."

Φ

The surveillance system disappeared? That's the last thing the mayor wanted to hear. Had someone taken it in the night, or did it even exist at all? Sheets of paper held the memories of every citizen, which meant it was within the realm of possibilities they could be altered. She stared out the large window that doubled as the back wall of her office. Landon had called her a short time before, informing her of the situation. She felt helpless. What could she do other than create announcements and give orders to the police? She tried making calls to outside towns and cities, but she only reached answering machines. What more could she do other than wait?

The rain had stopped for the time being, giving a clear view of the town to the east. A bolt of lightning in the distance startled Jessica, making her jump, and a clap of thunder followed thereafter. She stepped closer to the window when she saw smoke rising in the distance. Did the lightning strike start a fire? She watched the smoke rise awhile longer, then the telephone rang. She turned around and snatched it from the desk. "This is Mayor Dailey."

"Mayor, its Sheriff Landon," Landon spoke. "I received information from Officer Kent that lightning struck a rentable storage facility to the east called Safe Guard, and it started a fire. We will take a hose from the fire station and head to the facility."

The mayor could see several deputies running toward the smoke in the distance.

"Are there any specific orders you would like us to follow?" Landon asked.

"Do *not* let anyone get hurt. I would rather a storage facility burn down than have any of your men get injured or killed."

"Does that mean you want us to stand down and let it burn?"

The mayor contemplated the situation for a moment and a thought seemed to jab into her mind. She slid the left sleeve of the sweater up her arm and stared at the writing. SG-H30. SG... Safe Guard? Could that be it?

"Ma'am, are you there?"

Erased

"You said it is a rentable storage facility? What does that mean?" She asked.

"I'm assuming they have storage units you can rent to store your belongings in," he replied.

Jessica wasn't sure how she knew. Perhaps it was a hunch, or maybe it was a memory emerging somehow. "Save it," she ordered. "Keep the fire away from unit H30!"

"H30, ma'am?" Landon asked, confused at her instruction.

"Save the storage facility!"

Φ

"It will be very interesting to see what my grades were before all of this happened," Troy said as he and Kelly made their way to the school.

An oversized, black raincoat swaddled Kelly, and the hood covered most of her face. She shivered as a gust of wind blew by. "I'm sure you were a straight A student," she said as she withdrew her hands into the sleeves.

He turned to look at her as he hid his hands in the pockets of the black hoodie he wore. "Why do you say that?"

"Because," she responded. "I would never go out with a guy less than exceptional."

As he wasn't sure how to respond, he kept his mouth shut.

"So, Troy, are you ever going to look for your mom?" Kelly asked after several minutes of silence.

He shrugged. "Where would I even look for her? It's not as if I can search every single house in town. She may not even be in Lion's Glade. My dad, wherever he is, is working on a way of restoring our memories. I haven't heard from him today, but my journal says he's doing all right. If you can give me an idea where to search for my mom, tell me, please."

Kelly pressed her lips together and exhaled through her nose. She knew that even with his dad in town, Troy still felt incomplete without his mom. She felt the same way, especially since her father was also missing, if she even still had a father. Perhaps when they found their friends, things would be different, though one question nagged at her mind. Did she want to give up the time she spent with Troy, for a bunch of people she couldn't remember? Little did she know, Troy wondered the same thing.

Φ

"I don't understand it," Peter said as he read over the information on the computer screen. "Our system reset itself at midnight and didn't turn back on until six. There's no existing record to tell us if anybody left or entered the building until after six this morning. You're the only one it recorded today."

"I already know that! You must go *out* and find him!" Gray Eyes said as he stomped out of the room.

"Why is he *that* important?" Peter asked as he stood and followed after him. "He doesn't have the fungus in his brain, which is good news. It shows that our experiment has nothing to do with the memory loss."

The man spun around and glared at Peter. "Do you know *why* he still retains his memories though?"

Peter shrugged. "I'm assuming that the brain tumor is acting as a partial block to whatever is erasing memories. That information helps a lot. Now I can try to create a block of my own that may work in protecting *our* memories."

"Peter, that is your *last* priority. Your first priority is to find Mark and make sure he's safe. You will then do surgery to remove the tumor."

Erased

Peter ran a hand from his forehead over his slicked back hair. "I'm not qualified to do that," he blurted.

"I don't care what you *think* you're not qualified to do. You will follow my orders! Now get out there and go find my *brother* Mark!"

DAY FIVE: CHAPTER EIGHTEEN

A light rain fell by the time Troy and Kelly reached the school. They tugged on the front double doors, which didn't budge.

"Terrific," Kelly said with a sigh. "The school is locked. We walked all this way for nothing."

Troy rolled his eyes and walked around the side of the building. The school was large, for it held students from kindergarten all the way through the twelfth grade. The outward appearance was that of an old, red-brick building built in the nineteen seventies, though that was Troy's observation based on ... well, he didn't know for sure. Perhaps he had studied architecture at some point.

Kelly followed after him. "I hope we won't get in trouble," she mumbled.

Troy turned to look at her. "Kel, nobody gives a flipping doodah about this place. Besides, if we get in trouble, nobody will remember tomorrow!" He turned toward a large window he assumed led into a classroom. He reached to the ground, grabbed a rock the size of his hand, and chucked it. The rock hit and shattered the glass.

"Troy!" Kelly gasped. "I will *not* date a vandal!"

"Get over yourself, girl," Troy snapped. "Desperate times call for desperate measures!"

"We want to find the home addresses of other teens. I would *not* call that a desperate situation."

Troy walked over to the new hole and reached through with his arm to unlatch the window. He slid it up and pulled back when shards of glass fell to the grass. "If anybody asks, I'll tell them your mom told us to break into the school."

Erased

"You will not!" Kelly demanded.

Troy made sure the windowsill was clear of any glass and, placing his palms on it, pushed himself through the window. He poked his head out and looked at Kelly. "Are you coming?"

Kelly folded her arms and stamped her foot. "I don't want to get in trouble!"

"You're already an accessory to breaking and entering. If I get caught, I'm still telling them you helped me."

"This was *your* idea!" she whined.

"Actually, it was your mom's."

She glared at Troy, giving him the most frightening expression she could muster.

"It's up to you, but I will go find the names." He disappeared into the building.

"Wait," she called out, and Troy appeared once more. "Help me up."

Φ

Peter left the hospital feeling more than frustrated. Nobody there had seen or heard from anyone named Mark. He stared at his silver wristwatch and sighed. It was already early afternoon, and he was looking for someone he wasn't sure wanted to be found. How does a man wake up and leave right after having his head opened? Mark being Gray Eye's brother hurt matters. It added pressure to Peter's already stressful job. In all reality, he should follow the mayor's instructions and disregard Gray Eye's orders altogether, but he felt as though he must obey the strange man, or suffer the consequences.

He may have struck out at the hospital, but he left his cell phone number with the receptionist and instructed her to call him if she heard anything. His next stops would be Town Hall and the police station.

Lucas Heath

Φ

Deputy Kyle Anderaos had ridden as best he could in the pouring rain. There hadn't been many lightning flashes, and he wasn't too worried about being electrocuted, though water soaked his clothes. As he left town, he noticed how dead the ground looked, as if someone had built Lion's Glade in the middle of a desert. At least with the rain it didn't feel as hot or dry. He peddled hard, wanting to finish the job and be done with it. The next town shouldn't be too far away; at least he hoped it wasn't. After a while, the rain subsided.

He continued riding and hummed random melodies that popped into his head. After passing the *Welcome to Lion's Glade* sign, a silhouette appeared in the distance. As he got closer he saw a truck on the side of the road. He pulled on the handbrakes to stop, climbed off of the bike and set it on the ground, then removed his gun. Didn't he write about a red truck in his journal? Vehicles were illegal, but perhaps he would make an exception if he used it to complete his trip.

The figure of a man leaning forward, head resting on the steering wheel, caught Kyle's attention.

"Sir, get out of the truck!" Kyle called out, but the man didn't stir. "I order you to get out of your vehicle!" When the man didn't respond, Kyle approached the driver's door and pulled it open. The unbearable smell that escaped the vehicle made Kyle gag, and he had to force himself not to vomit. He could see a bald spot on the man's head with several staples imbedded into the skin. Whoever he was, he had defecated in his pants.

Kyle held his breath as he reached to check the man's pulse; it was faint. He pulled back when the body jerked.

The man's head turned and vacant eyes stared at Kyle. "Help me," he whispered before closing his eyes.

Kyle grimaced and turned away from the image. He could still use the vehicle, but not while this man was in it. He could either leave him on the side of the road or take him back to Lion's Glade. Either way, he would have the vehicle to use. Walking to the back of the truck, he unlatched the rear door. He inhaled a deep breath of fresh air, returned to the front, and went in for the man. He was careful to pull him off the seat and out of the truck. The man was light, as if he weighed almost nothing, and the paleness of his skin showed that sickness was the probable cause. Kyle lifted him and, with a gentle effort, placed him in the bed of the truck. He closed the end and walked over to his bike. There was enough room for that too.

It didn't take long for Kyle to rid the truck of the stench and fill it with the odor of cologne he had brought in a small backpack. He pulled himself onto the driver's seat, shut the door, and turned the key in the ignition. The truck roared to life sending a shiver of excitement through Kyle. He was a cop so he could justify doing anything considered illegal, except maybe the usage of drugs, though perhaps if he had a medical condition he could get away with that too. He pulled on the lever and shifted the car into drive, letting it move forward, toward Lion's Glade.

Φ

Peter reached the police station to find only the secretary and two dispatchers. The rest of the police were fighting a fire. "Aren't the firemen supposed to do that?" he had asked the secretary, but she remarked with a snide comment about showing his ugly face to the fire and it would kill itself. He retreated to Town Hall to speak with the mayor, but she wasn't in her office, so he walked back outside where the rain fell once again.

The phone in his pocket rang, and he snatched it up and answered. "This is Peter."

"Hello, Peter. My name is Bonnie and I work here at the hospital."

"Yes, Bonnie, hello. Do you have information for me?"

"Yes, I do. A cop just brought in a man with an ID that matches the name of the person you are looking for and he's in critical condition."

Peter walked toward the hospital. "Does he have staples in his head?"

"Yes, he does," she answered. "Is there something we should know?"

"You need to have him prepped for brain surgery. I will be there as soon as possible."

"Sir as far as I'm aware we have nobody with the skills to perform brain surgery. I suspect if somebody needed a surgery like that, we would have them sent to a city with qualified doctors."

"I'm the one who will do the surgery and I would rather do it at the hospital than in my laboratory. So get him prepped. That's an order!"

Φ

Deputy Anderaos sat in a chair in the hospital waiting room, watching fish swim around a large tank as the nurse made phone calls. She had asked him to wait until they had more information about the sick man. Waiting was fine with him. With a vehicle, it wouldn't take him long to get to the next town and figure out the answer to the question that plagued the self-appointed mayor, and her lackey the sheriff.

The woman behind the desk walked over to him with a concerned expression on her face. "I think we will need you here for a while longer," she said.

"Why, what's going on?" Kyle asked.

"Peter Benet is coming to the hospital and plans on performing brain surgery on the man you brought in, Mark Hood."

Kyle's left eyebrow rose. "Why is that a problem?"

"He's claims to be a biologist and doctor, but I don't think he has any training in neurology. Besides, how could he perform the surgery without his memories? He may end up killing this man."

"Then what do you want me to do, arrest him when he gets here? Do you want me to force him to leave or ask about his credentials?"

Erased

"I don't know," she replied. "Mark Hood is not in any condition for surgery. He may die within the next few days. His vitals are weakening."

"If Mark is dying, why shouldn't you let Peter do the surgery to help him?"

She shook her head. "We can't let that happen. If Mark dies of natural causes, then we aren't at fault, but if we let a random citizen come in and perform surgery, that's a lawsuit waiting to happen."

"You're worried about lawsuits in *this* chaos?" Kyle sighed. "I'll talk with Peter when he arrives."

Φ

"How long are you going to try breaking down that door?" Kelly asked with a frustrated groan.

"I think I almost got it," Troy said as he hit the handle again with a fire extinguisher. "I didn't expect them to have the office locked."

"You mean the office that has all those important documents that shouldn't be seen by normal eyes?" Kelly mocked. "Of *course* they would lock the office."

"Like I said, I almost got it." He swung again.

"You said that a while ago. Give it up and let's go."

"No," Troy said with a groan as he hit the door again. "I will not give up. That's not my style."

"Oh, so you have a style now?" Kelly snapped as she sat and leaned against the white-brick wall.

Troy looked around, trying to find something else that may help open the door. "You know, maybe we've been going about this the wrong way. Perhaps I should go up and over."

"Up and over, what are you talking about?" Kelly asked. "You want to go through an air vent? I doubt they are big enough."

Troy chuckled and pointed at the ceiling. "The ceiling is tiled. I could push it up and remove it, then slide through the ceiling to the other side, remove the second tile and drop into the office."

Kelly pressed her lips together. "I suppose that could work," she said, "unless the wall is higher than you think and extends all the way to the ceiling."

"It's worth a shot. Go grab one of those computer carts we saw along the wall. I'll need something to stand on."

Kelly stood and complied, and returned a short time later with the cart. She locked the wheels in place so it wouldn't roll.

Troy appeared from a janitor's closet further down the hall with three buckets.

"You *want* to do this, don't you?" she asked as he stacked them into a pyramid on the cart.

"This is the best day of my life," he said with a chuckle. "It's like I'm a secret agent!"

"So you know how secret agents act now?"

"I guess! Because I feel like one!" He laughed harder while stepping upon the cart and easing his way onto the first and second buckets. Kelly held them to prevent them from tipping. Troy pushed on the tiled slat and removed it, tossing it to the floor.

"Whoa, watch it!" Kelly rebuked.

"There's enough room to slide up here," he said with a large grin. He pulled himself up into the ceiling and disappeared.

It didn't take long before Kelly heard a tile break and a thump inside of the office.

"I'm okay," he called out, and within seconds the door opened.

"Troy, you're bleeding!" Kelly shrieked when she saw blood on his forehead.

"I scraped myself on some metal. It's not a big deal. Let's search this place!" He turned on a light and they walked over to the administrator counter.

"What are the odds that the file cabinets are locked as well?" Kelly wondered as Troy bent over and tried to open it.

"You jinxed us," he said with a groan when the drawer wouldn't open.

Kelly ignored the comment and stared down at papers on the front desk. "Troy, look at this," she said.

Troy joined her and read over her shoulder. "Wait, what is that?"

"March tenth through the twenty-forth, the Lion's Glade Academy is leaving on an out-of-state field trip," she read from a sheet of paper. "This is a complete list of the school's students." She handed him a list of at least two hundred names.

"They are organized by grade in alphabetical order," Troy muttered as he read through the list. Every name had a check mark by it showing their participation. When he got to the twelfth grade list, two names were unchecked. "Kelly, you have to look at this," he hissed and handed her the paper.

"What?" she wondered as her eyes glanced over the list of names. "They were taking the preschoolers too?" she asked aloud. She then saw what Troy had seen. She looked up at him, her eyes wide. "Our names are the only ones that aren't checked."

He nodded. "Yeah."

She looked back down at the paper. "But what does that mean?"

Troy's mouth formed into a half frown. "Well, if we assume every person that has a check by their name went on the trip, then I suppose it means that, other than possibly a few babies, you and I are the youngest people in town."

DAY FIVE: CHAPTER NINETEEN

"We can't be the only teens here!" Kelly gasped. "How are we the only youth left in Lion's Glade?"

"That's a question I can't answer," Troy responded. "Perhaps we skipped the trip to go on our date."

Kelly tossed the papers to the desk. "We should tell the mayor about this. I mean, if you and I are the only kids in town, then it's worse than we thought."

"I would not call us kids," Troy muttered.

"You know what I mean," she snapped. "I'm also wondering how the entire school left on a two-week trip the day *before* all of this happened. That seems *too* convenient. There's *more* to this memory loss issue than we realized; this is too weird!"

Troy looked over at the filing cabinet. "I want to get into those files." He left the room and retrieved a fire extinguisher.

"You would have more luck using a blowtorch to cut your way through, *without* damaging the files, than you would getting it open by smashing the extinguisher against it."

"That's a good idea!" Troy said with excitement in his voice.

"Troy, no!" Kelly ordered. "I will not allow you to use something dangerous like a blowtorch."

"And yet there's a gun in your purse," Troy countered.

"That's for emergencies," Kelly answered.

"This *is* an emergency." Troy groaned. "We need these files!"

"Why? We already know we're the only ones left."

Troy turned back to the filing cabinet. "Come on," he pleaded, though there was less enthusiasm in his voice.

"No," she said and stamped her foot. "We are done here. It's time to leave."

"You're right," he admitted with a huff. "Let's go."

Φ

Peter wasted no time getting to the hospital, and he squeezed through the automatic doors as they opened. "What room is he in?" he asked the receptionist the moment he saw her.

"To whom are you referring?" she asked.

"Mark!" he replied, exasperated. "You called *me*, remember? You told me he was here."

"Are you a family member?"

"No, but I'm here to save his life and remove a brain tumor."

"I'm sorry, but if you aren't family, I can't give out that information," she replied. "Officer Anderaos, please come here."

A man in a police uniform stood and walked over to Peter. His black eye was prominent, and Peter shuddered. According to his journal, this was the officer he had punched yesterday.

"Sir, I need to ask you to leave."

Peter folded his arms. "Excuse me, but Mark Hood is my patient and his brother gave me strict instructions to find him and save his life."

"Well, unless either Mark or his brother fills out a liability waver, we can't allow you to do surgery," she replied.

"You're Bonnie, right?" Peter asked.

Erased

"Yes, sir," she responded.

"I worked with your husband and he saved my son. The mayor hired me to help return our memories. Mark is crucial to helping me achieve that, and he won't be able to if he's dead."

"You're either lying or you have the wrong woman, because I don't have a husband," she replied. "And I don't care *who* hired you to help return our memories. Mark is a patient of this hospital, and unless he *or* a family member signs a form that releases the hospital of all liability in the event of his death, I cannot let you perform surgery on him. Officer, please escort Peter from the premises."

Peter held up his hand and removed the cell phone from his pocket. "Let me make a call." He found the contact he was looking for and dialed. "Hey, it's Peter. Do you want your brother to live?" There was a pause. "Good, then get down to the hospital!"

Φ

The mayor watched from afar as the police fought a fire desperate to keep burning. The flames had not gotten close to the section that contained the H storage units. However, the police prevented the mayor from entering the property until they extinguished the threat. Their protective nature annoyed her, but she understood they were doing their job. They had the fire under control, but putting it out altogether took longer than the mayor appreciated. Perhaps the letters and numbers on her arm meant nothing, or perhaps they didn't associate with these storage units, but she had to find out.

She waited and watched, hoping that soon they would be done and she could check out storage unit H30. Until then, she wouldn't move from her spot underneath the canopy of a grocery store across the street from the property. Forget about the afternoon announcements. This was more important.

Φ

"Do you think that was what your mom wanted you to learn?" Troy asked Kelly after leaving the school.

"What do you mean?"

"Do you think she wanted you to find out about the trip and that we're the only teens left?"

Kelly shrugged. "I suppose it's possible, though considering what we've been through, at this point *anything* seems possible."

"Except time travel," Troy countered. "And alien invasions."

"You are good at making life difficult for others, aren't you?"

"It's a gift," he said with a smirk. His expression changed to a frown. "I admit it's comforting to learn that the rest of the school got out of town before this happened. Can you imagine what it would be like for little kids to lose their memories? That would be devastating. I'm not sure how they would handle it."

Kelly nodded. "Agreed, but I hope whatever took *our* memories didn't affect the other youth at a later time. That would be more devastating to be away from your parents *without* your memory. Just look at *us*."

"Did the paper give details about the field trip's location? I forgot to look."

She shook her head. "Not that I saw. I find it strange that it was a two-week trip though."

"With every single grade," Troy said, his voice dropping to a whisper.

"Exactly! What school does that?"

"Something is screwed up with this whole situation. We need to inform the mayor about this development as soon as possible."

"What do you think we're doing now?"

"Right."

Φ

Peter sat in the waiting room next to Kyle Anderaos, writing in his notebook. It took a while before Gray Eyes arrived, and the scowl on his face revealed his disgust. He walked up to the front counter.

"My name is Thomas Hood and I am the brother of Mark, the man brought in here. He needs immediate brain surgery." He pointed over at Peter who stood and walked over to him. "That man is the one I selected to perform the surgery."

"I need to see proof of identification and you must fill out these forms," Bonnie said as she set a packet of papers onto the counter.

"I'm not filling out any paper work. Please escort Peter to my brother so he can prep him for surgery."

"You need to fill out paperwork in order for me to allow that," Bonnie replied.

"You heard the lady," deputy Anderaos said as he walked up behind Peter.

The movement was quick and fluid. Gray Eyes, now revealed as Thomas Hood, reached behind his back, removed a hidden gun, and pointed it at Kyle. "I will be the one to dictate what I will and will not do. I will also give the orders from here on out. Take your gun and set it on the floor."

Kyle quivered, but he obeyed and placed the weapon on the ground.

"Now, go sit down over there," Thomas commanded as he pointed his gun at the chair. He picked up the police weapon when Kyle turned his back and stuck it in the waistband of his pants. He turned back to the receptionist. "Now, please be a doll and escort Peter back to save my brother."

Lucas Heath

Φ

"When they brought him in, he had soiled himself, and we did our best to clean him," the nurse named Diana said as she led Peter into the hospital room.

"I need him taken to an operating table and sedated to make sure he stays asleep. Under normal circumstances, we would want the patient to stay awake, but considering the trauma already done, I don't want to take the chance of him jerking awake while I'm operating."

She nodded. "Yes, sir, right away." Within ten minutes, they had wheeled Mark to a sterilized operating room.

Diana led Peter to a locker room to change out of his business suit and into navy blue clothing the doctors at the hospital wore. She then took him to Mark.

Peter felt the pressure pushing down on his shoulders when he saw Mark's unconscious body on the operating table. He did not know what he was about to do, he could only hope and pray that he didn't kill this man.

Φ

"I think we are all clear," Landon said as he walked up to the mayor. He grinned from ear to ear and had two black smudges on his face from soot. "*That* was a thrilling experience."

Jessica nodded and returned the smile. "I am sure it was, Landon. Now, if you would be so kind, please lead me to compartment H30."

Landon took a deep breath. "What is so important in there?" he asked. "I mean, you tell me to keep my men safe, and then change your mind, demanding that we save this unit."

"I do not have to explain myself to you."

Landon nodded. "Actually, you do," he responded. "If you're the mayor, then you answer to the citizens of Lion's Glade. I don't know if I voted for you in the election, but if you are putting my men's lives on the line, and we are taking orders from you in a crisis, I have every right to ask you to explain the decisions you make."

"My goodness, Landon; I think that fire fried your brain."

"No, I'm seeing a lot clearer at the moment. Tell me why you wanted this place saved."

"I cannot," she said with a sigh. "It is only a feeling, but I know something important is hidden there."

"So you put our lives in danger for a feeling?" he asked.

"Landon, please. Come with me and we can find out together."

Landon nodded and led her through the property over to the large garage storage spaces. They reached the unit the mayor had been longing to see. There was a strong keyed padlock latching the door shut. "I don't see how we would break that," he said as he looked at the mayor. "We might pry it open with a crowbar," he began.

"Shoot it," she suggested.

"Excuse me?"

"Shoot it. That should work."

Landon knew this wasn't a battle he would win, and once the mayor was around the corner of the building, he removed his gun, aimed, and fired. The padlock broke and he removed it.

The mayor returned to the large, orange door and looked at Landon. "Well, here goes nothing," she said as she grabbed the handle and pulled it open. Landon helped push it the rest of the way. She gasped at the sight in front of her and Landon's eyes grew wide.

"I don't believe it," Landon said. "It's a car!"

DAY FIVE: CHAPTER TWENTY

"How's he doing?" Thomas Hood asked as Peter entered the waiting room. A few hours had passed, and the sky had already darkened for the closing of the day.

"He's stable," Peter informed. "I can't tell you how I succeeded without killing him. I don't understand it."

"Oh, come on, Peter. Don't be so modest. You're a great scientist."

Peter shook his head. "That's my point! I'm a scientist, meaning I know science, not the workings of the brain."

"Oh, really?" Thomas asked with a crafty smile. "Then how could you work on a project that pertained to memory loss? Sure, you needed to know biology to work with the fungus, but you also needed understanding the human brain."

"I never thought about that," Peter said. He looked past Thomas and saw Kyle Anderaos reading a magazine; the deputy looked up to eye the two men. "I removed the tumor, but I can't predict how this will affect him as a whole. We won't see the effects of the damage until he wakes."

"I'm sure he will be fine. He's a fighter." Thomas turned and stared at Kyle. "You may go now," he said and tossed Kyle his gun. "Don't even consider arresting me. By tomorrow morning, I would wake up somewhere else." Thomas smirked.

Kyle slipped the gun into the holster and left the hospital. There was something about Thomas' gray eyes that seemed to strike fear into his heart. Why that was, he didn't know and he didn't care. It was time for him to get back to his mission and journey to another town. He walked around the hospital to where he had hidden Mark's truck from prying eyes and climbed into the driver's seat. He started the engine and then pulled out of the parking lot, onto the road.

Erased

"I did the best I could," Peter said to Thomas. "Now, I need to figure out how to get *our* memories back. I may have an idea. Plus, I should call my son. I haven't spoken to him today."

Thomas nodded. "I'll go check on Mark. He and I have a lot to discuss when he awakes."

They shook hands before Peter left the hospital. He removed his cell phone from the pocket of the suit he had changed back into and found Kelly's number on speed dial. He waited for it to ring, and thereafter a girl answered. "Hello, Kelly? This is Mr. Benet."

Φ

The teens had been waiting for a couple hours on the plush couches in the mayor's office when Kelly's phone rang. She answered, then passed the phone to Troy.

The conversation didn't last long. Troy explained the new information they had discovered about the school and then asked about any new prospects on a cure for their memory loss. He said goodbye when the mayor entered the room.

"Oh, I was not expecting anybody to be here," she said as she walked to her desk.

"We have information you need to hear," Troy said as he and Kelly sat in the vacant chairs in front of the mayor's desk.

"Well then, spit it out."

Troy explained what they discovered though Kelly kept interrupting Troy to apologize for the vandalism.

The mayor didn't say a word until Troy finished. She pressed her lips together and stood. "This raises red flags," she said and turned to look out the large window behind her. "It looks as if someone purposely took the youth away before this event occurred."

"Do we even know anything about the citizens in town?" Troy asked. "There are still many unanswered questions and yet we don't know who is in Lion's Glade. How many people live here?"

The mayor nodded. "There are many questions still unanswered."

"Are you aware that Lion's Glade has no cars and yet we found an active gas station?" Kelly asked.

The mayor spun around and eyed the teens. "There is a working gas station here?" she asked.

Troy nodded. "It's west of here, near the school. The gas station is unlocked though nobody is working there. We found a ten dollar bill on the counter."

"This is interesting," she said and sighed. "I thank you for offering this information. Now, if you would, please leave. I have calls to make."

"One last question," Troy said. "In your announcement today, you promoted somebody else as the sheriff. What happened to Sheriff Orson? Our journals said he went missing yesterday."

"I am sorry to say he died in the line of duty," she answered. "Now, if you would," she motioned for the door.

The teens obeyed and left the office. "Do you believe he died because of us?" Kelly wondered.

Troy shrugged in response. "At least we can mark it down in our notebooks as a mystery solved."

"What should we do now?" Kelly asked.

Troy shrugged. "What more *can* we do? It's getting late. My dad is doing all right, so I don't have to worry about him. Let's go to your place and watch a movie. My journal says they are breathtaking." He grinned.

Kelly nodded. "I can make us dinner too. We haven't eaten since breakfast."

Troy frowned. "You can cook?"

"I guess we will find out, won't we?" she giggled. They passed Landon on the stairs and left Town Hall.

"Oh, I was about to call you," the mayor said as Landon entered the room.

He held a folder of notes as he approached the desk and sat down in the seat Troy had used. "Here are the notes you requested on the history of Lion's Glade."

"What about the car?"

"We don't have the keys for it, so we can't start it unless we want to hotwire it, though I would recommend against that. We found registration papers in the glove compartment and we will look them over tomorrow. Everyone is too tired from fighting the fire to do anything more tonight."

Jessica nodded. "Understandable. We can learn more tomorrow. I found out a disconcerting revelation from those teens you probably passed on the way in here." The mayor relayed the information Troy had given her.

"There aren't any kids in town? What does that mean?"

"I am not sure," she said. "It makes me wonder if someone targeted us. Perhaps we *are* the only ones dealing with this crisis."

"I suppose once Deputy Anderaos reports in, we will find out for sure."

The mayor sighed. "So, what did you learn about our humble home?"

"The book on Lion's Glade seems rather new as if someone recently printed it. The author is a man named Griffin Powell. An oddity about the book is that one word on every page is underlined. I can't say for sure if it's a code, but it makes me wonder."

"And the town's history?"

Lucas Heath

"Lion's Glade is in the State of Kansas. The Cherokee Indians first inhabited the land a couple thousand years ago. They farmed crops, hunted bison, and lived in peace. The land the town is built on used to be a small forest. In 1838, European settlers arrived and discovered gold. They created a small settlement and built a town. Because of this, war broke out between the natives and the settlers, but with the European's superior weapons, they drove the natives from their land.

"Many died, both Native American and European settlers, and the irony was that, after a while, the Europeans realized there was less gold than they expected. Some of the settlers joined in the Manifest Destiny movement to expand and take control of the rest of the continent while others stayed to make a new life for themselves. They took over the land and farmed it."

"I suppose that makes sense with all the farm land to the east as shown on the map."

"The story doesn't stop there. In the late eighteen-hundreds, one of the Cherokee chiefs claimed to have put a curse on the town. The settlers captured and killed him, but not before they had heard his words. He said that, just as the history of his people would be forgotten, the citizens of Lion's Glade would forget their own history."

The mayor's right eyebrow rose. "Is that a coincidence, or a prophecy now fulfilled?"

Landon shrugged. "I don't believe in curses. If this has any relation to our predicament, I would assume someone is enacting revenge upon us for what our ancestors did to theirs. It's a farfetched idea, but I figured you should be informed."

She nodded. "Thank you. This gives me a lot to ponder."

"The book goes over the history of each family that started the town. I made notes on that. Frankly, other than the mention of the curse, the book was boring. It contained no information that can help us. Learning about our country was more interesting. Those notes are included."

Erased

The mayor smiled. "Thank you and your men for the time you put into this. I will go over the notes."

Landon stood. "Is there anything else I can do for you before I leave? The men let me leave work early."

She pressed her lips together. "Something that boy said bothers me. We don't know who lives in Lion's Glade. If we assume that someone removed the youth from town right before this incident, then we should shift our focus to finding out who lives here. It's time for us to have a new census and learn what we can about our neighbors. For all we know, the one responsible for our predicament could live here."

"Have you ruled out that scientist Peter Benet and the fungus he developed? I learned about it from the notes Sheriff Orson wrote before he died."

"Mr. Benet called my phone last night and left a message, telling me he knows for sure the fungus is not responsible and that he has an idea on how to stop this."

"All right, so then tomorrow we learn more about the citizens," Landon confirmed.

"Right," she answered, "especially the one who owns that car."

Φ

Peter stared at a computer monitor, reading over data he had entered. Something Diana had said bothered him. After he had finished the surgery, Diana had asked him how Patient Zero was doing. When he questioned what she meant by that, she responded by saying that Mark was the first one to be infected by the memory loss virus. She showed him a security video of when someone brought Mark to the hospital one day before everybody woke up without their memories. He screamed about not remembering anything and wanted answers. Peter didn't tell Thomas what he had learned because he didn't trust him.

There was a question Peter kept asking himself. Mark was from California. At least that's what his driver's license said. Assuming that a virus *was* the perpetrator in causing everyone's memory loss, if Mark was the first person to experience it, did he bring the virus with him and infect the town? But then another question nagged at Peter's mind. Troy had informed him that every youth except him and Kelly had left on a field trip the day Mark showed the symptoms.

It seemed too convenient that every youth left on the same day. Did the teachers remove the kids from town to protect them from the threat? How did they get away without vehicles? Did someone infect Mark to contaminate Lion's Glade? Is the rest of the country infected and Mark brought it to town when coming to visit his brother? There were too many questions and not enough answers. Peter slammed his fist against the desk and groaned in frustration. He hoped they would learn those answers before anything else happened, and before anyone else died.

Φ

Landon sighed with relief as he removed the shoes from his aching feet. He ate the raspberry-filled donut a deputy had taken from a grocery store and then brushed his teeth to prepare for bed. He didn't forget about the experiment he wanted to conduct and wrote detailed information about the test and the purpose behind it. Tonight, he would sleep in one of the jail cells at the police station and have it locked. He had stopped by his house to retrieve a pair of shorts and t-shirt, then made his cell bed. He called Officer Barns into the back room.

"Sheriff Landon, are you sure you want to do this?"

Landon nodded. "Yes, this will prove once and for all whether something happens at night when we are all asleep."

With those final words, Barns shut Landon inside the small cell and turned the key. "Sleep well," he said as he left the room.

Landon held on to his journal and closed his eyes, allowing sleep to overtake him.

Erased

Φ

It was late by the time Kyle passed the *Welcome to Lion's Glade* sign for the third time that day. He had stopped to get gas and spent a good amount of time trying to cheat the cash register into giving him free fuel. He grabbed a bunch of snacks and piled them into the passenger seat of the truck, thinking they would fill his stomach during the trip. After the day he had, he felt fatigued and figured that his memories wouldn't be erased by taking a small nap, so he risked it, falling asleep for a couple hours. His phone woke him at eleven thirty and he felt more awake after chugging a soda he hoped had caffeine.

He drove and thought about everything that had happened at the hospital. That man, Thomas, sure had some nerve pointing a gun at him. He should have arrested him, but he knew better. Thomas was looking out for his brother, how could Kyle fault him for that?

He continued to drive, but the headlights were dim and he couldn't see very far in front of him. He drove at an unhurried speed for fear he may hit an animal or something else. It didn't take him long before he slammed on the brakes and stared out the windshield. He parked the truck and climbed out, looking from left to right, taking in the sight. "What the..." he cursed in disbelief. After a moment, he went for his knapsack. He groaned when he realized he had forgotten to bring a notebook and writing utensil. He flipped open his phone and attempted calling the police station; his phone beeped, telling him he had no service. "You gotta be kidding me!" he said as he climbed back in the truck and did a quick U-turn. He sped up and held the phone in front of him, watching and waiting for at least one bar to appear.

After driving for a short time, he let out a sigh of relief when he saw two bars replace the *no service* icon. He dialed the station.

"This is Deputy Barns," Barns answered.

"Barns, this is Kyle Anderaos. I need you to get me the sheriff."

"He's already off duty and the night crew is here. I'm about to head home myself. What do you need?"

"I found out something rather freaky! Lion's Glade is," he stopped talking and slammed on the brakes yet again. "What is that?" he asked aloud as he saw a light emanating from the town. "Barns, are you there?" he asked and shifted the truck into park. He climbed out to get a better view. The light continued increasing in intensity and power. It was almost unbearable to look at though Kyle couldn't turn away. "Barns!" he screamed into the phone.

No reply came from the other end, and before Kyle could say another word, the light consumed him and he fell to the ground unconscious. Day five had ended.

THE CITIZENS

DAY SIX: CHAPTER TWENTY—ONE

A beam of sunlight escaped through a thick layer of clouds, shining upon the town of Lion's Glade. It entered Landon's bedroom window and caressed his face, waking him from his slumber. He yawned and, after a short time, sat up and rubbed his eyes with his palms. How did he get home? Hadn't slept at the police station? His neck ached from an awkward sleeping position. After a moment he collapsed, letting his head rest against the plush pillow once more.

It didn't take long before he sat up again and stared at the mechanical clock on the wall though it wasn't to check the time. How did he remember that he had slept at the police station? He also remembered spending most of the day fighting a fire at a storage facility. Was this actually happening? Had he retained his memories from yesterday?

He yanked the covers aside and stood, then approached the bedroom window and pushed the curtains aside to let in more light. It wasn't a dream or a bad joke. Landon remembered everything that had happened yesterday. He remembered going to sleep in a jail cell to prove that something happens between the hours of twelve and six. His theory was correct, considering he was now at home, but that was only the beginning.

He rushed to the dresser where he kept his cell phone plugged in and looked through the contacts, finding the mayor's number. He called it and waited until the familiar voice answered.

"Yes, Landon, what can I do for you?"

"Please tell me you remember yesterday too," Landon said, hoping that he wasn't the only one affected.

"Of course," she said. "Perhaps the virus or fungus affecting our brain has finished its work. It is a good sign that we can return things to normal."

Erased

"We are a long way off from normal, but it's a great first step! I found out something important as well. Do you remember the test I wanted to conduct? Yesterday, the night crew disappeared, and I wanted to see if something happens between the hours of twelve and six."

The mayor grunted a little. "Yes, I remember. What did you discover?"

"Last night, I had myself locked in a jail cell at the police station and fell asleep there. I woke up in my bed at home this morning. I think that somehow, and I'm not even sure how, but when we sleep, we begin the next day back at our home. It's as if we teleport back to where we started the previous day."

"That sounds ridiculous," she said with a sigh.

"I'm not trying to get all science fiction on you," Landon said. "But I tested my theory and I am correct. If I'm right, the graveyard crew, once again, won't be at the police station. They will have woken up in their homes."

"Even if you are correct, what does that prove? Perhaps you slept walk and returned home when the jail cell became uncomfortable; and perhaps the night crew left on an emergency, forgot to return to the police station, and returned home too."

"Once again, I had myself locked inside one of the cells. And this proves that there's something even crazier going on here than we thought!"

"Well, let us worry about that another time. Who cares *where* we wake up as long as we keep our memories? I need to record the morning announcements. Everyone will want to know what is happening."

Landon sighed. "All right, ma'am. I'll get ready and be at the police station if you need me. The deputies and I will get that census started."

"Speaking of the census, as your men gather information from the people of Lion's Glade, I want them to record the word each citizen found on their arm when they awoke on day one."

"All right, that is doable. What if somebody doesn't answer the door?"

"If that is the case, you may enter with force, and depending on the situation, arrest the person, or persons hiding inside the house. We need to know everyone in our town, no matter what."

"But ma'am, that's illegal," Landon said.

"I am not concerned about what is deemed illegal by a government not here to help us," she said. "*We* are the government. *We* make the laws. This is to protect our people. I am not saying every house should be searched. I say that if somebody does not answer their door within the appropriate amount of time, you have every right to enter. This will also help get an exact count of how many live in town. I will include this information in the morning announcement so that people are aware of our plans."

"Fine, then that's what we will do."

"Good. Well, I must go now. Goodbye, Landon."

He hung up the phone and sighed. He didn't know what was happening, but perhaps learning more about the citizens of Lion's Glade from the census would shed light on the situation.

Φ

Peter awoke to a phone ringing in his ear. He lifted his head from the office desk and saw his cell phone an inch away. Had he fallen asleep at work again? He answered it. "This is Peter."

"Dad, it's Troy!" Troy's excited voice blared through the speaker. "I still have my memories from yesterday!"

Peter sat up as a rush of adrenaline filled his body. What was yesterday? He operated on Mark to remove the brain tumor. "I remember too," he said.

"But how and why? What changed?" Troy wanted to know.

"I have no clue, but I will find out. Is there anything you need me to do for you in the meantime?"

"Have you thought about looking for Mom?" Troy asked.

"If I'm being honest, I haven't. I'm preoccupied with trying to get our memories back. Not losing our memories while we slept last night is a great start. Returning our earlier memories is my next goal."

"Have you rallied the other scientists in town to help you with that?"

Peter sighed. "I don't trust them. One already committed suicide, and the others..." he paused for a moment. "I don't know who to trust. One of them could have caused all of this."

"Maybe it's time to get other help though," Troy said. "If you can't do it yourself, you need to find someone else who can help and give you refreshing ideas."

"You're right, son. I'll see what I can do. You stay safe and out of harm's way."

Troy chuckled. "Kelly and I will be fine, dad. Just get our memories back."

"All right," Peter agreed. "I will talk with you later, son." He hung up the phone and shoved it into his pocket. Before he contacted anyone for help, he would head over and see Mark at the hospital.

Φ

"It was blinding like an explosion," one deputy said as they waited for Landon to arrive and unlock the station door.

"Except there wasn't a mushroom cloud, not that I could see anyway," Officer Barns said.

"How could you tell?" another cop asked. "It was pure light. It seemed to penetrate the walls of the police station."

Lucas Heath

Landon pulled up on his bike and overheard the final parts of the conversation. "So I was right," he said. "The night crew disappeared again."

"We all woke up in our beds," a young woman said as she straightened the badge on her uniform.

Landon looked around and saw that the entire police force was in view. "What light are you guys talking about?" Landon asked as he inserted the key and unlocked the station doors.

"Around midnight, a bright light filled the town." Barns turned and looked up at the sky. The clouds were light gray and only threatened a drizzle, not a thunderstorm like yesterday. "The next thing anybody remembers, they awoke in their homes."

Landon shook his head. "That is too weird."

"That's why the night crew showed up," Barns said as he looked over at a group of police standing in the street. "We can assume that this happens every night at midnight. They can help us during the day."

Landon nodded as he opened the door and let the others enter. "We have a busy day today. The mayor has our task set."

"She does, does she?" Barns asked with a chuckle as he stepped inside and moved away from the entrance.

Landon nodded. "I'll explain it once everybody is situated."

Twenty minutes passed before Landon had the whole room quiet.

"We have come very far the past five days, and now we have retained our memories from yesterday. This will help us and everyone else in Lion's Glade. We have learned a lot about the history of our country and town. However, now we need to learn more about the Lion's Glade citizens. The mayor wants to have a census. We will divide into teams and head in different sections of town; going door to door and writing down the basic information, such as how many people live at each address, their names, ages, and gender. She also wants us to record the words each person found on their wrists when they awoke on day one."

"Why would she want the words from people's wrists?" Barns asked from the back.

Landon shrugged. "I'm not sure, but there's no reason why we shouldn't. We all have permission to force our way into a house if nobody answers. That way, we can find out if there are any unreported deaths or suicides. There may be elderly citizens who need help. So make sure you check out every house where no one answers."

"Isn't that illegal?" one deputy near the front asked.

"The mayor has declared Martial Law. She will explain it in the morning announcements."

"Can she do that?" someone in the back called out.

"At the moment, yes." Landon answered. "*We* enforce the laws. Who will the citizens complain to? Our job is simple. We will enter and search the houses where no one answers."

Barns walked through the group and up to the front. "Is this worth our time?" he asked. "Not to contradict your orders or anything. I'm wondering what the purpose is behind this."

"This is how the mayor and I see it. We don't know the current population of Lion's Glade or who lives here. It's possible the person who caused our memory loss is still here. We received word yesterday that the entire youth population has disappeared. It would be best to know who lives in our town."

"The youths are gone?" one of the female officers asked. "What about the two teens that have provided us with information?"

Landon nodded. "They are the only two left in town. At least, that's what the mayor told me. That's one reason this census needs to happen.

We have a lot more to learn. Are there any more questions before we start?"

"What if we need to report to an emergency?"

"Then the dispatchers will report it over the radio and the closest deputies will respond to the emergency," Landon said as he rolled his eyes. "Look guys, the citizens come first. If you get a report that someone nearby is hurt or needs police help, then report to the location. The census can wait. Just remember what houses you've visited. Are there other questions?"

The room remained silent.

Landon smiled. "Good," he said with a nod. "Then pair up. We can cover much more ground that way. One of you on each side of the street would work wonders."

The front door of the police station slammed, causing all eyes to turn away from Landon. A man dressed in a police uniform entered the room, panting. "Sorry I'm late guys. I overslept."

"And you would be," Landon asked and waited for an answer.

"You're kidding, right Landon? Please don't tell me I'm the only one who retained my memory from yesterday."

Landon shook his head. "I remember yesterday well, but I don't remember you."

"I'm Deputy Kyle Anderaos. You sent me out to find another town." The man looked at the others. "Come on, Barns, you remember me, don't you?"

Barns shook his head. "I'm sorry, but you don't look familiar."

Kyle turned to the others. "None of you remember me?" he asked, exasperated. He waited for a reply though none came.

Erased

"I'm sorry, Kyle," Landon said. "But it looks as though nobody knows who you are."

DAY SIX: CHAPTER TWENTY—TWO

"Hello, Bonnie, I'm here to see how Mark is doing."

Bonnie looked up from a card game on the computer. "He's not here."

Peter's head tilted in confusion. "He had brain surgery yesterday. Where would he go?"

Bonnie shrugged. "I can't answer that. He wasn't in his room when I arrived this morning. Sorry."

Peter turned away and scratched his head. He removed his phone and scrolled through the contacts. Thomas Hood's number had disappeared. A groan of frustration escaped Peter's lips, and he almost threw the phone at the wall. "He deleted his number from my phone... said he didn't want me remembering him."

"Who did?" she asked.

Peter turned back to her. "Thomas Hood. I wonder if he came by and took his brother away."

Bonnie shrugged. "I would suggest you ask the nurses on the graveyard shift, but none were in when I got here this morning, just like yesterday. I mean, I was twenty minutes late, but that doesn't give them a right to leave before I get on shift!"

Peter turned to leave. "Thanks for your help, Bonnie." He exited the hospital and gritted his teeth. Something wasn't right with Thomas. He had known that from the start, but helped him anyway to save the life of his brother. *Was* Mark, Thomas' brother? Peter wasn't sure, but he would find out. He needed to talk with the sheriff.

Φ

Erased

Landon sat at a table in Conference Room A, staring at the man opposite him. He had sent his deputies to begin the census, but stayed behind with Officer Barns to talk with the newcomer. Barns sat by the door to prevent any attempt of escape.

"To make sure I searched for the right person, what did you say your name is again?" Landon asked.

"Kyle Anderaos. I am a deputy here in Lion's Glade."

"A deputy of what?" Landon asked.

"A police officer," Kyle said and rolled his eyes. "Hence me wearing this uniform!"

"I looked through the records and we have no one named Kyle Anderaos on staff here at the station. Why don't you try changing your story again?"

Kyle stood and slammed his palms against the table. "I'm telling you the truth!" he turned to Barns. "Why would I lie about any of this?" He turned back to the sheriff. "I was here yesterday talking to you, Landon! I was reading the history books on Lion's Glade and our country, taking notes on paper, until you came in and sent me on a mission to bike my way through the storm to another town!"

"Please lower your voice, I'm sitting right in front of you," Landon said and huffed.

Kyle sat again. "You take detailed notes in your journals. I'm sure you wrote about me in there."

Landon removed two journals from a backpack at his side. "I looked through these too, and I see no mention of a Kyle Anderaos *anywhere*."

"If you didn't send me to bike to another town, who else did you send?" Kyle asked.

Landon shook his head. "I didn't send *anybody* to travel to another town. *I* attempted to leave a couple days ago, and the mayor had asked me to send somebody yesterday, but I didn't have the available manpower."

Barns jumped when someone knocked on the door. It opened and the secretary leaned in. "Peter Benet is here, sir," she said to Landon.

"Peter Benet!" Kyle yelled. "He was at the hospital yesterday doing brain surgery on a man named Mark! Mark's brother held me at gunpoint so Peter could operate!"

Landon stood. "Kyle, please lower your voice. I'll be back in a moment." He followed the secretary out of the room and shut the door behind him.

Peter stood at a desk and smiled when Landon approached. "Sheriff Landon, it's good to see you."

Landon nodded. "And you too. You're the one working on returning our memories, correct?"

Peter nodded. "That I am. I need you to put an APB out for a man named Thomas Hood and his brother Mark Hood. I performed brain surgery on Mark last night and I believe his brother has taken him from the hospital."

Landon's eyebrows furrowed, and he turned his head toward the conference room. "Why do you think his brother took him?"

"Mark wasn't there when the nurses showed up for work this morning. I'm guessing his brother removed him late last night."

Landon pressed his lips together and turned back to Peter. "I doubt anybody took him. Perhaps he returned to his home."

"Mark is from out of town and he *just* had brain surgery. There's no way he could leave the hospital on his own. I'm *sure* that Thomas removed him."

Erased

Landon sighed. "You will hear about this sooner or later, but I learned that around midnight our world resets itself. Everyone wakes up every morning in the same exact location they woke up the previous day. I tested this theory myself. Last night, I went to bed in a locked jail cell, and this morning, I awoke in my bed at home."

"That sounds crazy," Peter said.

Landon nodded. "I agree," he said. "However, it's the truth. I think it's possible that your man, Mark, was reset to wherever he has woken up for the past five days."

"If what you're saying is true, then where would that be?"

"That, my friend, is for *you* to figure out. I have a question though. Yesterday at the hospital, when you performed brain surgery on Mark, did his brother, Thomas, take any hostages during that time?"

Peter nodded. "He took the receptionist hostage to prevent her from calling the police. There was nobody else around that I saw. Why?"

Landon nodded and then shook his head. "No reason. Have a good day, sir." He watched Peter leave and returned to the conference room.

"Did you ask Peter about me?" Kyle asked. Anxiety ruled his demeanor.

"I'm sorry, but Peter doesn't remember you either. Care to change your story?" Landon asked as he sat in his seat again.

"This has to be the doing of the person who is messing with our memories! Think about it, Landon! The one day we keep our memories, you don't remember me?"

"Why would someone want to erase *you* of all people from everyone's memories?" Landon asked.

"What makes *you* so special?" Barns asked.

Kyle turned to him and shrugged. "I left Lion's Glade yesterday. Maybe this happened because of what I saw."

"What did you see?" Landon asked as his interest piqued.

"That's the thing. I can't remember! There is something several miles outside of town, but I don't remember what it was."

"Convenient," Barns scoffed. "Landon, I suggest we jail this guy until we are certain of who he is. Something doesn't feel right about him."

Landon shrugged. "What's the point? He will reset at midnight and appear somewhere else."

"At least it gets him off of the streets for the time being."

Landon nodded in agreement. "Good idea. I'll let you have the honor. I've wasted enough time here and I need to take information to the mayor."

Barns nodded, stood, and approached Kyle. He grabbed the uniform collar and lifted him to his feet. He made sure the cuffs around Kyle's wrists were tight and then led him out of the room.

Landon sighed and stood. He walked across the station to his office and picked up documents from the printer. The mayor would want to see them.

Φ

"Ma'am, may I enter?" Landon asked as he poked his head into the mayor's office.

"Come on in, Landon. I have been waiting for you." Jessica stared out the window at the horizon of dark clouds. She turned toward the sheriff and smiled. "Have a seat and tell me what you have found."

Landon sat and tossed a folder over to her. "The man who owns the car is Tucker White. He is a scientist working for the Midas Tech

Erased

Laboratory here in town. He has no criminal record that our system could find and he's the renter of the storage unit where we found the car."

"This is intriguing," she said as she read through the file.

"If we can talk with him and get the keys to the vehicle, we can use it to leave town and figure out if the outside world is affected by the same problem. That would at least answer one of our biggest questions."

She nodded and turned back toward the window. "So, shall we go meet him?"

Landon shrugged out of habit even though she wasn't looking at him. "I suppose so, if that's what *you* want to do."

"It would be good for me to meet him. I assume the other officers are on their way to begin the census?"

Landon nodded. "Yes, ma'am."

"Very good," she said with a large smile. "Then let's go meet Tucker White!"

Φ

"A census, huh?" Troy asked as he watched the mayor's announcement for the first time. "At least they listened to us yesterday."

"You know what stinks about remembering yesterday?" Kelly wondered aloud.

"What's that?" Troy asked.

"I still remember how listening to my mom's voice unnerved me."

"At least you have proof that your mom is alive and well. I still don't know where *my* mom is, or if she's even breathing anymore."

"I can't be sure if that *was* my mom though. It could have been anyone using her cell phone."

"I suppose that's true," he paused. "The mayor wants no one leaving their homes during this time, so I suppose we are stuck here. We could always watch more movies."

"I'm burned out on movies," Kelly complained. "Sure, the adrenalin rush is great, but I'm drained. I want to do something else, like go for a walk."

"The mayor asked us to stay here though."

"We have already done so much for her. I think as long as we tape a paper with the required information to our front doors, we will be fine."

Troy sighed. "Where would we walk?"

"I already have a place in mind," she said with a giggle.

"Which is where?"

"I want it to be a surprise."

"Kelly, where do you want to go? Tell me."

"No, I won't tell you. I will make you wait and let the suspense build."

Troy glared at her and folded his arms. "I will not go if you won't tell me."

"Don't be a big baby. Let me have fun for once."

"You could lead me off a cliff!"

"You won't be wearing a blindfold! What makes you think I would be stupid enough to lead you anywhere dangerous?"

"You've had your moments," Troy said with a smirk. "I'm not going if you don't tell me where."

She sighed and dropped her gaze to the floor. "*Fine*, I'll tell you." She looked up and stared into his eyes. "I want to go to a bar."

DAY SIX: CHAPTER TWENTY-THREE

"Hey, Bonnie, it's me again," Peter said as he approached the reception desk in the hospital waiting room. "I would have called, but my phone is about to die. Who brought Mark to the hospital yesterday?"

Bonnie looked up from her card game and gave him a blank stare. "I don't remember," she said.

"Please, try harder. I need to find out who found and brought him here."

She shook her head. "Sorry, I can't help you."

Peter grunted and turned toward the door.

"Actually," she said and pressed her lips together. "I think it was a man. I don't understand why it's so hard to picture him."

Peter turned back to her. "What *do* you remember about yesterday?"

"That lunatic, Thomas, held me hostage so you could perform the surgery. I have a vague recollection that a man brought Mark here. I thought I wrote down his name." She looked around the desk and under papers. "He had a unique name." She continued to search. She shrugged and looked back up at Peter. "It's not here. Sorry."

Peter sighed. "Thanks anyway."

"I wonder if," she said, and then bent over to look under the desk. There was a rustling of plastic and an excited laugh filled the room. "Got it!" She sat back up and held out a sticky note for Peter. "I suppose the other nurse threw it away last night after I left."

"Officer Kyle Anderaos? You didn't say he was with the police."

She shrugged. "I may remember most of what happened yesterday, but it looks as though I don't recall everything."

Lucas Heath

Peter read the name again. "I suppose it's time to go back to the police station."

Φ

"Okay, I've waited long enough," Troy said in exasperation. "Why do you want to go to a bar?"

Kelly giggled and kept walking.

"I'm serious, Kel. I never took you for a rebellious, underage drinker."

She stopped walking and gave him her death glare. "I'm not going there to drink, dummy."

"Well you've kept me in suspense long enough," he said as she began her journey once more.

"Fine if you *really* want to know."

"I do," he said with a sigh.

"This morning I received a text message from my mom."

Troy's eyes grew bigger in alarm. "And she wants you to meet her at a bar?"

She shook her head. "No, but she told me I need to stay anchored in reality and focus on the clues of my situation."

"And that leads you to a bar?"

She stopped and spun to look at him. She slid the sleeve of her sweater up, revealing the word on her arm. "See?"

"I don't understand the correlation, except for the word anchor."

"That's because I'm a better problem solver than you," she said with a grin. "It's a clue! Why would I write *anchor* on my arm, and then my mom tells me to stay *anchored* in reality?"

Erased

"Because she doesn't want you going off the deep end," Troy suggested. "Which is exactly what's happening right now."

"The 'A' is capitalized in Anchor on my arm and Anchored in my mom's text, and it shouldn't be capitalized in my mom's text, which suggests... it's a clue!"

"Uh huh," Troy said as he folded his arms.

"After I got the text message, I searched in the phone book for any place that had the word Anchor in it. There's only one in town, The Anchor Bar."

"And you think this will lead you to your parents, or what?"

She shrugged. "It's a start! Now let's hurry. It looks like it could rain."

Φ

Peter entered the police station and let the door slam behind him, startling the secretary and making her jump.

"Rude much?" she snapped.

Peter looked toward the door that led to the back offices. "Is Sheriff Landon here?"

She shook her head. "No, he left a short while ago. I think Officer Barns is still here though. You can head back if you wish."

Peter nodded and proceeded through the door into the office.

Officer Barns appeared from the bathroom and spotted Peter. "May I help you?"

"Yes, my name is Peter Benet. I am the scientist working on fixing our memory-loss problem."

"Oh, you showed up earlier. It's nice to meet you." He held out his hand and Peter shook it.

Lucas Heath

"I have a question about one of your officers. Does a Deputy Kyle Anderaos work here?"

Barns froze in place and eyed Peter. "No, but there's a man by that name in custody for impersonating an officer."

Peter bit his lip. "May I speak with him?"

"What's this about?" Barns asked.

"He dropped off a man at the hospital yesterday and I need to figure out where he found him."

Barns shrugged. "Be my guest. He's locked in the first cell at the back." He pointed toward a metal door at the end of the room. "I'll be here if you need me."

Peter nodded and walked toward the door where Barns pointed. He entered a dim room and saw a young man dressed in a police uniform sitting on a cot, his face resting against his palms. "You're Kyle, right?"

Kyle looked up and nodded. "And you're Peter Benet. It's good to see you again."

"We've met?" Peter asked.

Kyle groaned. "So you don't remember," he said. "Yes, we met yesterday at the hospital. It doesn't matter. Nobody remembers me anymore. I used to be a deputy here, and now I'm accused of impersonating one because nobody remembers me!"

"That sounds a little farfetched. I understand how somebody could lose their entire memory, but everybody forgetting a single individual is different."

"I understand that, which is why I'm not even going to bother explaining. There must be something you need if you came here to talk with me."

Erased

"A nurse at the hospital said you were the one who dropped off an individual named Mark Hood yesterday."

"She remembers me?" Kyle asked as he stood.

"Well, no, but she remembers that somebody dropped him off, and she had written your name."

"At least my name exists on paper *somewhere*. Yes, I brought Mark to the hospital. He was in bad shape."

"Where did you find him?"

"I suppose telling you won't help me out of here, but whatever. I found his truck parked off of the highway south of town." Kyle sat again.

"You mean he had a vehicle?"

"You didn't know that?"

Peter shook his head. "He's from out of state, but I didn't know he came in a vehicle."

"I drove it last night. I was trying to get to another town to find out if they are dealing with the same situation as us."

"Are they?"

Kyle shrugged. "I never made it because I discovered something bizarre and then blacked out. I can't remember what I saw, but I know that it was important. Next thing I remember, I woke up in my bed."

Peter smiled. "Thank you for your help, Kyle." He left the jail and walked back into the main section of the police station.

"Did you get the information?" Barns asked.

Peter nodded. "Yes. Now I know where to look."

Φ

Lucas Heath

"This is his house?" the mayor asked in awe at the mansion before them.

A giant fence enclosed the property and manicured, lush vegetation grew everywhere; someone maintained the grounds. Flowers in a rainbow of colors bordered the driveway leading up to the house, starting with red and ending in violet. Two giant trees grew several feet apart, covering a corner of the house with their branches and leaves.

As the gate was wide open, Landon and Jessica made their way to the front door and rang the bell. The doorbell played a symphony of music informing anyone inside they had visitors.

The door opened wide and a tall, slender man dressed in a white tank top, blue shorts, and flip flops stood before them. Pink sweat-bands covered his wrists. His blonde head had little hair, for it looked as though he had received a buzz cut. He couldn't have been more than thirty years old; at least, that was Jessica's opinion.

"Are you Tucker White?" Landon asked.

"That's what it says on my boxers," the man said with a chuckle. "What a surprise. I get a visit from the mayor *and* the sheriff at the same time! Come on in, my friends!" He ushered them to enter. "Can I get you anything, like lemonade or water perhaps?"

The mayor shook her head. "No thank you. We will not be staying long. Yesterday, we discovered a car you own in a storage unit you rented."

"That's wicked cool," Tucker said with a large smile. "I didn't know I owned a car!"

"Owning a car is a federal offense," Jessica said with a grim expression. "We need to impound it."

Tucker's demeanor seemed to wilt at the news. "Bummer, man. You got me all excited for a second."

Erased

"We are here to see if you still have the keys to the vehicle to help us move it," Landon said.

Tucker shrugged. "If they are, they would be in the garage. I haven't been out there at all. I'll be right back." He disappeared down a hallway and through a door.

"He is a scientist?" Jessica whispered. "He seems like an airheaded rich boy."

Tucker returned a minute later with a set of keys in hand. "Got em." He tossed them to Landon. "You sure I can't offer you fine couple some refreshments?"

"We are *not* a couple," Jessica rebuked. "And no, we will leave now. Thank you for your cooperation." She turned toward the door and opened it, stepping back outside into a light breeze.

"Have a good day," Landon said as he shut the door behind them.

"Well, that was embarrassing," she said with a sigh.

"Embarrassing or not, we have the keys to the car," Landon said as he held them up for her to see. "Want to go for a ride?"

Φ

Tucker White watched from the window as the mayor and the sheriff left the property. He laughed to himself and removed one of the sweatbands from his wrist, looking at the letters and number, *Car4JD*, written in black ink. The sentence *Car for Jessica Dailey* ran through his mind, which made him smile. Something told him that the plan was falling into place, and the next piece of the puzzle would be revealed soon.

DAY SIX: CHAPTER TWENTY—FOUR

"Please don't tell me you're going in there," Troy said as he looked at the old, brick building in front of them. "The place looks like it's falling apart. It's boarded up and condemned!"

"That's a clue right there! Why would a condemned building have a spot in the phonebook?" Kelly asked.

"Maybe the phonebook is old," Troy groaned and slapped his forehead. "You're taking this whole mystery thing too seriously."

"Says the boy who broke into the school, crawled through the ceiling to get into the office, *and* wanted to use a blowtorch to get into the filing cabinet," she countered.

"We were looking for the student addresses, not for a crazy mystery that's letting your mind run wild," Troy reminded.

"My mind isn't running wild, it's creeping carefully." She stuck out her tongue and turned back to the boarded-up window. "Let's see if there's any way to enter from the back."

"You can, but I'm staying here."

"Stop being a coward! I broke into the school with you! What if I get cut on a nail or glass and bleed to death?"

"Then I can tell you I told you so."

"You're so mean," she said and gave him a piercing glare.

"And yet you love me anyway," he said with a smirk.

"Love is such a strong word. Let's just say I occasionally enjoy your company."

Erased

"Says the girl who cuddled up to me while watching that vampire movie last night," Troy countered.

"It was such a romantic movie!"

"Vampires are *not* supposed to sparkle in the sunlight! They burn!"

"Who says? I don't remember that; how would *you* know?"

"I looked it up in my Mythical Creatures book this morning."

"You have one of those?" She huffed and stomped her foot. "Are you coming with me or not?"

"Not," he responded.

"Fine then, if I die, it will be your fault." She vanished around the side of the building.

Φ

Peter peddled hard as he rode the bike he had taken from the police station. He wasn't sure whose it was though he didn't care. He needed quicker transportation and would return it once he finished his search. After using a map to find which direction *south* was, he began his journey. Town Hall was closer to the center of town, so it would take him time to work his way to the highway. At least it wasn't raining. He wasn't sure if the sheriff's theory about people being reset every night was true, but what else could he do at this point? If Mark was unconscious in a truck somewhere, he needed to find him.

Φ

"This is a nice car!" Jessica Dailey exclaimed as she sat in the passenger seat of the blue vehicle.

"It's a 2005 Dodge Magnum," Landon said, taking the driver's seat.

"Whatever it is, it sure is comfortable."

"I'm surprised it fits in here. I suppose they built these storage units for automobiles."

"Have you searched any of the other units to see if they contain more vehicles?"

Landon shook his head. "No, do you want me to get the deputies to check?"

"Later," Jessica said as she opened the glove compartment. "Get us on the road. I want to get to another town as soon as possible."

"I can drive around town, but I don't think leaving Lion's Glade is the best course of action for you. You're still the mayor and you're needed here."

"The police have their assignments. If I stay here, I would sit in my office all day with nothing to do. If someone needs me, they can call my cell phone. Let's go check things out."

Landon sighed. "All right, ma'am, if you insist."

"I insist! We need to stop at Town Hall so I can put a note on the door and you can tell your secretary you are leaving."

Landon nodded as he placed the key in the ignition and started the vehicle. "There's half a tank left. We should get gas if possible."

"From what those teens said, there is a working gas station two miles west of Town Hall. We can head there afterward."

He nodded and shut the driver's door. Jessica closed her door, and he pulled out of the storage unit. "This feels so weird. I don't remember ever driving a vehicle, but it's as if my body knows how to do it." He applied the brakes as he turned the wheel. After a few minutes, they pulled out onto the road.

Φ

Erased

"Kelly, hurry!" Troy yelled, hoping she could hear him. She had yet to return and he worried something had happened. Perhaps he should have gone in with her. He waited a short while longer and walked toward the back of the building.

"Ouch," Kelly squeaked, and as Troy rounded the corner, he saw her emerging from a window of broken glass.

"Are you all right," he asked as he studied her.

"I'm fine," she said. "I got poked by a sliver of glass, but I'll live."

"Did you find anything at all?" he asked as his brows furrowed.

She shrugged. "Lots of broken alcohol bottles and wood from tables and chairs," she muttered.

"Did you find what you were hoping for?"

"Just take me home, Troy," she whispered. "Please, take me home."

Φ

"How do you even work this thing?" Landon asked as he stared at the gas pump.

Jessica got out of the car and joined his gaze. "You need money to pay for it."

"It's not as if I have any money on me," he muttered as he looked toward the vacant building.

Jessica reached into a pocket of her suit and removed a square piece of plastic. "I do; I found it in my desk drawer at the office." She slid the card through, and after a moment, lifted the nozzle and handed it to Landon. "Here you go." She sat back in the passenger seat and let him deal with the rest. She sighed and yawned. "So, what do you think is causing all of this?" she asked.

Landon shrugged. "Beats me," he muttered. "A part of me wants to believe this happened to the whole country because then we wouldn't be alone. But there's another part of me that thinks we're in an experiment of some sort. For what reason, I don't know, but those are my thoughts. What about you?"

"I have the same belief," she said. "Perhaps someone chose our town to be their test subjects or something. Maybe somebody chose our entire *country* for their sick game."

"Who could do that; the Chinese, the Russians, or the Germans?"

She shrugged. "Perhaps somebody from our own country. We may never know."

The handle clicked and stopped fueling, signaling that the gas tank was full. He removed the nozzle from the car and replaced it before screwing the cap back on and shutting the metal flap. He walked back to the driver's side, climbed in, shut the door, and started the engine. "So, are you ready to go?" he asked with a nervous chuckle as Jessica shut her door and buckled her seatbelt.

She nodded and grinned. "Of course! Let us see what lies beyond our town."

Φ

Peter didn't have to travel very far past the *Welcome to Lion's Glade* sign before he saw the outline of the red truck. He felt sweaty and drained. Biking in a business suit was an atrocious idea. Why hadn't he changed? His clothing had been the least of his worries. He needed to find Mark and make sure he was okay. Without the IV to provide him with fluids, Mark could be in danger. Peter peddled faster until he was several feet away and pulled on the hand brakes.

He climbed off, set the bike on the ground, and approached the driver's side door. Peering through the window, he groaned; the truck was empty. The keys were on the seat next to an mp3 player. Peter looked around the vast landscape; it looked like a barren desert. The ground was rocky and cracked, and not a single plant could be seen. Did Mark somehow wake up and wander away from the vehicle?

The sound of an engine caught his attention, and he turned to look down the road the way he had come. A blue car sped down the highway and came to an abrupt halt next to Peter.

Landon rolled down the window of the Dodge Magnum. "Peter; strange to see you out here," he said.

Jessica opened her door and stepped out. She stared at the truck. "Another vehicle?"

"This belongs to Mark, the man I'm searching for. With your theory about everyone resetting every night, I thought he would have appeared back at his truck. This is where Kyle Anderaos found him yesterday before taking him to the hospital."

"Kyle *was* at the hospital yesterday?" Landon asked.

Peter nodded. "Yes. He saved Mark's life. His theory about people forgetting him isn't that farfetched anymore."

"I think I should speak with Kyle when we return," Landon said as he looked in his side mirror, seeing the bike in the road. "Nice bike. It looks like mine."

"Peter, I assume you are the one still working on returning our memories," the mayor said.

"Yes, Mayor, I am, but I need to find this man first. He may have the answers we need."

"Well, get searching," she said as she climbed back into the car. "Take care of that truck. We may need it."

"We should be back later tonight," Landon said. "There's something I want to speak with you about when I return."

Peter nodded. "Sounds good."

The mayor said something Peter didn't understand, and the car moved forward.

Peter turned to the truck again. If he couldn't find Mark, then he would have to give in and contact the other scientists like Troy suggested. He picked up the bike, set it in the truck bed, and then climbed in to the driver's seat. When he started the engine, it purred to life. At least he had a motorized vehicle with which to return home.

Φ

"I wonder if this thing can play music," Jessica said as she pushed the buttons of the radio. "This thing has a CD player too."

"I imagine most vehicles did." He watched the road and saw the carcass of a dead rodent rotting away. After another mile, he could tell the gradient had shifted. It was a slight change, but Landon noticed an increase in the elevation. They were traveling up an incline.

Jessica turned a knob, bringing the speakers to life with static. She pushed more buttons though none of them changed the station. "Look, it's a CD!" she exclaimed when a compact disk slid out of a slot in the dashboard. "What..." she muttered when she read the words written in black ink on the top. "For Jessica Dailey."

"That CD is for you?" Landon asked as he turned to look.

"I do not understand. How could Tucker White know that I would be in his car?"

"Perhaps one of the other deputies who checked out the car somehow slipped it in to mess with you." He turned his eyes back on the road.

"That is unnerving." She placed the CD back into the slot and pushed the play button.

"You're going to listen to it?" Landon asked.

Erased

"Why not?" They waited for the CD to play, but the static remained. "It is not working. Maybe the CD player is broken." She pushed play two more times, but to no avail. She hit the eject button and grabbed the disk when it emerged, slipping it into a purple, velvet purse she had brought with her. "I guess I must listen to it when I get back." She turned the volume knob, silencing the static.

Landon watched as the road's incline continued and then leveled off before a decline began. His eyes grew wide as he saw what appeared before them. The mayor was too busy looking through her purse to notice. Now Landon understood what Kyle had meant when he said he saw something several miles outside of town. "Um, ma'am, you better look at this."

She set her purse down and followed Landon's gaze. A small gasp escaped her lips.

Landon slowed the car to a stop and put it in park. He opened the door and stepped out, and she did the same.

"Oh my," was all Jessica could say.

Landon turned his head both to the right and left of the highway. A large metal fence at least ten-feet tall, extended as far as the eye could see in both directions with an imposing gate secured across the road. The bars were an inch thick and continued every half foot, making him feel trapped in a giant prison cell. He could hear an electric hum coming from the fence. Touching it meant certain death.

"It *is* us," Jessica stammered.

"What?" Landon asked as he turned to her.

"Whatever caused our memory loss happened only to Lion's Glade," she said as she sucked in a gulp of air. "We were right, Landon. We *have* to be right. The citizens of Lion's Glade are test subjects in some screwed-up testing. Perhaps they chose our town because we were farthest away from other cities and towns. They put up this barrier to prevent us from escaping." She turned to him with tears running down her cheeks. "Landon, we are trapped."

DAY SIX: CHAPTER TWENTY—FIVE

Late evening had arrived by the time Landon and Mayor Dailey returned from their drive. Landon parked the car in front of the police station and turned to the mayor. "So, who do we tell about this?"

The mayor shook her head. "Nobody," she mumbled. "We do not want this to start a panic. As far as everyone is concerned, you and I got to another town and found out that the rest of our country is going through the same crisis we are. That should keep them satisfied; for a short while anyway."

"What's the town's name? What if people ask about uniting with them to help each other through this horror? Perhaps we should hide the car and pretend we never went."

"Peter saw us," she reminded.

"I need to go speak with him anyway. Perhaps I can explain the situation and ask him to keep quiet about it. I doubt he wants to start a panic either."

Jessica sighed once more and unbuckled her seatbelt. "That is fine. As far as anyone else is concerned, we never made it. The car broke down or something."

"I'll be honest with you. I don't remember who I was before all of this happened, but I know that I don't believe in lying. Where do we draw the line? Is lying ever okay, even to protect others?"

Jessica shrugged. "I know what you mean, but what is the alternative? If we tell people the entire town is surrounded by a large electrified fence, how do you think they would respond? They have already been through enough. Why should we impose on them any more fear? If we tell them about being trapped, we would admit to being test subjects in some sick experiment."

Landon nodded. "I suppose you're right, but I still don't like it."

"I am fine with you not liking it, but you have to honor my decision and think about the people above your own moral code."

Landon removed his cell phone and nodded. "You're right," he said as he looked through the contacts list. He found Peter's name and called the number. "Do whatever you need to do. I need to go meet with Peter."

She nodded and opened the car door. "Good night, Landon." She shut it behind her and walked to Town Hall.

"This is Peter," the scientist answered.

"Peter, it's Landon. We need to talk. Where are you?"

Φ

"Kelly, you have to tell me what happened today," Troy pleaded. He had tried shrugging off earlier events, but curiosity finally overcame his desire to keep quiet.

Kelly rolled her eyes and groaned. "Nothing happened! I walked into the abandoned bar, found broken glass everywhere, and left."

"Are you lying? Did you find something else?"

She stood from the couch and walked out of the room, into the kitchen.

Troy followed her. "Tell me," he said to her.

"I think it's time you left and went home," Kelly said. "I'm done watching movies and I wish to go to bed early."

"It's eight," Troy protested.

"I'm tired. I'm asking you to leave." She opened the refrigerator and removed a gallon of milk. She untwisted the top and drank straight from the jug.

Erased

"Kelly, you've been acting strange since we left the bar. Please tell me what you found."

"If you would have come with me like I wanted you to, you would have seen that everything was how I described it. Now, if you will excuse me, please leave my house."

"You're mad that I didn't go with you. That's it, isn't it? You're upset with me because I let you go in by yourself."

"Don't make me call the cops on you," she threatened as she put the milk back into the refrigerator.

"Fine, I'll go, but know that I'm sorry I offended you," he said as his head dropped. He walked back into the living room, retrieved his backpack, and left her house. It didn't take him long to return home and he couldn't shake the feeling that something had happened to Kelly. She had seen something inside of the bar, he was sure of it. He wished he knew what it was.

Φ

Landon pulled into the Midas Tech Laboratory parking lot and switched off the engine. He opened the door and stepped out into the cool night air. He shoved the keys into his pocket before approaching the large metal door at the side of the building where Peter had instructed him to go. The door opened and the scientist waved him inside.

"Glad you could make it," Peter said.

"I have some important information for you."

"That will have to wait. We are about to start the meeting."

"Meeting?"

Peter didn't respond. He led Landon down a hall with concrete floors, to a staircase past a metal gate. They walked down the stairs until they came to an elevator that waited with open doors.

"Is this where your company runs experiments?" Landon asked.

Peter nodded. "It is." He scanned a special card with a picture of his face and entered a code into a keypad. The elevator powered up, and the doors closed before descending underground.

"So, what's this meeting about, Peter?"

"Figuring out what caused the memory loss and how it can be reversed."

When the doors opened, they stepped into an underground office. Bright lights illuminated cubicles and other enclosed rooms. Peter led Landon down a hall to a conference room and opened the door, allowing Landon to enter first.

"Gentlemen, this is Sheriff Landon."

Landon studied the three men sitting around a conference table as Peter shut the door behind them and took a seat. "Sit down, Landon."

Landon complied.

"These are the scientists who worked on the fungus with me. Elizabeth is no longer with us. The man sitting next to me is Tucker White."

Tucker raised his hand as a greeting. He wore a florescent green t-shirt and a blonde wig, considering the length of his hair had grown longer since Landon had seen him earlier that day. "Dude, I totally remember you!" Tucker said with a large smile. "You came and got the keys to my car."

"This is Albert King. He's our geneticist." Peter pointed to the man sitting next to Landon. He wore a Hawaiian t-shirt that seemed like a shirt Tucker would wear. His black hair receded from his forehead and he was a larger guy than all the others.

"And this is Zane. I'm not even going to try pronouncing his last name. He's a psychologist, psychiatrist, and a bunch of other things I don't remember." Zane looked to be in his late forties. He was tall, slender, and had brown, combed-back hair. He wore a nice dress shirt, buttoned down the middle, and a tie.

"Nice to meet you all," Landon said. "What is this meeting about again?"

"We are coming up with possible theories about what caused our memory loss," Zane answered.

"Well, I can at least tell you it wasn't an accident. That's something you need to take into consideration when figuring this out."

"That's a variable we marked down," Peter said. "How do you know for sure?"

"What I'm about to tell you must be kept strictly within this room. If word gets out, it could start a panic. Someone has trapped us inside Lion's Glade."

"What do you mean by trapped?" Tucker asked with a frown.

"Several miles outside of town, a ten-foot, electrified fence blocks any escape to the world outside our borders. The mayor and I used your car, Tucker, and spent a few hours driving the perimeter. The fence surrounds the entire town; there's no escape. I don't know when they put up the fence, but they did it for the key reason of making sure nobody unexpected shows up to tell us the truth, and nobody can leave."

The room remained silent for several minutes.

Albert spoke. "If this is a planned attack on our town, and if what Landon says is true, this changes everything."

"How so?" Tucker asked.

"Think about it. Having a ten-foot electrified fence surrounding the town several miles out, far enough so that we can't even see it from here, would cost a significant amount of money. That proves a single individual couldn't have done this. Landon said it perfectly; he used the word *they*.

We are dealing with a group of people, like a company or an organization of sorts."

Peter nodded. "That's true."

Landon gasped, then inhaled and choked on his saliva. Once he could breathe again his eyes grew wide. "The cameras!"

"Cameras?" Zane wondered.

"The town is covered in cameras. They are recording everything that's happening. We found a computer with access to these cameras in the home of your former colleague Elizabeth, but it disappeared."

"These people have cameras throughout town, and they are watching our reactions to the memory loss?" Peter wondered. "What is their experiment? To see how fast we can get our society back up and running after our brains are fried? Are they seeing if we will find a cure? What is their goal?"

Landon shrugged. "I don't even know who *they* are. That's another mystery. I thought this information needed to be shared with you."

"Could they be watching us now?" Tucker asked.

Landon shrugged again. "It's possible, but I don't know."

"Well, whoever is listening, I want you to know that you are screwed in the head," Tucker said. "We will stop you!"

"The mayor and I discussed ramming the car into the gate to try and break it, but with the way it's built, I doubt we would succeed. And we don't know what's waiting on the other side." Landon stood. "I should get going. Peter, unless there's anything else you need from me, I'll talk with you tomorrow."

"What should we do about finding the people who caused this?" Zane asked.

"Leave that to me," Landon said. "Focus on returning our memories."

Erased

Φ

It was eleven thirty and Jessica Dailey sat at her desk, holding her aching head. What was she going to do? What could she do? Whatever type of mayor she had been before losing her memories, she wasn't the same now. She didn't feel up to the job. She felt like she needed to fix everything, though at the present moment, she wasn't sure how, which seemed to create an alarm in her head, causing it to hurt. In the next thirty minutes it wouldn't matter anyway. If Landon was right, she would fall asleep and wake up at home the next morning. That was the only reason she hadn't left the office. She wished to test his theory. Reaching into her purse for ibuprofen, her hand found the CD she had removed from the car. She pulled it out and stared at the words written across the face.

"For Jessica Dailey," she read aloud. She sighed and looked at the shelf that contained a stereo system. Perhaps before the memory loss she listened to symphonies. Maybe she would dance her cares away. The thought of it brought tears to her eyes. She wasn't yet willing to admit the truth to herself, but she felt alone. She doubted she had a husband, and there was no evidence she had a boyfriend either.

Taking the CD over to the stereo, Jessica pushed the eject button to open the top. She set the CD inside and closed the lid. She pushed play to listen.

"Jessica," a voice emerged from the speakers. It sounded like Peter. "Listen carefully."

There were no other words, and after a moment, a quiet hum filled the room. Jessica fell to the floor, clutching her temples. She screamed as a heat burned through her head. After several minutes, the hum subsided and she could stand. Her mind raced at high speed and adrenalin filled her body.

"Madam Mayor, are you all right?" Officer Barns burst into the room, his gun drawn. "It sounded like someone attacked you!" He looked around the office, finding it to be empty, except for the mayor.

She laughed and a large smile filled her face. "Officer Barns, I remember!"

"Remember what?" he asked with a frown.

"My past! All of my memories are coming back! I keep feeling more and more of them surfacing!"

"What do you mean?" He asked, dumbfounded. "How?"

She walked over to the stereo and opened the top. She removed the CD and showed it to him. "Landon and I found this in the car we discovered yesterday. I do not know how it works, but I listened to it and I have all my memories back! I know who I am now! It all makes sense!"

Officer Barn's brows furrowed. "You're serious," he hissed. "I was coming to give you a report on the census, but I guess I got here just in time."

"I must tell Peter! He needs to know about this. After all, it was his voice on the CD! He was the one who made sure I would find it!" She rushed over to the phone and picked up the receiver.

"Peter, what have you done now?" Officer Barns asked as he shook his head. He raised his gun and pointed it at the mayor. "Put down the phone."

Her eyes widened as she stared at the weapon. "What are you doing?"

Barns shrugged. "This is how I make my living," he said. "Now please, set down the phone."

She did as he ordered and replaced it. "What are you going to do, kill me?" She paused for a moment as she connected dots in her mind. "I understand everything now. I am a liability."

"Yes, you are," Barns said. "However, your death isn't for me to decide." He looked at the watch on his wrist. "I only need to keep you here for fifteen minutes. None of it will matter once the day resets." He walked over to a chair and sat, keeping the gun trained on her. "Have a seat," he said, ushering Jessica to sit down in her office chair. He removed a phone from his pocket and dialed a number. "Hey, it's Barns," he said. "We have a problem."

Φ

Night had fallen, bathing Lion's Glade in darkness. Kelly looked around to make sure no prying eyes watched from afar. She ran through her front yard to the sidewalk and made her way down the street. She took a right, heading toward the center of the town, and kept jogging at a steady pace until she reached a hardware store. Troy was right when he suspected something had happened inside of the bar. The moment Kelly had passed the broken window and was inside, the phone on the counter rang. She answered it and received instructions she would be sure to follow.

Kelly walked around to the back door of the hardware store and turned the handle. She stepped inside a hallway and wandered toward the front. A small light in an office to the right caught her attention, and she peered through a crack. A man dressed in a business suit sat at the desk, watching a computer.

"Come on in, Kel Bell," the man said and turned to the door.

Kelly pushed it open and entered, surveying the area. The small office was bare except for the desk and computer. The man was tall and slender; his stunning gray eyes seemed almost hypnotizing.

"I'm glad you came," he said with a warm smile.

She gave a half smile back and continued to stare into his eyes. After a moment, she responded. "Hi, dad, it's nice to meet you."

CHAPTER TWENTY—SIX

ONE DAY BEFORE 'THE AWAKENING'

The ticking of the blue mechanical clock attached to the yellow office wall caused a sliver of annoyance to etch its way underneath Thomas Hood's skin. He felt on edge, considering the day and the events that would soon unfold. He stared at a computer monitor, reading over the document his partner Peter Benet had sent him. His eyes skimmed over the text; he couldn't believe the words. He picked up a stapler and threw it at the time-telling device. The stapler hit the center of the clock, shattering the plastic cover and knocking it off the wall to the ground.

"Well, somebody is grumpy today," a blonde-haired woman chided as she entered the room. She wore a professional business suit and a pair of oval glasses rested on her nose. She had her hair tied in a bun at the back of her head.

"Monica, it's good to see you again," Thomas said as he stood and walked over to the visitor. He held out his hand, and she shook it before taking the extra chair in front of the desk. Thomas returned to his seat.

The office was rather small, containing the desk, the two chairs, and a bunch of filing cabinets behind Monica. She spoke. "Your associates told me you have a problem that needs to be addressed."

"There is," Thomas said with a nod. He opened one of the desk drawers and removed a folder full of papers. He tossed it over to her. "Only the documents on top are relevant."

She flipped the folder open and removed a small packet before pushing the folder back to Thomas. "Jessica Dailey?"

Thomas nodded. "Yes, she is the mayor of Lion's Glade. We thought she would cooperate, but we received intelligence that suggests she's a spy."

"A spy for whom?"

Thomas shrugged. "I don't know, but we don't want to take the chance. We need her eliminated."

"Define eliminated."

"We can't let her live."

"I am a *fixer*, a problem solver, not an assassin or murderer," she said with a scowl. "I cannot believe *you* of all people would ask me to do this."

"It's not a request, it's an order," Thomas said, and a sigh followed. "The decision is far above my rank. I am only relaying this assignment from the orchestrator. I don't condone it."

"This is disgusting," she spat. "Who do you guys think you are?"

"I don't like this anymore than you do, but it must be done," Thomas said with a grimace.

"Why not kill this woman yourselves? Why hire *me* for this?"

"Because your husband is on the team and the company likes to keep you accountable."

"What if I refuse this assignment? Will you punish him?"

Thomas rested an elbow on the desk and rubbed his forehead. "Not just him. We also have your son, Monica. I can't promise his safety if you don't follow the order."

"You know that he is my stepson, right? He and I were never close. He was a brat, always expecting everyone to owe him everything, like he owned the world. Threatening me with his life is *not* a convincing argument. And do not even get me started on my husband. We have been apart for some time now. I have not talked with him in almost a year since our jobs sent us to different quadrants."

Thomas shook his head and ran a hand through his hair. "Let me put it this way, Monica. If you don't follow the assignment, not only will the lives of your estranged husband and son be in jeopardy, but the company may end your job, if not your life, altogether. Trust me when I say I don't want this to happen. I tried fighting it, but they overruled me. So please, kill Jessica, for *all* our sakes."

Monica sighed and shook her head. "What are you guys doing out here that is important enough to solicit somebody to murder for you?"

"I am surprised your husband never told you. He was the one who developed this project in the first place *before* you two separated. Perhaps you should go talk with him."

Monica stood from her seat and walked over to the door. "I guess I have no choice."

"Oh, and Monica, Jessica needs to die today. We don't care how you do it. Just make sure she's dead." Monica left the room without a response and Thomas lifted the phone from its cradle, dialing another extension. The phone rang for a few seconds before somebody responded. "Hey, it's Thomas. Have you edited that photo yet?" he didn't have to wait long for the answer. "Good," he said with a smile. "They will never remember she was part of their family."

Φ

Monica grunted as she approached the blue, one-story house in which her husband and stepson lived. She had received the directions from Thomas' secretary and found her way. She didn't bother to knock as she grabbed the handle and pushed the door open. Monica set the suitcase by the front door and slammed it behind her.

"Back already?" she heard a man call out from the kitchen.

Erased

"Trust me, I would have rather stayed away," she snapped as she walked down the hall and through the arch.

Peter Benet froze for several moments as he stared at his wife.

"Look, I know I am attractive, but keep your eyes to yourself," she said as she walked in further and made a turn toward the refrigerator. She pulled it open. "I am hungry. Do you have anything to eat?"

"Monica, what are you doing here?" Peter asked with slight hesitation in his voice.

She shut the door and turned to him. "Who cares why *I* am here. What are *you* doing here? What messed up situation have you gotten yourself into, Peter?"

"Messed up situation? Everything is fine," he replied.

"Oh?" she snapped again. "So the company sent me here to assassinate the mayor for no reason? Do you realize that they are using you and Troy as leverage to get me to commit murder?"

Peter's mouth opened as if he would say something, and then it closed.

"Oh, so you have nothing to say to that?" she rolled her eyes. "What *is* this *project*?"

"It has to do with memory loss," he mumbled.

"I would give anything to forget about *you* right now." She turned back toward the refrigerator and opened it up again. She removed a turkey sandwich sealed in a Ziploc bag.

"So they want you to kill the mayor?" he asked as he watched her eat the sandwich. "I thought she might be a spy, but I didn't know they wanted to kill her."

"And like I said, they are forcing *me* to do it. They say it has to be done today before your experiment begins."

Peter nodded. "So will you kill her?"

"What other options do I have?" she asked in-between bites. "Where is Troy?"

"He's hanging out with Kelly, Thomas' daughter. They seem to like each other."

"At one point so did we," she said after swallowing the remaining piece of the sandwich. "*Now* I think I was just a rebound after your first wife died."

"How could you say that?" Peter asked as he approached her.

"Come on, Peter. Tell me the truth. Do you even love me anymore? *Did* you ever love me? You have not contacted me in almost a year."

"I've been busy," Peter said.

"You have been too busy to call your wife?" she asked. "You are pathetic. Answer my question. Do you love me?"

Peter paused and stared at the empty Ziploc bag.

"Answer the question!"

"No," Peter said. "I don't love you. You may be right. I used you as a rebound after Karen's death."

"See? Was the truth so hard?" she turned away from him and proceeded through the second arch into the living room.

"So you're staying here?" Peter asked as he followed her.

She threw herself onto the couch and yawned. "Until later this evening. If I kill the mayor, I should do it at night when there are no witnesses," she said with a smirk.

"You say that so coldly," he said with concern.

Erased

"Of course I do. When you left, I taught myself never to rely on my emotions. Emotions are for the weak. I focus on what needs to be done, and I do it. This will be another one of those times. Now, please leave me be; I need a nap."

Φ

It was after ten by the time Monica woke from her slumber. She yawned as she sat up from the couch. The room was dark, and she stumbled around until she found a lamp and bathed the room in light. She made her way into the kitchen and flipped the light switch.

"Good, you're up," Peter said as he entered through the opposite arch that led to the hall.

"I will leave in a moment and you will never have to see me again."

Peter walked over to her and embraced her in a hug. "I want you to know that I am sorry, and I want to make it up to you."

"It is a little too late for that," she breathed as she pulled herself away.

Peter shook his head. "No, it's not. Give me your arm."

"My arm? Why?" she asked as she made sure her hair was still in place.

"Please, Monica. Trust me."

She held out her arm with reluctance.

Peter pushed up her sleeve and took a marker from his pocket. She tried to jerk her arm away, but Peter held fast. "Monica, *trust* me!" he yelled. She watched him remove the cap and place the felt tip to her skin.

"What is that?" she asked as she read what he wrote.

"This is me making it up to you," he said with a sad smile. "We are safe guarding something. I know you will figure it out at a later time. You're incredibly smart."

She pulled her sleeve back down to cover the ink. "Whatever you say, Peter," she said as she walked through the arch and picked up the suitcase. "I will do my job and never bother you again." She opened the door and left the house.

Peter sighed and turned toward the dark hallway. "Did you get the CD into the car in time?"

Tucker White smiled as he emerged from the shadows. "You know me; stealthy and awesome."

"Good," Peter said with a nod. "Then I guess I've done everything I can do. Now I have to let God take care of the rest."

Φ

Jessica Dailey sat on the plush green sofa in her living room, holding a glass of wine in one hand and a novel in the other. The lamp behind her gave enough light to see, so she had turned off all the others. A knock on the door pulled her from the captivating world on paper and she looked at the clock. It was almost midnight. She stood and approached the front door, turning on the hall light so she could see.

Monica stood on the porch, a gun in hand. The streetlights hadn't turned on, giving her a cover of darkness. When the door opened she pushed her way inside and pointed the weapon at Jessica.

"What is the meaning of this?" Jessica demanded to know as her instincts screamed for her to run.

"Shut up," Monica snapped. "Listen. There are people here that want you dead. I do not know who you are, or who you work for, but I am *not* in the business of killing anyone. So I would recommend that you run. Run away and hide. Never come back." She kept the gun trained on the other woman. "I could kill you right now if I wanted, but that goes against everything I am as a person. I fix problems, *not* murder people."

Erased

"I don't understand," Jessica stammered as she tugged at her long, black hair. She seemed almost too skinny to be alive.

"Do you *have* to understand? I will give you five minutes to pack a bag and get out of here!"

"But they paid me to be here. I signed a contract and everything!"

"Do you care more about money or your life?" Monica snapped. "Stop being a fool, pack a bag, and leave. Don't even think about going to the police either, for I can guarantee they won't be able to protect you from those who want you dead."

Jessica seemed to realize the reality of the situation and disappeared for a short time into another room. She returned with a large suitcase. "What about the rest of my stuff?"

Monica rolled her eyes. "Forget about it. Just run like your life depends on it, because it does." She watched as Jessica lifted the suitcase off the ground and left the house, vanishing into the darkness. Monica shut the front door and wandered into the living room, collapsing onto the couch. She set the gun down and rubbed her eyes.

All she needed to do was convince Thomas that Jessica had already run away by the time she had arrived. She slid up her sleeve and looked at the letters and numbers on her wrist. SG-H30, what could that mean, and why did Peter write it on her skin?

The sound of the front door opening caught her attention. She grabbed the gun, stood, and spun around in time to take a projectile to the chest. Her weapon fell to the floor and the world faded to black.

"You were right, Peter. Monica would not kill Jessica," Thomas said as he entered the room with Peter.

"What can I say," Peter said with a chuckle. "I know my wife."

Thomas walked over to the limp body and nudged it with his foot. "The tranquilizer worked quicker than expected."

"So, what are you going to do with Jessica?"

"I will have Simon Orson take care of her. We won't be seeing her again."

"Did Monica pass the test? Will she be okay?"

Thomas nodded. "Yes, Peter. She passed with flying colors. When our experiment begins tomorrow, she will be the new Jessica Dailey."

DAY SEVEN: CHAPTER TWENTY—SEVEN

"Has Landon arrived yet?" Deputy Barns asked as he approached a group of officers standing in sunrays escaping through the clouds.

"Not yet," a female officer replied with an amused laugh. "If he had, we wouldn't be standing outside waiting for him to unlock the station."

"Fair enough," Barns muttered. He looked at his watch. It was seven thirty in the morning. Landon should have arrived by now with the key.

"Sorry I'm late!" Landon yelled as his shoes clapped against the pavement. "My bike disappeared." He made it to the front door and grabbed for the keys at his side. He unlocked the door, allowing everyone to enter.

"I take it we are still working on the census today. Is that correct?" Barns asked.

Landon inhaled to catch his breath and then exhaled. "Yes," he said with a quick nod. "If you could prepare the information you have for the mayor, I'll take it to her."

"The mayor?" Barns asked as his eyebrows furrowed. "Who's that?"

"Funny, Barns," Landon said with a roll of his eyes. "I'm talking about Jessica Dailey; she's the mayor of Lion's Glade."

"Landon, are you all right?" Barns asked. "Lion's Glade doesn't have a mayor."

"What are you talking about," Landon asked. "She's the one who has been giving us our tasks and assignments."

"Are you saying that nothing you've had us do has been your own idea?"

Lucas Heath

Landon shook his head. "Not at all. She works out of Town Hall. Do you honestly not remember her, or are you messing with me?" He turned to a passing officer. "Mike, you remember Mayor Jessica Dailey, don't you?"

Mike shook his head. "The name doesn't ring any bells."

"Stop the joke!" Landon yelled. "She has been the mayor of Lion's Glade since before we lost our memories." He pushed his way past Barns, into the main office space where most of the officers were talking with one another. "Excuse me," he said as he raised his voice. "Does anybody here remember the mayor of Lion's Glade? She always recorded the morning announcements for everybody."

Every head shook with the word no being murmured throughout the room.

"Landon," Barns said as he walked over to him. "*You* have been the one recording the announcements since the late Sheriff Orson died. We haven't *had* a mayor. *You* have been the one keeping us going." He placed his hand on Landon's shoulder. "Perhaps some of your memories are returning and mixing with your current reality. You should take a break today and let us handle everything. We are continuing the census. You don't need to help. However, you should go record the morning announcements and inform people of our plans."

Landon nodded as he took a seat on a roller chair. He removed the small pack from his back and set it next to him. His eyes lit up as a thought entered his head and he grabbed the bag, opened it up, and pulled out the two journals he had been writing in for the past six days. He flipped them open and began speed-reading through them. His heart sank when he couldn't find her name. He tossed the journals to the desk and looked toward the door that led to the jail cells.

Yesterday was a blur though he remembered the man named Kyle Anderaos. He claimed that everyone had forgotten him. Was it possible somehow he was telling the truth? Was the mayor erased from everybody's memories, or did she ever exist at all?

Erased

"Sir," Barns said, snapping Landon back to reality. "Are you okay? Can I get you water or coffee?"

Landon shook his head. "No," he mumbled and stood. "I'll be fine. I need to clear my head. A walk to the television station should help with that." He paused and turned back toward the door that led to the cells. "Kyle Anderaos isn't still in his cell, is he?"

"Who?" Barns asked with an expression of puzzlement on his face.

"I thought not," Landon said as he grabbed his journals and shoved them back into the bag. "I'll take a radio and let you know when the announcements are recorded. Then I'll join up with the deputies and help."

Barns nodded and a large smile spread across his face. "Sounds good, sir!"

Landon retrieved a radio and left the station, stepping out into the warming sunlight where all doubt faded away. The mayor must have existed. What they had found the night before was a huge revelation. Someone had fenced in the entire town and used the citizens for an experiment of sorts, which was why the mayor had vanished; he was sure of it. Whoever took her had erased her from everyone's memories and any trace of her. Why did *he* remember her though? Why wasn't his memory erased? How they'd even edited his journal was beyond his understanding, but it happened.

There was no use trying to find her. There was more happening than most could understand. The scientists understood though, which was why he had told them the truth. Now he needed to stay quiet and avoid attracting unwanted attention that could cause them to erase him next. He would step into Jessica's role and solve the mystery. Though first, he would begin with the morning announcements.

Φ

"Come on, dad. Pick up the phone," Troy screamed into the receiver. He paced around Kelly's living room with tears dripping down his cheeks.

"This is Peter Benet. I'm not available to answer your call. Please leave..."

Troy slammed the phone down and picked it up again. He dialed the number.

"This is Peter," Troy heard a live voice speak.

"Dad, Kelly is gone!" Troy yelled and held in a sob. "I got to her house this morning, and she is nowhere to be found. Her journal and cell phone are missing!"

"Okay, Troy, calm down," his dad whispered. "Inhale deeply and exhale slowly a few times."

Troy obeyed.

"I want to help you," Peter said. "But first, you have to tell me. Who is Kelly?"

Troy had no idea what it felt like to have his heart stop, but he was sure his had ceased to work in that moment. "Dad, this isn't a time for sick jokes!" he bellowed. "You know who Kelly is. She's my girlfriend!"

"Oh," Peter said. "Well, you haven't told me about her, how was I supposed to know?"

"You wrote about her in your journal," Troy said. "You should know about her."

Peter grunted and a long silence passed as he flipped through pages of his notebook. "I'm sorry, son, but I haven't written about her from what I can see. I can tell she's important to you. What would you like me to do? Once I get the other scientists started on our work, I can come help you search for her."

Troy shook his head, hoping it would shake all the fear and confusion free from his mind. "No," he said. "Keep working on getting our memories back. I'll look for her." He hung up the phone and sobbed.

Erased

He fell to the floor and curled into a ball. What in the world was wrong with him? What was with the tears? Kelly was just some girl, a friend. No, she was more than a friend and Troy knew that. Even with all the arguments and annoyances, there was no doubt in his mind that Kelly was the girl he loved.

He wasn't sure how long he cried though it felt like an eternity. What was worse, he imagined Kelly getting home and walking in to find him crying. Oh boy, how she would tease him for that. Where would she have gone? Why did she leave? She had been acting different since they returned from that bar. He pulled himself together and wiped his face clear of tears. The Anchor bar would be the first place he would search.

Φ

"Wake up, honey," a strong male voice seemed to reach in and pull Kelly out of her slumber. Her eyes opened, and she yawned. "What's going on?" she asked as she sat up and rubbed her eyes with her palms. "Where am I?"

Thomas sat on the edge of her bed with a grin on his face.

"Dad, oh my gosh!" Kelly bolted toward her father and tackled him into a hug. "I've missed you so much. What's going on in Lion's Glade? Why did everybody lose their memories? Why can I remember everything now?"

"I can't answer your questions yet."

Kelly pulled back from the hug and stared at her father's unique gray eyes. "Where have you been? Why didn't you come back for me sooner?"

"I wanted to, but they wouldn't allow me to get you. I can't talk about this right now. I brought you here for your help."

"My help?" she asked as her mouth fell open for a moment. "I don't think you've ever asked me for my help, except for chores."

Thomas chuckled and stood.

Kelly looked around the almost blinding-white room. The bed frame was a dull gray, though the rest of the sheets were solid white like the walls, ceiling, and floor. There were no windows or any other furniture. Kelly's pink sweater and blue jeans stood out in the sheer whiteness. "Are we in a hospital?" she wondered aloud.

Thomas nodded. "Yes." He held out his hand. "Come with me."

Φ

Peter sat at the conference table, looking through a bunch of documents. He passed them around to the three other scientists: Tucker, Zane, and Albert. "So, this is what we know," he began. "Our town is surrounded by an electrified fence that keeps us separated from the rest of the world. We can assume the fence is there to prevent us from escaping this..." he paused and thought for a moment "... whatever *this* is. If it's an experiment, it's a twisted one."

"I second that," Zane agreed.

"Our fifth member, Elizabeth, killed herself around the time we all lost our memories," Peter continued.

"Are we sure she killed herself?" Zane asked. "I can't deny that it would be the most logical assumption she took her own life. It's conceivable that someone would commit suicide because they don't want to live without their memories, but is that the truth?"

"I don't think we will ever know for certain," Tucker said with a frown.

"Maybe not," Zane said with a nod. "However, what if we assumed someone murdered her?"

"What's the point of making assumptions?" Albert asked. "She's dead and won't be joining us in figuring out this mystery, so why dwell on what happened?"

"Because I don't want to end up like her," Zane stated. "You're right when you say we can't make assumptions based on information we do not have, but I want to know that I'll be safe pursuing this mystery, and that someone won't kill me for sticking my nose where it doesn't belong."

Peter frowned. "I've been trying to solve this problem since the beginning, and I haven't died yet."

"For all I know, you're the mastermind behind this whole thing," Zane snapped.

Tucker sighed. "He was the one who called us all together. Don't make him the enemy. We all want our memories back, just as much as you do. In order for that to happen, we need to work together."

"You're right," Zane said as he lowered his head. "I'm sorry. This whole thing puts me on edge. Where do we even begin to figure this out?"

Peter motioned to the whiteboard. "Let's come up with theories, no matter how outlandish they may seem."

"Space aliens," Tucker said. "They wanted to experiment on us. How else could a fence be built miles around town with none of us knowing beforehand?"

Peter paused. "You may be on to something," he said as he looked at the board. He stood and grabbed a dry erase marker, uncapped it, and wrote.

"You *can't* consider that," Albert argued.

"Not the alien theory, no, but Tucker brings up a valid point," Peter said as he wrote the words *electric fence* on the board. "How could those conducting this experiment have built a fence around the whole town with no one questioning it? It would have taken quite a while to set something like that up, right?"

"You would think that anyone traveling into or out of town would ask about it. Did we know about the fence before we lost our memories, and if we did, why didn't we stop it?"

"That's *another* mystery," Tucker said with a sigh.

Peter nodded. "Yeah, it's just another mystery."

Φ

"Where are we going?" Kelly asked as she followed her father down a pure-white hall. They passed several women dressed it light-blue pajamas, holding clipboards. "Why is everything so white?"

Thomas grinned and continued walking.

"Where are we in town?" Kelly asked. "Are we even in Lion's Glade?"

"Kelly, you need to stop asking so many questions," he replied, his smile being replaced with a frown.

"How can I *not* ask questions? For the past week, every time I went to bed at night, I lost my memory. I would forget about Troy and you, and Mom, and everything else!"

"I'm glad your mom hacked into the system and sent you those clues," he whispered.

"Where *is* Mom?"

"How's it going between you and Troy?" he asked.

"It's great," she said with a smile. "He's adorable most of the time. He often says things that annoy me, but I get over them. He's worth it."

"That's good," Thomas responded. "We are here."

Thomas stopped at a door and opened it, allowing Kelly to walk in first.

"Uncle Mark!" she squeaked when she saw him lying in the hospital bed. A bandage wrapped around the top of his head.

Erased

"Hey kiddo," he responded with a tired smile. "How's it going?"

DAY SEVEN: CHAPTER TWENTY—EIGHT

Kelly ran to Mark and embraced him in a careful hug. "What happened to you?" She asked, noticing his head.

"Kel, I need to get back to work. Please look after Mark while I'm gone. I'll be back this evening."

Kelly nodded and watched her father leave, and as the door shut behind him, she turned back to her uncle. "Uncle Mark, what's going on?" she asked.

He shook his head and winced. "I don't know," he said. "I don't remember much; only that I had a brain tumor removed a short time ago. I don't know how I got here from home. Where *are* we?"

"Kansas," Kelly said. "At least I believe we're in Kansas. That's what dad told me when we moved here."

Mark nodded. "That sounds about right," he said. "The doctors say I'm lucky to be alive. It amazes everyone I'm awake and can talk. However, right now I can't move my legs."

"You're paralyzed?" Kelly gasped.

Mark shrugged. "I've been out of surgery for about a day and a half. It's probable that my legs will work again. I didn't break my neck and there was no damage to my spine. My brain is having a problem telling my legs what to do. I don't know the science behind it."

"Who performed the surgery?" she wondered as she sat on the chair by his bed. Mark's room appeared almost whiter than the room in which she awoke.

"Peter did," Mark said with a smile. "I can't even tell you how many times that guy has saved my life." He laughed. "When we were kids, he saved me from a starving wolf, using a slinky."

Erased

"I don't know how that's possible, but I love that man more than I did," she said with a giggle.

"I heard he may be your father-in-law someday."

Kelly sighed. "Has my dad been blabbing away again?" she muttered. "It's possible, but who knows? I still don't know what's going on in town. I wish my dad would tell me why people lost their memories."

Mark sighed. "Don't worry about that for now," he said. "Tell me about your life the past couple of years. Tell me about Troy."

Φ

Though Landon recorded the morning announcements, he felt defeated as he left the news station. The mayor's disappearance after what they discovered the day before seemed to weave a thread of fear around his throat. He struggled to swallow, his palms were sweaty, and beads of sweat formed at his brow – although the air felt cold. Was he supposed to pretend as if she never existed? If he pursued any more investigations, would he end up meeting with the same fate?

Landon sighed and looked toward the storage units they had saved from a fire two days ago. The Dodge Magnum had disappeared from the side of the road by the time Landon had woken up that morning. It probably reset like people did at midnight, which would mean it was back in the storage unit several blocks away.

The car keys remained attached to his group of home and police keys. How did the whole reset thing work? Did bigger objects reset and smaller objects didn't? What was the reason, if there was one?

"Command control to squad leaders," the dispatcher Bobby called over the radio. "We have received a report of a young man breaking into an abandoned pub on Maplewood and Grover Avenue."

Landon pulled out a map to study. He grabbed the radio and pushed down the button to reply. "This is Sheriff Landon. I'm right by the location; I will check it out."

"Copy that," Bobby said, and the radio went silent.

He grunted and looked down the road toward the storage units again. He didn't need a car at the moment and he preferred to walk. Taking a left, he walked down the road toward Maplewood and Grover.

Φ

Troy pushed his way through the broken window into the dim room. The only light came from the sun through a skylight. None of the light switches worked. He wandered down the ancient-looking, wooden hallway and entered a larger room. He could have sworn it still smelled like cigarettes, as if someone had been smoking there recently.

The room was as Kelly had described it: turned over rotten tables, broken glass from smashed bottles, yet nothing stood out that would explain why Kelly changed. He walked around the room, making sure not to miss anything.

After a short while, he admitted defeat, picked up an unbroken bottle and screamed in frustration as he threw it at the wall. It shattered and pieces flew in all directions.

"Put your hands where I can see them," a voice thundered.

Troy spun around and raised his hands. "Oh, it's you, Sheriff," Troy said with a sigh of relief. He let his arms fall to his sides.

"I didn't tell you to put your hands down," Landon said, still aiming the gun at Troy.

Troy raised them again.

Erased

"Trespassing and vandalism," Landon said as he removed his handcuffs. "If we want to get our town back to normal, we need to make sure the law is enforced."

"I was here looking for clues to why my girlfriend disappeared!" Troy defended.

Landon's muscles tensed. "Who's your girlfriend? I thought you were the only teenager in town. You're Peter's son, right?"

Troy nodded and then shook his head. "I *am* Peter's son, but I wasn't the only teen in town. Kelly and I are best friends. We've supported each other since this all started. We came here yesterday because of a clue on her arm. I stayed outside while she came in here. She seemed weird when she came back to me, and today she vanished. You saw me with her a couple days ago!"

"I did?" Landon asked. "When?"

"She and I went to give Mayor Dailey information we found about the school."

Landon lowered the gun. "You remember the mayor?"

Troy lowered his arms down to his sides. "Why wouldn't I?"

Landon replaced the gun into the holster and rubbed his forehead. "You're the only one I've found who remembers her," he said. "I don't remember your friend, but if she also disappeared, it's likely you would be the only person to remember."

"My dad didn't remember her."

Landon nodded. "I still have to arrest you," he said.

The strength in Troy's legs weakened. "For what? I came here looking for Kelly! She needs me!"

Landon nodded. "I know. I'm not charging you with trespassing or breaking and entering, but I still need to charge you for vandalism."

Lucas Heath

"What did I vandalize?" Troy snapped.

"You threw a bottle against the wall, getting glass everywhere."

"In a condemned building! There's already glass everywhere!" Troy countered.

"Doesn't matter. You will be safer in police custody." He walked over to Troy and pulled his arms behind his back. He cuffed them and led Troy to the front door, which opened after a kick to the center.

"I need to find Kelly, why are you doing this?" Troy asked. "Please, let me go find her!"

"I can't," Landon said with a sigh. "She's gone for a reason. Maybe she saw something she shouldn't have, like the mayor did. Maybe that's why they took her."

"Who are *they*?" Troy asked as Landon led him out into the rays of sunlight. The clouds moved toward the east and no longer posed a threat of raining on Lion's Glade again.

"I know you won't understand it, but the safest place for you to be is in one of our cells. Your father is trying to figure out what caused our memory loss. I can't have something happen to you that would delay him."

"What about Kelly?" Troy asked as tears sprang to his eyes. "I need to find her," he repeated.

"You're better off *not* looking for her," Landon said as he walked next to Troy. "God only knows where that would lead."

A tear dripped off Troy's cheek, hitting the pavement. "I only hope God *protects* her."

Φ

After a while, the police station came into view and Landon sighed with relief. There were several times he expected Troy to make a run for it, and Troy's willingness to follow his orders impressed him. He led the young man into a cell and removed the handcuffs.

"You will be safe here," Landon said with a smile as he left the cell and shut the door. "I'm doing this to protect you. The more you look into her disappearance, the more likely it is they will take you next."

Troy didn't reply. He sat on the cot and cried again. Landon left the room and walked out into the main office of the station.

"Officer Alison to Sheriff Landon," a woman's voice cracked over the radio.

"This is Sheriff Landon, go ahead," he answered.

"We are at 1452 Penn Avenue. Sir, you need to see this."

Φ

Almost an hour later, Landon arrived at the home across town. Officer Alison was waiting for him as he approached.

"Sir, glad you could make it."

"Sorry it took so long," he said as he tried to catch his breath. "I somehow became mixed up on street names and got lost."

She motioned him to enter. "A published author named Griffin Powell owned this house." She walked from the main hall into the living room. There were framed family photos on the cream-colored walls, but other than that, the hall was empty – no entry table, no carpet, just a wooden floor.

The living room was more vibrant in color. Though the walls were bare, they had an emerald green color that clashed with the violet carpet. Near one wall, a small tube television rested on a black wooden stand. A leather sofa positioned in the room's center had a brown coffee table in front it of it, and on that coffee table was a book. Landon leaned down to take a look.

Lucas Heath

"The history of Lion's Glade," he read aloud. "Griffin Powell wrote this book."

"Come with me, but plug your nose," she said, heading through another door into the kitchen.

Landon understood why she suggested plugging his nose. The place smelled like something, or someone, had died. The smell grew stronger as they entered the kitchen and he saw the body a moment later. "That's him?" he asked, trying hard to breathe through his mouth.

Another deputy named Myles stood by the body, taking notes on a small pad of paper. "We found him like this when we didn't get a response from knocking," he said.

The deceased in question had a head full of white hair and looked to be in his late seventies. Judging by the decay, it appeared he had been dead for several days. The old man was face down on the table holding an open marker in his right hand and his left arm dangled at his side; a wooden cane lay on the floor several feet away.

"I have nurses coming for the body," Alison said as she noticed Landon staring at the sight before him.

Landon nodded and walked over to the corpse. He reached out and lifted the left arm. "Twelve, twenty-one, fifty-four," he read aloud from the numbers written in black ink.

Officer Myles wrote down the numbers on his pad of paper.

"What do you think it means?" Alison asked.

Landon pressed his lips together in thought before responding. "He wrote this right before he died, which means it was important to him. The question is why." He paused and sighed. "It looks like we have yet *another* mystery on our hands."

DAY SEVEN: CHAPTER TWENTY—NINE

The day passed rather fast for the citizens of Lion's Glade. The police continued their census and recorded the data they discovered.

"We only need another couple of hours and we should be finished," Officer Barns informed Landon over the radio.

"Sounds good," Landon replied as he sat on the leather couch in Griffin Powell's living room. The nurses had taken the body away hours ago, but he had stuck around, hoping he would somehow find clues to their predicament.

"Why do you expect answers to be in Griffin Powell's house?" Landon asked himself as he closed his eyes. "He wrote about the town, but that doesn't mean he had any more information than you do."

"True, but those numbers must have been important to him if writing them on his arm was the last thing he did," Landon heard his own voice reply. Was he talking to himself? "They are simple numbers though," he said with a groan. "It looks more like a date than a code. Besides, I didn't find a safe anywhere in the house."

He opened his eyes and yawned. It was still early evening, and he felt exhausted. Without the mayor, he was in charge of everything now. He didn't like that; it added pressure he didn't need. He stood and brushed off his uniform. Perhaps he should follow Barn's earlier suggestion and take the rest of the day to relax.

Landon left the house, shutting the door behind him. He would head back to the police station and write everything that had happened in the past couple of days. He neglected to do that, taking his memory for granted. However, anything was possible. Anything could happen, and he wanted to make sure he had a record of *everything*.

Φ

Lucas Heath

Kelly spent the whole day with her uncle, catching him up on her life before and after the memory loss. He listened to every word and detail, throwing in his own ideas and thoughts to what was happening, but none of them seemed to connect or make sense.

At one point, Kelly tried leaving the room to find a bathroom, but found the door locked. She had to wait for a nurse to escort her.

"This place gives me the creeps," Kelly told her uncle with a sigh.

"You won't be here much longer," Mark replied. "Me on the other hand..." He looked down at his legs.

There was a knock on the door and Thomas entered. "Ah, Kelly, you're still here. Good."

"As if I could have gone anywhere else," Kelly mumbled.

"I didn't want you to wander around and get in people's way," Thomas said with a smile as he wrapped an arm around her shoulders. "We need to get you back soon."

"Back?" Kelly replied. "Back where?"

"I'll return later, Mark."

"Bye, Uncle Mark. I hope I can see you again soon!"

Thomas and Kelly left the room and the door shut behind them.

"Saying you need to get me *back* implies we *aren't* at Lion's Glade."

Thomas shrugged. "If that's how you want to interpret my words, go ahead. I need to get you home though."

"At least I get to see Troy. That will be awesome!" she said with an excited squeal. "I'll be able to tell him about all the things I remember about our relationship!"

Thomas nodded. "Perhaps."

Erased

She turned to him. "If I remember everything, does that mean you have the cure to the memory-loss problem?"

He continued walking, unfazed by the question.

She paused and pulled on Thomas' arm to get him to stop. "Dad, answer me."

Thomas shrugged. "You could say that."

"Then why haven't you used it yet?"

"It's not the right time," he answered, choosing his words with care.

"What do you mean? People are in trouble out there!" the pitch of her voice rose.

Thomas reached for something in his back pocket and walked up to Kelly, embracing her in a hug. "I'm sorry, but I can't tell you everything right now." He removed the cap from the needle with his thumb and pushed on the syringe, squirting the liquid out to remove any air bubbles. He pulled away, and with a quick gesture, pushed the needle into her neck, injecting the formula. "I'm sorry, Kel Bell."

Her world faded to black as two female nurses ran over to help Thomas carry her.

"Do you think she will remember that?" a nurse asked.

Thomas sighed. "I hope not, or she may never forgive me."

Φ

"You will not get away with this, you creeps!" Monica yelled from a small padded room. The chamber was snow white and almost blinding. The only thing missing was a straightjacket. A door made of thick, heavy metal prevented her from leaving.

"Mayor, is that you?" a voice entered the room.

Monica looked around and, for the first time noticed a small vent near the ceiling.

How should she respond? The voice did not sound familiar, but if the people she worked for knew who she was, why would they call her mayor? Could this be a trap? They had put her in this experiment, albeit without her permission or her knowledge, to play the role of Jessica Dailey. Was that their plan when they ordered her to kill Jessica? Well, that's who she had thought she was for the past week; she might as well keep playing the role.

"Yes, it is me," she blurted.

"Oh, thank goodness. It's me, Kyle Anderaos."

The name sounded familiar. He was a police officer serving under Landon.

"Yes, I remember you," she said.

"Where *are* we?" he asked. "Yesterday, people didn't remember I existed, and today I woke up *here*."

"You do *not* want to know."

"I'm scared," he said. "I don't understand what's happening."

"That makes two of us," she answered. Monica sat and fell backward, her back and head resting on the plush material. She didn't know what to say next or even if she should say anything at all. She closed her eyes and let sleep overtake her.

Φ

"Those are a lot of good theories," Peter said as he finished writing them all in his notebook. "Today has been productive which is a nice surprise." He looked at the whiteboard of data.

Erased

"So how are we going to test these theories and solve our problem?" the psychologist, Zane, asked. He turned to the others. "I mean, trying to figure out what's causing this is great, but how do we even test our theories?"

"Very carefully, away from prying eyes and cameras," Tucker White answered. "It's already late. Let's focus on that tomorrow. I want to go home and eat. That tuna wrap for lunch wasn't enough to fill my stomach."

The others nodded and placed the daily notes into their briefcases.

"Tomorrow then," Peter said with a grin. "I think soon enough we will have our answers."

Tucker nodded. "I don't doubt it. Good night, brochachos!" he hurried from the room.

"Brochachos?" Zane asked as he stared at the door. "He acts like a teenager. Sometimes I wonder if he's sane."

"You need a bit of insanity in you to be a scientist, right?" Peter asked with a short laugh.

The others dismissed the question.

Peter finished packing his folders and left the meeting room. He walked to his office and removed the blue tie from around his neck. He hated his suit. Every time he woke up, he was wearing it. "Maybe if I tried burning it," he mumbled, and then realized that if he did that, he may wake up naked next time.

He looked at the clock. It was after eleven. The flash of light would soon cover the town and everything would be reset. At least, that's what *could* happen. By now, Peter had decided he would never try to expect something specific to occur at any point in time, at least until the crisis was over and they got their memories back.

Troy came to his mind, and he thought about how his son was panicking over a girl Peter didn't even know existed. He sat at his desk, picked up the phone and dialed home, but didn't get an answer. He hoped Troy was safe although something told him his son often took care of himself.

Peter yawned and rested his head on his arms. Thinking of the many theories hurt his brain and wore him out. If this was the life of a scientist, he wanted no part of it.

Φ

"Monica, get up," a deep voice ordered. A man she didn't recognize stood over her. He reached down and grabbed her arm, lifting her to her feet.

"Let go of me, you brute!" she ordered, though her words had about as much effect as telling Troy to mow the lawn or unload the dishwasher.

Entering a whitewashed hall, she could see another man holding Kyle Anderaos by the neck, leading him in the same direction.

"It's time for you to go back in," Thomas Hood said with a smile as they passed him.

"You are despicable," she spat at him.

Thomas sighed. "You don't understand, but that's fine. I hope you enjoy your stay in Lion's Glade. I would tell you to say hello to Peter for me, but you won't remember tomorrow morning." He watched as the two men led Monica and Kyle away, and then proceeded down the hall. His cell phone buzzed and he answered.

"This is Thomas." He paused and listened to the person on the other end. "Yes, sir, we are right on schedule. We had a couple hiccups, but we are back on track."

"What kind of hiccups?" the voice screamed at him.

"Somehow, somebody got a car within the Lion's Glade boundaries without us knowing. We had to detain the mayor for a day, but she's going back in as I speak." He listened to the voice on the other end for a moment longer. "Thank you, sir. I'll contact you when I can. Goodbye."

Φ

Landon had finished writing all the happenings of the past two days and went to check on Troy, who was asleep on the small bed in the cell. He walked back to his office and looked at the clock. There were two officers still unaccounted for, the two he had met up with earlier in the day, Myles and Alison. The rest had dropped off their information on the census. Alison and Myles had ten minutes left to return before the strange light filled the sky and reset the town. Landon *assumed* that's what would happen anyway.

He tried calling and radioing the deputies, but to no avail. The rest of his officers had already gone home for the night at the command of their sheriff.

The front door to the station opened, and a commotion reached his ears.

"Stop fighting me," Landon heard a woman yell. It sounded like Officer Alison. He left his office in time to see her and Myles round the corner, holding a flailing middle-aged man.

"Sheriff, help us here! Get him into a cell."

Landon ran over and did as requested. In no time at all, the man, still handcuffed, paced around the cell furthest from Troy.

Troy had woken up and glared at the others in the room.

"Why did we put him in there?" Landon whispered to Alison. "Everything will reset in just a few moments."

"I'm not too sure about *everything*," she said. "You'll want to hear what he has to say."

"I'm trapped, trapped," the man muttered. It looked as though he hadn't changed his clothing or showered for at least a week. His noticeable greasy hair matched the color of his unkempt black beard. "Must get out, must, have to, escape," he said. His eyes darted back and forth. "Please, they can't find me. I must hide." He tried sliding underneath the cot, but without luck.

"He's crazy," Landon observed.

"You will be safe here. *They* won't find you. Tell the sheriff what you told us," Myles told the man.

The man spun to look at him and then turned to Landon. He tapped his fingers on his forehead and muttered incoherent words under his breath. "Light, the light," he spoke. "The light will fill the sky in minutes!" he paced around the cell once more. "You all sleep, when the light hits, you sleep. But then you don't!"

Landon's right eyebrow rose, and he looked at the others. He turned back to the man. "Well we wake up after sleeping."

"Not waking up," the man said and turned to look at his shoes. He leaned down and rubbed one of them as if he was expecting a magic genie to appear. "Zombies," the man said. "Awake, but not awake. Alive, yet not, simultaneously. I've seen this. The light makes you do it!"

"What is he talking about?" Landon asked as he turned to the others.

"So, you are awake past midnight?" Myles asked the man.

The man nodded his head. "Of course! I never sleep! Not at night. Only day. I see everything! I see where the light comes from!"

Myles handed Landon his notepad. "I already wrote this in my notes."

Landon read the information. "A tower?" he asked as he looked at the strange man.

Erased

"The tower..." the man said and laughed, "... the light comes from the tower!"

As if the man spoke a prophetic word, the light filled the sky, covering Lion's Glade, rendering the town unconscious; except for one.

"Good night, good night," the strange man said and laughed again as he curled into the fetal position in the corner of the cell.

Day seven had ended.

CHAPTER THIRTY

TWO DAYS BEFORE 'THE AWAKENING'

"Hey, dad, do you know where mom is?" Kelly asked as she stepped into the pristine kitchen. The smell of lemon soap filled the air as Thomas hand-washed the dishes.

He nodded. "I thought she told you. The company sent her over to the west coast for some special assignment. It's just you and I for the next while, kiddo."

Kelly groaned. "Why does she always do this? She knows I have a date with Troy coming up and I need her help to look beautiful!"

"Come on, honey. Can't you rely on your old man to help with that?" he asked with a wink.

"Not unless you were a female in a past life."

"You and Troy have been on several dates now, what makes this date so special?"

"I don't know if this will happen for sure, but I heard from Elizabeth, who heard from Peter, that Troy is giving me a promise ring!"

Thomas grinned and dried his hands on a towel. "Well, I hope it works out for you. Troy is a good kid. He's changed a lot since they first moved here."

Kelly nodded. "Yeah, I agree. He has such a good heart. I can't say I love him, but a part of me is leaning in that direction."

"Don't let him do anything I wouldn't approve of. You're still my daughter. As that ancient saying goes, guns don't kill people, fathers with beautiful daughters do."

Erased

"Come on, dad, Troy isn't like that!"

"That's good," Thomas said with a wink. "Well, I need to leave for work. I'll talk with you later, okay?" He kissed her on the forehead and walked out of the kitchen.

Kelly giggled and reached into her pocket, removing a pink cell phone. She flipped it open and accessed her text messages. Troy wanted her to pick the place for their date that night. She smiled and sent a reply. She knew where they should go.

Φ

"Hey, Kathy," Thomas greeted his secretary as he entered the building.

"Good afternoon, Thomas," she replied. "Mr. Harding is waiting for you in your office."

Thomas felt his blood run cold. "Mr. Harding is *here*?" he whispered to her. "Why?"

She shrugged. "Maybe to see how the project is going. It doesn't seem that farfetched that your boss would want an update."

"But in person?" He groaned. "All right." Thomas trudged his way to his office in the back. He opened the door and stepped inside, seeing the short, brown-haired man sitting in his chair. He wore a very expensive silver suit that sparkled in the room light.

"Thomas, it's good of you to show up to work," Harding said with a devious grin. "I know you are surprised to see me, but the shock will fade. I came to inform you of a change in our plans. It felt safer to tell you in person than over the phone where someone could bug the lines."

"What kind of change?"

Mr. Harding stood and leaned forward, placing his hands on the desk. "Peter reported that he thought there may be a spy amongst your town folk."

"If the spy you're referring to is Jessica Dailey, then Peter has reported the same thing to me."

"And you've done nothing about it?"

Thomas shook his head. "I've been a little preoccupied getting everything in order. I've seen nothing suspicious that would lead me to believe Peter's allegations are true."

"Yet you haven't even looked into them," Harding countered. "I'm not here to cast blame. I'm here to inform you of how we will handle this. First, we will get rid of her."

"But we need a mayor," Thomas objected, "especially for the experiment."

"We do. Peter has given us a perfect candidate for the next mayor; his wife Monica."

"He chose Monica? Why? She's a Fixer, not a woman trained in leadership."

"Peter suggests she has a good heart and can do the job."

"Are you sure? She always seemed coldhearted and distant. She never liked people; well, other than Peter."

"That's why we will put her through a test. She will arrive tomorrow."

"What test?" Thomas asked with a frown.

Harding chuckled and rubbed his scalp with his palm. "I will let Peter be the one to explain it." He sat back down and motioned for Thomas to sit in one of the guest chairs. "There is one more thing to discuss."

Thomas sighed. "Which is?"

Erased

"We are moving up the experiment date."

"You're joking, right? Do you know how much more work we have left?"

"If Jessica Dailey is a spy, she could have told her employers our plans. We need to start this now!"

"How many days do we have left to finish preparing?" Thomas asked.

"Less than two," Harding informed. "Tomorrow night at midnight, everything will begin."

"That's insane!" Thomas yelled. "How do you expect me to prepare everything in that short amount of time?"

"Get Peter, Tucker, Zane, Elizabeth, and Albert to help you, they are *your* scientists after all. Oh, and there's one other thing you should know. We are including them in the experiment."

"What do you mean?"

Harding sighed and shook his head. "Do I need to spell everything out for you? We will erase their lives and memories, along with everyone else."

"Peter invented this whole thing," Thomas replied. "Why would you subject him to his own experiment?"

"Your job is not to ask why, but to do as you are told. You wouldn't want anything to happen to your daughter now, would you?"

"Don't you *dare* threaten my daughter," Thomas growled.

"Oh, she will be fine. We are erasing her memories too, but that's only to keep you in line."

"She is *not* part of the experiment!"

"She is now. With all of your talking back, I have to show you how serious I am," Harding said with a laugh. "Don't worry though, I'm sure Peter's son, Troy will protect her. I would also recommend you not saying another word. Threatening me is a death sentence, and your daughter needs you in her life. Do you understand everything I have told you?"

Thomas nodded.

"Good," Harding said. He stood and walked over to the office door. "Then I look forward to hearing how everything goes." He exited the room, leaving Thomas by himself.

Thomas groaned and slammed his fists against the desk. Moving up the date changed everything, but how could he go against orders? If he warned anyone or tried to fight the commands, his wife and Kelly would be in danger, which was unacceptable. He would have to include Peter and the other scientists in the experiment; even his own daughter.

Φ

"Peter, I have been wondering something," Tucker White said as he typed away at a computer console in the Midas Tech Laboratory. He sat across from Peter who studied information on a screen.

"Wonder away," Peter said.

"Why did you sign your wife up for this experiment? You told me you haven't talked with her in almost a year."

Peter grunted. "I figured that if we get a new mayor, she should be firm, caring, and someone we can secretly manipulate."

"Manipulate?" Tucker asked as his eyebrows rose for a moment.

"We need to be able to control the mayor's actions without fail."

"But why?"

Peter lowered his voice. "Because we need her for what's about to happen."

Tucker sighed. "But why *her* of all people?"

"Because she's a Fixer, and we will require her help if we want to bring down Harding and his people."

Tucker gagged on his own saliva. "What?"

Peter turned to him. "I bugged Thomas' office. My fear has been confirmed. Harding has given him the order to include us in the experiment."

Tucker shook his head. "No way, man. I will not have my memory erased."

"And how do you expect to prevent that from happening? You can't leave. They would just lock you up until tomorrow night when they begin the experiment."

Tucker closed his eyes and groaned. "They're starting the experiment tomorrow night? This will suck!"

Peter shrugged. "I'm quite interested to see how things will play out with us being included."

"If he's including us, how do you plan on stopping Harding?"

Peter grinned. "That, my friend, is where I will need your help."

"What do you need me to do?"

"We need to make sure we provide a way for Monica to get her memory back. You still have your Dodge Magnum stored at Safe Guard Storage, right?"

Φ

Lucas Heath

Troy stared at the building before him. "You want to have our date here?" he drawled, trying to grasp Kelly's reasoning.

"Yes!" She said with a large smile.

The brick building looked condemned and planks covered the windows. A laminated sign nailed to the door informed passersby what Troy had already suspected.

"I don't understand. Why take me to a condemned bar?"

She smiled and giggled. "The Anchor Bar is more than *just* a bar. It's a place full of memories."

"Such as drinking beer with convicted felons?"

"Funny," she said and rolled her eyes. "My dad ran the bar before they decided that the structure was unsafe. It means a lot to me. My dad and mom are my anchors in life. Even if I don't like their decisions, I still know they care about me and want what's best for me. This bar has sentimental value."

"Which is the *only* value it has," Troy responded.

"The building isn't dangerous. I come here often to be alone and think. I won my first game of pool and saw my first bar fight here."

"Great memories," Troy said as he rolled his eyes.

"Come on, Troy, please. I want you to join me. Just this once."

Troy sighed and nodded. "Fine, but *only* this once."

They made their way to the back and slipped in through a broken window. A blanket with plates and food laid across the floor. Troy nodded with approval when he saw the chicken drumsticks in a plastic container. "Well then, let's eat!"

Φ

Erased

It was late evening when Troy returned, his stomach full of delicious food.

"How was the date?" Peter called out from the kitchen as Troy entered the house.

Troy kicked off his shoes and shut the door before responding. "It went well; she sure can cook," he responded with a laugh. He walked into the kitchen where his dad spread mayonnaise on a slice of bread.

"At least someone in this family can," Peter said with a laugh as he placed a leaf of lettuce onto a thin strip of meat.

"She's not part of our family yet," Troy said.

"Yeah, but I know she will be. Are you still giving her the ring?"

Troy nodded. "Yeah, I am. Saturday night."

Peter laughed. "Well, son, I hope it goes well. By the way, I lost my cell phone. I need to use yours for a while until I can get it replaced."

Troy nodded and pulled his phone from his jeans pocket. "Yeah, sure, let me text Kel and let her know. I wouldn't want her sending you anything embarrassing."

Peter's eyes narrowed on his son. "Like what?"

Troy laughed. "Nothing bad, dad. We have inside jokes and stuff. You wouldn't want her sending a text saying she loves you, would you?"

Peter shrugged. "At least *someone* would say it," he said with a wink.

"Ha, you're funny." Troy punched out a text message and sent it, then handed over the phone.

"Thanks," Peter said as he placed it into his pocket. "Well, I have a busy day tomorrow. Sleep well!"

Troy walked over to his dad and hugged him. "I love you, dad. Sleep well yourself."

Φ

"I'm glad you're home," Thomas said when Kelly returned.

"Stalker dad much?" she said with a nervous giggle. "It's normal for you to be in bed by this time. Did you wait up just to see me?"

He nodded. "Yes, I did. I needed to ask you something. You remember the Anchor Bar, right?"

She paused and stared into his eyes. "Funny you would ask that, I had my date there with Troy tonight. Why?"

"If something ever happens, that's our designated safe zone, all right?"

"Um, what?" Kelly's right eyebrow rose.

Thomas removed a marker from his back pocket and handed it to her. "Write the word Anchor on your arm, with a capital A."

"I'm confused. Why?" she asked.

"Please, Kel Bell, do as I ask. Don't wash it off and don't let it fade. It needs to be your reminder where to go in case of an emergency."

She grabbed the marker without taking her eyes off his and removed the cover. "Are you expecting an emergency?"

Thomas shrugged. "I can't answer that. Please, just do as I ask."

She obeyed and wrote the word Anchor on her arm before capping and handing the marker back to him. "Satisfied?"

"Yes." He nodded and embraced her. "I love you, Kelly, never forget that."

"I won't forget, dad," she whispered. "I'll never forget."

THE TOWER

DAY EIGHT: CHAPTER THIRTY—ONE

This day is not beginning well, Thomas Hood thought as he gripped the cellular phone in his hand. He waited for his superior to respond to the disturbing news Thomas had just given.

"What do you mean he's missing?" Mr. Harding growled.

"Charles escaped last night before Dale Barns could get to him."

"How has Charles avoided being affected like the others?"

"I don't know, sir." Thomas took a deep, silent breath to help him stay cool under the pressure. "He had all his memories erased on day one, but he seems to be unaffected by the subsequent memory wipes. We think it has something to do with a malfunction with his implant. When we tried capturing him to figure out why, he escaped and has been hiding out in Lion's Glade. We didn't think he would do anything to cause trouble, considering he didn't have his memories, but last night, Officers Myles and Alison found him and he told them about the tower."

"He told them about the tower?" there was an annoyed huff. "The reset happened though," Harding said. "Please tell me you erased all evidence of the tower's involvement."

"Of course. I'm not stupid, sir. There was only a small notebook I needed to alter."

"That still leaves Charles. How did he escape from the jail?"

Thomas sighed. "The prison cells are set to open electronically a few minutes after the flash, to make it easier to reset everything. Since Charles was unaffected, he slipped away. Per your instructions, the cameras turn off after midnight, so we can't track him to see where he went. He seems to be out of his mind."

"Explain."

Erased

"From the tapes we reviewed, he was acting insane, almost as if he didn't have a grip on reality. I'm wondering if something happened to him after the first memory wipe."

"Well, whatever happened, you need to stop him before he ruins this experiment. Get Officer Barns to help you. Kill Charles if you have to, but don't let him reveal anything about that tower!"

"You're willing to have your son killed?" Thomas asked and then held his breath while he waited for an answer.

"He ceased to be my son the moment he tried to take my life."

"Well, I hope it doesn't come to that."

"Don't *conveniently* forget to keep me updated."

"All right, sir. I'll make sure you hear about everything."

Φ

"Kelly!" The cry escaped Troy's throat as he flung the sheets off his body and almost fell out of bed. His heart pounded and adrenaline pumped through his veins. Tears poured down his cheeks. He caught his balance, sat upright, and hugged his knees close to himself.

Looking around the room, he saw the navy blue walls covered with newspaper clippings, band posters, and a small whiteboard calendar. He turned toward the computer on the desk, his mind trying to figure out where he was. The room felt familiar, but he couldn't figure out why. Could it be his? Why couldn't he remember? He sat there for several minutes, hoping his brain would fill in the missing details. Who was Kelly? Why had he yelled her name? Why did every fiber in his being scream at him to find her?

He climbed out of bed, his bare feet sinking into the plush carpet. He rubbed his eyes and then gripped his pounding head. A green spiral notebook in the center of the floor caught his attention. The word *Memories* titled the notebook with the sentence *Troy Read Now* below it.

Lucas Heath

Was his name Troy? That felt right though he wasn't sure. The fading letters and numbers on his arm, *Troy18*, seemed to confirm his identity.

He reached down, picked up the notebook, and read. As his eyes passed over his own words, Troy couldn't say for a fact that his memory returned, but what he read felt familiar to him. Somewhere deep in his mind, buried memories pushed to the surface, as to give him confirmation of the truth. He understood his reality.

Kelly was his friend; his best friend and girlfriend. She was the one who made him smile and laugh, even in the crisis their town faced. She poked fun at him, and he at her, and they bickered like siblings, but they loved each other. Troy could feel that love burning deep down in his heart. He loved that amazing young woman. She was the girl of his dreams, and he needed to make sure she was safe.

Φ

A huge yawn overwhelmed Landon and his body shook from exhaustion. Coffee didn't seem to help wake him up either. He sat in his office chair, his notebooks sitting on the desk in front of him. Flipping them open, he dove into their mystery. He had read enough when he awoke to give him a sense of what was going on, and after a short shower, he put on the uniform and made his way to the police station.

He looked at the plaques on the wall that bore a name that seemed familiar. Simon Orson had been the sheriff before Landon and had died in the line of duty. Landon took his job. At least, that's what his journals said. He continued to read through the past seven days. The more he read, the more anxiety he felt. Something sinister was happening. The proof was in the mayor's disappearance the previous day and the fact he and only one other person had remembered her existence. There were great forces behind this memory loss, that much was obvious, though the reasons *why* and *how* remained unknown.

After he finished reading the journals, Landon reached into his desk and removed a stack of papers from the census they had been taking the past couple of days. Last night, he had written something about the data that bugged him. According to a census done two years before, the population of Lion's Glade had been 1305 people. However, according to the newest data, 425 citizens lived there now. Why would a town's population decrease by two thirds in two years?

He continued reading through the information. The people's names, ages, and the words written on their arms filled the papers. There was something specific Landon was looking for, but he didn't find it on any list. He shook his head in disbelief. The two teens were right. Other than Troy Benet and Kelly Hood, there wasn't a single person under the age of twenty. There were no children, no infants, and the youngest person, not including Troy and Kelly, was twenty-five.

"What on earth is going on?" he muttered as he looked up at the clock. Half of his officers would show up for the morning shift in a few minutes. The other half would come in at four and work until the flash ended the day and everything reset again. Now that they had completed the census, there wasn't a lot they could do. Landon hoped that the scientists he wrote about in his journal would come up with a cure or solution to their problem.

Φ

Kyle Anderaos stood before his bathroom mirror, finishing up shaving the whiskers off his cheeks. Under the circumstances, he felt rather calm. He had read his log book when he woke up, and his mind felt at ease with the situation.

An enchanting melody surfaced in his mind, and he hummed, which seemed to set him further into a state of peace. He finished up, wiped his face clean of shaving cream, and left the bathroom to get dressed. He was about to put on his uniform when a sharp pain shot through his neck and he fell to his knees.

It looked as if someone had draped a white sheet over his eyes, for the world faded into a colorless void. With a sudden shift in perspective, two large men led him and a woman down a white corridor. Someone held his neck and pushed him forward. "It's time for you to go back in," a man with a devious smile said to the woman as they passed him in the hall.

The image faded. The white hall vanished and Kyle was back in his bedroom. He reached back and felt the spot on his neck where the pain had started. It felt as if there was a small bump right below his hairline though that could have been from hitting his head or something else that he couldn't remember.

What was the image he had seen? Was it a hidden memory or was it a delusion? He pushed the images away for the time being and stood. Kyle needed to get to work. He finished getting ready and, after grabbing a set of keys, left the house.

Φ

"Doctor, come look at this," a young woman dressed in a lab coat called to a middle-aged man standing on the opposite side of the room.

The doctor wore a bleached-white shirt and pants. His skin appeared almost as white as his clothes, as if he had never seen sunlight a day in his life. The only thing that stood out were the black-framed glasses that perched on his nose. He walked over to the woman and checked the readings on the computer monitor. "This was the man we put back in, correct?"

She nodded. "The connection between his implant and neural pathways seems to be degrading."

The doctor grunted. "That shouldn't happen!"

She agreed and bit a piece of skin off of her lower lip. She pointed to a small bar in the corner of the screen. "A moment ago, the Stuller bar fluctuated. I think his memories are trying to resurface. That could be the reason for the degradation."

Erased

"I should inform Thomas of this right away," the doctor said as he ran over to a door and left the room.

The woman turned back toward the computer and watched the stats. "I warned them this would happen," she said to the people on her left. "A person's brain isn't meant to be reprogrammed."

Φ

Mayor Jessica Dailey stumbled over herself as she made her way to the news station to record the morning announcements for the citizens of Lion's Glade. She had an eventful morning of personal freak outs and then journal reading before she got a grasp on her current reality. She was the mayor and needed to act like it. Her people came first, and they needed to know what was happening.

Her diary, journal, whatever somebody wanted to call it, informed her that the town census had finished the previous day, which was good. She would have information to look through once she acquired it from the sheriff. They would need to figure out the cause of this memory problem, and fast. Before she knew it, she was at the large, brick building that held the Channel Five Studio. She looked up at the logo and her muscles tensed as a thought occurred to her: how did she know how to get here?

Perhaps it was instinct. She didn't need a map, for she knew where the station was. The sign in front felt familiar, as though she had been here many times. According to her journal, she had. She walked up to the entrance and unlocked the door with a key in her pocket. How she even had the key was a mystery.

Jessica stepped inside to the smell of fresh office supplies and paper. She walked up a familiar flight of stairs to the second floor and made her way through the offices until she reached the studio. She stared at the electronic panel of buttons, and without the need to look at a manual, worked her magic.

Φ

"Kelly, it's Troy. Answer the door!" he pleaded as he continued to knock on the front door of her house. "Please tell me you're in there!"

"I'm here. Hold your horses," she yelled. She opened the door and Troy charged toward her, embracing her in a hug.

Kelly stood still, unsure of how to react. She used her hands to push him away. "Clingy much?" she asked and rolled her eyes.

"I had this dream that something bad happened to you. I needed to make sure you were okay!"

"Right," she said unconvinced.

"I'm so... glad to see you," Troy stammered.

"It's nice to see you too?" She wasn't sure whether that should have been a statement or a question.

Troy smiled. "The mayor should give the announcements any moment. Now that I'm here, we can watch together!" Without needing guidance, he walked into the family room and turned on the television to channel five.

A smile spread across Kelly's face and she nodded with approval. Based on that brief meet, she already knew he was better than she had written.

Φ

In a closed-up shop across the street from the police station, a man hid behind a counter displaying sunglasses, coins, and other items people had pawned. He held a pair of binoculars and peered through them, watching the police station and the men entering it as they arrived for their morning shift. One man caught his eye, and he shuddered. He was one of them, the people who didn't sleep after the flash; the redheaded police officer could not be trusted.

Erased

The man munched on a bag of chips, waited, and watched. He needed the sheriff to leave the police station, and then he could continue his plan. The sheriff was good; that much was certain; he could be trusted. The man needed to make sure he timed everything with accuracy, or he could be in trouble. He had disabled the two cameras in the pawn shop last night while they were offline. The evil people wouldn't risk sending in a team to repair them before the next flash, but by then, everything would have changed. He needed things to change.

He smiled and laughed as he thought through his plan. It was a good plan, a good plan indeed, though he had to wait for the right moment. He knew how to wait; waiting was something he had mastered. By the end of the day, everything would be radically different.

DAY EIGHT: CHAPTER THIRTY—TWO

"So, boss man, what's the next step in this investigation?" Kyle Anderaos asked as he leaned back in a roller chair and placed his feet on a desk he had claimed.

Landon shrugged. "At this moment, I don't know. We have all these clues, but I'm still not sure how they fit together. I don't even know how to find the clues that would link *these* clues."

"Maybe the mayor will have an idea," Kyle said with a shrug.

Landon turned to him. "The mayor?"

Kyle nodded. "Yes, the mayor. My logs were clear that Mayor Jessica Dailey runs the town."

Landon pressed his lips together and his eyebrows furrowed. "I wonder if she returned. My own journals say she disappeared yesterday, and that nobody remembered she existed."

Kyle shrugged and the chair almost fell backward. He caught himself in time and planted his feet on the floor. "I had nothing written about her disappearing, but then again, maybe I was one who forgot her."

"This whole thing is a mess," Landon grunted. "My journal confuses me."

Landon sat on the edge of a desk and looked over at Barns leaving the bathroom. "Barns, what do you know about the mayor?"

"She should be at Town Hall after recording her announcements. Why?"

Landon sighed. "She's back."

"Back from where?" Barns asked.

Erased

Landon shrugged. "Who knows? I don't even know what the heck I'm talking about!"

"Have you discovered any clues from the census; anything that could help us?" Kyle asked.

Landon nodded. "Not a single person under the age of eighteen is in Lion's Glade."

"You're joking," Barns said.

"Not at all," Landon said with a sigh. "I also noticed something else. Everybody in town woke up on day one with a word written on their forearm. You may find it interesting to know that every word is exactly six characters long. No more, no less." Landon looked at a paper he had with him. "The mayor had SG-H30 and I have the word Bishop. There are other words like fiddle, anchor, puzzle, spring, and victim. Some are just digits; like a dead writer we found yesterday with the numbers: 12, 21, and 54."

"All six characters? That sounds suspicious," Kyle said as he stood and held out his hand for the list. Landon passed it to him. "If people wrote clues on their own arms, they would write over six letters, right?"

"It makes you wonder," Barns said with a sigh.

"Yeah," Landon mumbled so the others couldn't hear. "It makes me wonder if *we* were the ones who wrote on our arms, or if the people who took our memories did it themselves."

Φ

Peter Benet spent his morning reading through the journals laying next to his head when he awoke. He was in his office in the Midas Tech Laboratory, a place he had awoken many times before, at least that's what his personal journal said. He wore an uncomfortable navy blue business suit, and he removed the tie and outer coat, revealing the white dress shirt. Loosening his belt, he pulled the shirt from his pants. He felt better.

Lucas Heath

His son Troy had called him and the conversation had lasted less than a minute. He wanted to inform Peter that he was all right and wish him luck in finding a solution to their memory loss.

Peter sighed when he found a page with a list of names and numbers of the other scientists that had helped him yesterday. He would need to call and get them together so they could continue searching for a solution to their problem. He had written down an idea for a way to prevent the midnight resets, which had to do with creating a special block around a certain part of the brain, and needed to tell the others.

Picking up the phone, he dialed the first number. Tucker White answered after a couple rings.

"I knew you would call me soon," he said with much enthusiasm. "I made a bet against myself that you would call around nine-thirty. It's almost ten, so it was close enough. I win."

According to Peter's notes, Tucker appeared to be an oddball, though he had a brilliant mind. "Can you get to the laboratory soon? We need to get started on this memory solution. I have a great idea."

Tucker laughed. "I'll be there in four shakes of a lamb's tail!"

Peter sighed as he hung up the phone, "One down, two more to go."

Φ

"Mr. Hood!" A young woman sporting a white lab coat ran toward the older gentleman. "I have news for you. We believe we know where Charles is hiding."

Thomas' right eyebrow rose, and he pursed his lips together. With his hand, he motioned her to continue.

"Two cameras have shut down in the pawn shop across the street from the police station. We can assume it was Charles since he's not anywhere else that we can see."

Erased

"Well then, that's good news."

"What would you like us to do, sir?"

Thomas sighed as he rubbed the bridge of his nose. "We can't risk sending in a team to get him during the day, and I don't trust Officer Barns' abilities to capture, or even kill him. Charles is too smart for that. Just keep an eye on the building, and right before tonight's reset, we will get him."

The woman grimaced. "I trust that Doctor Jones told you about Kyle Anderaos?"

Thomas nodded. "He did. Kyle could be a problem. Keep an eye on his data readings and I will inform Barns to watch him."

"Yes, sir." She turned around and made her way back to the observation center, leaving him alone.

Thomas groaned. "So many problems arising," he muttered. "This was *not* how we planned the experiment." He needed a break. He hadn't had time to sit down and relax for quite a while. At this moment, the others didn't need him. Other than the situation with Charles, everything was under control. He decided that taking a much-needed rest was best.

Φ

Kelly brought in a bowl of popcorn and two glasses of pink lemonade she had mixed that morning.

Troy read through his journal and looked back up to the television screen where the mayor gave the daily announcements and instructions. "May I see your journal?" he asked Kelly as she sat the beverages and bowl on the coffee table.

"What for?" she asked. She hesitated, for she didn't want Troy seeing what she had written about him.

"Check the latest entry and tell me what the day is."

She opened to the last page with writing. "My last entry talks about the bar we visited because I thought it could be a clue, and then I came home and went to sleep."

"But what was the day?"

"The day or the date?"

"Either of them! We should be on day seven, correct?"

She looked through her notebook a minute more and nodded. "Yes."

"Then why did the mayor announce that today was the eighth day? She said they finished the census yesterday, but I don't think they could have finished it in one day."

"So you think we are missing a day?"

"Maybe," Troy said with a frown. "For two people who are so adamant about keeping up with their journals, why wouldn't we write a single thing about yesterday?"

Kelly shrugged. "Perhaps we forgot to write."

Troy shook his head. "I doubt we would have forgotten. I woke up this morning feeling like you were in trouble, so I wonder if something we aren't aware of happened yesterday."

"Does it matter? We are safe and sound. We have each other now."

Troy wanted to agree, but something felt wrong. He felt as though he spent most of yesterday searching for her, as if she had disappeared. Maybe she had, but that begged the question as to why she was here now.

She sat on the floor with him and pulled him into a close hug. "We'll be fine, Troy. Stop worrying so much. Your dad will figure it out."

Troy tried his hardest to smile though even that seemed to fail. "All right," he said. "Everything will be all right."

"Of course it will!" Kelly said with a giggle. "Now, let's watch a movie. There's this one about vampires I want to see."

Ф

Landon sat in his office, reading over the census papers. A question nagged at him. If the people who created this experiment, or torture, or whatever it was, wrote the six-character phrases and words on the citizens' arms, then did they have meaning? Could the word *bishop* on Landon's wrist be a clue? Was this a twisted game somebody had created? Out of all the words he read through, none of them seemed to stand out. The writing on the mayor's arm was the only actual clue that led to something important. But that didn't prove the rest of them had any meaning.

He groaned and had the urge to mope, but at the moment he needed to be an example and a leader. No matter how defeated he felt, he would pretend that the nagging beast inside of him did not exist.

The phone rang, making him jump. He answered. "This is Sheriff Landon, how can I help you?" That greeting didn't sound right. He would have to come up with something else next time.

"Hello, Sheriff, this is Mayor Dailey. With the census completed, I would appreciate if you brought me all of your findings. We can look them over together."

Landon breathed a sigh of relief. He wouldn't have to do the problem solving all on his own. "Yes, ma'am, I will bring the information to you right away."

"I look forward to it."

Landon hung up the phone, picked up a small stack of papers, and shoved them into a manila folder. He pushed against the paper on all sides to make the stack even and then stood from his seat. He left his office and walked to the front of the station. "I'm headed to see the mayor," he told the receptionist before stepping outside. He took a deep breath of fresh air and stood still for a moment to enjoy a breeze.

Lucas Heath

His attention turned to a neon *open* sign in the window of a pawn shop across the street. It had flickered to life. "I didn't know people were opening businesses again," he muttered. Landon almost turned toward Town Hall, but the sign's light faded. He studied the shop and stared at the sign for a moment longer. He couldn't see through the windows, for darkness consumed the store. The sign flickered on again.

Landon gripped the folder tighter and crossed the street. By the time he reached the opposite sidewalk, the light had turned off again. He tried peering through the glass though he couldn't see anybody. With his curiosity getting the best of him, he made his way to the front door and tugged on the handle. The door opened without resistance. "What is going on here?" he muttered as he stepped inside the store. "Hello?"

"Please come in, Landon," a voice called out from behind a counter in the back.

Landon approached the dark outline of a man. The only light came from the front windows.

"What are you doing in here? Who are you?"

"Sir, my name is Charles, and we have to talk."

Landon stopped walking and stared at a man he could now see.

Charles had black hair, a full beard, and brown eyes. He appeared in his late thirties or early forties, was five-feet, eight-inches tall, and had a very slender frame.

"Did you flash the sign to get me in here?" Landon wondered aloud.

Charles nodded. "This needed to be a meeting between you and me. I couldn't step outside for fear that I would be seen by the wrong person. The hidden cameras in here have been disabled, so we should be safe."

"So there *are* cameras throughout town? I only know what my journal says."

Erased

Charles nodded. "Yes. I brought you here so I could tell you everything I know."

"Everything you know about what?"

"About the experiment being performed on the people of Lion's Glade," he replied.

"You know something about that?"

Charles nodded. "Not much, but I know where you should look for answers. You and your people need to check out the tower."

"What's so special about a tower?" Landon asked.

"The tower controls *everything*. If you disable it, the resets should end."

DAY EIGHT: CHAPTER THIRTY—THREE

"What is the tower, and how does it work?" Landon prodded. "Give me more information."

"It's a cellular tower on the hill to the west." Silence ensued for several moments.

"That's all? You *must* know something more. Why else would you suspect the tower has a role in this?"

"That's what makes the light. There *has* to be a connection. The tower is also surrounded by an electric fence with an armed guard."

"The light?" Was the man referring to the light that fills the sky at midnight? Landon had written about it on two separate occasions.

"The tower gives off a piercing light every night at midnight. It makes everybody fall asleep and begins the reset for the next day. I've seen this happen seven times now. I don't fall asleep or reset like everyone else. Whenever I'm around people, or near a camera, I act like I'm out of my mind. That way, the those running this experiment think I'm harmless and don't pursue me. After last night, they have increased their efforts to find and take me out of Lion's Glade."

"What specific things *do* you see?" Landon walked closer and set the folder on the counter.

"Everyone falls asleep when the light flashes, and after a short time, those affected get up and make their way back to where they awoke on day one, as if they are in a trance. They don't talk or do much else. Sometimes those who can't make it to their starting point get help from several spies throughout town that aren't affected by the light."

"There are other people who don't fall asleep at midnight?" Landon wasn't sure how to react to that. "Who are they?"

Erased

"I can't tell you that, for I fear that if they are found out, they would be killed by the Lion's Glade citizens or those conducting the experiment. I don't want their deaths on my head."

"We need to worry about ending this, not about the deaths of those keeping us trapped like lab rats!"

"That may be your opinion, but I can't give that information away. I'm sorry. I've given you enough information. If shutting down the tower does what I think it will, it won't matter who the spies are anyway."

"Fine," the words slipped out as a groan. "Do you remember everything from the beginning? Your memory doesn't get reset at all?"

Charles shook his head. "No. I awoke on day one like the rest of you, without my memories. However, they don't reset anymore. I've been in hiding the past week, moving from house to house to avoid being found. Your deputies got lucky when they found me last night. After I met you, I realized I could trust you to help."

"So we met last night," Landon said, eyeing the man.

Charles nodded. "Yes. We've talked enough for now. You must go get people to help you. You must bring down the tower. Once you do, there should be no reason for these people to come after me anymore and I'll be able to help you further."

Landon nodded. "I hope you're correct about this."

Charles sighed. "So do I."

Φ

"Peter, I understand the data you found, but I'm not sure if we could create something like what you're suggesting."

Albert King, the geneticist pessimist. Peter thought. "Mark's tumor helped him keep his memory, but how? What exactly is the connection?

This is the reason of our gathering, to figure out this mystery. I think it acted as a blocker and protected him from an outside source."

"What outside source are you thinking?" Tucker White asked.

"Hypnosis is a possibility," Peter suggested.

"Hypnosis isn't powerful enough to erase every memory from people's minds, is it?" Tucker wondered.

"It would explain why we keep our skills and understanding of things. We know what objects are, but we have no memories of our lives." Albert saw Peter's reasoning.

"If we could create a device, something as simple as a helmet that blocks any waves from getting to the brain, and someone wore it at midnight, that person may be unaffected by the reset." The cell phone in Peter's pocket vibrated, and he reached for it. "It's the sheriff, hold on," he said as he hit the answer button and lifted the phone to his ear. "Hello, Sheriff."

"This is Peter Benet I assume?" Landon asked.

"Yes, sir. What can I do for you?"

"I need you and your team of scientists to come down to the police station as soon as possible."

The sudden change in Peter's expression caused a sense of anxiety to pass to the others. "Why?"

"I'm not sure, but it's possible we may have discovered a way to end the resets and we'll need your help."

Φ

Thomas yawned and made his way to the room where he had Mark moved. He placed his hand on a pad by the door that scanned his fingerprints and waited for a computerized beep. The door slid open into the wall. Thomas stepped inside and saw Mark sitting up in bed, a book in hand. The room had a splash of color; sea foam green walls and a dark turquoise carpet. The bed sheets were still plain white and the bed frame was a dark gray. Another door to Thomas' right led to a bathroom, which contained toiletries and towels.

Mark looked up and smiled. "I wondered when you'd visit."

"I apologize," Thomas said as the door slid shut behind him. "Work is chaotic. I'm sorry I haven't been around to see you."

"It's all right. I've been catching up on my reading here anyway."

Thomas sat on a gray foldable chair near the bed.

"I have questions," Mark said as he closed the book and set it on his lap. "What happened to me in Lion's Glade? I remember everything up until I got to town, but then my memories go black after that."

"From what I understand, when you arrived in Lion's Glade, the gate was already open, but not for you. A supply truck was leaving. Due to a lack of communication, the guards on duty didn't know of your approved arrival, so they raised an alarm when they saw your truck." Thomas yawned and then continued.

"Instead of coming to find me first, you went straight to the motel you had stayed in the last time you were here and rented a room. Because of your condition, the men sent to protect the town assumed you were carrying a virus. Considering where we are, they couldn't take that chance. They abducted you and brought you to the hospital for tests."

Mark reached up and touched a tender part of his head causing him to wince. "I think the memories from the last time I was here mixed with my recent ones." He paused and sighed. "How did I get back in my truck on the side of the road?"

Thomas shook his head. "I didn't know you were here until after Peter took you to the laboratory. Nobody told me, and I had assumed you got lost or decided not to come. I'm the overseer of the experiment being conducted in Lion's Glade. There are others who run everything else. I'm only called if there's a major problem. The others used you as part of the experiment. Because of your tumor, the experiment didn't affect you the same way as the citizens."

"Yes, I remember that. Peter wanted to study my brain when he learned I still had vague memories."

"It was only at *that* point when someone informed me that a citizen of Lion's Glade had retained some of their memory. When I found out it was you, I had to step into the experiment myself and, without giving too much information away, convince Peter to perform your surgery."

Mark nodded. "So what is this experiment about?"

Thomas smiled and shook his head. "I can't tell you that. Not now anyway. I wasn't even supposed to pull Kelly out, but I got away with it by using the excuse that I was testing a theory. In a way, I was. It's looking like this experiment will be over quicker than we expected."

"Why?"

Thomas chuckled. "Let's talk about something else. How are *you* feeling?"

Φ

It took a while before everyone that needed to be at the police station had arrived. Landon would not take any chances. He called in most of the police force. If the tower had an armed guard like Charles thought, then he needed help to capture and disable it.

Peter and his gaggle of scientists showed up after a short time. Landon had already prepared himself for the mission; he was going in with full power, a loaded, double-barrel shotgun.

"So, why do you need us?" Peter asked as he poked his head into Landon's office.

Erased

Landon made sure he had extra shells in a pocket and then tugged on his bulletproof vest to make sure it was snug. If the previous sheriff, Simon Orson, had worn one, he might still be alive. "Someone informed me of a tower that *may* be the key to this mystery. We have to see if it's causing our memory loss."

"Why do you need me and my group though?" Peter inquired.

"Once we take the tower, we need you and your scientist friends to study the technology inside and turn it off, maybe even reverse the process."

"What about the mayor? What does she think about all this?"

Landon walked over to the door and slipped past Peter.

Peter followed.

"She approved of this plan. She will join us soon."

The moment Landon spoke the words, Jessica entered through the door. She looked around at all the police and scientists talking about the assault on the tower. She saw Peter with Landon and approached them both, a giant smile on her face. "Well then, what do we have here?" she asked as she came to a stop. "Hey honey," she said to Peter and kissed him on the lips. She pulled away and froze. "I am *so* sorry; I do not know why I did that." She blushed.

Peter shrugged. "Someone has been messing with our minds the past week. *Anything* at this point is a possibility." He smiled at Jessica and laughed. "We'll pretend like that never happened."

She nodded and looked at the sheriff. "Anything else I should know about?" she attempted to change the subject.

Landon shrugged. "Our normal dispatchers haven't arrived yet for work, so we should leave two guys here. That's about it."

Jessica nodded and turned toward the rest of the chatting people. "May I have your attention please," she called out. The room hushed. "Now, I do not know what we will find at this tower, but stay alert. Be ready for anything." She turned to Landon. "Do you have anything to say?"

Landon shook his head.

"Good," she replied. "I want two deputies to stay here, in case someone calls with an emergency." She looked around the room and pointed at Kyle. "You will stay."

"Dang it, I wanted to go," Kyle said with an annoyed groan.

"And you," Jessica said, pointing to Officer Barns.

"Seriously?" Dale Barns shook his head in disbelief.

"Seriously," the mayor countered. "The rest of you will follow the sheriff."

Landon held the shotgun close as he made his way out of the police station and toward the tower in the distance. A rush of adrenalin surged through his body as the realization hit him with sudden force. This could lead to the end of their nightmare, and answers.

Φ

Thomas stood from the metal folding chair to stretch when the phone in his pocket rang. "Hold on just a sec," he told Mark and answered it. "This is Thomas."

"Thomas, it's Dale," Officer Barns said in a hushed whisper.

"I told you not to call me again unless it's an emergency."

"It *is*, sir. Landon and his squad of police are on their way to take over the tower!"

It felt as though someone had injected ice into Thomas' veins. "You're kidding me! How did they find out? We erased all the evidence!"

"It's possible that Charles contacted Landon, but I don't know when. Landon has been here all morning, except to see the mayor. However Charles did it, it's done. A large group just left for the tower and they are armed."

"Thanks for letting me know. I need to contact Mr. Harding. I'll get back to you." He hung up the phone.

"Problems?" Mark asked.

"I have to go," Thomas said as he turned toward the door and placed his hand against a pad on the wall. It scanned his fingerprints, and the door slid open. "Goodbye, Mark." He stepped out into the hall and the door slid shut, leaving Mark alone.

Φ

"But, sir, how should I stop them from going to the tower?" the words were meaningless, for Thomas had ended the call. Barns grunted in annoyance and stomped his foot against the concrete floor of the jail. He had stepped away to make the phone call. "What am I going to do?" he muttered.

"You will tell me who you *really* are."

The voice caused Barns to spin around, and he almost lost his balance. Kyle stood by the door that led into the main office area of the police station. He aimed his gun at Barns.

"Kyle, I can explain. Lower your weapon."

"You're one of them, aren't ya? You're one of the people doing this to us. Come out into the office, but slowly." Kyle stepped backward, making sure Barns obeyed.

He followed Kyle into the office. "It's not what you think," Barns said. His body shook.

Lucas Heath

Kyle kept the gun trained on his suspect and tossed Barns his pair of handcuffs. "Put these on behind your back."

Barns obeyed and, per Kyle's orders, turned around to show that the cuffs were secured. He sat when Kyle motioned toward a roller chair.

"I may get valuable information from you. If this thing with the tower doesn't work out, I'll be a hero. Now, tell me, who are you working for, Barns? What is the purpose of erasing our memories?"

Without warning, an ear shattering gunshot echoed throughout the room and Kyle's head whipped forward. He slumped to the ground, landing face first, revealing a bullet hole the size of a quarter.

Barns stared in shock at his rescuer.

She wore black jeans and a black t-shirt, had brown hair tied into a ponytail that extended down to her neck. A strange fire burned in her eyes that Barns hadn't seen for quite a while. It was the former sheriff's wife, Bonnie Orson.

"Bonnie, I don't know why you're here, but thank you."

She walked over to Kyle's body, grabbed the handcuff keys and freed Barns. "Where is my husband?" she demanded to know. "I want to see him, *now*!"

DAY EIGHT: CHAPTER THIRTY—FOUR

Thomas winced as his boss, Mr. Harding, let a series of curses fly in his direction. "How could you let this happen?" He bellowed. Thomas couldn't see him, but he was sure Mr. Harding's face was scarlet from his yelling.

"Sir," Thomas tried interrupting. "What do you want me to do?"

"There's nothing you *can* do, is there? The reset can only happen once every twenty hours to avoid brain damage and machine overload."

"Sir, to be honest I don't think it matters much anyway. I've been testing certain theories, and the more we reset people's memories, the more they are remembering. I think the effect is fading. Implants of several subjects are malfunctioning. I don't think there's a point to this experiment anymore. We've got more than enough data for what we need. We've erased their memories eight times now, done full erases, partial erases, and tried implanting memories. I would say this experiment is a success. Perhaps it's time we return things to normal."

Harding grunted. "No. Let the tower fall, but this experiment isn't finished."

"What do you want me to do, sir?"

"Continue to monitor everyone's implants and record as much data as you can. Without the resets, we need to study how people's minds try to heal themselves. Also, prepare to go dark. You will lose all camera functionality if they shut down the tower."

"Wait, what do you mean?"

"The tower transmits the live camera feeds to you. Once that's gone, you won't be able to view what's happening."

"*That's* good to know," Thomas muttered. "What do you want me to do about Charles?"

"He's already ruined everything; leave him be. If he knows about nothing more than the tower, then he won't find you."

"All right then," Thomas paused, unsure of what to say next. "Is there anything else?"

"No, not right now. Goodbye, Thomas."

Thomas hung up the phone, fell backward into a wall and slid down until he was sitting on the white, linoleum floor. He needed to get Kelly out of Lion's Glade though he wasn't sure how. Harding had people everywhere, watching his every move. Harding used Kelly for leverage, and until Thomas could come up with a way to help her escape, she would stay a victim in this messed-up experiment.

Φ

The group of ten police officers, four scientists, and the mayor, stood before a large chain-link fence surrounding a tower that rose two hundred feet in the air. It looked like an old triangular cell phone tower that had stood for countless generations. Rust covered the array in its entirety. It was a wonder it was still standing, let alone active. The tower stood next to a small, one-story building.

"That's it?" A deputy asked aloud. "*That* thing can erase our memories?"

"Looks can deceive," Landon reminded. "If they use something that looks unusable, nobody would suspect it."

"Makes sense," Jessica said as she approached the gate. "I can hear a hum coming from the fence here," she said and stepped backward. "It's electrified."

Landon nodded. "I heard that it would be."

Erased

"How do you plan on getting through without dying?" A deputy who Landon only knew as Myles asked. "I doubt we could shoot it open."

Landon chewed on his lip for a moment and his eyes grew wide. "I got it. Tucker, come with me."

Tucker tilted his head, showing his confusion.

"We will be back soon. I have an idea."

Tucker joined Landon.

"Where are you going?" Jessica asked.

Landon grinned. "We shouldn't be long. We are going to pick up a car."

Φ

"Barns, where are we going?" Bonnie demanded to know.

"To the hospital!" he snapped and rolled his eyes.

"We are going the wrong way," she said and grabbed his shoulder.

Barns spun around and stared into her eyes. "Look here, lady. You only got your memory back this morning. I spent a lot of time studying every camera's location in this town, and I'm taking us through the dark areas to avoid being seen. So please follow me and trust I know what I'm doing."

She glared at him and then nodded. "Lead the way."

Φ

The group at the tower didn't have long to wait before Tucker and Landon returned with the Dodge Magnum. Landon came to a stop a short distance from the gate and got out of the car, leaving it running. Tucker sat in the passenger seat.

"You're planning on running that car into the fence?" Peter asked. "Logically, it should work."

"I want all of you to step back. There's no telling where sparks or shards of metal could fly." Landon returned to the car and climbed inside, shutting the door. He latched his seatbelt and waited until everyone moved away from the gate. "Are you ready?" he asked Tucker.

A large goofy smile spread across Tucker's face. "Oh boy, am I ever!"

Landon shifted the vehicle into reverse and backed up a hundred feet. "Here we go." He shifted the car into drive and slammed down the gas pedal with his foot. The car lurched forward with a sickening jolt and, after gaining significant speed, collided with the gate, bending it inward and breaking it off the main fence. Sparks flew and rained down upon the car. The men inside the vehicle could feel their hair rising from the electricity in the air. Landon hit the brakes and the large, broken gate collided with the side of the building before falling to the ground.

Landon left the car and turned toward the crowd now gathering at the entrance. "Come on in," he waved. "Just be careful not to touch the fence."

Those armed had their guns ready as they surrounded the building and tower. Landon stood at the only door to the oversized shack and grabbed the knob. It was unlocked. He turned it until the door unlatched and pushed it ajar. He backed up, readied his gun, and kicked open the door. "Police, don't move," he yelled as he rushed inside the building. Four other officers joined him.

The room was small and built out of wood and drywall. The walls were a dull white, as was the ceiling, and the floor was a wooden brown. In the far corner of the room was a filing cabinet and a potted cactus. Straight ahead sat a desk with at least four computer monitors and two desktop computers. Two other strange machines were against the wall next to the desk. To Landon's left, a door led into a small bathroom with a sink and toilet.

Erased

He and two others approached an office chair in front of the computers. A body of a man in his early twenties slumped over a keyboard. Landon touched the man's neck and attempted to find a pulse. "Whoever he was, he's dead now," Landon said as he motioned for his deputies to pull the body out of the building. "Peter, get your scientists in here," Landon called out.

Peter rushed inside with Tucker, Albert, and Zane behind him. They stared wide-eyed at all the equipment before them.

"This is it?" Peter asked.

Landon shrugged. "It looks that way. I thought we would have more opposition."

Peter sat at the computer and searched through the files. "This may take time. We don't need everyone here anymore, now that we know it's safe. Keep two of your men here and send the rest home or something. I doubt we will be bothered. They should know by now their experiment is over."

Landon frowned. "I'll stay here with you, as will Officers Myles and Alison. I'm sure the mayor will stay."

Peter nodded. "Please, just keep out of our way as we study these systems."

"Agreed," Landon said and left the building to dismiss most of the police.

Peter sighed and looked at his group. "Well men, we have work to do!"

Φ

Barns and Bonnie made their way to the back of the hospital, which, if Barns was correct in remembering, had no cameras watching it. He had a key to get through the locked door at the rear of the building. Before long, they were sneaking down a dark hallway.

"We need to be careful. There are many cameras here, but they are easy to spot."

They continued through one hall and down another.

"I never understood why a small town needed such a large hospital," Bonnie said with a frown. She continued to follow Barns until they came to an elevator.

Barns tapped the down arrow key, and they waited for it to open.

"So, are you going to explain what's going on?" she whispered. "You were so cryptic this morning."

Barns nodded. "I know, and I'm sorry. I will explain everything once I'm sure it's safe."

The door slid open, and they stepped inside the elevator. Barns stuck a strange key into a metal slot and turned it. The elevator doors closed, and it descended into the ground.

Barns' eyebrows furrowed in thought. "Someone told me there was an accident here two years ago. I don't know if an explosion caused it, but the stairwell to the lower floor collapsed. They used that floor to store unwanted supplies so it didn't matter to Midas. It would cost too much money to rebuild, and the building foundation wasn't in jeopardy, so they saw no reason to try. They moved most of the excess supplies they needed with the help of the elevator and stopped coming down here altogether." The doors slid open and they stepped out into a dim hall. "The elevator was the only access point from that moment on, and to prevent unauthorized people from coming down here, they created two keys."

They walked to the end of the hall to two latched double doors. A keypad on the wall had glowing numbers, zero through nine.

"How were you lucky enough to find a key?" Bonnie asked.

Erased

"I know the woman who made them," he said as he entered a five-digit code. The doors unlatched and he pushed one of them open, allowing Bonnie to step into the new room.

The room appeared to be an intensive care unit. It was well lit and beds lined the walls several feet from each other, each one separated by a curtain. Bonnie could hear heart monitors beeping. A woman wearing a light-green shirt and pajama pants stood at the end of the room. She placed a clipboard into a slot on the end of a bed, then turned toward the newcomers.

"Barns, you're back!" she said as she rushed toward him and embraced him in a quick hug.

"I would like you to meet Bonnie, Simon's wife."

The woman nodded and smiled. She held out her hand. "My name is Elizabeth Muhammad, pleased to meet you."

Bonnie looked confused and didn't reach for Elizabeth's hand. "You're supposed to be dead," she said. "We were looking for your body in the morgue, but it disappeared."

"My body was never in the morgue to begin with," Elizabeth said with a short laugh. "Back in the beginning, before all of this happened, I had to fake my suicide to prevent anyone from coming to look for me. It wasn't hard, considering I had a good friend on the police force."

Bonnie looked at Barns. "You helped fake her death?"

Barns shook his head. "No, your husband did. This was before we knew that everyone's memories would be erased. Simon was the…" Barns raised his hands and gestured imaginary quotes in the air, "… first one on the scene, filled out the report, and took her body to the hospital." He closed his quotes. "He fabricated quite a few of those files. She's been hiding down here since then."

Bonnie shook her head in disbelief. "Well then, you said you would take me to my husband. Where is he?"

Φ

Zane, Peter's scientist colleague, stared at a document on one of the computer screens and nodded. "This explains it. I think I know how to shut off the tower. Those devices next to the desk are generators and power up this facility. If we can deactivate one, then the tower should be offline. Leaving one running will keep the computers working."

"Excellent!" Jessica Dailey exclaimed and laughed. "This experiment is finished. We will be free of this!" Tears of joy ran down her cheeks.

"Hold up," Peter said and rubbed his ear. "Is there a way to reverse the memory wipes so we can get our memories back?"

Zane shrugged. "I don't know if I've ever used this technology before, and I don't know how to reverse it. I could end up doing serious damage to our brains if I mess with it. The coding in these computers isn't familiar. It may be best to disable it for now and figure out a different way of getting our memories back."

"Bad news guys," Landon said as he entered the shack. "A deputy found Kyle Anderaos dead at the police station, and Dale Barns is missing. I don't know what this means, but it's not good."

"It's time we end this," Peter said. "Zane, pull the plug."

Zane complied and typed commands into the computers. He stood from his seat and walked over to the generators. "Here goes nothing," he said as he flipped the switch. For the final time, a bright light filled the sky, and all but a few of the population of Lion's Glade fell to the ground unconscious.

Φ

"You need to be quiet," Elizabeth warned Bonnie. "There are others sleeping, as is your husband. He took two bullets to the chest. He's recovering, but he needs all the rest he can get." She moved a curtain aside revealing Simon Orson lying in a hospital bed, eyes closed. Several tubes protruded from his arms, connecting to different liquid solutions hanging on a metal rack.

Bonnie started to speak, but without warning she collapsed to the ground.

"Did she faint?" Barns asked as he knelt down to check her pulse.

Elizabeth shook her head. "No. I felt the vibration. Another reset affected her."

CHAPTER THIRTY—FIVE

THREE DAYS BEFORE 'THE AWAKENING'

Thomas' office seemed empty as Peter approached the door. No light flickered between the slats of the blinds, but the secretary at the front of the building said that Thomas hadn't left yet. Peter knocked on the door and heard an annoyed grunt.

"Come in," Thomas' voice passed through the door.

Peter pulled down on the handle and pushed the door open, stepping inside the near pitch-black room.

"You can leave the door open, but don't turn on the lights."

"You've been sleeping?"

Thomas yawned as he sat up, a strip of light from the hallway covering him. "Yeah, I didn't sleep at all last night."

Peter approached one of the guest chairs and pulled one away from the desk to sit. "Does it have to do with Julie's new assignment in Oregon?"

Thomas nodded. "She was up all night packing; you know how she is. The adrenalin rush from all the excitement prevented her from sleeping, which prevented *me* from sleeping. All she wanted to do was talk about Kelly and how I'm supposed to look after her while she's gone."

"Well, you *are* her father."

"Exactly," Thomas muttered. "I *know* how to take care of my little girl." He sighed and yawned again.

"So when does Julie leave?"

Erased

"Her flight takes off later this evening. She should be gone for three weeks. I'm not worried about being alone; this project keeps me busy."

Peter nodded. "I understand. Speaking of the project, I came to inform you that we finished the video recordings of the *fake* experiments. Anyone who watches them won't have a doubt in their mind that a fungus is responsible for their memory loss. That's assuming somebody is intelligent enough to find the videos."

"Someone will find them. We'll spread enough clues that lead to the laboratory. It's better to throw people off the trail so they don't suspect the tower is involved. That could be disastrous. I'm glad the recordings are finished though, it's another thing we can cross off the list."

"How many days do you think this experiment will last?" Peter asked as he stood, raised his arms in the air, and stretched. His blue flannel shirt lifted above the belt line revealing a part of his stomach.

"We aren't sure, but the estimated running time is two weeks. If the citizens can't figure out the mystery by then, we should have recorded enough data to end the experiment."

Peter nodded and pressed his lips together in thought. "Sounds about right," he said. "Well then, I should get going. I've still got a lot of stuff to do."

Thomas smiled, stood, and held out his hand. "Thanks for coming. You can turn the light on when you leave."

Peter shook Thomas' hand and left the office, flipping the light switch on his way out.

Thomas fell back in his chair, his eyes clenched shut. He forced them open until they could withstand the bright bulbs screwed into the ceiling. He yawned once again and reached to turn on the computer monitor when the phone on his desk rang, startling him. Grabbing the phone, he lifted it to his ear. "This is Thomas."

"Hey, Thomas, it's your brother Mark."

Lucas Heath

Mark was calling him *now*? Thomas hadn't talked with his brother in close to a year. A short time after his move to Lion's Glade, they had lost contact.

Mark was three years younger than him and had the brain of a genius though he had been arrested several time for possession of drugs and alcohol consumption.

Thomas loved his brother, but he couldn't deny that he enjoyed the past year without being dragged into one of Mark's problems. Thomas wasn't sure how to reply, but he got his lips to move. "It's been a while."

"Yes," Mark replied. "Look, I'm sure you would rather not talk with me, and I understand why. I wanted to let you know something," he paused, waiting to see if Thomas had hung up on him.

"Go on," Thomas replied. It was common for Mark to pause and wait for a response.

"I'm dying, Thomas. I don't have much time to live. This will be the last time you will hear from me."

The words felt like a bag of bricks slamming into Thomas' chest. "Dying," he responded, not wanting to give off any signs the information alarmed him. "Why are you dying?"

"I'm not sure," Mark answered. "None of my doctors know. Some think that I have a tumor, and others think I have a genetic abnormality that is making my brain swell. Another doctor thinks it could be a parasite in my brain. None of them know enough to help me. I've accepted this, Thomas. I called because I want to apologize for everything I've done to you and our family."

Thomas rubbed his forehead with his empty hand. "I forgive you... I do, but there has to be a way for you to get treatment."

"Not here," Mark stated.

Erased

There was a lull in conversation as Thomas contemplated the options. "Maybe it's time you came to Lion's Glade," he said. "Peter is here, and he's the best neurologist left in the country. He might have the knowledge to help you."

Now, a long pause without a word from Mark followed, though Thomas could hear breathing on the other end. "It may take me a couple days to get there."

"Do what it takes," Thomas said. "Even if Peter can't find the problem, at least I get to see my brother, right?"

Mark sighed. "Right," he whispered.

"Get a piece of paper and a pencil so you can write down the directions."

"I already know how to get there," Mark reminded. "I dropped off furniture for that old lady last year, remember?"

Thomas had forgotten about that. It was the last time he had seen his brother. "Well if you're *sure* you remember."

"I remember. Is there anything else I should know?" Mark asked before he hung up the phone.

"Someone will monitor the gate and will open it for you when you arrive."

Mark mumbled something that Thomas couldn't hear and ended the call.

Thomas replaced the phone on the cradle and rubbed his forehead again. Even through the family drama and work chaos, Thomas loved his brother, and he would do whatever he could to keep him alive.

Φ

Lucas Heath

"Simon, what are we going to do?" Dale Barns asked the sheriff as he munched on one of the homemade chocolate chip cookies Bonnie Orson had made that morning.

"What do you mean *do*? We will make sure we stick with the plan." Simon Orson removed the gun from its holster. He was the sheriff of Lion's Glade, a fitting position for a man of his caliber.

"That's my point. We still don't know what these guys are scheming, not fully anyway. That man, Peter, is already getting suspicious of Jessica. If he finds out who she is, that kills our whole plan." Officer Barns finished the rest of the cookie and grabbed another one from the tin Simon had brought with him to the station.

"Even if she is found out, she's not the puzzle piece holding this thing together. As long as one of us remains alive, our mission will succeed," Simon responded as he leaned back in his office chair.

"That's if we can figure out where their laboratory is," Barns grunted and ran a hand through his short, red hair. "I've been meaning to ask you for a while now, why did you bring Bonnie here with you? That seems dangerous."

"Public image," he stated with a chortle. "I don't think I would have gotten the job here without her. They wanted to know that I had someone in my life worth protecting and that I would do my job right."

"You were the police chief in Athens, Georgia. That on its own should have been enough of a resume. Especially with what went down last winter."

Simon nodded. "Yes, but this job is different. Think about where we are and those around us. Midas needed to make sure they had a sheriff of Lion's Glade they could control. All they have to do is threaten Bonnie's life for me to follow their orders."

"You *want* them to threaten her life?"

Erased

Simon shook his head. "Not at all, but I knew that if I gave them leverage over me, I would be hired into this position. It was the only way."

"If you say so," Barns muttered. He didn't understand the genius behind it all, but that was all right.

"I say so. Just follow the plan and we will find out where their fortress is. Once that is done, we can take back what they stole and finish this."

Deputy Barns nodded. "All right, sir. I'll head out on patrol and keep watch." He stood from his seat and grabbed the final cookie from the tin before leaving.

Simon stood and grabbed a coat. It was time for him to head home for the day and spend time with his wife.

Φ

"Honey, can you get that suitcase for me?" Julie Hood asked as she tried her best to open the front door with the tips of her fingers.

Thomas ran to her aid, taking the red purse and coat about to slip from her grasp. She turned the handle and pulled the door open as a chilling gust of wind entered. A car waited outside for her. "What does Kelly think of this?" he asked as he handed her the coat and purse.

"She didn't say anything when I told her, though she's always on that phone so I'm not sure if she heard me. I'll be back in three weeks though, so it shouldn't be an issue. Please grab the rest of my stuff," she said, pointing to the large, black suitcase in the corner.

Thomas grabbed the handle and attempted to lift it into the air. "What do you have in here?" he muttered as he removed it from the ground.

"A couple dozen bricks," she joked as she walked outside, toward her ride.

Thomas carried the suitcase to the car and heaved it into the trunk. He shut it with a thud and walked over to his wife. He was taller by almost a foot and looked down at the woman he loved. Stroking her black hair, he embraced her. "I will miss you," he said before kissing her on the lips.

"I'll miss you *and* Kelly," she replied as she stared into his gray eyes, one of her favorite features about him. "I don't know how much I'll be able to contact you, but I'll try to send Kelly a message before her date with Troy."

Thomas nodded. "All right, have a safe flight."

She nodded and winked as she climbed into the back of the vehicle. "I love you!"

"I love you too."

Julie shut the door, and the car pulled onto the road, heading toward the plane that awaited her.

Thomas sighed and turned back toward the house. Now that Julie had left, he could return to work.

DAY NINE: CHAPTER THIRTY—SIX

Troy awoke with a large yawn and looked down at Kelly's head on his stomach. Did they fall asleep? The last thing he remembered, they had been lying on the family room floor of Kelly's house, talking about their future. A trickle of sunlight crept in through a window and spread itself over Troy's legs. He turned his head toward the pink cell phone next to Kelly and reached for it, tapping a button to see the time. It was seven in the morning.

Adrenalin flooded his body. He shook Kelly's shoulder. "Wake up, Kelly!"

She groaned and her eyes opened. "What? Did I fall asleep?"

"We both did!" Troy said. "It's already morning!"

Kelly sat up and snatched the phone from Troy's hand. "Morning?" she looked at the clock. "Holey cheese!" she cried out. "We slept a long time!"

Troy sat up and stared into her eyes. "Kelly, we still remember."

She turned to him and, as what had occurred dawned on her, a light seemed to fill her eyes. "Your dad did it?"

"*Somebody* did," Troy said with a large smile. "What does it matter *who* did? We still have our memories from yesterday... and we didn't reset, waking up in our own beds!"

"Now we need to get the lost memories back!" Kelly stood and grinned. "You should call your dad." She tossed her phone back to Troy.

Troy caught it, found the number for Peter, and called.

Φ

Peter stirred when the ringtone for Kelly's number played. He fumbled through the pockets of his pants with his eyes closed and found it. He brought the phone to his ear and answered. "This is Peter."

"Dad, its Troy! Kelly and I remember everything from yesterday! Our memories weren't reset last night!"

Peter pushed himself up and looked around the room. He sat in the small building that held the equipment for the tower. Landon, the other scientists, and the mayor were all asleep on the floor. "The reset didn't happen," Peter said as the realization sunk into his brain. "The reset didn't happen!" he screamed with such excitement that Troy had to pull the phone away from his ear.

Everyone in the room stirred and awoke to Peter dancing around in place.

Landon sat up and rubbed his eyes. The reset didn't happen? They shut down the tower yesterday, and yet they still fell asleep, but why?

Peter stepped out into the open air to talk privately with Troy.

"I am quite hungry," Jessica said as she held an arm around her stomach.

"I'm sure we all are," Landon said as he looked at his cell phone. "We've been asleep for almost eighteen hours."

Zane walked over to the computers and looked through the data displayed on the screen. "It was an electrical safety feature," he said. "The tower's built up energy had to release one final burst before deactivating. That's why we fell asleep."

"I am glad it did not erase our memories," Jessica said.

"It didn't even reset our location," Landon added.

Erased

"From what I read yesterday, the reset system has three steps." Zane opened a file he remembered from the day before and read aloud. "The first step is for the light to flash. It's ironic that the flash has nothing to do with our memories. It informs planted citizens, or I guess you could call them spies, that midnight had come, and to prepare for step three."

"But that does not seem possible," Jessica said as she poked her head out the door and looked up at the tall metal contraption. It looked like a normal tower though she could see a tiny sphere at the top. "I see a bulb, but I doubt a light that bright or powerful could come from it."

"Are you sure?" Zane asked. "Remember, we are dealing with technology of which we have no understanding."

"True," Landon said with a frown.

Zane turned back to the computer. "Step two begins a moment after step one starts. It releases a radio wave containing hypnotic suggestions. The wave puts us *susceptible* citizens to sleep."

"But how?" Landon asked.

"I'm only reading this off of a document. I don't know how it works, but does it matter? The *point* is that it works." Zane continued. "The third step begins a couple minutes after the first two steps initiate. Another hypnotic radio wave is released, which has everyone wake up long enough to make their way home, get ready for bed, and go to sleep. It's almost like sleepwalking."

"Why would *I* keep waking up in my office though instead of my bed at home?" Peter asked as he entered the building and joined the conversation.

"Perhaps they programmed the hypnotic suggestion to return you to your office. I don't have that answer." Zane sighed. "There are no other comments here about the process."

"So that explains about the physical reset," Jessica said with an understanding nod. "What about the mental reset? How are our memories erased?"

Zane shrugged. "Like I said, nothing else is written here to offer anymore answers."

"Does this tower even have anything to do with our memories being reset?" Landon asked. He doubted they had solved the problem.

Peter burst out laughing, drawing everyone's attention. "Who cares? We woke up this morning in the last place we were yesterday, retaining our memories from yesterday. Whoever was doing this to us is finished now. They can't continue!"

Landon nodded. "Let's hope so."

"We still do not know who started this or why," Jessica said and pointed to each of the scientists. "You all need to figure out how to return our missing memories. That is your next task. Until then, I need to eat, make myself look pretty, and record the daily announcements." She turned and left the building.

Landon breathed in and exhaled in an attempt to control the raw emotion swirling in his gut. "Well then, I suppose we can now try returning things to normal, if that's even possible. Let me know if there's anything I can do to help you guys. I will keep two of my officers up here, in case you run into any trouble."

Peter nodded and smiled. "Thank you for everything you've done," he said. "You *are* a great sheriff."

Landon forced a smile and nodded before leaving the building. Myles and Alison stood at attention, waiting for Landon's orders. "You both, stay here. I will return to the station and send someone to release you. Go home, take a shower, relax, and report to the station by four o'clock this afternoon."

Erased

They nodded in agreement and he walked over to the Dodge Magnum. Could it still work after crashing it through an electric fence? He slipped inside, found the key still in the ignition, and turned it. It took a couple tries, but the engine sputtered to life. "Success!" he said with a laugh and the doubts slipped away. Perhaps the mayor was right. They could return things to normal and move on with their lives.

Φ

Troy had a large smile spread across his face, unable to contain the happiness he felt. He stared at the figurative and literal girl of his dreams until she broke the stare.

"Come on, Troy! How could I expect to win a staring contest when I have to see that goofy grin the whole time?" she teased. She stood and walked over to the window, peering out at the vast blue sky. "I want to go for a walk," she said.

Troy nodded. "I wouldn't mind, but where?"

Kelly shrugged. "Let's head north. On the town map there's a forest with hiking trails. Let's check them out."

Troy nodded. "Are you sure you're up for it?"

"Why wouldn't I be?"

Troy shrugged. "I don't know," he said. "I never thought of you as much of a hiker."

"Why?" she prodded.

"My journal says that every time we walked somewhere, you complained about your feet getting tired."

"I did not!" she squeaked. "I wrote in *my* journal *you* were the one complaining the whole time."

"I'm a man; I don't complain!"

"I'm Kelly; I'm always right."

"That is definitely not true."

"There's one way to find out. Let's go on that hike! The first one to complain owes the other twenty dollars."

Troy nodded. "Deal!"

Φ

"Bonnie, wake up," Dale Barns' voice sounded muffled, as if it were far away.

"Do you think the reset erased her memory from yesterday?" Elizabeth asked.

Barns shrugged. "I hope not because I don't have the CD with me. She should wake up soon… I hope."

"I still don't understand how or *why* you took the risk to return her memories."

Barns shrugged as he stared at Bonnie lying across a stretcher. "The CD that Peter made for the fake Jessica Dailey was helpful; though I'm sure his plan didn't go the way he expected. When they came to get her after the reset, nobody even questioned how her memory returned. They assumed it was a glitch in their technology and *I* kept the CD."

"But why did you give *Bonnie* her memories back? What was the logic behind that? Her husband is in a coma. I'm trapped here, and now *you* are hiding from Thomas' people."

"Exactly," Barns said, "That's why I need Bonnie's help. She's our last chance to complete our mission."

"And you didn't think you can convince Landon and the others to help you?" Elizabeth sighed.

Erased

"Are you aware of what Landon did before the experiment began? I read his file, and as nice as he appears, I don't trust him; I will never trust him – not for something like this. The same goes for all the others in town."

Elizabeth frowned. "Thomas betrayed Peter and trapped him in his own experiment. Don't you think *Peter* would help you? He knows where the laboratory is."

Barns nodded. "You have an excellent point. Perhaps that's not a bad idea."

"See?" Elizabeth poked Barns and grinned. "I *have* good ideas."

Barns nodded. "That you do. I need to figure out how I'll do this."

"How you'll do what? Convince Peter to help you?"

Barns shook his head. "No, I need to figure out how I'll abduct him."

DAY NINE: CHAPTER THIRTY—SEVEN

"It's warm out today," Troy commented as he and Kelly made their way to the north part of town.

"I wish we had bikes. Getting around would be much easier."

Troy laughed. "Walking is better exercise for you."

"I'm not worried about exercise. I want to view the beauty of nature and getting there faster would be preferable."

Troy remained quiet, not wanting to say anything stupid to upset her.

"Aren't you going to reply with a snide or witty comment?" she asked.

He shook his head. "No, I'm not."

Kelly wrapped her arm around his back and rested her head on his shoulder as they walked.

"Do you really want to go hiking?" he asked. "We can always find something else to do, like play Frisbee at the park."

She shook her head. "Don't tell me your legs are getting tired already."

He shook his head and laughed. "Not at all; I'm just not up for hiking."

"You don't have to come with me if you don't want to go."

"Kelly," he said. "Forget I said anything. Anywhere you are is where I want to be."

Φ

By early afternoon, Jessica Dailey had gone home, showered, eaten, walked to the television station, recorded the town announcements, and returned to the police station. She passed two nurses wheeling out a long, black bag on a stretcher.

"That was Kyle Anderaos' body," Landon said as he met Jessica at the front door. "Deputy Barns is still missing. We still don't know what happened here."

"I cannot explain why, but a part of me thinks Barns is a spy for the people running the experiment."

"Really?" Landon asked. "Out of everything I've written about him in my journal, there weren't any red flags that would suggest he's anything more than genuine."

"Like I said, I cannot explain it. Call it instinct if you wish. That is why I chose him to stay back at the station when we left to raid the tower."

"You weren't selecting at random?"

She shook her head. "I do not trust him."

"Well, we will keep an eye out for him. He left his cell phone on a desk here and it might hold a clue, though I'm not holding my breath."

"Keep me informed; I will be in my office." She left Landon and walked over to Town Hall. The front desk was empty as it had been yesterday and every other day. She needed to change that and hire a secretary, or at least figure out who had been her assistant. She made her way up the plush red steps and approached her office; a loud grumble from inside reached her ears. She pushed open the door and stared at the man sitting behind her desk. He was reading her papers. "Who do you think you are?" she demanded to know.

He turned to her with a smile and stood with a salute. "Captain on the bridge!"

"Excuse me?"

"You're the captain of this ship, are you not?"

Jessica took two hesitant steps forward, not knowing if she would need to run for her life in a moment. "What ship?"

The man rolled his eyes and came out from behind the desk, causing the mayor to step back toward the door. "Never mind. My name is Charles. I'm the one who informed Landon of the tower."

The name clicked in the mayor's mind and a smile appeared across her face. "Ah, so *you* are Charles. It is good to put a face to the name."

"Precisely, which is why I showed up to introduce myself. With the tower deactivated, their cameras no longer work. I've checked many, and they are all offline."

"What do you know about this experiment?" Jessica asked as she walked over to the couches in the corner of the room and sat. She motioned for him to join her. He followed her gesture and took a seat.

"I know as much as you do. The tower was the key, and now it's deactivated. You won."

Jessica rubbed her neck and frowned. "We still do not have our old memories back. We have not won *yet*."

"Are you willing to face the possibility they may never come back?"

The mayor shook her head. "I will not accept that. There has to be a way."

Charles shrugged. "Maybe, but maybe not; I don't have the answer. It's only a question."

"That is a question I cannot afford to ask myself. Our scientists are busy working to find a solution."

"Well, I hope they find one for the sake of everyone here. Speaking of which, while you were at the tower, I read through your files and the information taken during the census. I find it rather intriguing."

"How so?" she wondered.

Erased

"I find it odd that there are only two individuals in town under the age of twenty-four. What do you make of that?"

The mayor shrugged. "I cannot answer that; school field trip maybe? Perhaps the people running the experiment figured out a way to get them out of Lion's Glade."

"What about the writing on everybody's arms?"

She shrugged again. "I am still trying to figure that one out."

"Fair enough," Charles said. "Well then, I must be going." He stood and walked over to the desk. He picked up a book and held it up for the mayor to see. "I'm taking the book written about the town. History intrigues me."

The mayor nodded. "I doubt I will need it again. Enjoy."

He nodded and bowed before leaving her office.

Jessica walked over to her desk and sat in the chair. Charles had a lot of good, brain-numbing questions. How would she ever be able to find answers for them? She hoped the scientists figured out how to reverse the process before things got worse.

Φ

"She's waking up," Elizabeth said as she saw Bonnie's eyes open.

"It's about time. I've never seen the tower knock somebody unconscious for over a day."

"The scientists created the tower to be used once every twenty hours to prevent system problems and brain damage. The premature reset may have had a negative effect on her brain and it needed to correct itself. Also, she had all her memories when it happened, which may account for a longer sleep."

"I'm fine," Bonnie mumbled as she sat up and yawned. "Where am I?"

"The hospital," Barns said. "Don't you remember?"

Bonnie rubbed her head. "Yes, I came with you to see Simon."

Elizabeth sighed with relief. Bonnie still had her memories.

"What happened?" the older woman asked.

"Another reset happened, but it only knocked you unconscious and nothing more."

"Oh," Bonnie said. "I have a massive headache. Do you have any medication for that?"

Elizabeth nodded and walked over to a cabinet on the other side of the room.

"I expect you to explain what's going on," she said to Barns. "Tell me everything."

Barns sighed as he sat on a wooden stool near the stretcher where Bonnie rested. "About a year and a half ago, a man working for the Helios Company approached your husband. The company specializes in advancing technology to get our country on top and protected again. They have come out with revolutionary new ideas."

Bonnie nodded. The company had a reputation for technological breakthroughs.

"The man from Helios explained to Simon that another company, Midas, had stolen their technology and planned on using it for their own personal advancement. Midas had already prepared for a major test in Lion's Glade to see how far the technology could go. Helios hired Simon to infiltrate this place, retrieve the stolen technology, and destroy all records of its existence."

Erased

Bonnie's mouth hung open and the look in her eyes seemed to burn straight through Barns. "How did Simon know this guy was telling the truth? How did he know the technology was the Helios Company's as the man claimed, and that Simon wasn't getting in the middle of a corporate feud?"

"Take this," Elizabeth said as she handed Bonnie a glass of water and two pills.

Bonnie swallowed them and downed the water in one breath. She handed the glass back and once again focused on Barns.

"Because, the man who approached Simon was my father, and every word he told your husband is true. The man who stole from Helios, my father's company, killed my best friend Ken. It took much effort, but I convinced my father to let me go with Simon to help him. It took nearly a year to infiltrate this place and get hired, but Simon and I succeeded. A woman named Jessica Dailey also worked for us, and Midas hired her to become Lion's Glade's mayor, though right before the experiment began, Midas discovered she was a spy and killed her."

Bonnie nodded, understanding. "And where does *she* fit in to all of this?" she asked, pointing at Elizabeth.

"Simon, Elizabeth, and I grew up in the same neighborhood. When we first moved here, we reconnected with Elizabeth and it shocked us to find out she worked on the project we planned to destroy. We didn't tell her anything for a while, but several days before the experiment began, we confided in her."

"You both grew up with Simon? How old *are* you?" Bonnie asked.

"A *lot* older than I look," Barns admitted.

Elizabeth sighed. "If I would have known what Midas' intentions were, I wouldn't have worked with them."

"Why didn't you end the project then? I'm sure you could have sabotaged it!" Bonnie accused.

Elizabeth shook her head. "No, I couldn't have. My job kept me at the tower the whole time. I never found out where their main facility is. Plus, with the man Midas hired to guard me, I wouldn't have been able to do anything."

"They hired a man to guard you?" Bonnie wondered.

The doctor nodded. "Because of my last name, they hired a man of Saudi Arabian descent to watch over me. The overseer, Thomas, wanted people to think Ahmed, and I were married, so that none of the men here in town would try anything. The problem was that, over time, Ahmed developed unhealthy feelings for me. He followed me everywhere, and living in the same house together made things worse. He attempted to control me and even forced me to take *my* moose head down in *my* office! I couldn't get away from him, which was another reason I faked my death."

"Ahmed was the one who shot your husband," Barns informed Bonnie. "Thankfully, it happened a few moments before the reset. Once everyone was unconscious, and the cameras turned off, I placed Simon in a wheelbarrow and ran the entire way to the hospital, to Elizabeth. I thought he was a goner for sure, but he's a fighter and proved me wrong."

"That sounds like him," Bonnie whispered.

Several moments of silence passed before Elizabeth spoke. "What are you thinking?"

"What were you and Simon waiting for, exactly? Why haven't you gone after the technology yet?"

Barns grunted and ran a hand through his hair. "Because we don't know where their laboratory is. There was a time when Simon believed he knew where it could be, but he never shared that information with me. We assumed that we would have weeks to look; though the scientists moved up the test date once they figured out the real Jessica was a spy. Right before the experiment began, men came to the police station and took Simon away. I think it was because he refused to kill Jessica. They didn't appreciate his disobedience. Thomas' called me into his office and informed me of the experiment's beginning. They chose me to be one of their *watchmen* as they call it. Simon wasn't so lucky. He had his memory erased and then got shot a couple days later."

Another period of silence pursued as Bonnie processed the information. She looked up at the others. "Now what?"

"We need your help," Barns admitted. "I think that Peter is our only chance of finding the laboratory. We need him, even if we have to take him by force."

Bonnie stood and stretched. "Well then, what would you like me to do?"

DAY NINE: CHAPTER THIRTY—EIGHT

"This place is beautiful!" Kelly gawked at the plants and trees along the dirt path.

Troy nodded in agreement though he didn't hear a word she said. He pondered what his dad had told him over the phone. Peter had confirmed that someone used the Lion's Glade citizens as test subjects. Kelly didn't seem affected by the information, but something about the revelation bothered him.

"What's on your mind," Kelly asked as she stopped and tugged on his arm.

"Nothing," he replied.

"Like I'm stupid enough to believe that," she muttered. "What's going through that brain of yours?

"Something is bothering me, something I don't understand."

"Such as," Kelly prodded.

"Where are your parents? Where is my mom? I haven't written about her once in the past few days."

"And that's a problem?" Kelly asked.

Troy frowned and his eyebrows furrowed. "Are you serious? You don't care where your parents are?"

She shrugged. "I care about *you*. I don't even remember them."

"I don't remember my parents either, yet I miss them. At least I believe I do. I'm not sure what I'm feeling."

"We're teenagers. We aren't *supposed* to understand our feelings."

Erased

"Something just doesn't click though," Troy said with an annoyed grunt. "When I woke up yesterday without my memory, I was freaking out. Not because I couldn't remember anything, but because I thought you were in trouble, even though I didn't remember who you were."

"That's not a bad thing."

"It's not?" Troy's volume rose. "When I talked with my dad on the phone this morning, I heard excitement in his voice, but it was wrong!"

Kelly's eyebrows furrowed and her head tilted to one side. "Wrong, how?"

"It was almost like a false excitement."

"How can excitement be false? You think he was faking it?"

Troy shook his head. "No, not faking; it was genuine. It was a genuine fakeness. I can't explain it," Troy groaned in frustration. "I wish I understood! I noticed something in myself yesterday too, but I couldn't recognize the problem until I learned that we are in an experiment. Every time I laugh at something, it's wrong, like the laughter isn't real. It almost feels like I laugh because it's the right time to, not because something is funny. I feel like my emotions are on autopilot."

"We've been through a lot, Troy." Kelly grabbed his arm. "Think about what these people have done to our minds! Of *course* we're messed up right now!"

"And another question: why haven't there been more problems?" Troy asked.

"What do you mean?"

"Why hasn't there been more chaos in Lion's Glade? I've written down every announcement the mayor has given from day one. Each day she has announced the fatalities, assaults, and suicides, but after the first couple of days, she stopped reporting on them. Why weren't there more?

There should have been more rebellion and anarchy in the streets. There should have been more people looking for answers!"

"Perhaps she wanted to report good news and not negativity that would bring others into *more* chaos or confusion."

Troy shook his head. "Yesterday she reported that the death toll from the past eight days was fourteen people."

"Troy, I don't understand what you are getting at, but none of this matters anymore. Let's just walk and enjoy nature. Please?"

"I think there's more to this memory loss experiment than all of us have realized. Perhaps nobody noticed because our memories were reset every day, but I believe these people are also messing with our emotions." Troy turned toward a tree off the path and walked away from Kelly. He reached toward a branch covered in strange, green, diamond-shaped leaves and grabbed one.

Kelly watched him stare at the odd leaves and he looked up at her.

"I wrote in my journal several days ago that the people we've interacted with have acted awkward; they seemed almost emotionless. I thought that was because they weren't sure how to cope with their new reality, but now I wonder."

"Troy, you're thinking too much. Let's continue our walk, please."

He shook his head. "No, we need to head back. I think it's time I tell my dad that something else is happening to us."

"So if you think all of our emotions aren't real? Then what about our friendship and the love we have for each other?"

Troy shook his head and she could see a sad expression on his face. "I don't know, Kelly. Even at this moment I give off the impression of sadness, and I *should* feel sadness, but I can't *feel* it." He turned his attention back to the leaf in his hand and rubbed it between his fingers.

Erased

"What in the world?" he mumbled as he tried ripping the leaf in half. "Kelly, look at this."

She walked over to him and stared at the plant life in his hand. He handed her the leaf and reached up, breaking a branch from the tree. He touched every part. "As if losing our memories and emotions weren't enough..." his voice faded.

Kelly turned the leaf around in her hands and shook her head. "I don't understand." She jogged over to another tree and checked its leaves. "It's the same on this tree."

They walked around for several minutes, looking at each tree, though they found the same issue with every single one.

"What's the purpose of this?" Kelly asked, though she knew Troy wouldn't be able to answer her question. She knelt down at a bush and touched the stems and flower stalks. "These are the same."

Troy shrugged and shook his head. "I don't know."

"They look so real!"

He nodded, his mind full of wonder, or maybe it was confusion, Troy wasn't sure anymore. "It doesn't matter how *real* they look, but if the rest of the trees are like the ones we checked, then this entire forest is fake."

Φ

"Mayor!" A voice called out to Jessica as she left Town Hall to head home for the night. There was nothing more for her to do, and she felt too much anxiety to sit around all evening waiting for answers.

"Oh, Charles," she said when she saw him bounding down the sidewalk toward her.

"I think I figured it out!" By the time he stood before her, he gasped for air. He clutched the book on the town's history in his hand. "I need to read your files again. Please, come with me," he said. He entered Town

Hall and ran up the steps with Jessica following behind him. He made his way through the hall, into her office, and over to her desk.

"What could you have discovered in several hours that none of my police did through days of searching?"

Charles grabbed a paper that had data from the census and read through it after opening the history book. He flipped through the pages and a large smile stretched across his face. He turned to the mayor and winked.

"Did you find something?"

He nodded. "When I left earlier, I went to the park down the road and read the book. Something odd stood out. One word on each page is underlined. I wasn't sure if it was a puzzle, but I tried searching for any patterns to the underlined words. I hit a block for several moments, but then something popped into my mind I couldn't seem to shake. A police report said that the book's author, Griffin Powel, died at his home."

The mayor nodded. "Yes, that is what I read."

"He had written numbers on his arm right before he died! So I tried to remember what the numbers were, but I had read through so many names I couldn't think of them. I have them here now though." He held up the paper. "My theory was right. How I even came up with it, I don't have a clue, but I did, and I was right, so *bam*!" he shouted out the last word. "Each pair of numbers on his arm is a page number of his own book. This guy was a genius! He wanted to create a clue that most likely only *he* could figure out and solve."

"Then he wrote a message on his arm with six numbers?" She admired the writer's ingenuity *and* Charles for solving a case her own police force couldn't crack.

"We have three words here, on pages twelve, twenty-one, and fifty-four. The words underlined on the corresponding pages are '*search the basement*'."

Erased

The mayor shook her head in amazement. "He left a clue for himself to solve, to search his basement. That's genius."

Charles nodded. "So, are you ready to go?"

The mayor's right eyebrow rose. "Go where?"

"To Griffin Powel's home. I have the address right here. Don't you want to know what he left himself?"

The mayor shrugged. "Does it matter? He might have hid personal items to help him remember who he was."

"Are you so sure?" Charles asked with a mysterious grin. "If he went to all the trouble to hide something from others, I'm sure it would be more than *just* keepsakes."

She shrugged again. "Perhaps, but I am rather tired right now. We can continue this tomorrow."

"Don't be lazy, Jessica," Charles rebuked. "Either you come with me, or I'm going without you."

"Fine," she huffed. "We have a vehicle to use, so that will help."

Charles smiled. "So you're coming with me then?"

She nodded. "Yes, I am coming with you. Let us go and find what this writer hid."

Ф

"Sheriff, we need to borrow the car," Jessica informed as she entered his office at the police station.

He picked up a set of keys on his desk and tossed them her way. She caught them with ease. "I've been doing more investigating into Kyle's death. Our front desk clerk, Linda, was using the bathroom at the time of the shooting. She heard the shots and hid in a stall. That's where she woke up this morning."

"Quite an unpleasant place to wake up, I am sure," Jessica muttered.

"Linda said that she heard a female voice talking with someone after the shooting. At this moment, we can assume the shooter was this unknown female, or Barns."

"Make sure your men keep an eye out for him. I want him found and questioned."

Landon nodded. "Where are you headed with the car?"

"Your friend Charles discovered another possible clue. Care to join us?"

"Let me send information to my men and I'll be right with you."

The mayor nodded and left the office.

Landon sighed and looked at the clock. How had the day gone by so fast? At least he had something interesting to end it.

DAY NINE: CHAPTER THIRTY—NINE

The teenagers made their way through the forest, a small pile of leaves in hand. They continued checking every plant and tree on their way out, all with the same results. After a time, Troy retrieved Kelly's cell phone from his pocket and called his dad. Several rings passed before he heard the familiar voice.

"Troy! Good to hear from you, son."

"Dad, something is wrong and I need to talk with you in person. Where are you?"

"I'm at the cell tower. It should be easy to spot from anywhere in town. I'll be here for a while longer if you want to come by and see me."

"Yes," Troy replied. "Yeah, I can see it. We'll talk when I get there." He ended the call and handed the phone to Kelly.

"You could have told him what we discovered over the phone."

Troy shrugged. "I'm tired of talking on the stupid phone and I want to see him in person. Besides, I doubt he would believe me unless he sees it for himself."

"Well then, since you know where he is, lead the way."

Φ

"It's official," Albert King said as he entered the small building next to the tower. "The dead man we found here seems to have died of a brain aneurism. I'm guessing all the resets caused it. He was too close to those pulses the tower gave off."

"This technology can do that?" Tucker wondered in amazement.

Zane frowned. "I'm not too sure the tower caused his death, based on my own findings about what it does."

"Peter, I sent the two officers home for the evening. With the tower deactivated, I doubt we will have any problems," Albert mentioned.

"Works for me." Peter stood over Zane's shoulder, watching him search the coding of the computer programs that ran the tower's functions.

"This will sound strange, but I have confirmed that the tower has nothing to do with our memories being erased," Zane informed.

"Are you serious?" Tucker asked and shook his head. "So then it only had to do with the resets?"

Zane nodded. "It looks that way."

Peter stared at the information on the screen and looked down at the cell phone in his hand. "You said that the tower is inactive now, correct?"

Zane nodded again. "Yes, there's no power. Why?"

"If there's no power, then how is my cell phone receiving a signal? How did I just talk with my son?"

Zane grinned like he knew something they didn't. "This isn't a tower for cell phones. I know that's what it appears to be, but it's not. The equipment in here doesn't even support cell service. This tower strictly worked for the experiment."

"Then how do our cell phones have a signal?" Peter asked.

Zane shrugged. "I can't answer that. This is the only tower I remember seeing in town, so there must be a satellite dish somewhere that connects all of our phones."

"Knock, knock," a woman's voice called from outside.

The four scientists turned around and saw an older woman waving at them.

Erased

"The door is wide open. You may enter," Peter said.

She nodded and joined the group. She wore dark blue denim jeans, a white blouse, and had her brown hair tied into a ponytail. "My name is Bonnie and I'm a nurse at the hospital."

Peter nodded. "Ah, yes, I wrote about you in my journal. What can I do for you?"

She smiled and nodded at the others to acknowledge their presence. "I'm looking for a Peter Benet. The receptionist at the police station said he would be here."

"That would be me," Peter said. "How may I help you?"

"I think we may have discovered a cure for everybody's memory loss. I need you to come with me to the hospital."

Peter's eyes grew wide for a moment. "Really? Well, I would like to come with you, but I can't yet. I'm waiting for my son and his girlfriend to arrive." He turned to the other scientists. "You three should go with her and I can meet you down at the hospital afterward."

She shook her head. "I only need you, Peter, and we need to go now."

"I do apologize, but I can't just yet," Peter said. "I need to wait for my boy. You'll be just fine with the others until I get there."

Bonnie rolled her eyes and reached behind her back. She removed a pistol and pointed it at Peter. "You are so stubborn! All you had to do was come with me. So much for your plan, Barns," she called out.

Barns appeared at the door. "It was worth a shot. I didn't want to resort to this." He had a roll of duct tape and threw it at Peter, forcing him to catch it or be hit in the face. "I want you to tape everyone else up, Pete. Their legs and arms shouldn't be able to move."

"Why are you doing this? What's going on?" Peter asked.

"I'll explain it once we are long gone from here. Now, get to work."

Φ

"This house smells like death," Jessica said as she plugged her nose. They had stepped inside the entryway of Griffin Powel's home.

"We can leave the front door open and let the house air out more," Charles suggested.

Landon shook his head. "No, keep the door shut. We want nobody to know we are in here."

"And yet the only car in town is parked out front," Jessica reminded.

"Let's get to the basement. It should smell better."

The three searched the house for a short time before Landon found the door to the basement. They all made their way down the steps. Charles flipped a switch at the bottom of the stairs, bathing the room in light. Several boxes, tools, two rusted bicycles, a workbench, and jars of fruit filled the cellar.

"So, I guess we search," Jessica said as she lifted a box off another and set it on the ground.

"Just don't stress about it," Landon said. "We have the time now. Don't worry about being reset at midnight."

"Oh *please* do not let it take *that* long," Jessica begged.

Charles laughed. "Then let's get started, shall we?"

Φ

The sky had blackened, and the stars were visible by the time the teens arrived at the tower.

"Hello, anyone in here?" Troy knocked on the door. His dad should have been there though there was no answer.

"Perhaps they left to get food," Kelly suggested.

Erased

"Then dad would have called to tell me," Troy snapped. He tried turning the handle. "It's locked. Dad!" he called out.

Kelly checked her phone. "Troy, the phone battery is dead. That's why he couldn't call. Come on, they aren't here."

"Something's wrong," Troy said as he took a step back and slammed the bottom of his right foot into the door. It had no effect, except for a sharp pain shooting through his leg. "Yow, that hurts." He hopped around on one foot until the pain subsided.

"Troy, stop it!" Kelly said and grabbed his arm.

"Trust me; something isn't right!" He pulled away and threw all his weight into another kick. The door flew open and splintered wood rained to the floor.

"Sometimes you can be idiotic, Troy," Kelly rebuked.

After a moment of intense pain, he could walk again and limped into the building. There was a desk with computer monitors in one corner of the room, and over in the opposite corner were three bodies sprawled across the floor.

"Oh my gosh, Kelly!" he called out. "Help me!" He hobbled over to them and could see their chests rising. Each one had red marks on their faces, as if someone had hit them with something hard. Tape bound their wrists and legs, and a strip covered their mouths.

The room seemed to fade away for a moment as Troy found himself shirtless in a dark basement, taped to a chair. A trickle of fear touch him and he shuddered. Was he remembering something? The room faded back into existence and he, with Kelly's help, unbound the men. One of them opened his eyes. "Where's my dad?" Troy asked.

"Officer Barns took him," the man said before his eyes closed again.

"An officer took your father?" Kelly wondered aloud. "Why would he do that? And why would he bind and knockout the scientists?"

Troy shrugged. "Perhaps someone at the police station would know. We can send help once we get there. Let's go."

Φ

"We looked through all these boxes, and we have not found one helpful thing," Jessica said with a sigh as she sat on a dusty chair.

Charles matched her sigh and shook his head. "There *has* to be something here! The clue was specific!"

"Maybe the people running the experiment figured out the clue already and found whatever he had hidden down here," the mayor suggested.

Landon rubbed his forehead. "That would be lame."

"We need to think through this. Who was Griffin Powel? How did he think?" Charles walked around the basement, eyeing everything. "Look at the dirt here," he pointed to an area in the center of the room.

"This is a basement," Jessica reminded. "All basements are dirty."

"That's a generalization, but you're not wrong. However, most basements wouldn't have dirt all over the floor unless someone has been digging. There isn't much here though." He kicked empty boxes around, eyeing every detail of the concrete floor. He approached the work bench. "There's more dirt here." He grabbed an end and lifted it up, rotating the bench away from a hidden hole. "Look at what we have here."

The mayor and sheriff stood and made their way to the discovery. "It's a box in a hole," Landon said unimpressed.

"Thank you, Sheriff Obvious," Charles said with a smile. He reached down, and with a little effort removed the container. It was about the size of a loaf of bread and a padlock kept it shut. "This is sturdy wood," Charles observed. "The lock and clasps are well done too. I don't think we will get this thing open without tools." He bit down on his lip and motioned toward Landon. "I didn't see any tools down here. Are there any at the police station?"

Landon nodded. "It's possible, but I'm not sure."

"That may be the best place to open this thing anyway. We want as many witnesses and as much protection as possible."

"How can you be so sure of its value?" Jessica asked.

Charles shook his head. "I don't know. It feels familiar, like I saw it before losing my memory. I may have been to this house before and the name Griffin Powel resonates with me. Somehow, I knew this man before the experiment began. Perhaps he told me about his plan to hide this; I'm not sure. This could be something very important. We need to take it to the police station."

Landon nodded. "All right, but it's getting late. We could always save opening the box until tomorrow."

Charles shook his head. "No, we need to open it as soon as possible."

"You are sure about this," Jessica commented, hearing the urgency in his voice.

"Yes," Charles said. "Yes I am."

"All right then," Landon said with a frown. "Off to the police station we go!"

CHAPTER FORTY

ONE YEAR AGO

"Peter, you need to do something about your son!" Monica cried with exasperation as she entered their bedroom. She glared at her husband Peter who was lying in bed, reading a book.

"What did he do this time?"

"I only asked him to unload the dishwasher, and he gave me a smart-alecky response! It is not as if I asked him to wash the dishes by hand!"

"He's a teenager. He will grow out of that rebellious phase."

"He is seventeen; almost an adult. He needs to grow out of it *now*, especially with the world out there!"

Peter sighed. "I'll talk with him in the morning. Leave it alone for now."

"He frustrates me!" Monica said as tears filled her eyes. "I try so hard to be a good mom, and he rejects me at every turn."

"That's the problem," Peter said as he set aside the book and motioned for her to sit. She joined him and snuggled up to him. "You're trying too hard to replace the mom he lost. He won't accept that."

"Then what am I supposed to do?" she asked.

Peter sighed and rested his head on hers. "Stop trying so hard. Just be yourself. Be that happy, spunky, cheerful woman that captured my heart. You've lost a lot of that."

She nodded, causing his chin to bob. "It has been hard with work. They keep sending me all over, and I feel as if you and I do not connect anymore, like we have drifted apart. And now I have this new job offer, which takes me across the country, I do not know what to do."

"Is it a job you want to take?" Peter asked.

She nodded again, causing his head to bob. "Yes, I do. It would be an amazing job."

"Then take it."

She pulled her head away from his and looked into his eyes. "Are you serious?"

He laughed and nodded. "I want you to be happy, and if this job looks like it's good for you, then go for it!"

"What about you and Troy? I would have to move and leave you two unless you came with me."

Peter shrugged. "I'm meeting my old friend Thomas tomorrow for a job interview. He wants me to get involved with a project of sorts."

"That is great!" Monica's eyes widened. "I am so glad you are finally going for a job! I hope it works out."

"As do I," Peter said. "It's not as if the country needs neurologists these days, all things considered."

Monica climbed off the bed and yawned. "I want to make myself a strawberry smoothie, would you like one?"

"No, thank you. It's getting late and my meeting is early in the morning. I need to sleep."

Monica nodded. "All right then, good night," she said and blew him a kiss. She left the room and shut the door behind her. She was right, and she could see it on Peter's face. They were drifting apart. Maybe it was for the best though. Maybe it was time they went their separate ways. Monica wanted Peter to be happy, even if that meant she had to leave both him and Troy.

Lucas Heath

Φ

"Good morning," Peter said as he held out his hand.

"Good morning, Peter. It has been a long while," Thomas said as he gave his friend a handshake and then a hug. They stood in a large office furnished with a desk, multiple bookshelves of old books, couches, chairs, and tables. The carpet was a dark blue, the walls were an eggshell white, and it seemed cozy to Peter.

"How's Mark doing?" Peter asked as they sat on the couches. "Has he run into any hungry wolves lately?"

Thomas shrugged. "I couldn't tell you. I don't talk with him much anymore. He has gone off-track in life and has done his own thing."

"That doesn't sound like the Mark I remember."

"He changed a lot the past several years," Thomas said. "My family disowned him."

"Yikes," Peter mumbled. "I can't imagine Troy doing anything that would cause me to reject him."

"How *is* Troy?" Thomas asked. "I haven't seen him since he was a little kid."

"He's doing great. He's been going through a rebellious stage the past couple of years, which began when his mom died. And then when I married Monica, it got worse."

"Is she a good woman?" Thomas wondered.

Peter nodded. "She is. She tries so hard to fit into our family. However, I realized that, and I'm sure this sounds bad, but I'm not ready for another woman in my life."

"It doesn't matter whether you are ready or not, you already married her," Thomas said with a chuckle.

Erased

"Well, not to get too personal, but she and I haven't ever been," he paused, being careful to choose his words. "Intimate… if you know what I mean. I feel like I would be cheating on Karen. I understand that she died a long while ago, but it wouldn't feel right. Monica is only by my side for moral support, I suppose."

"That's a natural response, but I wouldn't let that trouble you. Perhaps your relationship will change when you get hired for this new project."

"Which is what?"

"I'm waiting for two more guests. They will hold the interview."

There came a knock at the office door.

"Speak of the devils. That should be them." Thomas stood, walked over to the door, and opened it. "Charles, it's good to see you again," he said as he shook his new guest's hand. "And you too sir," he said, shaking a second man's hand. "Come join us. We can have the interview on the couches since they are far more comfortable."

Two men walked into the room; both wore gray suits and blue ties. One of them looked to be in his late thirties, had clean-cut, black hair, and had a clean-shaven face. He seemed sure of himself. The other was an older gentleman in his seventies, had a head full of white hair, and walked with a cane.

Peter stood and approached them. "I am Peter; it's nice to meet you."

"I am Charles Harding, and this is my grandfather, Griffin Powell Harding. It's a pleasure to meet you."

They all shook hands and sat on the sofas across from each other, Peter and Thomas on one, Griffin and Charles on the other.

"So, what is this project Thomas mentioned?" Peter wondered.

Charles looked at Thomas. "Oh, so you didn't tell him yet?"

Thomas shook his head. "I wanted you to have the honor."

Charles smiled and nodded. "Well," he said and cleared his throat. "We, the Midas Technology Company, are looking for a neurologist to work with us on an experiment we will be conducting." He paused, making sure Peter could speak if needed.

"I'm listening," Peter said with a nod. "Please continue."

"This experiment involves," Charles paused and tilted his head upwards, as though he was searching for a thought. "Well, let's just say it involves a lot of things, one of them being memory loss."

"I've worked with patients with memory loss. It can be a catastrophic experience," Peter said.

"Exactly," Griffin chimed in with a mischievous grin. "And that's one reason we want your help. We want to make it less problematic."

"I don't follow," Peter said.

Charles smirked. "Right now, we are in control of a small town known as Lion's Glade."

"I've never heard of it," Peter said.

Charles cleared his throat before continuing. "I don't imagine you would have. It's an old town in the state of Kansas, or what used to be Kansas, that we turned into a prison colony. We have land for miles to work with, and it's surrounded by a sturdy, electrified, twelve-foot fence, so nobody can escape. It's not like there's anywhere to go anyway. There's nothing but desert for many miles beyond the gate. Most of the convicts are there for thefts, assaults, and drug usage, though we have a few imprisoned for manslaughter. We want our scientists to be safe. We don't accept murderers unless it's an accidental killing."

Griffin placed his hand on his grandson's leg to inform him he wanted to speak. "Lion's Glade is the most luxurious, open-aired prison colony in the country. Anyone convicted of a crime who wants to be transferred to Lion's Glade has signed a form allowing us to use them for experimental purposes. That was our only requirement. They get their own homes and jobs; it's a fantastic program. We keep the usage of vehicles to a minimum to prevent anyone from breaking through the fence. There are cameras throughout the town, so we monitor everything."

"Interesting," Peter said as he leaned forward, intent on hearing more.

Charles continued. "About two years ago, we acquired off of an island some technology we've been trying to perfect. It involves manipulating memories and emotions. We can't get it to work, and we expect that someone who understands the human brain may have a better chance of completing this project."

"And you're assuming I would be that *someone* to help you?"

"Exactly!" Charles exclaimed. "Think about it. What would our country be like if we could erase the memories of criminals and the emotions that came with their offenses? We are beginning with what you might call the mild-mannered criminal. In the future, we may be able to transform a serial killer into a model citizen."

"I wouldn't go that far," Peter said with visible hesitation.

"I'm thinking far ahead," Charles explained. "Right now, we need to get this technology working. We want to hand this experiment over to you. You can do what you want with it. You would have free rein. Thomas will be the overseer of the project, and we will provide you with the resources, scientists, and protection you need. We plan on hiring a well-known law enforcer to take over the sheriff's position in Lion's Glade and we're getting a new mayor too. We want to turn this into a realistic town. Will you join us?"

"What about my son?" Peter asked. "Troy is still in high school."

"We have a school building, but there aren't any youth in town other than Thomas' daughter Kelly. None of the convicts had children they wished to bring. Some of them have spouses, but most are single. The school is never used, but we could arrange for a personal tutor like the one Kelly, has."

Thomas nodded. "She learns a lot from her instructor. She does all her work at home."

"Your wife is already thinking about joining us," Griffin informed.

"My wife?" Peter paused for a moment. "You're the one who offered her a job?"

Charles nodded. "We did. Everything will work out splendidly!"

"This seems more like recruitment than an interview," Peter pointed out.

Charles nodded. "Thomas speaks well of you. We know that you're the one to work for us if you accept."

Peter gave a single nod. "I need to contemplate this and talk with Monica."

"Sure," Charles agreed. "We would like an answer within the next few days."

"I can do that."

Everyone stood, shook hands, and said their goodbyes. The Hardings left and Thomas sat alone with Peter.

"So, what are your thoughts?" Thomas asked.

"Do your wife and daughter like it there? They aren't threatened being surrounded by convicts?"

Thomas shook his head. "Not at all," he said. "Most of the convicts are nice people. Many had problems with drugs and others stole food to feed themselves. There are no drugs in Lion's Glade and we offer enough food. I have been able to spend time with some of the best folks you could imagine. They just needed a second chance."

"That's another thing I'm wondering. How *do* you provide food for them?"

Erased

"We have a truck that brings shipments every week." He paused "And we grow our own food… without the domes." Thomas said with a grin.

Peter's mouth dropped open. "Impossible!"

"It's *very* possible," Thomas said. "What Charles didn't tell you, is that Midas Technology is revolutionizing our planet. They have been working with genetically manipulated plants that can grow in actual soil without being infected by the V3 virus. We *don't* need to grow food in domes anymore. We have already grown our own trees, though I will admit they turned out to be rather abnormal. The leaves have the consistency of rubber, and the wood feels petrified, but at least they still act like normal trees, providing the planet with air. The same goes for other plants and flowers."

Peter shook his head. "This is too good to be true! What other experiments are going on there that you aren't telling me about?"

"How about you take the job and move to Lion's Glade to find out?"

Peter nodded. "I need to talk with Monica first, but I believe I've already decided."

Φ

"So, what do you think?" Peter asked Monica after he told her how the interview went. He had left out every detail about Lion's Glade, only telling her they needed a neurologist for important work.

"I think it is wonderful," she said with a far from genuine smile. "Are you going to take it?"

Peter nodded. "I think so. This would work out well! You can take the job they are offering you too, and we can both be doing something we love."

"I suppose."

"So, you think I should take it?" Peter asked.

She nodded. "Yes, Peter. If this would please you, I would say take the job."

A huge smile stretched across Peter's face and he embraced Monica. He pulled back and removed a cell phone from his pocket. "I will call Thomas and let him know."

He left Monica alone in the kitchen and she sighed, trying to contain her emotions. She knew that in a short time, they would separate. Their lives pulled them in two different directions, but perhaps that was best.

THE FACILITY

DAY TEN: CHAPTER FORTY—ONE

"It's after midnight, how much longer are we going to wait?" Troy bellowed as he stood from his seat at the police station. "Yo, cop boy, when is the sheriff going to arrive?" He asked an officer sitting at a desk.

"Sheriff Landon already went home for the night. He's not answering his cell phone."

"Then give me his address and I'll go to his house myself!" Troy snapped.

"Troy, calm down," Kelly begged.

Troy turned and sneered. "Calm down? Are you kidding me? A rogue cop kidnapped my father! How do you expect me to calm down?"

"I can't give out addresses," the man behind the desk said and Troy stomped over to him.

"Then call every off-duty and on-duty police officer you can, and find my father!"

The man rolled his eyes. "Look, kid, you need to calm down or I may have to lock you up until morning."

"And what would you charge me with, oh mighty officer?" Troy mocked.

"Harassment, or a possible danger to yourself and others. I could find several things if I wanted. I'll continue to call the sheriff, but until then, take a chill pill."

Troy turned around and returned to Kelly. He sat and buried his face in his hands. "I want my dad."

"I know you do," Kelly said as she wrapped her arm around him. "I know you do."

Erased

Φ

"Don't expect me to tell you anything." Peter sat tied to a chair in a dim room underneath the hospital. Bonnie and Barns had already played the CD for him, but even with Peter's returned memories, he refused to speak.

"Come on, Peter, don't be stupid. Bonnie and I can end this horrific experiment, for everyone's sakes. But you must tell us where to find the laboratory."

Peter shook his head. "The experiment is already finished. The tower is deactivated and can't be used again."

"And yet nobody has their long-term memories back."

"Perhaps it's better that way," Peter snapped. "Where did you even get the CD to return memories anyway?"

"I got it from the mayor after she listened to it. You may be disappointed to hear that, once her memories returned, Thomas found out and erased them again."

"No," Peter hissed. "That should not have happened!"

"Well, whatever you planned failed. Now, tell me what I want to know."

Peter shook his head. "I've seen what these people have done with the technology. I won't allow you to steal it and use it for your own gain."

"It was mine to begin with!" Barns snapped. "Midas Tech stole from us!"

"Then let me correct myself. I won't allow you to steal *back* a dangerous technology for your own gain. How's that for you?"

"Gah!" Barns yelled in frustration. He turned to Bonnie. "Go get her."

"You think she can help?"

"I don't know, just get her!" he screamed as he pointed toward the door.

Bonnie scrambled out of the room, leaving Barns alone with Peter.

"Nobody will look for you for a while. The sheriff is stranded and I doubt he remembers how to navigate the town by night." Barns shook his head and stared into Peter's eyes. "I will get that information from you, Peter. No matter what."

Φ

Jessica, Charles, and Landon trudged their way down the sidewalk toward the police station. Charles carried the box underneath his arm, holding it tight.

"So much for the only car in town," Jessica spoke for the first time in an hour.

"It only needs a new tire," Charles said with a small laugh.

"Do you see any spare tires anywhere?" she replied and rolled her eyes. "Why in the world did it flatten?"

"It looked deliberate," Landon said.

Charles shrugged. "It may have been. I told you there are people out there who want to stop us from finding the truth."

"Thanks for staying with us," Landon said. "I wouldn't be able to get back in the dark without a map. I also have to admit that it's nice not having to worry about a midnight deadline."

Charles smiled and nodded. "It has been my pleasure."

They took a little longer than expected, but they reached the station. Landon removed his keys and unlocked the front door. Earlier, the officers had decided that after nine at night, the station doors would stay locked until eight in the morning. Now that the midnight resets no longer occurred, the station would be manned around the clock. After everyone stepped inside the station, Landon shut the door behind them, locking it again.

They made their way to the back room, seeing the two teenagers sitting on a bench against a wall. The boy had his head resting on the girl's shoulder and he had his eyes closed; it appeared as though he was sleeping. The girl was awake and smiled when she saw the arriving trio.

"Sheriff, these kids are here to see you," the deputy behind the desk informed.

Kelly shook Troy awake.

He opened his eyes, sat up straight, and yawned.

"It's the sheriff," she informed him.

"Deputy, go find any tools we have in the station and bring them back here. We need to pry open a box."

The man obeyed and left the room.

"What can I do for you two?" Landon asked the teens.

"Sir, I'm Kelly, and this here is Troy. His dad is Peter Benet, who I'm sure you've met."

"Ah, yes I know him."

"Someone abducted him," Troy blurted. "I need your help to find him."

The deputy reentered the room with a case of tools and set them on a desk. "I tried calling you sir, but you didn't respond."

Charles grabbed pliers out of the bag and worked on the hinges of the box.

Landon nodded. "I forgot my cell phone here at the station. I apologize. What's the situation?"

"According to these kids, officer Barns subdued the scientists and abducted Peter. I sent Paul and Riley to help take them to the hospital and get their statements."

"Please find my dad," Troy said. "He's the only parent I have left. My mom died of cancer a few years ago."

"She did?" Kelly asked. Her mouth hung open and her eyes grew wide. "How do you remember that?"

Troy stared at her with a confused look on his face. "What do you mean?"

"Your memories... are they returning?" she asked.

"Maybe," he whispered. "I need to make sure my dad is okay."

"Got it!" Charles screamed in excitement. He removed the box lid.

"What was the point of even putting a lock on it if it was that easy to get into?" the mayor wondered.

There were two objects in the box, a square card and a piece of paper. Charles unfolded the paper and read.

"We also found something interesting." Kelly removed the strange leaves from her pockets and held them out for Landon.

He took and studied each one. "What on earth..." he muttered.

"These are leaves from the forest to the north. The plant life is phony; all of it."

"*All* the trees?" Landon asked.

Erased

"I'm sure we checked at least a hundred different plants, and they're all the same. I may not remember ever touching plant life, but this doesn't feel right to me," Kelly interjected.

"This is interesting," Charles said as he looked up from the paper.

"What did you find?" Jessica asked as she pulled a roller chair from underneath a desk and sat.

"Let me read this letter to you."

"My name is Griffin Powel Harding. If you found this box and letter, then I may be correct in assuming I didn't make it through the first reset. Or maybe I am the one reading this without my memory. Either way, it makes no difference, as long as somebody knows the truth. I am the one at fault for everything that has happened in Lion's Glade.

"Back when I first received this technology, I thought of so many uses that would benefit our country, especially for rebuilding it. It could be a powerful tool, or a powerful weapon. Either way, it was useful. My son Jacob did not share my enthusiasm to use this technology to help our nation, at least, not for the sake of the people. He wanted to experiment with it and gain power for the company.

"I humored him for a while, until I realized the extent of his psychosis. I don't understand how it came to this; Jacob was such a nice kid. I adopted him when he was fifteen and I was thirty. I mentored him, cared for him, and I was a loving father. Sure, he got in trouble every once in a while, and had a baby by the time he was eighteen, but that didn't matter to me. I'm glad his son didn't end up like him.

"Two years ago, Jacob went on a rampage and tried killing his own son for disagreeing with him over the direction of the company. I had Jacob locked up in a mental institution to get the help he needed, and took my grandson Charles under my wing, promoting him to his father's position. He and I worked well together. The peace didn't last; six months ago, Jacob returned with a group of scientists and soldiers he had gathered to take over the project. He banished me and Charles to Lion's

Glade where we would become part of the experiment. The original scientists and staff were stuck and forced to continue working. I hope they are safe.

"I have little time left, for the testing is about to begin. Jacob has twisted everything and ruined what I built. Please, whoever is reading this, even if it's me, stop Jacob. Stop the experiment.

"Inside this box is a keycard, which will allow you access to the facility in the woods up north. That is where the head of operations is, and the technology that makes this experiment possible. I'm sure it's heavily guarded, and it's surrounded by an electric fence, though the card will open the gate. Remember to thank Peter Benet for providing me with this key. He has been an abundance of help.

"I have told Peter and Charles about the hiding place beneath my workbench, so perhaps if Peter succeeds in his plan to have his memory returned by his wife, he will come find the box. If you are reading this, Peter, thank you. I need to stop writing now. The experiment will begin in just a few minutes. I wish the reader of this letter good luck, and God speed. Griffin Powel Harding."

Silence filled the room.

"So this Jacob Harding guy is your father?" Landon asked.

"This reminds me of that movie with the light side and dark side, and the good guy had to kill his father who was a bad guy," Troy said.

"Troy, we never watched a movie like that," Kelly said. "Your memories are returning. They have to be!"

"So what do we do now?" Jessica asked.

"We need to figure out what happened to *my* father," Troy reminded.

"It's possible the people running the experiment have your father, Troy," Charles said. "Perhaps they want to use him for something more sinister."

Erased

"It's the best lead we have," Landon said.

"So back to my question, what should we do now?" Jessica asked again.

Charles lifted the keycard out of the box and let it dangle in the air off the metal chain attached to it. "We head to the forest."

DAY TEN: CHAPTER FORTY—TWO

Shock registered on Peter's face the instant Elizabeth stepped into the room. He didn't speak as he studied every detail of her face, trying to decide if he was hallucinating.

"Hello, Peter. It's good to see you again," Elizabeth said with a sincere smile.

"But you're dead."

"Obviously not," she replied. "Look, Peter, you need to help Barns and Bonnie. *Please*. It's important that they end this experiment once and for all. They can stop Jacob and take the technology far away from here. They can finish everything!"

"I can't do that," Peter said with a groan.

"Why not? What's your reasoning?"

"I can't let these people have technology this dangerous."

"So you would rather Jacob holds onto it?" Elizabeth countered.

Peter shook his head. "No. If I escape from here, I will destroy It all."

"It shouldn't be destroyed, Peter. You of all people know how much *good* potential it has."

"I also see the *bad* potential. I can't take that risk. Imagine if someone used this technology to erase and edit the memories of every person on the planet! They could make anyone their slave, and if they learned how to eliminate emotions along with memories, people would be nothing more than drones."

"So you won't help us?"

Peter shook his head. "No, I won't."

Elizabeth sighed. She turned around and poked her head out the door. "He won't tell us."

Barns reentered the room and shook his head. "Then we will have to take more drastic measures. Call Bonnie and tell her it's a go to get Peter's son."

"Do we have to resort to that? Troy is a boy."

Barns nodded. "Yes, call her."

Peter growled with frustration and attempted to pull away from his restraints. "Don't you dare touch my son!" he screamed.

"Don't worry, *she* won't be touching him; the bullet will though," Barns said. "All you have to do is give me the information to prevent that from happening. I'm *not* a murderer. I'm trying to get back what belongs to my father. If Troy dies, then that's on *your* head as a father by not protecting him. You can save him by telling us where to find the facility!"

Peter cried out one final time before becoming silent. He stared toward the ground and shook his head. "Fine," he spat. "I'll tell you."

"Good! See, was that so hard? Now, where is it? Could it be underground or outside of the fence?"

Peter shook his head. "It's in the forest to the north."

"That's excellent," Barns said and gave an approving nod. "I suspected that for a while, but never had the time to search. I'm sure there's security. What do I have to contend with, Peter?"

"An electric fence, armed guards, and you need a keycard."

Barns nodded. "I'm sure, but I also know you and Thomas are close. If I use you as a hostage, he would *have* to let me pass, but we will worry about that in the morning. I hope you sleep well in that chair. You will need it." He left the room leaving Elizabeth alone with Peter once again.

"Why do you work with Barns? Didn't you see what he planned to do to Troy?"

Elizabeth shook her head. "I won't deny that he makes mistakes, but it's for the right reason. We will be back to get you in several hours." She left and shut the door, leaving Peter alone in the small room.

Φ

"So, when are we going to go get my dad?" Troy asked as Landon, Charles, Jessica, and two other officers stepped out of the meeting room.

"Tomorrow morning," Landon said. "That way we can sleep tonight and be rested. Once the other officers arrive for the day shift, we can use their help. We need all the man power we can get."

"But my dad's in danger *now*!"

"And we will be too if we can't see where we're going," Charles stated. "It's the best choice."

"Then I'm going without you guys," Troy informed as he turned to leave the building.

Landon grabbed Troy, pulled his hands together, and handcuffed him before the boy knew what had happened.

"What do you think you're doing?" Troy yelled as he tried to twist away.

"Troy, stop it," Kelly said as she ran over to him. "You can't go without these guys. You might be killed!"

With the help of two other officers, Landon forced Troy into one of the jail cells. He shut the gate and locked it, and tossed the handcuff key to the teen. "You can take the handcuffs off, but you're not leaving that cell until morning."

"This isn't fair! He's my dad!" Troy screamed and then began to cry.

Erased

Landon sighed and placed the cell key into his pocket. He walked out of the room with the other officers.

"It will be all right," Kelly tried comforting. "They won't kill your dad. He's the smartest man I know."

Ignoring the handcuff key, Troy crumpled to the floor from exhaustion. Within a few minutes, he cried himself to sleep.

Kelly lay down on the floor and stuck her arm through the bars. She took Troy's cuffed hands into hers and fell asleep too.

Φ

Landon sighed and ran a hand through his hair. "Where's Jessica?" He asked Charles, who sat on the floor, leaning against a wall.

"She went home for the night, but promised to be back by eight."

Landon nodded. "I was thinking about doing that, but I'll take one of the emergency bedrolls and sleep in my office. What about you?"

"I've been sleeping in dark and gloomy basements all week. Taking the floor here would be fine."

"There are several bedrolls. You could always sleep in one of the conference rooms, or a cell where there's a cot."

Charles nodded and smiled. "I would like that."

Landon looked toward the door that led to the cells. "I'm not sure Troy should come with us tomorrow."

Charles nodded in agreement. "He shouldn't. If his dad *is* there, then that could be a horrific combination."

"Yet leaving him in the cell may also have a terrible outcome."

Charles stood. "Sleep on it. Rest up and decide in the morning when your mind is clear."

Landon nodded. "Sounds like a plan."

Charles smiled. "Good, now let's go get those bed rolls."

Φ

Peter spent most of the night in thought, for sleep eluded him. Elizabeth came into the room twice to give him a drink of water. Tape bound his wrists and legs to a chair, preventing him from moving. The image of Troy taped to the chair the day Mohammed kidnapped him entered Peter's mind. He now realized that, during that time, he may have felt fear, but he hadn't felt the pure terror that reemerged now.

He shook his head and closed his eyes. "So they got the full experiment and technology working after all. They can alter emotions," he exhaled. Peter drifted off to sleep; it was a restless one.

Φ

"Thomas, if you are calling me at this hour, then I have to assume you have good news for me?" Jacob Harding asked as his tired, graveled voice seeped through the phone speaker.

"Sir, I'm sorry to say I have the opposite to report. Peter's implant is offline, and his son's implant is breaking. It is possible they will both have their memories again soon."

There was a sigh on the other end of the phone. "There will be a team arriving later in the morning to remove the technology from your facility. The experiment is over. Disassemble *everything*. We are done."

"We are abandoning the colony? What about returning the citizens' memories?"

Jacob Harding scoffed. "Those convicts don't need their memories returned. Just let them live their new lives. Let them gain new memories. Perhaps old ones will surface over time, but we won't be responsible for that."

Erased

Thomas bit his lip hard enough to make it bleed. "All right, sir. I will make sure everything is ready to move by late morning," he said, though there was a grimace of disgust on his face.

"Good, then that's settled. I will send a transport vehicle to take you, the team of technicians, and the guards away from Lion's Glade."

"What about Peter and his group? What about my daughter?"

"Peter and his scientists may be of further use to us. I will expect them to join you. Your daughter can go with you if you wish."

"Is there anybody else you would like to join us, like your son perhaps?"

"No," Harding replied. "That's it. Have a good night, Thomas."

Thomas hung up the phone, and after putting it into his pocket, rubbed his eyes. Harding had ended the experiment. Perhaps after they packed everything and left Lion's Glade, he could get much-needed rest.

Φ

Jessica Dailey tossed and turned as she attempted to sleep. Something nagged at her. Before the group had left for the tower, she had kissed Peter. They had spent no time together the past week, so why were the feelings so strong? Nothing could have developed in that amount of time, right? Before the experiment, she had known him and loved him, though she wasn't sure how she knew.

She kicked the covers away in agitation, sat up, grabbed the covers now at her feet, and pulled them back over her body. "What is going on?" she cried out. She fell backward, her head landing in the center of the fluffy pillow. She took a deep breath and exhaled, a technique she had learned a long time ago to help relax the muscles.

Wait... a long time ago? Her eyes fluttered open. She learned the technique from a doctor in New York though she couldn't remember his name. She remembered seeing the ruins of the Statue of Liberty on her trip. It was a sight that should have affected her, but it didn't. While others mourned, she went on with her day.

She closed her eyes again. "Monica," she heard somebody call out, though it came from a memory. She stood in front of a broken stone monument of a man on a chair. He had been a president around the birth of the country. She turned to face the man who called her name. Peter! She rushed to hug him, then kissed him on the lips. He hugged her back, and she jerked up in bed, letting the image disappear. She kicked the bedding away again and stood. She ignored the blood rushing to her head and made her way to the bathroom.

Without turning on the light, she found the sink and splashed water over her face. She closed her eyes as the cool liquid made contact and she saw herself in an apartment with Peter and Troy. She turned off the water faucet, dried her face with a towel, and reentered her room. An overwhelming feeling flooded her body, and before she understood what was happening, she collapsed to the floor. Everything faded away, and then she was unconscious.

DAY TEN: CHAPTER FORTY—THREE

"Rise and shine, Peter," Barns called out as he stepped into the room.

Peter straightened his posture and a devious smile stretched across his face. "Good morning, Dale. I have a deal for you."

Dale Barns narrowed his eyes at Peter and folded his arms. "You're not in a place to be making deals."

Peter nodded. "That's true, but I trust you'll want to hear what I have to say."

"All right, shoot."

"You weren't planning on killing my son, were you? It was all a ploy."

"How do you figure that?" Barns asked.

"Troy is an innocent kid. Bonnie wouldn't dare kill him. She may have killed a drug addict, child abuser, and thief like Kyle, but she wouldn't kill Troy."

"What's your point?"

"I know you were bluffing."

"So I may have been bluffing," Barns admitted. "Perhaps Bonnie hadn't even left the other room when I told Elizabeth to call her. It doesn't matter anymore. You gave me the information I need and I have you."

"Exactly! You *do* have me. This whole time, I was thinking about keeping this technology out of the hands of others, and I hadn't even considered what *I* could do with it if I had more time. You will need experts to help you out."

"My company already has engineers and scientists."

"But you don't have someone who has worked with *this* technology. We would save you years of pointless experimenting. Think of how much data we recorded during this experiment alone!"

The glare of suspicion on Barns' face was clear. "So then, what do you propose?"

"I want to join your team. I can get the other scientists on board with me; even Thomas. We never wanted to work under Jacob, but he forced us with threats of death. They trapped us in our own experiment!"

"How do I know you aren't planning on destroying the technology?"

Peter shook his head. "I thought about this last night and I concluded that whether I destroy the technology or not, if I run, Midas will come after me. But if I had an ally to protect me, I would rather work for them."

Barns licked his lips and nodded. "It's a fair explanation, I'll give you that."

"I have a son I want protected and Thomas has his daughter. Maybe it's time we jump ship and join you."

Barns nodded. "I must think about that. For now, let's get ready to move out. When the time comes, I'll let you know."

"You must decide before we get to the facility."

Barns smiled and nodded once more. "Trust me. I will."

Φ

"We deactivated the technology and will load it up once the truck gets here," a young tech informed Thomas as he passed.

A guard dressed in a white uniform motioned for Thomas to stop. "Sir, what do you want to do about the other scientists and Peter?"

Erased

"One of our watchmen has reported that Peter's scientists are back at the tower. Send a small team of men to take them. As for Peter, he seems to have disappeared. I have people searching for him."

The guard nodded and hurried down the white halls to round up more men and start on his task.

Nobody needed Thomas at the moment so he made a trip to see Mark. He let the machine scan his fingerprints and entered the room when the door slid open.

Mark looked up from a new book in his hands. "Thomas, back so soon?" he joked.

"We are moving you to a new facility."

"Why is that? Did you tire of keeping me here?"

"I'm going with you. Kelly will join us once my people find her."

"You need somebody to find her? Is she lost?"

"I think you'll enjoy the new place. It's on the east coast."

"I've always wanted to visit the east, but never got my passport."

"Well, now you get to visit." Thomas turned back toward the open door. "I'll be back once we are ready." He left the room and closed the door behind him. Jacob Harding never said Thomas could bring his brother, but then again, he didn't know his brother was there. If Thomas could help it, Harding would never know.

Φ

"Landon, it's after eight and the mayor still isn't here." Charles fidgeted. "What if they got her?"

"She may have overslept," Landon suggested. "In all honesty, the mayor shouldn't come with us. It's too dangerous. We should go without her."

"Are you sure?"

"You can stay here and wait for her if you wish." Landon turned to the others.

"No, I'll go with you."

"All right, men, you know what to expect. This could be the day we get our memories back. Be on guard and be careful. We know that this facility is somewhere in the forest though we aren't sure where. We will split into two groups to cover more ground."

"What about Troy?" Kelly asked as she joined.

"You and Troy will stay here. I don't want you two hurt. This is a dangerous situation."

"I understand and respect that, but Peter is Troy's father. He should be a part of this. Troy is eighteen, not a minor."

"He's not going and my decision is final." Landon turned to the others and divided them into two groups.

"Troy will not like this," Kelly said to Charles.

"He doesn't have much of a choice; he's in jail." Charles left Kelly and joined his assigned group.

Landon smiled as he watched the groups form. "Let's go folks; we have a facility to find!"

The groups departed, leaving Kelly with Bobby the dispatcher. He sat at his desk reading a book, waiting for any phone calls.

Kelly walked to the jail room and found Troy doing sit-ups. "Um, Troy, what are you doing?"

Troy sat up, moved into a position where his knees were on the floor, placed his hands at shoulder width, and stretched out his legs so his toes and hands were touching the ground. He began a set of pushups. "Isn't this

Erased

what prisoners do?" Troy asked with a snarl. "They workout to get stronger so they can take on the outside world when they escape."

"Don't get mad at *me*. I didn't put you in here."

Troy pushed himself into a seated position. "You also haven't tried helping me get out either."

"Troy, it's for your own good. Please don't hate me. I agree with the sheriff. You wouldn't be safe if you went with the group."

"You know who else *isn't* safe? My father!"

Kelly grabbed onto the bars of his cell, pressed her head against them, and sighed. She heard the door behind her open and she turned to see Jessica Dailey enter the room. "Hello, mayor."

Troy jumped to his feet.

"Troy, we have to get you out of here and find Peter," Jessica said.

"Good luck with that. The sheriff has the key," Kelly informed.

Jessica nodded. "I figured. Kelly, back away to the other side of the room. Troy, get on your stomach and cover your head with your arms."

"Why?" Troy asked.

The mayor produced a gun from her purse and pointed it at the lock on the cell door.

Both teens did as Jessica told them.

"I do not know if this will work, but there is no harm in trying, as long as nobody gets hurt." She took a step back and fired the gun twice into the metal lock. Sparks flew, and the door opened. Wires hung out of the holes the bullets had made. Jessica stepped into the cell, and once Troy was standing again, she embraced him into a hug. "I have missed you," she said and kissed him on the forehead.

"Whoa, what in the world?" he stammered.

"I know you do not remember now, but I am your stepmom. My memory has returned. Your dad and I got married almost two years ago. We can talk about that later, but we need to get going!" She turned around and rushed out of the room to explain to the dispatcher why he heard gunshots.

"That's your stepmom?" Kelly asked with a grin.

"I guess?" Troy wasn't sure what to say.

"She's so cool! She broke you out of jail!"

Troy laughed. "I suppose so. Come on, let's go find my father."

Φ

Peter, Dale, and Bonnie made their way through the forest, down tiny, secluded paths.

"This forest is bigger than I thought. I've never been out here," Barns commented.

"They grew this forest to hide their facility from prying eyes. They grew other trees and plants in the park though none of the convicts ever seemed to go there."

"I don't blame them. The grass doesn't even feel real."

"It doesn't matter how strange or rubbery plants feel, at least we have them, right?"

Barns nodded in agreement. "Does Midas Tech plan on growing these trees anywhere else?"

Peter shrugged. "I don't know. Griffin Harding wanted to, but once his son took over, everything changed."

Erased

"I would love to get the formula for this, for my company," Barns said in awe.

"If you let me join, I'm sure I could get that information for you." Peter winked at him. "Have you made your decision yet?"

Barns shook his head. "Not yet, no.

Peter couldn't point, for tape bound his hands behind his back. "Well, you better decide now. The facility is up ahead."

DAY TEN: CHAPTER FORTY—FOUR

The building looked much bigger than what Barns or Bonnie expected. It stood three-stories tall, and they weren't sure how long or wide it was. It seemed to extend for quite a distance.

"Just because the cameras in town shut down when we deactivated the tower, that doesn't mean the cameras on this building aren't working. Before we approach any further, I need your guarantee that your company will keep my family and Thomas' family safe." A low roar of a vehicle could be heard in the distance. Peter stopped walking and peered around a tree. He could see a large semi-truck driving toward the facility on the hidden dirt road he had ridden on many times himself.

"Including the scientists?" Barns asked.

Peter nodded. "Including my scientists, Tucker, Albert, and Zane; and I already know you have Elizabeth covered. The other scientists are Jacob Harding's people." He watched the truck disappear into the facility and then turned to Barns, waiting for an answer.

Barns nodded. "Elizabeth wants to stay in Lion's Glade and won't come with us. But yes, you have my word that my father and I will take care of you, as long as you work for us and let us have the technology."

Peter smiled and nodded. "You heard him, right Bonnie?"

"I did."

"That's all I needed to know." Without warning, Peter ran for the electric fence surrounding the building. "Help!" he screamed.

"Stop him!" Bonnie yelled at Barns.

Barns charged after Peter.

Erased

"Someone help me! These freaks are after me!" The closer he got to the fence, the more he understood there was no other choice.

Two guards dressed in white aimed large hunting rifles at the men running toward them.

Peter couldn't wave his hands, but it didn't matter. He knew the men wouldn't shoot. He dove to the ground a few feet away from the fence. One man aimed the gun at Peter while the other aimed his at Barns.

"Don't move," he commanded Barns.

The ex-police officer froze, his hands raised high. "Don't shoot," he begged and fell to his knees.

Peter turned his head toward the cowering man and smiled. He turned back to the guards. "My name is Peter Benet. Get Thomas out here, now!"

Φ

"So you're Troy's stepmom?" Kelly asked as they made their way to the forest.

"My name is Monica Benet. Jessica Dailey was the name these people gave me for their experiment."

"Well then, Monica. Tell me; what was Troy like before he moved to Lion's Glade?"

Troy turned to Kelly with a confused expression on his face.

"I'm curious. I don't remember what you were like when you moved here, so I figured that if somebody does, why not ask?"

Monica laughed. "Well, he loved studying science and math. He was quite the inventor, knew how to fix anything that broke, and he hated doing the dishes."

"I didn't hate doing the dishes," Troy responded. "I hated that you asked me to do the dishes."

Kelly and Monica stopped walking. "You remember?" Kelly asked.

Troy nodded. "Not everything, but more and more memories keep coming back."

"I wonder why I still don't remember anything," Kelly said.

"Perhaps the effect of the tower wears off at different intervals for different people," Troy suggested.

"Troy, what do you mean by what you said? You hated that I asked you to do the dishes?"

Troy nodded. "My mom always asked me to do the dishes. I hated that you kept trying to take her place. If you took her place, then she would be gone for good. Moving to Lion's Glade allowed me to deal with the pain. Kelly helped with that."

Monica took a step toward Troy and embraced him in a hug. "Troy, I am sorry. I was trying to be there for you."

"I didn't need it then," Troy pulled away and looked her in the eyes. "But I *do* need it now. Thank you. Now, let's go find dad."

Φ

Peter and Barns stood before Thomas in his office, with two guards in white standing behind them. Tape still bound Peter's hands and handcuffs embraced Barn's wrists.

Thomas smiled. "Peter, it's good to see you. Thanks again for saving my brother; I don't know if that's a debt I can ever repay."

"Maybe you can," Peter said. "I want to return to experimenting and designing. This lunatic kidnapped me," he motioned to Barns, "and wanted to use me as leverage to get in and destroy the technology."

"Is that true?" Thomas asked Barns as he turned his cold gray eyes in his direction.

Erased

Barns remained silent.

"Sir," a man entered through the door behind the captives. "Peter's scientists have arrived. We also found the wife of Simon Orson attempting to leave the forest. What should we do with her?"

"Lock her up," Thomas ordered. "Take this man with you too. He's of no use." He waved at Barns and the man behind him pulled him toward the door.

"Screw you, Peter!" Barns screamed. "I'll find and kill you!"

Two guards hauled him from the room.

"You can free Peter's wrists and leave us be," Thomas told the other guard.

The guard obeyed and used a knife to cut the tape and give Peter his hands back. "You're sure I shouldn't stay?" the guard asked.

"Peter is harmless. Leave us be."

The man nodded and left the room, shutting the door behind him.

"Now, Peter. Tell me what's been going on out there."

"No," Peter said. "You tell *me* something. Do you want to leave this company and take Kelly to safety?"

Thomas stared at Peter without a response.

"I want an honest answer. Do you want to get out of here?"

Thomas nodded and pointed at the lamp on his desk. "Peter, I obvious don't, or I would have left a long time ago. I like it here. You should be careful what you say or they may get rid of you." Thomas mouthed the words *they listen* and pointed at the lamp again.

Peter nodded, understanding.

"Good. I was hoping you would say that because I wish to be wherever you are. We wouldn't want to separate Troy and Kelly."

Thomas handed Peter a piece of paper and pen and then spoke as Peter wrote. Once Peter spoke, Thomas read the words and replied. This process continued until Thomas understood the plan.

"Well then," Peter said. "If you can get someone to bring Troy and Kelly here, that would be great."

"They are already on their way. My watchmen in Lion's Glade have reported that a group of police officers are coming for us. Your son and my daughter are behind them a short distance, accompanied by Monica."

Peter's eyes grew wide. "How do they know where we are?"

Thomas shrugged. "I don't have a clue. After you disabled the tower, our cameras went offline."

"But you're sure they are coming *here?*"

Thomas nodded. "They should be here within the hour."

Peter pressed his lips together and bobbed his head up and down in thought. "I never looked at the dossier of every citizen in town. How many of the police are convicted criminals?"

Thomas chuckled a little. "All but two of them are convicted felons. Other than Barns, Simon Orson was the one we hired from the outside, to keep everybody in line and to train them."

"That may work to our advantage."

"How so?" Thomas asked as his right eyebrow rose.

"I think it's time you told them who they are."

Φ

Erased

"What do you think will happen once we get there?" Kelly wondered as they made their way through the forest.

"We don't even know where *there* is. It could be anywhere in this forest," Troy said.

"Do you have any memories of coming out here with your dad?" Monica asked Troy.

He shook his head. "I've never been to the facility. I was always at home working on school work, or with Kelly."

Monica sighed and looked around for any signs they could be near a structure of sorts. "I never came out here either. When I met with Thomas, it was in an office in town."

The snapping of twigs behind the trio caused them to turn toward the sound. Five men dressed in white pants and shirts stood in a line, each one holding a hunting rifle.

"Did these guys escape from a mental institution or something?" Kelly asked as she stared at the weapons pointed at her.

"You will come with us," one of the men spoke. "Thomas and Peter are waiting for you."

"Who is Thomas?" Kelly asked.

"He's your dad," Troy whispered.

As if those words set off a chain reaction of chemicals, Kelly saw multiple images of a man with silver eyes flash through her brain. "Daddy," she whispered without letting the others hear.

"Let's go, Kel, I'm sure Thomas and my father will give us all the answers we want."

"Well," Monica said as they walked in the direction the men herded them. "This is about to get interesting."

DAY TEN: CHAPTER FORTY—FIVE

"How hard could it be to find a facility in a forest?" Landon asked and groaned in frustration.

"Harder than expected, considering we haven't found it yet," Charles replied.

Officers Myles and Alison accompanied Landon and Charles, forming group one out of two. The second group searched in the opposite direction. They had radios, so if one group found something, the other could hear about it and join them.

They continued to search, looking left and right, making sure they wouldn't miss anything.

After a short while, Charles pointed. "I see something!" He ran forward.

"Charles, hold up!" Landon called.

The older man stopped and nodded. "It's a building." They could see a chain link, barbwire fence in the distance.

"So, how do we get in without being seen? We have the keycard, but now what?"

"This facility is huge. I expect they will have both a back and front entrance. I'm thinking that perhaps we send your officers to the front, and while they cause a commotion, you and I slip in the back."

Landon shook his head. "Two of us alone would be a bad idea."

"No it wouldn't. It would be the best idea. We have no hope of getting through the front with all the guards. We need to go in the back and find the technology. Perhaps if we can steal it, I can figure out how to use it and restore everybody's memories."

Erased

Landon sighed and closed his eyes. He rubbed the bridge of his nose. "The others will be in danger though."

"They are police," Charles reminded. "They knew what they were getting into when they took the job. I'm not saying they need to fire their weapons, but we need a distraction big enough to lure the guards away from the back."

"We can do it, sir," Myles said. "We can create that distraction."

"Fine," Landon said. "Radio the other group. Once they join us, we'll figure out what to do."

Φ

"Dad!" Troy yelled when he entered Thomas' office. He ran over to Peter and embraced him. "I'm remembering everything!"

Thomas' attention turned to the young woman standing by the door. She wore a light blue skirt, white shirt, and gray hiking shoes that seemed out of place. "Hello, Kel Bell."

"You're Thomas, my father," she stated.

He nodded. "Peter, we have to get Kelly her memory back."

Peter ended the hug with Troy and shrugged. "You of all people should know that with all the technology being disassembled, that's not possible right now. Unless you can get the CD from Barns."

"What CD?" Thomas asked as his brows furrowed.

"Barns has a CD he found that restores people's memories. That's how he gave Bonnie Orson her memories back."

"Dad, Monica is waiting outside," Troy informed as he touched Peter's arm. "She isn't sure you want to see her."

Peter walked over to the lamp on Thomas' desk, unplugged it from the wall, and grabbed the base.

"What are you doing?" Thomas asked.

"I'm helping you pack your office. We are leaving soon, aren't we?" He winked and walked out of the room and into a hallway littered with boxes. He placed the lamp inside an empty box and saw Monica leaning against the wall a short distance away. "Monica, come here, please." He turned and walked back into the office.

Monica joined the group and Peter shut the door.

"We don't have a lot of time, and I can only answer some of your questions," Peter said. He turned to Thomas. "I'll be honest; I doubt we'll have time to get the CD from Barns. We need to move fast before they suspect anything. I don't know if Kelly's memories will return like Troy's and Monica's."

"How did their memories return and mine haven't?" Kelly asked.

Peter shrugged. "I don't know. Perhaps their brains broke through the mental barrier. This technology isn't foolproof. The effect *should* last forever, but it may not for some people. Once we join Barn's people, we can see about using the technology to restore her brain synapses to normal."

"Kelly needs her memories back *now*," Thomas informed.

She shook her head. "No, dad, I don't. At least not at the moment. If I have to wait for them to return, then that's fine."

"But what if they don't return?" Troy asked her. "We've had awesome times together."

"I already have images of returning memories, so I'm not worried. And even if my memories didn't come back, we will make more until your dad can use the technology to return them," Kelly said. She turned to Peter and Thomas. "Tell us what's happening."

Thomas began. "A few years ago we acquired powerful technology we tried to understand. It was too complex to use, but we knew it could

Erased

alter a person's brain chemistry and affect memories. It wasn't until Peter studied it that he found out the full potential of what it could do."

"What *does* it do?" Troy asked.

"It can manipulate core parts of your mind, such as memories, emotions, skills, and instincts," Peter explained.

Thomas continued. "From the perspective of everyone in town, the only thing we messed with is their memories. However, we did so much more experimenting than that. For example, Troy, remember back on day one when Ahmed Mohammed chased you from home?"

Troy nodded. "I'm assuming he's the Arab who kidnapped me."

"Yes," Thomas confirmed. "Remember how you jumped over that fence when you were running away? I'm sure it felt natural to your muscles. We gave you that skill. Not at that exact moment, but we programmed it into you while you slept that night. The next evening it was something different, and the evening after that, something else. You may not have used all of them, but we kept trying new things on you, and to the rest of the citizens."

Monica interrupted. "How can there be a technology *so* advanced with the ability to manipulate someone like that? It does not seem possible."

"Didn't any of you find it odd that the murder and suicide rate was so low during such a catastrophic experience? We were dealing with a town full of convicts. We needed to make sure they wouldn't kill each other."

"Yet people *did* kill out of fear," Monica stated. "Like the woman on day one who shot her husband in front of my home – well, Jessica's home!"

"You're right," Thomas said and nodded. "We had to make constant adjustments to different citizens. We tried taking away fear and anxiety from the situation. There was trial and error, but after a couple days, the citizens woke up and responded the way we wished they would; complacent, at least to some degree."

"You turned them into robots," Kelly said.

Thomas shook his head. "I wouldn't say that. We made them numb to the situation, but they could still feel happiness and joy, at least until Harding wanted that changed too."

"Which I knew he would," Peter added.

"So what was the purpose of this experiment in the first place? What were you trying to prove?" Monica asked as she folded her arms.

"The original orchestrator, Griffin Powel, wanted to use this technology for several reasons. One was to learn how to target memories and block them from a person's mind. That way we could erase phobias and help people. There's a problem with that logic. Even though you may not have a memory of a traumatizing event, you could still have the subconscious effects."

Troy's eyes grew wide. "Like the example in the book on your desk! If as a child you almost drown, you may not have retained that memory when you become an adult, but whenever you see a body of water, you may freak out."

Peter nodded. "That's why people have such odd quirks, phobias, and issues, because something happened to them, or they developed them at an impressionable time of their life and don't remember. The unique thing about *this* technology is that it can eliminate the emotions along with the memory. Not only could we remove emotions, we learned that we could add them, just like we could add skills. If we could add more positive emotions and skills to people, we could rebuild this country at a faster pace."

"Who created the technology?" Troy asked. "Is it from outer space or something? Maybe a time traveler brought it from the future?"

Peter laughed. "We don't know who designed it, per say, but I highly doubt it's alien in origin."

Erased

"I'm curious about something," Kelly said as she raised her hand. "If you could manipulate people's emotions and remove them, then what happened with the Arab who kidnapped Troy and me? He kept claiming Peter was the reason his wife killed herself."

Troy turned to her, a big smile on his face. "That happened a few days ago. Now *you* are remembering!"

Thomas nodded and sighed. "Something about his implant went haywire. We couldn't figure out what it was until it was too late and we could only reset his mind every night at midnight with everyone else. Removing his emotions did not work."

"We need to get going now," Peter said.

"No, I have one more question," Monica said. "What is an implant, and how did the tower play into this whole thing?"

There was a knock on the door and a guard dressed in white entered. "Sir, there's a group of Lion's Glade police storming the front of the building."

"Here we go," Thomas said and smiled at Peter. "You know what to do."

Peter nodded. "I'll answer Monica's question. You go deal with the cops."

Thomas left the room and followed the guard, shutting the door behind him.

"In a nut shell, the implants are miniscule devices connected to the brainstem. It allows us to transmit wireless data to the brain of someone who has one and monitor the brain activity. Every night, the reset instructions came from this building, where the machine is located."

"Then how could deactivating the tower stop our memories from resetting?"

Lucas Heath

Peter grinned at Monica's question. "When we first experimented with the technology, it was useless and we couldn't get it working. Through research and study, I realized that our brains have a natural barrier to protect us from any intrusion, which is why hypnosis can only go so far. Somebody who's hypnotized can't be forced to do something that would go against their morals. For the technology to work, I had to put everyone into a special form of hypnotic sleep that let down the barriers in the mind. It was only then that the reprogramming could begin."

"So without the tower and hypnotic sleep, the technology is useless." Troy understood.

"I'm glad you understand, but we *need* to go. I will take you all to the truck that will get you away from Lion's Glade." Peter opened the door and walked down the hall. He turned back to make sure the others were following.

After traveling down several corridors, they arrived at a door that led into a loading dock. A camouflaged truck with a green canopy sat in front of a rollup door. Troy could see people already under the canopy.

"Get in," Peter instructed.

"Where will this take us?" Troy asked.

"Away from here," Peter answered. "Now go. I'll be back to join you."

Troy turned to Kelly and took her hand in his.

"What about all our stuff at home?" Kelly asked.

"Who cares," Troy said. "The only one worth anything is holding my hand."

Kelly blushed, and they made their way toward the truck.

"They are cute together," Monica said with a smile as she watched them. She turned to Peter. "I have to ask. What about us?"

Erased

Peter pulled Monica into a hug. "I can't explain everything that's about to happen, but trust me. I've had a lot to think about over the past year, and I want us to be a family again. A *real* family though."

"But when I first got here, you said…"

"I know what I said, and I was a jerk for saying it, but I didn't mean it. I'm sorry, and I hope you will forgive me."

She nodded. "Yes, I can forgive you."

"But *will* you?"

She smiled and nodded. "Yes, I will forgive you. I want to come home."

"Good," Peter said with a nod and pulled away. "I need to finish what I started." The look of confusion on her face made him laugh. He leaned forward and whispered into her ear. "I'm going to break someone out of jail."

DAY TEN: CHAPTER FORTY—SIX

"Your men must be causing a stir. Those guards left their posts fast," Charles said as they made their way toward the back gate of the building. They approached it with caution and Charles held the card over the scanner. The gate slid open, unblocking their path. "Don't touch the fence. I can hear that it's still electrified. I'm assuming the gate is on a timer and should shut in a moment."

They made their way into the compound and, not seeing any guards, approached a door to the inside of the building. Charles scanned the card again over a dark pad, causing the door to unlock, and then he grabbed the handle and pulled it open. They stepped into an unlit corridor.

"It's possible they either cleared out this section already or they never used it," Charles suggested. Once the door shut, darkness reigned and sight became an issue.

Landon removed his cell phone and turned it on to use it as a flashlight. "I'm glad I remembered to bring it with me this time," he joked, and they walked through the passageway. "Where should we go? Neither of us knows this place."

"You're right," Charles agreed. "We should head to the loading dock for trucks and shipments. That's where the military truck went. I'm sure they are packing up and leaving. It's what I would do if I didn't want to deal with angry police officers or townsfolk."

"Or other angry scientists?"

"That too," Charles said. "The loading dock would be somewhere to our right."

"Then let's go. We don't have much time left."

Φ

Erased

"Well, that plan worked," sarcasm dripped from Bonnie's words as she pouted in the corner of a padded room. It seemed more like a mental hospital isolation room and not an actual prison cell. The guards had thrown both her and Barns into the same one. The room was dark, except for a small window in the door which let in a single beam of light.

"Be patient, Bonnie," Barns replied.

"You want me to be patient? I may never see my husband again!"

Both captives heard a click in the lock and the door opened.

Peter stood at the opening, ushering them out with his hand. "Come on," he said. "It's time to go."

Barns jumped to his feet. "So I was right," he said with a smirk.

"You doubted me?" Peter asked.

"At first, yes, but when you told Thomas I came here to destroy the technology and not steal it, I figured you were trying to let me know you were on our side."

Peter nodded.

"And you couldn't have told me this?" Bonnie asked.

"I could have, but I didn't know if this room is bugged. What's the plan, Peter?"

The scientist checked his watch. "Thomas is dealing with a group of angry police officers from Lion's Glade. We need to deactivate the satellite dish on the roof of this building to knock out all communications to the outside world. We can't have Harding's guards calling for reinforcements."

"Logical," Barns agreed. "That would hinder us from using cell phones though."

"It won't matter once we are out of here." Peter jogged down the hall. "Come on, we don't have much time. If Thomas doesn't succeed at bringing peace, a war between the police and Harding's men will begin."

Φ

Thomas felt the tension in the air. To calm the convict officers, he had told them the truth about where they were and who they were. The only thing he didn't list off was their personal rap sheet. Though the cops were all on the opposite side of the electric fence and couldn't touch Thomas, they all had guns, and bullets were small enough to pass through the barrier. Thomas had three of the guards in white on either side of him and almost ten on the roof of the building, aiming down at the aggravated police.

"We want to leave this facility in peace," Thomas informed. "If you turn around and go home now, nobody will get hurt. We are packing up as I speak and will be out of Lion's Glade as soon as possible."

"We want our memories back!" one cop screamed.

"But *why*?" Thomas asked in sheer amazement. "You are all convicted felons with messed up histories! Why would you want to remember them? Start a new life; make new memories. Forget about who you used to be and embrace who you are *now*. You are people chosen to uphold the law and protect the citizens. It's time you all start fresh without worry of your past. The choice is yours." Thomas added with a genuine smile, to encourage the convicts to see things his way. He paused for a moment for effect and then continued. "Just make sure you're willing to face the consequences of your actions. If you try to take this facility, you will die. There are more of my men on the way. I would suggest you head back to town." Without saying another word, Thomas turned and walked back into the building.

A guard followed him. "Great speech, sir," he said.

"Thank you. I hope I got through to them."

Erased

"After seeing the looks on their faces, I'm sure you did."

"I suppose we'll see. I rounded up everyone Harding requested we bring back with us. I'll go let the caravan know that it's time to move out."

The guard nodded. "Very well; get to safety."

Φ

"You didn't do much to disable the dish. Won't Harding's men be able to repair it?" Barns asked as he, Bonnie, and Peter made their way down from the roof.

"I didn't want to destroy it. I know that someone will repair the dish, which is a good thing. The citizens of Lion's Glade will need the ability to use their cell phones. I only deactivated it to give us time to get away."

"And what is the plan?" Barns asked.

"We need to get to the loading dock. Thomas will join us."

The three got to the bottom of the stairs and made their way through hall after hall. The lack of guards confirmed that the police had made enough of a ruckus to pose a threat, which was more than Peter could have asked. They made it to the loading dock where two guards waited by the rollup door.

Peter, Barns, and Bonnie walked by without a response. As far as the guards knew, the three were just scientists about to leave. Four vehicles were ready; three of the large trucks with canopies over them contained the many scientists that made the project possible, and a large semi-truck, which contained all the computers, panels, and technology. They walked to the back of the truck that Troy, Kelly, and Monica were in and Peter waved to the three scientists he had personally hired.

Tucker, Zane, and Albert waved back. Peter, Barns, and Bonnie climbed in, and after a swift apology about Peter's abduction, explained the plan to the scientists, asking them if they wished to join. There were no objections, which pleased Barns. Peter saw Mark lying on a small makeshift bed in the back. According to the others, the nurse who wheeled him in gave him a sedative.

The sound of a banging door caused Peter to stick his head out of the canopy. Landon and Charles entered the room through a side door, guns visible. Without warning they opened fire on the two guards in white before they had time to retaliate. The men slumped to the ground, deep red bloodstains marring the once spotless white suits they wore.

The scientists in the other vehicles stuck their heads out to see what had happened.

"Get back inside," Landon ordered. He waved his gun at them and they shrunk back.

Peter jumped off the truck. "Guys, glad you could make it," he called out.

The two turned to him, guns ready. "Oh, Peter, thank goodness," Landon relaxed and jogged over to him. He saw everyone else in the back of the vehicle as he approached. "What are you doing?"

"I don't have time to explain, but we are getting out of here."

"You're going with Jacob Harding's men? What's Barns doing here?"

Peter breathed in a huge gulp of air and talked at a rapid pace, explaining to Charles and Landon the history of the town and purpose for the experiment.

Landon tilted his head to the side, not knowing how to take in the information. "So, everybody in Lion's Glade is a convicted felon?"

Peter nodded. "Except for the scientists, the late Sheriff Orson, Charles next to you, and the handful of people you see here in this vehicle, everyone else is a criminal. Landon, even you."

Landon shook his head. "This makes no sense. I'm a police officer. I'm the sheriff."

Erased

Bonnie climbed out of the vehicle. "I want to stay here in Lion's Glade with Elizabeth," she informed. "My husband is still alive and my life is here now."

"Simon is alive?" Peter asked.

"Your husband works for my father," Barns reminded. "He will leave and come back to us."

"Not if he doesn't have his memory restored," Bonnie said. She turned to Landon. "What they are saying is true, Landon. That doesn't mean it's the end of the world. I know of a CD that returns your memory when it's played. We could restore the memories of everyone here, but you have to ask yourself the question: do you want to remember your past, now that you know what you know?"

"I'm not sure."

"Charles, if you come with us, we could help you fight against your father," Peter said.

Charles looked at him, his expression blank. "Other than what you told us, I don't know what's happening."

Peter placed his hand on Charles' shoulder. "Then we will tell you, but you should come with us."

Charles pulled away. "We need to use the technology and return everyone's memories."

Peter shook his head. "You have the CD for that, which Bonnie can get for you. You don't need the technology itself. We are taking it far away from here where your father can never use it again. It's so unique in its design I'm doubtful it could be duplicated. But the question remains: is it better to return everybody's memories, or try starting a new life and getting the town up and running?"

Landon shook his head. "Once again, I'm not sure. Would we ever regain our memories without the CD or technology?"

Peter shrugged. "It's probable that your brain could bring the memories back at a natural speed. It's also a safer alternative to let them come back at a gradual pace than all at once; if they even come back at all."

A door to the loading dock opened and Thomas entered. He shut the door behind him and walked down a set of concrete steps toward the small group gathered behind the truck.

"What's going on?" He saw Charles and a smile appeared on his face. "Charles, it's good to see you again."

Peter answered Thomas. "We explained what's happening and they know their options now. They can choose whether they want to return everybody's memories or not. We will be far from the town by then, so what they decide will not affect us."

"We need to get out of here now," Thomas said. "I subdued the vehicle drivers, and the guards have realized cellular communications are disabled."

"If we are criminals, we can't leave town," Landon replied. "How will we get supplies?"

Barns jumped off of the truck. "I will make sure supplies are sent to you every month. However, we will expect compensation. We can help you turn Lion's Glade into a real town and not a prison colony."

"The government doesn't even know you exist," Thomas informed. "Jacob Harding made sure of that. To the outside world, you are all dead. You can begin a new life here, with or without your memories. The decision is up to you, but *we* have to go." Thomas jogged over to the metal rollup doors and pushed a green button, causing them to rise and expose the sun. He glanced at the bodies on the ground and returned to the vehicle, pretending he didn't see them.

"So, you aren't coming with us, Charles?" Peter asked.

Charles shook his head. "No, I'll stay here for now."

Erased

"Thomas, Mark is asleep in the back of the truck here," Peter mentioned.

Thomas turned to Landon. "I think I should let you know that if you decide you don't want your memories back, but you want to know what you were in Lion's Glade for, the computer in the tower's building has that information. All you need to do is access the program titled Dossier, and when it asks for a password, enter the six-digit word on your arm. It will get you into your secured files."

"So the words on our arms are passwords?" Landon asked.

Thomas shrugged. "Sort of, but they were shorter titles the scientists here gave you to help keep track of all the inmates. We know you as Bishop, Officer Myles is Spring, so on and so forth. They were simple words to identify you."

"What about the word on my arm?" Kelly asked.

"That was an exception," Thomas said.

"Thomas, enough with the explanations; it won't take the guards long to realize what we're doing." Peter groaned. They were cutting it close.

Thomas nodded and motioned for Barns. "You're riding with me in the semi. Peter will drive this truck and follow behind us."

"Do you have the keys?" Barns asked.

Thomas reached into his pocket and held them up with a grin. He removed another set of keys and tossed them to Peter before making his way over to the semi.

"All right then, Charles, it's been nice knowing you," Peter said as he held out his hand for Charles to shake.

"I wish the same could be said of you."

"Once we leave, we aren't coming back," Peter reminded Bonnie.

"My husband is alive, Peter. He may be in a coma, but he's still alive. I'm not going anywhere."

"Fair enough," Peter said with a nod. "Troy, come ride with me in the front. We should talk. Monica can ride in the back for now."

Troy turned to Kelly who gave him a nod. He jumped down from the back and made his way to the passenger side.

Peter climbed in, slid the key into the ignition, and started up the engine. He waited for Thomas to drive forward after the gate ahead of them opened, and then pulled behind him. They traveled down the dirt road and watched as Landon, Bonnie, and Charles disappeared into the forest.

"You don't have to worry about those men using the other vehicles to come after us, I took care of them." Troy held up several wires and hoses.

"When did you have time to do that?" Peter asked in astonishment.

"When Kelly was flirting with the guards."

Peter laughed. "That's my boy."

"Dad, there's something I have to ask, and please be honest. I know what you told Landon, but will the inmates ever have their memories returned?"

Peter shook his head. "There's a possibility, but without the CD, it's improbable. Even if they removed their implants, it wouldn't matter."

"Monica and I didn't need the CD to regain our memories. Kelly is even remembering."

Peter smiled and nodded. "That's because I made special adjustments to your implants. I needed a backup plan, in case Monica didn't get the CD. I made sure that Kelly's, Monica's, and your memories would resurface, and I did the same thing for myself and the scientists who helped me with the project."

Erased

"So then the citizens of Lion's Glade can begin their lives again without their shaded histories haunting them?"

Peter nodded. "If that's what Landon chooses, then yes, they can."

Troy smiled and nodded his head in approval. "So, where are we headed now? Won't Jacob and his company try coming after us? We *are* stealing his technology."

Peter nodded. "Yes, I'm sure Jacob will want to come after us, but I'm not too worried. We have new friends to protect us now."

"And our destination?" Troy asked.

Peter turned his head for a moment to look at his boy, and a grin of excitement spread across his face. "We are moving to a place I've always wanted to go; Washington State."

EPILOGUE

Two months passed and the town of Lion's Glade flourished. Dale Barns set up a trade route like he had promised and they traded supplies for strange new fruits and vegetables that grew on the farmland to the east of town. To the citizens' disappointment, the old man Lion's Glade traded with didn't know English, so they never received updates from the outside world, though most thought it for the best.

The rest of Midas Tech vanished without a trace, except for an empty facility hidden in the forest and one empty laboratory in town. None of the employees had returned, nor would they ever.

Faced with whether or not to return the memories of the population, Landon had decided against it. Peter and Thomas had been right. People could start their lives new and fresh and didn't need to remember their past mistakes. He let Charles play the CD to regain his memories and then locked it away in a safe in the mayor's office. Charles disappeared.

Even though the police force knew the truth about the town, they never told another soul. They kept their jobs of protecting the citizens and keeping the peace.

Simon Orson awoke from his coma, and after months of therapy, retook his position as the sheriff, but not before the town elected Landon the new mayor of Lion's Glade.

Nobody dared venture outside of the town, or even past the now-open gate surrounding it. They had everything they needed; everyone felt content.

Julie Hood, Thomas' wife, vanished from her assignment in Oregon, never to be seen again by her employers. Peter, Thomas, and their families disappeared, though rumors being spread within the Midas Technology Corporation suggest they now work for Helios and are in hiding. The technology would never be found.

Erased

Φ

Landon stepped into the small, abandoned building he and Simon Orson had secured. Nobody had touched the computers in six months. Landon shut the door behind him and walked over to the electronic device, pushing the power button. He waited for the desktop to load and clicked on the small icon titled Dossier. The screen went black and then green text appeared asking to input a password.

Landon no longer had the word on his arm though he remembered what it had been; *Bishop*. He typed it in and the screen loaded. Information scrolled across the monitor, followed by his picture. He read over the data and it felt as if his heart had stopped.

Landon Grayson, Age 24.

Mother: Unknown, Father: Unknown.

Convicted of Manslaughter in the fourth degree

Sentenced to 40 years in Alabama State Prison

Transferred to Lion's Glade January 16th, 2280

It wasn't his crime that made his blood run cold, it was the date.

It wasn't the year 2017 like everyone thought, it was the year 2280.

ABOUT THE AUTHOR

Author Lucas Heath was born and raised in the Puget Sound region of Washington State. From an early age, the fanciful worlds and characters he has created have found their way onto paper and with his developing skills, Lucas completed his first novel, Erased, at the age of 22. He sat on the manuscript for over a year before self-publishing it, after already having released the shorter sequel, BoX.

Switching gears from the mystery/thriller genre, Lucas returned to his work on the Domain: Virtual Takeover series – a project he had been developing for the past ten years. Thus Betawolf and Sightless were written.

In writing, Lucas aims to be the epitome of a mischievous story teller, one who weaves tales of mystery and suspense, pulling readers deeper until they can't escape from his grasp.

You can read his blog and sign up for the mailing list to receive updates and discounts on future books by visiting the official website.

http://www.DreamWalkerBooks.com

Or visit the official author Facebook page!

http://www.facebook.com/LucasHeathAuthor

Check out a preview of **BoX**, the novella sequel to Erased.

1: Marsha and Barry

The room was a cube. It was twenty feet in height, length, and width, and the walls seemed to glow a stunning white that surpassed the purity of fresh-fallen snow. There were no windows, no doors, and no blemishes of any kind, just solid walls that boxed the young girl inside with no way of escape.

Her fragile body lay sprawled upon the solid white ground, shaking from cold. Fear had yet to settle in, for she had not yet awakened.

As time ticked away, her eyes opened and her head jerked up from the floor of her prison. Her head pivoted and tilted as she surveyed her surroundings. The beat of her heart quickened as she realized her predicament.

She remembered her identity, and where she was from, though why she was in this strange place escaped her memory. She sat up and grabbed at her neck, letting trembling fingers glide across the soft, tan skin. A bump where somebody had stuck a needle, found its place underneath her index finger and she rubbed at the spot, ignoring the pain. Someone had drugged her though the reason as to why eluded her.

Panic threatened to overtake her mind. The fight-or-flight instinct gripped at her heart, but with a deep breath she pushed the feelings away. Her father had always said, "Marsha, fear is an illusion that makes you weak. You either learn to control it, or it will control you." She agreed with that statement and made destroying fear in her life a goal.

Marsha stood and felt her legs wobbling underneath her. Using the wall for support, she steadied herself and took another deep breath, letting it out at slow pace. A pedestal in the center of the room drew her attention. Sitting atop the square stand was a single pistol, though she didn't know what kind it was, or if it had ammunition.

Deciding to avoid the death device, Marsha turned toward a wall and ran her hands over it. It was smooth like marble and radiated a luminescent light that gave the room its glow. If it weren't for these walls, floor, and ceiling, darkness would reign. She followed the wall around the entire cube, feeling for any switches or hidden panels, though she found nothing.

After a final pass, Marsha leaned against and slid down a wall until her bottom hit the ground. She rested her head against her knees and cried.

****

Barry had a different reaction to his predicament, which began with a panic attack and then a surge of rage. He was alone, trapped in a glowing white cube with no food or water. He spent an hour kicking and slamming his fists against the walls, but left no sign he had done so. They were solid and seemed unbreakable. He had tried grabbing the gun from the pedestal in the center of the room, but a strong surge of electricity knocked him off his feet the moment he touched it. He wept and fumed as he stomped around the room, trying to figure out what he could do to change his circumstances.

"I don't deserve this!" He ranted for a while, though he wasn't sure if anyone was even listening. Someone *had* to be listening, right? They wouldn't just lock him up and leave him be, would they? Who were *they*? Why take *him*? Barry was a waiter at a small restaurant in Buffalo, New York. Why was *he* so special?

He sat and looked at the clothing he was wearing. Someone had changed him while he was unconscious. He wore gray sweatpants, a gray sweatshirt with his name embroidered on the left side of the chest, and he was barefoot. Allowing him to have socks and underwear would be too much of a luxury.

What if he had to go to the bathroom? There weren't any toilets or sinks, or even a bucket. How would he get food? The walls were solid and left no indication they could contain a door. There weren't even any vents in the room so the thought of running out of air made him calm and breathe at a steady pace. He stared for a while at the bloody knuckles he had gotten from punching a wall and wiped them against the leg of his sweatpants.

Something had to happen soon, and he would have to wait until that moment came.

2: Chuck and Elisa

The room was silent as her eyes fluttered open. She stared at the glowing white ceiling of the cube and a smile formed at the corners of her mouth; she had committed suicide and was now in Heaven. Sitting up, her head pounded to its own beat. The light added to her headache. She looked down at the black cross tattooed onto the back of her dark brown hand. Even from looking upside down, she could see her name, Elisa, embroidered into the gray sweatshirt she now wore. Wasn't she supposed to get a new body?

Elisa stood and gazed around the room with a look of confusion displayed on her face. Could she be in a holding room before seeing God? That didn't sound right. The glowing walls seemed to dim as if answering her mental plea for less light. In the center of the room rose a pedestal with a gun resting on top. She walked over and studied it.

"Where am I?" The words escaped her mouth in a British accent and echoed as though she were in a cave or tunnel. "This can't be hell, can it? It's too beautiful." She dismissed the gun and walked around the room, looking for any clues that would define her reality.

Elisa's mind raced at the possibilities of her location. Perhaps aliens had abducted her after taking the pills. No, that idea was absurd. Maybe someone had found her dying and called for help. Perhaps they had locked her in a mental hospital though that wouldn't explain the gun in the center of the room *and* the walls would have thick padding.

"Hello, can anyone hear me?" She called out as she looked toward the ceiling corners, hoping to see a camera watching her. "Hello?" The thick accent filled the room once more and Elisa sat cross-legged on the cold, glowing floor. Perhaps she needed to wait for an angel to come get her. She leaned up against a wall and closed her eyes. Other than her breathing and the pounding of her head, there were no noises coming from anywhere, as though the strange cube was soundproof. She expected to at least hear harps playing.

Another possibility nagged at her. Perhaps the pills put her in a coma and this was just a dream. That theory seemed more probable considering her situation didn't match up to what she had grown up learning in church. She didn't feel depressed anymore, that much was obvious, and she enjoyed the mental freedom. Perhaps the cube represented her brain, and she was trapped inside a coma. No matter the answer, as long as she wouldn't have to face the outside world, she felt at peace with where she was.

****

The moment Chuck awoke, he jumped to his feet and spun around to study his prison. "Four walls, one floor, one ceiling, estimated between fifteen and twenty feet. It's a cube," he said to himself as he took frantic mental notes. "Light emits from every direction preventing shadows. A single pistol rests on a podium in the center of the room." He walked over to the gun and reached down to touch it. He yanked his hand back the moment he felt and saw the hairs on the back of his hand stand on end. "Electrified; interesting," he mumbled. He ran a hand through his thick, black hair and circled the pedestal.

He moved over to one wall and knocked on it. "Solid, yet smooth, but not stone, possibly glass," he continued to mutter. "Though I'm sure it's unbreakable," he added as if he were trying to convince himself of that idea.

Chuck closed his eyes to recall what had happened. He had been sitting on a train, traveling from Mississippi to New Jersey, when a sharp pain shot through his neck and he awoke in the cube.

He reached for the right side of his neck and found the bump he had been expecting. "Sedative," he confirmed with a nod to himself and sat. "I know who you are," he called out as he looked around the cube. "I know what you're doing." He waited in silence. "I promise that I will stop you. You didn't win last time and you *won't* win this time." A grin appeared on Chuck's face and he stared at the gun. He already knew he was a lab rat in an experiment and he would not lose.

The light in the room increased, causing Chuck to shield his eyes while they adjusted. A voice echoed throughout the room as if it were coming from every direction.

"Participants, we selected you at random for this upcoming experiment." The deep gravel voice was that of an older man; it sounded as though the announcer had smoked most of his life. "My name is Jacob Harding and I would like to welcome you to The Box."

www.ingramcontent.com/pod-product-compliance
Lightning Source LLC
Chambersburg PA
CBHW060147260626
47160CB00001B/165